K

Collected Short Stories

JAMES PLUNKETT

POOLBEG PRESS: DUBLIN

This collection first published 1977 by Poolbeg Press Ltd.,
Knocksedan House, Swords, Co. Dublin, Ireland

HANDO £.50

Printed by Cahill (1976) Limited, Dublin 3

Contents

	Page
The Trusting and the Maimed	7
A Walk Through the Summer	34
The Scoop	64
Weep for Our Pride	84
The Wearin' of the Green	98
The Damned	130
The Half-Crown	140
Mercy	153
Dublin Fusilier	168
The Web	182
Janey Mary	200
The Eagles and the Trumpets	208
The Trout	236
The Plain People	252
Finegan's Ark	274
A Touch of Genius	280
The Boy on the Capstan	284
Ferris Moore and the Earwig	292

The assistance of The Arts Council (An Chomhairle Ealaion) in the publication of this book is gratefully acknowledged.

The Trusting and the Maimed

AT about eleven o'clock the pigeon came slowly and uncertainly from the west, leaving behind it the rim of encircling mountains. Its wings beat heavily. It flew low. Some miles to the east the sandy surface of a road broke the monotony of the moors. The pigeon hovered. There was no movement anywhere; no small whitewashed houses with windows to flash as they returned the sun; no men bending their backs in labour over the harvest, no loaded carts swaying and trundling behind sweating horses. All that lay behind. Eastwards, where the pavements began, were the serried hall doors, the spires and factory chimneys, the smoke and hustle which was home. The pigeon desired the city, not this wilderness; these worked-out turf cuttings with water too black to reflect the sun, this marshy ground too poor to bear anything but heather and reeds and an odd cluster of purple frocans. The pigeon distrusted the moor, the absence of life, the silence. But its wounded leg throbbed more painfully, its wings beat with decreasing strength. When suspicion and fear could no longer sustain it, it dropped quietly to earth and began to push a passageway into the tangled heather. Under the thick growth was the darkness of a smaller and more tangible world. It was companionless without the exuded warmth of other pigeons but it was bounded like the pigeon hutch at home. It gave an illusion of safety. The pigeon rested, waiting for its strength to return, every instinct yearning and quivering for the city.

From the top windows of the Georgian house the mountains which encircled the moor were clearly visible, but Florrie, busy sweeping the top landing, hardly noticed them. She had other things on her mind. Sweat had left a thin ring of dirt around the nape of her neck and made dark smears down her plump young arms. The deliberate banging of her sweeping brush against the bedroom door had failed to bring any response. The failure irritated her. She leaned across the banisters. Warm, unpleasant odours from the kitchen rose unremarked about her flushed face. It was the boarding-house odour she had grown up with. Behind her, in the sunlight shafting from the window, dust swam wildly.

"Ma," she yelled.

"What is it?"

"Mr. Casey isn't stirring, Ma."

"Then for the love of God go and rouse him," her mother screamed back. "Tell him it's eleven o'clock. He'll be sacked out of his office."

Florrie bundled her hair under her kerchief and re-tied it before selecting the key for the door. She was used to them all – the junior clerks from insurance offices, the lonely, elderly men with no known occupation, the university students who had lived in bed-sitting-rooms in her mother's house for as long as she could remember. Without embarrassment she pushed the door open. The bed which had not been slept in stopped her short in the doorway like an affront; the fact that after all the banging and the brushing there was nobody there overawed her. A set of underwear and a soiled shirt, bundled roughly for Monday's laundry, lay in the corner. She looked enquiringly from the picture of St. Rita, patroness of hopeless cases, to a glossy photograph of a pin-up girl in a swim suit and then to a family group of Casey in a sailor's suit, sitting on a table which stood between his mother and father. On the dressing-table, between a crushed tie and a sticky bottle of hair dressing, lay an envelope. Florrie picked it up, detected the faint odour of perfume, and sat down on the bed to read. Some time later, when her sweeping-brush slid sideways and fell, she paid no attention.

8

Dear Joe,

After I got home last night I just couldn't sleep the words we had and no sign yet although it's nearly eight weeks now. Ma asked me where I was I suppose my face looked a fright was I crying a lot. You upset me talking about those people you want me to see on Monday. Joe please understand I just can't do it. It was bad enough taking those pills but what you suggest now is something so terrible it's against everything against the law and against the church. If you loved me there is a way out even now but you don't. I realise that and that makes it even more awful. I'm in this trouble because I loved you I suppose I was a fool in the first place. But I won't see those men although I think now mother is beginning to suspect something or will soon. I will get this to you by hand or somehow and please Joe see me tomorrow so that we can talk.

In haste,

Rita

Florrie rose quietly and went out once more to the landing. In the shifting sunlight dust no longer swam.

"Ma."

"What is it now?"

"Come up, Ma. Mr. Casey's not here."

"Not there."

"No, Ma. I think . . . I think he's done a bunk."

Florrie anticipated with accuracy the sudden flurry of ascending feet.

By the hour of eleven the office of Pigott & Turrow had settled down to the dusty routine of the day. It was a small office at the top of the building and from its windows also the mountains were visible. Across a jumble of roofs and chimney pots their tranquil shapes rose blue and clear-cut in the autumn sunshine. The small office was quiet. Rita Kilshaw bit her lip over the letter she was attempting to type and made more mistakes than usual. After each sentence she breathed "Dear God, don't let it happen, please don't let it happen," because she hoped if she said that often enough it really wouldn't happen. She

9

had cried so much these past few weeks that by now the relief of easy tears was no longer left to her. But the small pale hands which seemed always to be smudged with carbon seldom stopped fidgeting. She had developed the habit of drawing the corner of her lip between her teeth and looking up miserably under arched eyebrows at images which passed from time to time before her mind. She looked around sometimes at the grey head of Miss Bates as it bent over the work of the day, or said, "Yes, Mr. Turrow," in a gulping voice when the large bulk of her boss materialised beside her. There were moments of terror when she believed they knew all about it, that their voices were engaging her in conversation only that their eyes might search the lines of her body the more diligently. In the middle of her third attempt at the letter before her she stopped and opened the petty cash box. She said, trying to pitch her voice casually: "We've run rather short of stamps, Miss Bates. Do you think I should slip out for some?" Miss Bates, a little surprised, raised her head and stared at a straight, uncommunicative back.

"Can't you get them as usual on your way to lunch?"

"I suppose so."

Miss Bates, catching the note of defeat in her voice, asked with customary kindness:

"Did you want to go out for something else?"

"I've such a splitting headache," the girl lied, "I thought some fresh air might clear it."

Miss Bates, ironically misconstruing the headache, said pleasantly, "Get the stamps by all means and call at the chemist on your way."

The girl took off her overall and went down a flight to wash. Through the open window of the toilet, which looked out over a flat zinc roof at the weathered brick of walls and chimney stacks, pleasant autumn odours of the city stole in, a breeze astringent with the smell of the sea and the smoke of burning leaves in public parks. The girl examined her face in the mirror for reassurance that it was hers, that it betrayed nothing more than tiredness, bit her lip and arched her eyebrows and asked herself if she was going mad. She would have liked to have gone mad, to have escaped into sickness and fever. But the thoughts tapped out rationally and logically, as clear-cut as the zinc roof and the chimney pots, miserably sane. She took up her handbag, went through the hall which always smelled coldly of garbage, and found herself in the street.

"For you," Higgins said, pitching the instrument neatly into the tray in front of Ellis. Ellis, startled by the bump, looked up irritably from his work.

"Who is it?"

"Some bird," Higgins conveyed.

"What bird?" Ellis insisted, putting his hand over the receiver. "Why the hell don't you get a name?"

"Some mutual bird," Higgins explained. "She asked for Casey – then for you."

Ellis, glancing down the office before answering, guessed the caller before he heard the voice. No views of distant mountains troubled the air-conditioned comfort of the Municipal Insurance Office, no windows allowed the sunlight to challenge the discretion of its artificial lighting. Telephones, when they rang, did so with regulated emphasis. Ellis addressed himself reluctantly to the instrument in his hand.

"Oh Rita, hello. Yes, this is Bob Ellis. No – not so far. I don't know. He didn't send in any word either. No, it's not like him. Did you try his digs? Yes, call me back and let me know. Good luck."

Ellis cut off, considered thoughtfully, and requested another number. During the second conversation he frowned and looked around two or three times at the vacant chair. He let down the receiver again and sauntered down the office, sedulously avoiding the eye of Mr. Pringle, the Chief Clerk. Pringle, Ellis knew, was deeply wounded by Casey's non-appearance. It was unbusinesslike, it was not worthy of the high tradition of the Accident Department. But Ellis, lacking an explanation, lifted the hinged leaf of the counter and tried to convey by the expression on his face that the business of

11

the Municipal was absorbing his whole attention. He made his way past the serried desks with their serried batons of fluorescent lighting and found Connolly leaning against a filing cabinet in the Whole Life Department.

"I want to talk to you," he said.

Connolly, gravely regarding a sheet of figures, which he held in his hand, asked, "Have you something good for the Curragh?"

"Not bloody horses," Ellis answered, "something serious."

"Horses are serious," Connolly said. "I dropped a tenner at Leopardstown on Saturday on a flaming certainty Higgins gave me. Every penny I could borrow."

Ellis, ignoring him for a moment, measured interrogatively the space which separated them from the nearest clerk, and dropped his voice.

"Your man Casey hasn't turned in this morning. I 'phoned his digs a while ago but the skivvy only knows his bed hasn't been slept in."

"What do you suspect?"

"I'm uneasy. The two of us have an appointment for tonight with the crowd I was telling you about."

"The crowd who were to do the what-you-may-call-it?"

"Exactly."

"And the woman – is she willing to chance it?"

"I don't know. Casey was to put it to her on Saturday and let me know today. He can't expect me to meet them on my own. It's dangerous. I don't mind being a friend, but I'm not going to be made a scapegoat. I'm wondering should I chance asking the woman about it myself."

When Connolly continued to regard him silently he added, "It's a bit embarrassing."

"Take my tip," Connolly said at last, "steer clear of it."

"But what about the woman. She's just been 'phoning me?"

"Is the poor bitch terrified?"

"Naturally," Ellis said. But the contempt in the

12

question angered him, He liked the girl.

"Let her go to hell," Connolly said. "What do you want to get mixed up in it for? It's highly dangerous. And it's immoral. It's bloody immoral. You know what'll happen if you're caught."

"I know. But I'm sorry for the woman. She's a nice girl."

"That's Casey's affair."

"I wish to God he was here," Ellis said miserably. "It's a bit thick leaving me to carry the baby."

Connolly looked at him with disapproval. "An unfortunate expression," he said finally.

Later in the morning Pringle spoke to him.

"Mr. Casey has not reported for duty. Do you know anything about him?"

"No, Mr. Pringle," Ellis said. "I expect he's ill."

Pringle looked at the clock on the far wall.

"Extraordinary," he said.

The expression, Ellis gathered, was intended to convey that no word to that effect had been received although it was now fifteen minutes past twelve.

"Perhaps he could get nobody to bring a report in," Ellis offered lamely. "He may be seriously ill."

"I should hope so," Pringle said, "it seems the only charitable explanation."

The interview was cut short through Higgins' intervention.

"A telephone call for Mr. Ellis," he said apologetically to Pringle. When they got out of earshot Ellis said, "Who is it?"

"The same bird," Higgins said. "You know you ought to do your courting in your own time."

With sudden venom Ellis said:

"It's Casey's bloody bird."

"That only makes it worse, doesn't it?" Higgins answered, smiling.

After the fluorescent lighting Ellis found the October sunlight strong and irritating. He fretted at the delay when he was held up at traffic crossings and wondered why he had been such a fool as to ask her to lunch in the first place. But when he joined her in Stapley's he knew the answer. Rita Kilshaw was a nice girl. She was petite and dark with a childlike air which moved him tenderly. He had met her first at a hop in the tennis club but Casey had won the day. Casey was more enterprising and besides he was two years senior. At twenty-four Ellis still felt that that counted. So he gave Casey a clear field and did the best he could with her girl friend. When the affair developed on more serious lines Rita Kilshaw became forbidden territory. Ellis was prepared to chance a lot – all the chaps in Municipal were. But where a friend had staked a claim you tried not to cut in. If he got into trouble you were expected to help him. If he wanted a loan of a dinner jacket or was stuck for a few quid, you came to his rescue. If he was in more serious trouble there was a fund of commonly available information on ways and means of putting matters right. At the worst somebody always knew somebody. Unfortunately the simple remedies had failed in the present case. Ellis, looking down at Rita Kilshaw for a moment before drawing out his chair, was bitterly sorry. It was one thing taking your fun where you could and looking for a soft thing when the mood was on you, but it was quite another when things went wrong. The girl had her family, sober, sodality-minded parents who were likely to kick up holy murder. Casey's job might be at stake, because the Board had high standards of morality. The chairman, for instance, had two sons in the Jesuits. Ellis felt the whole business was disastrous.

"Did you order?" he asked.

He was answered with a look of such detached misery that he felt suddenly chilled.

"Look," he said humbly, "I don't mean to start any silly chin-up look-on-the-bright-side business. Honest. I know how you feel."

They sat in silence. The meal was going to be a hopeless affair. He tried again.

"I know it's embarrassing," he said. "I find it embarrassing too. I mean third party and so on. I know how you feel. But we've got to talk."

Her gaze was fixed on the fork which she was jabbing lightly at the tablecloth. She said:

"He wasn't at his digs last night. They think he's gone away."

"Nonsense," Ellis said, with an attempt at conviction. "He'll turn up. I wouldn't worry about that end of it."

A waitress was hovering at his shoulder. He ordered for himself. The girl would have coffee.

"Nothing else?"

"No."

"But, Rita."

"Please . . . just coffee."

The waitress went away.

"Rita," he said, "did Joe tell you he was talking to some people?"

"He did. I told him I wouldn't see them."

"It's a chance."

"Aren't things bad enough already?"

"But this may be a way out."

"There are other ways out."

"Rita, for the love of God, don't start talking like that."

"Like what?"

"About other ways out. We've got to keep our heads." Ellis realised that once again he was involving himself. Why should he say "We?" It was Casey's jam, not his. He looked down at his plate and the food filled him with disgust. He heard the girl saying:

"I think I'm going mad."

"Rita," he said, "Casey will turn up. I'm sure of it. But in the meanwhile don't let this chance pass."

15

"I'm not going."

"Then what are we to do?"

She had let down the fork. Her hands were tightly clenched, her face was full of so much suffering that Ellis felt every eye in the hot, sticky restaurant must be drawn by it. He sensed a crisis approaching and felt the urgent necessity for deflecting it.

"Rita," he said, gently touching her sleeve, "please don't cry. Not here. We'd have everyone staring."

"I've no intention of crying."

He knew that was a lie. She looked like somebody who at any moment might start to scream. He sighed but said nothing. The rest of the meal passed more or less silently. He led her by crowded tables. People sweated over their food, people who came in from surrounding offices and eat always in a hurry. The clatter of knives and plates helped in its own way to set nerves on edge. It was a relief to pass out once more into sunlight, to push through lunch-hurrying crowds until they reached the river wall. She began to walk towards the dock area. They passed a public convenience and a car park packed with cars. The river wall was spattered here and there with gull droppings. Ellis, glancing at a public clock, said:

"What time have you to be back at?"

"I'm not going back."

His anxiety was now mixed with irritation. He hid it but it brought him to standstill. She was being difficult at a time when a little mutual trust meant so much.

"You'll only make things worse, Rita."

"What do *you* care?"

She turned towards the river and looked down at the green slime which showed above the low water. A light breeze was irrelevantly stirring her hair. Ellis covered her hand gently, almost shyly, with his.

"Rita," he said, "that's not fair. After all, I don't have to get mixed up with this at all. It's dangerous for me, too. I could say it's not my business. I could walk off and say to hell with it."

"Then why don't you?"

"I don't know. I suppose because I'm a pal of Casey's. Or because I like you, Rita. Maybe I like you more than I should. I can't help that — Casey or no Casey. I asked you to lunch when I knew you were feeling pretty low."

She considered this for a moment in silence. Then without looking at him, she said: "I'm sorry. I know you don't have to do this. I'm behaving like a bitch."

"Oh, no."

"Yes, I am. It's the things that keep coming into my head. When we lived in the country we had a maid. She hid it for nine months. Then she locked the bedroom door and the baby was born. Daddy packed her off. I remember the things we said about her. About skivvies and soldiers and not being able to watch them. We thought she was dirt and what could you expect. Now I keep thinking of what she suffered in that nine months — binding herself up, not pretending when she was sick, praying that it was all a nightmare."

"Rita — if you know all that why can't you do something about it? Why won't you chance these other people?"

"No."

"I'm seeing them tonight . . ."

"No."

"Then what are you to do?"

"There are plenty of things I can do," she said, looking down at the water. He caught the look.

"Rita," he urged. Her mood distressed him.

Insulating herself in her own world once more, she said: "You'll be late back at the office."

"And what about you?"

"I've the afternoon off. I told Miss Bates I was sick."

"Rita . . . please . . ."

"Do go."

He left her leaning against the wall. Ellis found it a little incomprehensible. If you were in trouble you had to go deeper to get out. It was undesirable, of course, but

17

beggars couldn't be choosers. The chaps in the Municipal were often enough in trouble; over horses, over drink and not doing their work properly, and now and then, like Casey, over women. Life was a succession of small deceits and subterfuges, snatched pleasures and social inconveniences. There was only one commandment which demanded absolute regard, the eleventh commandment – don't be caught. The rest could be discreetly tampered with. The thought filled his mind when he arrived back at the office and he found Casey's chair still empty. Casey had been caught. And like the cute customer he was, Casey had run out on them. Ellis was convinced of it.

The pigeon, having found the darkness under loose heather reassuring, burrowed in further and was suddenly gripped by a hand. It was Casey's hand. He made no conscious decision to grab at the pigeon; the action was automatic. But the effort made him turn a little to one side and that hurt his injured leg. Pain twisted his face. For a moment after drawing the pigeon towards him he was tempted to kill it, to exorcise the pain forcibly through some act of violence. Then he noticed that the pigeon's left leg was almost severed at the joint. Under the raw and bloody skin a single tendon joined it to the upper half. Its breast feathers and the leg itself were smeared with clay and grass. The right leg, uninjured, carried a silver ring. Casey looked down at his own broken leg and felt his self-pity large enough to embrace the maimed pigeon. Its suffering, its fright, its heart beating with terrified warmth and softness under his hand, took his mind for a moment away from his own plight.

"You poor little bastard," he murmured gently. He drew the pigeon under his jacket and with extreme caution lowered his body again until he was stretched out on the heather, the stems rough against the side of his face. There was grit about his lips because he had sucked moss to ease his thirst. The sun, high overhead, drew a warm, soft, hungry odour from the moor. A short distance away, but too far as yet for Casey's thirst to brace him for the almost unbearable ordeal of dragging his way towards it, the small stream reflected the sky, a vast blueness with one small white cloud, a slow argosy in a motionless sea.

After a night spent on the open moor, the sun had come as a trusted friend. But its heat aggravated his thirst, its light forced him to turn his head into uncomfortable positions. Casey had not known how cold the moors could be at night, how hot in the day. The pain of his broken leg, the shock of exposure were bad enough, but the brutality of these extremes he had not reckoned on. It filled him with a new fear and called out new reserves of cunning. The other fear had been his constant companion for weeks. It followed him into the office in the morning and walked home beside him in the evening. It kept him awake in his room at night, contemplating the disastrous consequences should anything misfire in his dealing with the men Ellis knew, and the equally disastrous consequences of letting things take their course. It had become unbearable after Mass on Sunday and drove him in flight from the company of the lodgers, from the necessity of behaving as though nothing was wrong, from the misery of another depressing evening with Rita Kilshaw.

The mountains had provided some measure of peace which encouraged him to carry on across the moors. There was peace and there were no people. He had been aware, of course, that one day's respite was no solution, that the sight of the first lights stringing along the first suburban road would bring back all the suffering and indecision once more, but up to the moment when he caught his foot in the hole and pitched forward heavily he had known a calm which had not been his for weeks. It was a calm in which it had occurred to him that he might marry her after all. It would be difficult to arrange, it would be hard to find money and set up a home. But when it was all smoothed over it might work out successfully. The idea had begun to engage his serious

19

consideration.

The pigeon stirred against his breast and he stroked it until it settled down again, accepting his friendliness now without further question, so reassured and quiet that after a while Casey forgot all about it. He closed his eyes. They would be wondering where he was, Florrie when she found his room unoccupied, Ellis when he failed to turn up at the office, Rita Kilshaw when she received no letter and no telephone call.

"Is there any change?" he had asked with growing hopelessness every day. There had been moments when he loved her wildly; when he left her home on the night of their first meeting; on the golf links when intimacy had first offered. They had spent the whole August day on the beach; swimming, throwing a beach ball from one to the other afterwards and lying lazily in the sun until the time came to make tea on the oil stoves the others had brought. Everyone shared spoons and laughed because sand had found its way into some of the sandwiches. When he wanted milk and sugar for his tea she had said, "Let me do it" in a way which gave him to understand that it was her pleasure to perform such a trivial and everyday service for him, that she was playfully attempting to transform it from ordinariness into some kind of smiling sacramental. He touched her arm as she leaned over him. It was cool and streaked intimately with fine sand. Afterwards, when the rest went on to dance in the seaside town, they lingered behind but promised to follow.

Much later, when it was already dusk, they did so, crossing the golf links alone together. Mooncast shadows made the ground deceptive. She said to him, "Look at the moon on the sea." They stood still on the cliffs. Then without any further word they sat down. The night was soft and warm. Below them one broad path of moonlit silver cleaved the dark symmetry of the ocean. To their right, about a mile away, the curved arm of the bay winked with coloured lights, the amplifier in a fairground sent a popular tune drifting tentatively towards them over the dark interval of water. The light breeze left a salt taste which mingled with the odour of clipped grass. He kissed her. She said:

"We're going to miss the rest."

"Does it matter?"

"No."

Somewhere in the back of his head a gaily coloured beach ball was floating to and fro amid disembodied laughter, the desirable coolness of arms was streaked irresponsibly with fine white sand. All day he had been living beyond his means because it was Bank Holiday, all day acting an opulent lie. Now, becoming himself, he said with engaging modesty:

"I wish I had money."

"Haven't you?"

"A clerk in the Municipal – a clerk anywhere?"

"It's quite respectable to be a clerk."

"A salary scale starting at three quid a week and rising by annual increments over twenty-one years to a max of ten pounds. Sign the clock in at nine and sign it out at five. Three weeks paid leave every year and a contributory pension scheme. That's being a clerk."

"Isn't there promotion?"

"Yes. If you study at night for ten years. Do your accountancy or secretarial. Go bald and lose your teeth. I want money while I'm young."

"Money is nice."

"Money is everything. Money is a yacht of your own. Money is a coloured beach ball. Money buys the sun we had today and the moon we have tonight. Money is short drinks in expensive hotel lounges. Money is making love to a nice girl like you."

"And to a nice boy like you."

"Rita."

She lay back in the grass and laughed. "Let's make a litany again about money," she suggested.

"Rita," he repeated, and bent down to her. He took her in his arms. After a while he amended, "Money isn't everything."

"What is everything?"

Her coolness, her shapeliness, the faint fragrance of the sea clinging about her, sent the coloured ball flashing as it crossed and re-crossed. She was no longer a bit of fluff or a dame or a date. He found her transformed and incredibly beautiful. "This," he had said, kissing her again. She stroked his hair. A warm voluptuous flood engulfed him.

Casey twisted without due caution and sweated again with vicious pain. "Jesus," he breathed. Pain and hunger and heat racked him with nausea. The pigeon began to flutter wildly. "Stop it," he breathed. "Give over." He had been lying still for too long in the sun. His eyes were momentarily blinded, a luminous brown blindness which terrified him. It was like trying to waken from a nightmare and not being able. He raised himself on his elbow and waited. The pigeon quietened. His eyes cleared. There was no sound but the unceasing murmur of the nearby stream. Under the arched sky with its becalmed white cloud the sun-filled moor was empty.

III

The river was now quite full. It flowed in a brown flood quietly between slime-encrusted walls and smelled of the sea. Spires and towers cluttered in smoky disorder the horizon ahead. A Franciscan church rose behind ugly railings to her right and on the opposite bank the hands of a public clock stood at five – almost tea-time. After leaving Ellis she had walked down-river until the rattle of cranes unloading ships warned her that the dock area was just ahead. She had turned back and walked up-river then, pausing often to note the swirling conflict when the tide began to force its way against the river. Gulls circled with sharp cries. Going home was out of the question. She could not sit down at table with the family in the drab loneliness of the kitchen to lie to them when she was asked why she had not been home to lunch. She could not sit listening to the radio in the front room with the holy pictures staring at her from the walls. The water she had considered but dismissed. There were too many people. Besides it was a mortal sin. If she did that she would go straight to hell. She would plunge deep down through the turmoil of river and tide into flames and everlasting torment. So it was either home or walk on and on or the church. While she hesitated a woman passed her and she prayed, "Jesus, O Jesus," because the woman was big with child. She had the habit of prayer. She prayed the weather would be fine for the club outing and she prayed her brother would get through his Leaving Cert, and she prayed the pastry wouldn't burn if she made tarts on a Sunday. She prayed to St. Anthony when she mislaid the petty cash book in the office. He found it for her. She prayed to St. Francis when the dog got sick and the dog got better. The habit drove her into the church. You prayed to St. Anne for childing mothers, but did that apply to unmarried ones? The church was large and restfully dark, lit only by the wavering shrine candles and the solitary lamp which burned before the tabernacle. There was no saint now to pray to or, if there was, she had not been informed. Having an illegitimate baby was unthinkable. Miss Bates would tell Mr. Turrow when it all came out and the tennis club and the social club would say Rita Kilshaw of all people. The months would pass and she would get bigger and bigger and they would say he thought her good enough for that but not good enough to marry. No one had told her who was the patron saint of skivvies and prostitutes. She would pray to the Sacred Heart. They got the *Messenger of the Sacred Heart* at home and it was wonderful the favours and miracles which the devotion elicited. Incurable disease disappears, job secured when all seemed hopeless, two hundred and sixty-three favours notified to our office this month, father cured of excessive drinking, rent obtained and eviction notice quashed at last moment. It was all listed. She began to pray to the Sacred Heart, fervently, in short ejaculations, until the tension inside her eased and her attention began to wander. A ragged man with cord tied about his coat for a belt was doing the Stations of the Cross. A stout, heavily built friar crossed the altar, genuflected and came down the church. He had a large grey face and his pendulant rosary rattled as he walked. He carried a stole in his hand. Without ceremony he entered a confessional to her left. People moved over. She found herself rising, genuflecting and taking her place with them. She made no examination of conscience, no preliminary confessing to God, no act of contrition. She had lived with conscience and contrition for weeks. The first penitent entered. The rest moved up. Clenching her hands in the hypnotic dimness she neither prayed nor thought. She waited. Terror found an inlet, seeped through, invaded her to the finger-tips. She sweated, but refrained from prayer or thought. She waited.

"I can't tell them, Father, I can't."

"What else can you do *but* tell them, my child."

"My father is a religious man. He won't have me under his roof."

"He must learn to be a more religious one and do his duty. He must protect you and look after you in the trial ahead of you. Later on I can offer some help too."

"They'll never forgive me."

"Tell them God has forgiven you. You have made your peace. You have had absolution and you are worthy of the sacraments. If they withhold forgiveness they will render an account for it. But you must have courage, my child. You must trust in God."

"Yes, Father."

"Tell them the moment you go home. And come back to me in one week. I can help you. I can give you a note, perhaps, to the Reverend Mother of a community who do good work. They'll look after you. Now promise God, solemnly promise God in His sacrament of penance, to tell your parents!"

"I promise."

"Don't, when you feel lost and hopeless and unloved, give way to despair. The devil will tempt you often to despair and that is when you will most need God's grace and strength to help you. Remember God is your Friend. And as His priest I am here to help you too. You will come to see me again in a week?"

"I promise."

"For your penance say three *Hail Marys* and three *Glorias*. Now make a good Act of Contrition."

The penance was trivial, less than you would get for immoderate love-making or for reading an immoral book. Did it mean God took account of how she had suffered, how she would be made suffer in the months ahead? Feeling that God's compassion and His absolution flowed quietly over her through the priest, she finished her Act of Contrition and felt her lashes sticky with tears.

"Now go in peace. And pray for me."

"And ... for me, Father?"

"God bless you, child."

The slide clicked shut. One moment a large head leaning on a huge hand, soft voice weary with the tribulation of the world. Then a blank wooden wall. Had he been there at all?

IV

Not for the first time it occurred to Casey that he might die. During the first hours of pain, during the cold of the previous night, during the unbearable heat of the early afternoon, the thought had suggested itself. He had pushed it away. It was too melodramatic, too unthinkable. He was within eight miles of the city, within eight miles of hospitals, X-ray apparatus, ambulances, of blood plasma and surgical instruments and anaesthetics. You turned on a tap and you got water, you turned a knob for music, you touched a switch for light. Eight miles was nothing; two minutes by plane, twenty slowly by car, less than an hour by bicycle. If he could walk he would be there in a little over two hours. But he could not walk because his leg was broken. It was as simple as that. He could not even reach the stream some yards away, although thirst had driven him several times to suck the moss which grew near his hand. So if nobody came this way, he would die. It seemed unlikely that anyone would, unless the weekend brought someone else hiking along the same stretch of moor. The weekend would be too late. He had no food and the nights were too damp and cold. He had seen no houses. The road was some miles ahead, but it was used by turf-cutters and the turf-cutting season was over. A shepherd? There had been sheep at the foot of the mountains, but not here. Casey, raised on his elbow, his arm now chilled and numbed by the damp earth, looked at his enemy the moor, a dark and empty expanse, now silently waiting the approach of night. The lower slopes of the mountains gleamed here and there in unaccountable light, but the summits and the sky over them were draped in rainy blackness. A wind rippled the purple loneliness of the heather, gripped and tossed his sleeves and the lapels of his jacket. Its coldness attacked his courage. He looked to the west. The sun had left an angry afterglow, a ragged sprawl of clouds and crimson light. Looking into its glowing caverns, his heart failing, Casey thought of God and sin and eternity. He had never outgrown the idea that the gateways to heaven and hell were somewhere in the sky; dreadful portals to trial and judgment which still, as in childhood, he saw in a rent cloud or an angry sunset. He was small and sick and maimed and mortal. The moor was immense, the sun straddled civilisations, the sky was infinite, like God. They were all enemies. Out of such a sunset the trumpets would blast, the Son of God in power and majesty come signing for a Cessation. Those who went to their duties, the daily communicants and the sodality men, the sayers of family rosaries and the women who went to evening devotions, these would be called in; people like Pringle and Rita Kilshaw's father and the Chairman of the Board who had two sons in the Jesuits. And outside would be left the dogs and the sorcerers, the whoremongers and the fornicators. Casey knew his category. It filled him with fear, but it moved him also with a desperate cunning. He began to weigh again the odds against him, the possibilities of escape. He wanted desperately to escape, not so much now his pain and the indifference of the moor, but the trumpets and the judgment, the onset of eternity and its glowing cauldron of condemnation. God was Just, they said, and God was Merciful. But he had always been suspicious of the mercy end of it. He had never noticed much of it knocking round, not when it came to the point. Death and eternity he would push aside and cheat. It was easy in town. If they nagged you you simply stopped thinking about them, by switching on the radio or dropping down to the social club or by figuring out a crossword. Here you did it by going over again the ways of escape. It was hard though. It was nearly impossible. He was beginning to stare at the sunset again with hopeless foreboding when the pigeon occurred to him. It was a racing pigeon – he knew that by the silver ring. It would fly for home. When you'd wings a broken leg did not matter so long as you got off the ground. Wings were a kind of double indemnity. Casey could see it got off the ground. He could throw it into the air. It was only necessary to write a note, describing where he was, stuff it into the ring, and the pigeon would deliver it. Pigeons were pretty fast.

Casey tore a page from his diary and did so. It was difficult to be any way accurate about where he was, but what he had written would serve. He drew the pigeon from under his coat and began to insert the folded paper between the ring and the flesh. It was difficult. The ring was tight and the pigeon grew restless. He tore up what he had written and did it again, writing smaller this time so as

27

to use less paper. It was still difficult to insert. He tried several times. When at last he got it small enough and had a quarter of its length inserted the pigeon, jerking suddenly, half freed itself, so that Casey in surprise pulled hard at the injured leg. "Wait, you bastard," he breathed. The leg tore again before he released it. His arm was almost at the end of its reach, so that the pigeon, half-thrown, rolled rather than flew into the air. It struggled, its wings flapping wildly, its leg dangling useless. But the piece of paper remained in the ring and the pigeon regained control and rose. Then, having resisted with his last effort until he saw it winging steadily towards the east, Casey fainted with the pain which his effort had cost him.

V

"Search me," Ellis said feelingly, "I've tried every pub and rendezvous in this flipping town."

"And the lassie is not keen either?" asked the big man in the bowler. He sounded gloomy and disillusioned.

"That's putting it mildly," Ellis said.

"It's clear to me," the little man with the red lump on his forehead observed, "from what this young fella has been telling us, that she's highly dangerous material anyway. And the other fella has hopped it. It's not honourable, but there it is."

"Now you have it in a nutshell," Ellis said.

The big man sighed deeply.

"Taking it by and large," he said, "I think it's healthier we called it a day."

"Me too," the little man said.

"I'm sorry," Ellis apologised.

"That's all right," the little man assured him gloomily. "You've acted honourable. It's not your fault."

"Thanks," Ellis said. "I'm glad you see it that way."

They drank in silence. Then the other two left and Ellis, grateful to be alone, ordered himself a beer. From time to time Casey's cowardice made him frown and pucker his lips. He felt doubly betrayed. He had risked a lot to save him, and he had stood aside and let him have a clear field with Rita Kilshaw. But mostly he thought of Rita Kilshaw. She had not been very kind to him; she had certainly not been grateful. But he would have given her anything she asked in return for one responsive word. He hoped she would do nothing desperate. Gradually withdrawing from the smoke-filled lounge he stared in alcoholic melancholy at the uncurtained window. It was dark. Blobs of rain were breaking on it into flowing rivulets. Gradually these spread until below him the lights of street standards and passing traffic began to look like melting stars.

VI

"I don't know if I can let this pass without some sort of formal report to the Board. You are extremely late. And you've broken your leg."

"I'm sorry, Mr. Pringle, I was out walking when it got caught in a hole which was hidden under the bracken. I pitched forward and twisted on it. I can only assure you that it was quite unintentional."

"I must accept your word I suppose. But how did you get here?"

"At first I crawled. Then I hailed a passing pigeon, which very kindly offered me a lift. It had a leg on it and one of its rings was broken."

"I see. You know I've warned you before about coming in improperly attired. On one occasion you were wearing a pyjama jacket but you wore your tie with it in the hope it would pass as a shirt. That was outrageous."

"I believe I apologised."

29

"You did. And I overlooked it, which you will admit was very fair of me."

"I know, Mr. Pringle. I suppose I should go home."

"If you could even make it look a bit more tidy. The bone is sticking out through the skin. Isn't that uncomfortable?"

"It is. But when I try to put it back the pain is unbearable."

"I see."

"May I go to my desk?"

"I suppose you may. But tidy it up somehow. The Chairman of the Board may appear at any moment in great power and majesty to judge the living and the dead. We can't let him find you like this – can we? Perhaps if you happen to hear the trumpets in time you will take steps to ... well ... to discreetly absent yourself."

"I will, Mr. Pringle."

"In the meantime turn up your collar, it's beginning to rain. If you look round you will notice the rest of the staff have wisely provided themselves with heads. It keeps the rain off their umbrellas."

"But where is the roof, Mr. Pringle? Has somebody taken it?"

"The roof?"

"There used to be a roof. I remember it distinctly."

"You are a little feverish, Mr. Casey."

"But there was. There ought to be a roof."

"Roof?"

"Yes, a roof. Wasn't there? Surely there was a roof?"

"No roof, Mr. Casey. Cold rain and no roof. Curl up on the floor here, I think, yes, here on the green inlaid linoleum by the thin tubular legs of this desk. Turn up your collar and curl up coldly under the cold rain. Why, Mr. Casey, you are shivering."

VII

The rain had crept in on the city just as the public lamps were being lit. It was a soft, cold curtain of rain which swung sadly over the streets and flecked noiselessly on the dark waters of the river. To Rita Kilshaw it symbolised the end of any little comfort the streets could offer. Drop by drop it adulterated and washed out forever the clinging sediment of hope. She went home. The light in the front window told her where the family had gathered. Letting herself in quietly she went straight to the kitchen. She stood for some time in the darkness, her hair wet, her bag clasped under her arm. Her thoughts were slow and confused and in the back of her head was a low incessant murmuring. She knew she had been heard. It was not possible to open the hall door and go down the narrow strairs without being heard. But though she waited tensely for some time nobody called. She repeated to herself:

"He said you're to forgive me that God has already forgiven me. He said to tell you. He said God has forgiven me and that's why I'm to tell you that if God has forgiven me you are to forgive me too." But it was difficult to put it right going over it in the darkness and feeling your hair heavy and wet and your bag tight under your arm. It was difficult with the murmuring in her head incessantly dragging her from concentration. She bit her lip. She knew she looked a fright and she would shock them standing in the doorway for a while waiting for the words to come. But there was nothing else for it. As she went up the hall again the murmuring grew. She flung open the front room door. It took her some time to realise that the murmuring had not been in her head. Her father and mother and her two younger brothers and sisters were all on their knees. Her mother looked around first. They were saying the family rosary.

VIII

The pigeon met the full fury of the rain as it approached the suburbs. First the darkness had closed in and then a breeze from the right, strengthening to a wind, buffeted it. But home was in the wind too, home and the reek of smoke, the smell of little gardens, the promise of lit windows under thousands of cosy roofs, the darkness and safety of the pigeon hutch. It struggled on. Near the end the rain almost drove it to earth again. The pigeon persisted. Darkness and rain would end with home; food and ease were within reach. It was quite dark when it reached its destination, so dark that only for the flurry of its fall and the fact that it scrambled forward noisily because of its useless leg, the boy waiting for it at the window would not have known it had arrived. He shouted to his father: "He's here. I heard him. There's something wrong." He rushed out. The pigeon, frightened by its skid, suspecting another trap, was flapping its wings blindly and fighting for balance on the muddy soil. It went round in frantic circles. When the boy caught it at last he shouted to his father, "He's hurt. Pingy is hurt."

"Bring him in," his father commanded. The boy, his hair already matted with rain, took the pigeon gently against his breast and brought it indoors. They examined the wounded leg under the kitchen light. "This is bad," the boy's father said, shaking his head, "poor old Pingy." For a while apprehension kept the boy silent. Then he asked: "What can we do?"

"Not much," his father said. "Give him food and bind it up until the morning. Then we can do him in. Quietly."

"No," the boy said, "it'll mend. I won't let you."

"It's kinder that way," his father said. "He's in pain and it won't mend. It's damn nearly torn off." The boy, looking at the pigeon with love, said, "Pingy."

"It won't take long," his father told him gently. "The air-gun upstairs – or a twist of the neck. It'll be all over in a second. It's better than suffering."

"If I knew who done it," the boy said in sudden fury, "I'd give *them* the air-gun."

He was trying not to cry. His father said nothing. He was skilfully binding the leg. Rain rattled in a tumultuous gust against the window.

"By God," the boy's father said, "that's a night and a half."

Ellis, making his way home along the wall of the river, turned up his collar and said the same thing. It startled Florrie, who was assessing for her mother the value of what was left in the tenantless room with its set of soiled underwear and its bottle of sticky hair dressing. Rain covered mountain and moor and city in an unremitting downpour. It made a torrent of the little stream, nearer which Casey now lay, his shoulders hunched, his arms across his breast, summoning his yielding and outnumbered garrison to stand desperately against this latest assault. It battered the soft earth of the garden and beat to pulp the piece of paper which the pigeon had dislodged from its ring in its first frantic efforts to find balance. It drummed loudly on the corrugated roof of the pigeon hutch. But the pigeon was undisturbed. Surrounded by familiar odours it dozed comfortably and warmly after the painful length of the day. It was fed and at ease now, and confident once more of love.

A Walk Through the Summer

AT intervals while he walked the man, who was old, allowed his stick to touch the railings which bounded the plot about the ivy-covered church. It was not a very well-cared plot. The grasses had grown high with summer and there were tall dandelions about the notice-board. The notice itself had loosened with heat. Already one corner folded limply away from the wood. The loose end made no stir, the grasses stood perfectly still under the glowing sky. The notice read, "I Am The Way The Truth And The Life." It was the end of a summer evening.

Almost opposite the board, the print on which was large and aggressive, the old man stood still and listened. He was blind. He was also lost. He stood at the edge of the path and would have crossed if he had known for certain that some light still remained. But the silence, the heavy feel of the air about his face, the motionlessness and warmth suggested summer darkness. He allowed his stick to rest against the path's edge until a distant door dragged on its weather board. Then the blind man began to make tapping noises without moving from his position.

Casey stepped out into the summer evening. The quietness made him hesitate before descending the steps. He acknowledged the sky with its remote streaks of colour behind long rolling furrows of black cloud. For Casey it was a pregnant evening, an hour of decision. He thought uneasily of Barbara, who had probably spent the day at the sea with John and the children. His own evening had gone on some exercises in couterpoint, several dreary and unrewarding hours spent in the over-furnished room which Mrs. O'Keeffe provided in addition to his meals for the all-in sum of three pounds per week. It was reasonable, Casey knew. Yet he found it expensive. The weekend trip to Galway was likely to prove expensive too. After a moment he dropped his cigarette over the railings, dug one hand deep into his pocket and took the steps slowly.

In a house some miles away Barbara shook sand from a towel and heard John leaving the bathroom upstairs. He always bathed immediately on their return from the sea. She shouted up to him:

"Who's coming tonight? Will there be a crowd?"

"Only the Manpowers. He wants to discuss the Cork trip. I put all the rest off as best I could."

"My God – why didn't you say. Did you ask them for dinner?"

"No. I can take the Manpowers in small doses only."

"Did you put Tom off?"

"Who?"

"Tom Casey."

"Why?"

"Because I think I asked him. It could be embarrassing. I didn't know about the ghastly Manpowers."

She listened carefully for his answer.

"Don't worry. We'll have some music anyway." She folded the brightly coloured towel before resuming.

"What shall we play?"

"Darling, let's not gossip. I'm mother naked."

"Sorry."

"We'll put on the new issues from the Haydn Society. Do you think?"

"Chamber music. The Manpowers will be furious."

"Damn the Manpowers," John shouted back. "Just give them plenty to drink."

She heard him scampering towards the bedroom.

They met at the notice-board. The aggressive letters were familiar to Casey.

"Can I help you?"

"I was looking for Ravensdale Avenue."

"It's certainly not around here."

"A road with houses only just built."

"There are no new houses around here. A little further

35

on there's the river. Then Ballsbridge."

"Them railings behind me?"

"They surround the church."

The blind man misunderstood and crossed himself. Casey smiled. "It's not that kind of church," he said gently.

The blind man cursed at his mistake.

"I've a little time to spare. I'll help you to try some of the back roads."

The blind man allowed him to take his arm and shuffled along beside him, muttering angrily to himself. Casey, without minding very much, noticed he had not been thanked.

The girl who looked after the children for Barbara got them to bed. They were overtired and cross. They emptied little mounds of fine sand from their sandals and quarrelled with each other. There were three of them, two boys and a girl. Then she made tea in Russian fashion for Barbara who liked it that way after a day on the sands. She would sit for an hour perhaps, being lazy, hardly talking, until it seemed time to ask John to pour a drink while she changed and prepared for her guests.

The girl sat down dutifully opposite to her. She was a Pole, a refugee Barbara had offered to take care of. A couple of years before she had come from a world of devastated homes, a chaos of maimed people and orphaned children, so remote from the untouched safety of Dublin that few who met her realised that it had had any real existence. But they treated her with kindness. She was almost, but not quite, one of the family. Barbara sipped the tea and studied the young, grave face which seemed absorbed in the piece of knitting she had automatically picked up. It was not a pretty face, but foreign and strange and therefore different enough, Barbara knew, to prove attractive. Barbara herself was very pretty, in a well-groomed very feminine way. Her hands were particularly beautiful and delicate; her face, at thirty-four,

36

quite unlined and untouched, perhaps because whatever she thought or felt never seemed quite to reach it. Nature had shaped her to go with the rich, warm room, the novels, the records, the Russian tea. And Barbara, for her part, encouraged nature.

"You had a dreadfully boring afternoon, I'm sure." Her voice, too, was very beautiful.

The head above the knitting shook emphatically.

"Oh, no."

"It's such a nuisance not having room. John and I were wishing you were with us."

"That was kind."

"If I'd known John was going to Cork tomorrow I could have got out of weekending with the Burkes. But he never tells me these things. You'll have the children to manage all on your own."

"I do not mind."

"It's only for the weekend of course. I'll get back on Monday afternoon."

"I hope you have a lovely time."

"Not in Galway, dear. Lough Corrib is such a bore. Festooned with fishermen."

The brows puckered for a moment at the unfamiliar phrase, the eyes lifted enquiringly, then returned to the knitting. Barbara sipped her tea. Everything was working out nicely.

II

"If I could only get the feel of the streets," the blind man complained. He hurried his step. There was no purpose in doing so, Casey knew, but he quickened also. It was quite a hopeless quest. Two or three times, when asked what road they were on, Casey was unable to say.

"Can't you ask someone?"

"There's no one about."

"You live near at hand. It seems queer you don't know."

"There are no name-plates," Casey patiently explained. "You can't read name-plates in the dark, anyway."

"It's not altogether dark."

"The dark leaves you just as helpless as I am. You don't have to make excuses. I'm not a fool."

Casey, his arm linked in that of the blind man, grew tired and noticed that his companion smelled. It was a faint smell, a pitiable smell really because it sprang, in all probability, from helplessness and infirmity. It was also, of course, the result of poverty. Poverty nearly always smelled. Casey, for all he himself knew, might possess his own peculiar odour. It would be fainter though, because he was a little more capable and a little less poor. It was all very natural. Clothes worn for too long often caused it. Also a condition of the health. Casey was aware always of living on the fringe of such a world, saved only from its indignity by youth and a touch of fastidiousness.

They emerged from the leafy quietude of an elegant backwater on to the main road. Traffic passed on its way down the coast. Neon signs flashed in various colours, though not brilliantly, for the sky was not as yet dark. The clock of the Royal Dublin Society chimed.

"Where are we now?" the old man enquired.

"Ballsbridge," Casey told him. He found himself saying it with a touch of triumph, as though it had been necessary to prove it by demonstration. That brought both of them to a standstill.

"Look," Casey said, "it's ten o'clock."

The blind man screwed up his face unpleasantly.

"I mightn't be able to see," he said, "but I can hear a clock as well as the next."

"You might let me finish," Casey objected. "It's ten o'clock and I want a drink before they close at half past. Would you like one?"

"Is it far?"

"Across the road."

"I've no money."

"I'll stand you one."

"All right so," the blind man said, "but watch the traffic."

"I think you can trust me."

"Damn the thing I'll trust for many a long day after this." As they crossed the road the blind man explained himself.

"I'll have nothing but the height of bad luck this night," he predicted, "and me after saluting a bloody Protestant church."

The bar was pretty crowded. They moved down towards the end. As people were clearing a passage for the blind man a familiar voice rang out. It was Ellis.

Ellis, like Casey, knew the loneliness of furnished rooms and moved in a world of small salaries. In return for such respectabilities as a Post Office savings account and the renunciation of alcohol and tobacco it offered a tenuous measure of security — even the possibility, ultimately, of marriage to a respectable girl. These were ideals which Ellis had deliberately pondered and then contemptuously rejected.

As they came over he lowered his paper and there was a pint of stout on the counter in front of him.

"What'll you have?"

"A pint," Casey said.

"And your friend?"

"I'll leave it to yourself," the blind man answered.

"That's what the jarvey said. I suppose it means whiskey."

He called for a pint and a small Jameson.

"Not Jameson," the blind man said. "Jameson's is a Protestant crowd. Get me Powers."

Ellis raised his eyebrows at Casey. Casey smiled tolerantly. Ellis shrugged and amended the order. Then he tapped the racing page with the back of his hand and said:

"There's where I should have gone today. The

Curragh. I'd have had the first two favourites. Then I'd have backed Canty's mount – I'd reliable information and it came in at tens."

Casey, his mind on Barbara and the fact that he was on the eve of arranging an adulterous weekend, found it hard to concentrate. But he managed to say:

"What put you off?"

"Oul Pringle had a liver on in the office and I didn't want to ask for the time off. So instead I went to the dogs after tea and lost a bloody stack. Here's health."

The drinks had arrived. Ellis put the whiskey glass in the blind man's hand and poured some water into it.

"There's a drop of holy water to go with it," he said. The blind man's hand shook with anger.

"Don't mock at God, young man," he said, "don't try to be smart about God." He raised the glass unexpectedly and emptied it at a swallow. Then he put it down with a bang which very nearly shattered it. Ellis waited for some time for the customary salutation. None came.

Motioning him not to mind, Casey said, "Good luck."

Ellis acknowledged and said, "I suppose you spent the day in virtuous pursuits."

"At harmony and counterpoint exercises."

"Ah. Messrs. Bach and Beethoven. How are they keeping?"

Casey smiled and said, "Deceased – I fear."

"For God's sake," Ellis exclaimed, as though the news was unexpected. "That was very sudden."

"It's the way of us all," Casey said, falling in with his mood. "Here today and gone tomorrow."

"It's Mrs. Bach I pity most. All them children. Twenty – isn't it?"

"Twenty-seven," Casey corrected.

Ellis made a slow, clicking noise with his tongue.

"Have you two gentlemen lost someone," the blind man asked. He had gathered little of the conversation.

"Bach and Beethoven," Ellis explained. "It's a great shock."

The blind man's face grimaced unpleasantly once again. He said, "Death comes for all." There was a belligerent note in his voice. The thought seemed to satisfy some need in him. Perhaps it was the fact that all infirmity fell away in that one universal infirmity. Ultimately all men would be equal.

"You're right," Casey agreed. "That's a day we'll all see."

"If God spares us," Ellis added without a smile.

It was Ellis who posed the question at closing-time. They had drunk rather fast, partly because the blind man kept emptying everything immediately it was placed in front of him. He knocked each drink back and then stared ahead of him, his jaws champing most of the time and his lips dribbling now and then from one side. At times some inner anger showed in his face, at other times greed. Near closing-time Ellis asked:

"Are you going out to John's?"

"What put that into your head?"

"It's Friday. Don't you want to hear some music?"

"I've had my bellyful of music today," Casey evaded. He had hoped Ellis would not be going.

"Then — the divine Barbara . . . ?" Ellis had said similar things in the past. Casey found it hard to assess just how much he guessed. He decided not to comment.

"What about our friend?"

"Shunt him off."

"We can't do that. He's still lost."

"We'd better bring him with us so. We haven't time to go messing round."

"What about John?"

"John is a philanthropist."

Casey doubtfully supposed it would be all right. It was an unexpected complication.

"You'll get a meal," Ellis said to the blind man. "And we'll get you home."

The blind man hesitantly accepted. He appeared to be suspicious.

They took a bus. Ellis deliberately deposited the blind man in a seat apart and led Casey to the back.

"That's not a very appealing specimen of afflicted humanity," he explained.

"What can we do. If we left him home we'd miss our last bus."

Ellis said: "I know. Duty before everything. I hope you have the fare."

"Barely."

"That's why I'm going to John's, if you want to know. I'm going to knock him for a tenner."

"Everybody knocks John for money. It's a bit thick, in a way."

"Better than knocking him for his wife."

Casey stiffened. Ellis only meant it as a joke.

"I don't think that's funny."

"Don't mind me," Ellis said, "I like saying things like that. As a matter of fact, she has an eye for you. You could nearly have a go there."

"I don't want to discuss it."

But Ellis kept on. He pushed his hat back and produced two packets of potato crisps from his pocket.

"Have a chew," he offered.

Casey refused. Ellis put back the second packet and tore his own open. He stuffed a wad of crisps into his mouth.

"I'm not offering jembo over there any. He drank enough free whiskey to satisfy a bishop. That's another good reason for going to John's. We'll get something to eat. I'd nothing for tea except a sandwich I managed to lift in the canteen today. It fell off one of the trays on to the floor."

"What did you do — put your foot on it?"

"Dropped my napkin over it. A bloody lovely sandwich. You should have seen your woman when she came back to pick it up and throw it out. She didn't know Ellis had it safe in his arse pocket."

Casey smiled again and looked out the window. The bus had swung on to a looping road which skirted the

Bay. Tall street lamps spread long orange streaks on the full waters and the stream of air which raked through the open glass panel smelled of the sea. Ellis crumpled the empty crisp bag with a sigh and flung it on the floor.

"That'd be a pleasurable night's work," he observed.

"What?"

"The fair Barbara."

Casey once again controlled the anger which in the eyes of Ellis would betray him, if he allowed it to show. Ellis, he felt, was pumping for information.

"I want happiness – not pleasure."

"Happiness is not without pleasure."

"But pleasure can be without happiness."

Ellis looked astounded. He opened the second packet of crisps.

"I'll need a bit of nourishment to sort that one out," he said.

"Happiness is the object – pleasure merely the accident. The object is legitimate, but the accident may operate in conflict with the object."

"Illustration required," Ellis invited, his mouth full of crisps.

"All right. Drink too much and you get a head. Result – unhappiness. Eat too much and you get sick. Result – ditto."

"Mysterioso Profundo."

"You should read Aquinas."

"Ah. Aquinas. How's he keeping?"

"Deceased also," Casey said, to draw the subject further away from its beginnings.

"It's terrible," Ellis said, "all the old crowd dropping off one by one." He shook out the bag and three small crisps fell into his hand. He gazed at them sadly, then showed them to Casey.

"There you are," he said, "there's only a few of us left."

"I think that's about all," Mr. Manpower said. "The main thing is to keep the American end interested."

When he spoke of business he spoke with authority.

"Bloody dreary," John said and Mrs. Manpower, a refined, spinsterish woman, looked startled. Mr. Manpower used such expressions frequently. But a well-bred person, who had been to university. And before the ladies.

"Why can't Wallace come to Dublin?" John complained.

"He never does. He never flies from New York. Always comes by boat. And he won't trust any form of Irish transport." Mr. Manpower paused. "You keep a good drop, John," he added, eyeing his glass with great friendliness.

"Have some more," John invited.

"Henry," Mrs. Manpower warned.

"Do me good," Mr. Manpower said easily.

A gentle snore drew their attention to a presence they had almost forgotten. A long, thin, aristocratic form lay sleeping in an easy chair.

"Poor Haddington," Barbara apologised. She gently relieved the long fingers of a glass which dangled perilously from them and placed it on a shelf.

"How did he get here. He couldn't have driven out."

"The bus," John explained. "He comes now and then. He was a dear friend of my father's."

"One doesn't expect it really," Mrs. Manpower suggested carefully, "certainly not from a professor."

"That's what you call scholarly drinking," Mr. Manpower enthused.

"I think it most unbecoming," Mrs. Manpower reproved, making it clear that she was going to stick to her guns.

Mr. Manpower winked vulgarly at John. "Good thing for her," he said jovially, indicating his infuriated spouse, "that I'm only half educated."

John pretended to be amused, and Barbara, because Mr. Manpower was of considerable financial importance, managed a thin smile. Then she said sweetly:

"Don't you think, darling, a little music would be amusing."

IV

The bus left them at its lonely terminus, a point of the bay marked by a few shops and a road which ran steeply uphill between tall hedges. As they climbed, the blind man linked between them, they saw it reverse and make its way back along the road below, a small smear of light pursued at water level by its own reflection. The blind man, who was puffing with exertion, stopped and suddenly lost his temper.

"What sort of a fool am I to be led on a wild goose chase like this?" he demanded. "What class of a heathen hideout are youse heading for at this unholy hour of the night?"

"We're heading for records and novelties," Ellis assured him, "long hair and sturdy bank balances. You'll find it eminently respectable."

After a while they turned into the tree-lined avenue. At the end stood the house, well lit, self-assured, master of its own well-kept grounds.

"How do you think they'll take it," Ellis asked, meaning the blind man.

"You're the one who said it was going to be all right."

"That was approximately an hour ago."

"So you've changed your mind?"

"That is what distinguishes man from the brute. The cow chews the cud. But does it get any nearer inventing the milking machine? When man ruminates he moves from idea to idea. I have been ruminating."

"I'll say this for your friend," the blind man confessed to Casey, "he's an eolquent young blade."

"You mean you've developed cold feet," Casey grumbled. "You'd better go to the front door with our friend. I'll slip round the back and explain matters."

The french windows at the back stood open to the night. A piano trio of Haydn grew louder as Casey approached, his feet crunching on the gravel. The occupants of the room sat around in various attitudes of attention. Each had a drink. Though he had sat in it so many times the soft lighting and the warm luxury of the room affected Casey pleasantly. Money and graciousness did not always go together as they did so flawlessly here. Barbara, who was facing the windows sat up and said:

"Tom."

"My dear Tom," John greeted, rising.

"I'm interrupting," Casey apologised. Then he explained quickly about the blind man.

"Delighted," John said. "Is he a musician?"

"No. An ignorant and rather aggressive old man who smells."

"Oh, no," Barbara said.

The Manpowers detached themselves from contemplation of the music in order to look surprised.

"This is delightful," John said. "Bring him in."

"Good evening, everybody," Casey said generally. The Manpowers switched on automatic smiles and went back with alacrity to the music. Casey went through to the hall door where Ellis was waiting with the blind man. Between them they brought him into the room and seated him down. John asked him if he would have a drink but Barbara said, "Please, John." John smiled at everybody and said sorry. When the music had finished the guests expressed their opinions.

"Damn good," Mr. Manpower applauded. "You're a powerful man for the music." His wife made a great show of pleasure and said rapturously, "I adore Haydn."

Haddington, who was half awake, murmured

approvingly but incoherently. Casey recognised him as the author of a number of difficult philosophical books.

"Mr. and Mrs. Manpower," John introduced. "Meet Mr. Casey . . . Mr. Ellis."

"Glad to know you," Manpower responded heartily.

"Delighted," Mrs. Manpower confirmed, but coolly. She had noted that they were rather shabbily dressed.

"And of course, Professor Haddington."

Haddington mumbled unintelligibly but with great courtesy and politeness. Casey remembered that he was said to rise at six o'clock every morning and work until noon. At noon, but never before, he opened his first bottle of whiskey. The professor had the reputation of being a man of unshakable habit. No one had ever known him to utter anything intelligible after five o'clock.

"And your friend?" John asked.

There was a noticeable pause.

"They never asked me, mister," the blind man said triumphantly. "It's Moore . . . Tom Moore."

"Our national poet," Mrs. Manpower said sweetly, but to John and Barbara only.

"A shoneen, ma'am," the blind man contradicted, "who aped the English gentry because he took them to be his betters."

There was a pause. John decided to offer drinks. Sara, who was still smiling a little at the Rondo which had just concluded, rose to get glasses.

"Don't fuss, dear," Barbara said, "I'll get them." When she had gone a little while she called out to Casey. He joined her in the dining-room.

"Well?" he questioned.

"Everything is beautiful."

"John is definitely going?"

"Tomorrow, by train. He made no fuss at all about leaving the car when I told him I'd like to spend the weekend with the Burkes. That was the only thing which worried me."

"What?"

"I thought he might bitch about leaving the car." She paused.

"Aren't you going to say it's wonderful?"

"Of course," Casey said. He kissed her. It was all that was required to spark off his desire. But he regretted just a little that such things had to be planned. It would be so much easier if they just happened. They remained in each other's arms for some moments. Barbara said:

"Don't let John delay you tonight by offering you the car. Leave with the Manpowers. They'll drop you home."

"But why?"

"I don't want you to take the car. I must have it fairly early tomorrow morning."

"What on earth for?"

"Don't ask so many questions, darling."

"The Manpowers don't look very musical to me."

"They're ghastly. Business friends of John. At least he is. She's just a drip. And poor, dear, befuddled Haddington. What a collection."

"Wait till the blind man gets going."

"Why on earth did you bring him along?"

Casey held her closer, pressing his face against her hair and reflected why. Love? Because you just could not meet a blind man who was lost without putting him right? Superstition? For some dark primitive reason his infirmity gave him the right to your service? Incompetence? Why not get a policeman to look after everything.

"Love," Casey said.

"Little Sir Christopher," Barbara murmured. Casey, knowing she had probably meant to say Saint Christopher, disengaged himself without pointing out the mistake. She handed him glasses.

"Take these in while I get Sara to give you something to eat."

V

John filled out whiskey and put on another trio. John's measures were liberal. This time it took the blind man two gulps to finish it. When John noticed he filled the glass again. An empty glass in the hands of a guest made him feel restless. His generosity was misguided. The blind man threw it back. Some minutes later, cutting across the music and the reverent silence, he said loudly, "You're a gentleman."

Mrs. Manpower shot upright. Her husband showed a moment's surprise, then grinned happily.

"Thank you," John said with a smile. The blind man wiped his lips noisily.

"Don't think I'm trying to scratch your back."

"Not at all."

"I'm not that class. There's a lot of our people and when they get thrown in with moneyed people they lose themselves in embarrassment. But I'm an Irish Catholic and I'm not ashamed to be what I am whether I'm in the company of Protestants or Communists."

Nobody answered, in the hope that in that way their desire to listen to the music might register most forcibly. It worked for some minutes. Then the blind man groped for his stick and made a fumbling attempt to rise.

"I can see I'm not wanted."

John jumped up and went across. "Please," he said, pushing him back gently into the chair.

"Then why does nobody talk to me?"

"We were listening to the music."

"Can't you listen and talk."

"Really," Mrs. Manpower observed. "What a peculiar way to behave."

"Don't you think because I'm blind that I lack for education. I'd the school for the blind to go to when I was young. And the nuns still come to read to me once a week."

John, with a grimace of resignation, went over and

touched the reject button. The music gave up.

"What a shame," Mrs. Manpower whispered. Mr. Manpower looked relieved. Casey felt responsible and consequently embarrassed. He was also a little surprised that anything stupid could happen on a night of such importance to Barbara and himself. In the silence Haddington, registering that something was missing but unable to give it a name, began a vague and incompetent search of his pockets.

"Do have a drink or something," John invited. He began to fill the glasses and gave an extra large helping to the blind man. Barbara and Sara reappeared with sandwiches. They placed a plate between Ellis and Casey and one on a special table beside the blind man. Barbara arranged herself gracefully and asked for some music. Casey, contemplating her with tenderness, was startled by a half-choked exclamation from the blind man.

"Holy God," he spluttered.

"Is something wrong?"

"Meat," the blind man said. "Meat of a Friday. And I swallowed some of it."

"Is it meat?" John asked wearily.

"Of course it's meat," Barbara snapped, "how was I to know."

Ellis guffawed, sending a shower of crumbs about the carpet.

"Do you find it so amusing?" Barbara shot at him.

"Gas," Ellis confirmed. He winked at Mrs. Manpower, who glared. Barbara asked Sara to get some cheese and tomato sandwiches and when they arrived Barbara put them beside the blind man and said, "Now for goodness' sake let's have some music."

"I'd like this one from the beginning if nobody minds," John said to the rest.

Everyone appeared to approve.

While John adjusted the record player the blind man began to eat. He attacked his sandwiches ravenously and not by any means quietly. The task of satisfying his appetite absorbed him. Casey saw Barbara turn away her eyes in disgust, but in a remarkably short time the blind man disposed of the sandwiches and brushed the crumbs from his lap. Then he became abstracted. It was possible at last to attend to the music. Barbara, no longer irritated, smiled at Casey and bowed her head to listen. There was a grace about everything she did, an appositeness of word and gesture which, though studied, was nevertheless quite charming. It had been so a year before, when Casey met her on a road some miles beyond the town of Galway. She had been marooned in her car in the middle of a flock of sheep then, unable to go forwards or backwards. The air was full of the smell of animals and their bleating calls, the sun drew waves of heat from the long stretches of moor and rock. Casey, who was on foot, picked his way slowly through the woolly mass and as he passed her she threw him a grimace of humorous resignation which had the effect of fixing her image pleasantly in his mind for some considerable time. About half an hour later her car drew in beside him.

"You look so dusty," she invited. "Hop in."

He eased the rucksack from his shoulder and accepted. The car, which was roomy and luxurious, smelled in the heat. It was a comfortably expensive smell.

"Clifden any use?"

"That's where I'm going," he said.

"On foot?"

She sounded surprised.

"It's a hobby of mine."

"Have you been fishing or shooting somewhere?"

"No. Collecting folk music."

"Oh. Is that another hobby?"

"No. I'm doing that for a thesis."

"Any luck?"

"No. In fact I've spent most of my time teaching the people their own folk tunes. I must say they found them quaint and interesting."

"Too bad for the thesis."

"Not if you're inventive enough. After all, it isn't difficult to make up a folk tune or two."

He offered a cigarette.

"Don't the examiners know the difference?"

"Either they don't, or they don't examine them very closely."

She remained smiling for some time.

Lakes came up to the edge of the road at times and then were left behind, the sheer and desolate mountains lifting steeply on their right accompanied them mile by mile.

"What beautiful country," she remarked.

They stayed at the same hotel. They went about together for some days. There were the beach and dancing and quiet walks. Some love-making too which she made no effort to discourage. One evening when they were sitting in the lounge she was called to the telephone to take a trunk call and when she returned she remained silent for so long that he asked her if it had been bad news.

"No," she said, "it was just about my ring."

"Your ring?"

"My wedding ring. I left it on the dressing-table at the Burkes' place. They 'phoned to tell me it was safe." Casey found it impossible to say anything. He waited. After a while she said, "Well . . . now you know."

Casey noted that for a moment she seemed to have lost her studied elegance. She was hunched, even miserable. This proved an even greater shock than the first, until it occurred to him that this too fitted perfectly. It was both touching and disarming. Next morning she was her sophisticated self and before she left asked him to visit them when he got back to the city. John, she said, adored music.

VI

The look on the blind man's face held Casey's uneasy attention for some time before he realised that anything was going to happen. At first it was unusually pale, with saliva showing at the side of his mouth. His head began to nod from side to side, as though in rhythm with the music. Then his fingers tightened on the arms of his chair as he heaved himself to his feet. He was half-way across the floor before the others realised what was happening, and before Casey could reach him he got violently sick. Mrs. Manpower gave a little scream and gazed in horror at the carpet.

"Good God!" Barbara exclaimed.

The blind man, whom Casey had gripped and helped back to his chair, shuddered all over. When he had recovered he said: "It was the food. Tomatoes and cheese is far too rich for me. You shouldn't have given them to me."

"Sorry," John said.

"It's all right," the blind man said, "it can't be helped now."

"I like that," Barbara exploded, "what the hell did you eat it for if it wasn't going to agree with you?"

"Why does anybody eat anything that doesn't agree with him," the blind man snarled back.

"The pleasure principle," Ellis contributed, addressing Casey exclusively. "The man is a philosopher."

"I hear the fellow with the smart talk," the blind man said.

"Can't you shut up, Ellis," Casey complained, "you always manage to make things a good deal worse."

Sara, who had left the room immediately the incident happened, returned now with a bucket and some cloths.

"Poor Sara," Barbara sympathised. The rest withdrew, including Haddington, who made his way after them. It required remarkable concentration, but he managed it unaided. The Manpowers, once on their feet, gently declined the invitation to move into another room. They had had a most interesting evening, Mrs. Manpower said, but it was quite late and time to go home.

Mr. Manpower agreed. He offered lifts. "We'll take Professor Haddington."

"Of course," Mrs. Manpower said.

Haddington acknowledged courteously, waved a vague leave-taking and shuffled out into the night.

"The back seat, Professor," Mrs. Manpower called out after him, with great sweetness. Haddington's unintelligible reply made her smile at the others.

"Such a curious man," she said, "but, after all, so brilliant."

Mr. Manpower extended the offer to Casey, Ellis and the blind man.

"But we'd hardly have room, dear."

"We've managed six before," Mr. Manpower said hospitably.

But the blind man was found to be very unsteady and upset still.

"I think you'd better leave us," Casey said regretfully.

"Yes, do," John urged. "Tom here can take our car. We won't need it."

"But we do, dear. I wanted it tomorrow morning."

"Tom can bring it back early."

Barbara said, "Never in history has Tom been known to bring back a car early."

She appealed to Casey, "Couldn't you manage him?" She looked at him in a way which conveyed the very special nature of her appeal.

"He's not well enough at the moment," Casey resisted. "Put him in a car now and he'll be sick all over again."

"We mustn't keep the professor waiting," Mrs. Manpower said, failing to hide her alarm.

Everybody accompanied them to their car, the gravel crunching under their feet and the night warm about them.

"Hello," Mr. Manpower exclaimed when he had

54

opened the door, "where's Haddington?"

There was no one in the back seat and no one to be seen anywhere near. A search proved fruitless. They called out several times but got no answer. The night had swallowed Haddington.

"Let's spread out and search the grounds," John said. It was obvious that he was finding it difficult to remain calm.

VII

In the now silent house Sara bent over her unpleasant task. There was a shadow of suffering on her face but her voice betrayed no note of complaint.

"Who are you?" the blind man asked.

"I am Sara," she said.

"A foreigner?"

"Yes — a refugee."

"One of the crowd that gets everything while the poor of Ireland gets nothing. I wonder if you know how lucky you are."

"I think I do."

She was mopping the floor, her task half completed.

"From where?"

"I beg your pardon?"

"Where do you come from?"

"From Poland."

"You're a Catholic so?"

"Yes. I am a Catholic."

"What do you think of them giving me meat of a Friday. What would you do if it happened to you?"

"Probably I would eat it."

That brought him to a standstill. But only for a moment. He took it up again.

"No doubt," he said. 'Foreign Catholics is notorious luke-warmers. They're not a patch on Irish Catholics. The

Pope himself said that."

The girl squeezed the cloth into the bucket and the water slopped about.

"Is there a cigarette handy?"

"Please . . . in one moment."

"Don't hurry yourself. Irish Catholics didn't get it soft like you. They suffered for the Faith."

"Please . . . ?"

"Never mind. You're a foreign Catholic. Brought up in indifference. Then taken into good homes where you get the height of good feeding. You never suffered."

"I think we suffered."

"No. You've a loose way of living, you foreign Catholics. Not like Irish Catholics. What about that cigarette?"

The girl went out to empty the bucket, washed her hands and returned with a cigarette. She lit it for him and he rattled on. He talked about the great faith of the Irish and about all they suffered. Some people didn't appreciate how lucky they were, living free in comfortable Irish homes. As she tidied up he asked her questions. She made no answers. For some reason she had begun to weep. But quietly. She did not want him to know.

VIII

The rest failed to find Haddington and after half an hour the Manpowers gave up and drove off. As the wheels crunched on the gravel Barbara waved for a moment and then linked Casey's arm. They moved together towards the house. John and Ellis were still searching. They saw Sara going across to join them.

"We'll search the house," Barbara shouted.

"He couldn't possibly be in the house," John shouted back.

"No harm trying," she answered. "He must be

somewhere."

Barbara and Casey went from room to room. In the children's room he was about to switch on the light when she stopped him. It would waken them, she said. They passed through into Sara's room, leaving the door open. A small, illuminated cross glowed red in a covering of glass. The air in the room was warm still from the earlier sunshine. It was a small room. On a bed at one side the pillow and sheets looked extraordinarily white.

"You let the Manpowers go," she accused.

With a shrug he said, "What could I do?"

"You'll have to take the car now, of course. But you must promise to bring it back early in the morning. It's quite important."

"Won't it do in the afternoon. We'll have the whole day driving down."

"The shops close. There are things I want which can't be got just anywhere."

"Such as?"

She moved into his arms.

"Don't be such a dumb idiot," she said in a small embarrassed voice.

He realised then what she meant. There were certain preparations; there were the necessary womanly precautions.

"I'm sorry," he said. "Put it down to my peasant stupidity."

After that Casey was silent. He had made a humiliating discovery. He was not as sophisticated as he had believed.

IX

The rest of the night was hardly more successful. They had some more drinks and listened to some more records. But for some reason there was no point of contact between them. The blind man lay back in his chair, looking very

57

pale and breathing heavily. Ellis was unusually subdued. Sara kept her head bowed, her natural gravity emphasised by the lack of communication between the others. Casey looked from Barbara to John and felt the situation keenly. He knew that John had his own infidelities from time to time. He felt, however, that it was not quite the same thing; or rather, that in matters of the kind he himself was not made of quite same clay. The prospect of the long trip, the excuses, the lies which would inevitably be necessary, began to suggest themselves in a new light. The situation would pass and give way to new situations, but for the moment he saw clearly that it would require a betrayal of his personality which he would have to sustain for many months, perhaps even for life. He felt about such matters at a far deeper level than either Barbara or John, for whom money and well-trained manners had rounded the edges of reality. He saw beyond the situation to its effects. He was not himself pure and he was far from being a prude. But he could not help seeing impurity as a state and not simply as a word. So palpable was it that in a moment of alarming comprehension it had stood before him. It was a brown shroud stiff with the remains which stuck to it, sticky to touch – if one dared. He had seen it a moment before, when the reason why Barbara wanted the car had suddenly become clear to him.

Between his mood and the innocent good humour of the Haydn trio there was a gap which no effort of concentration could close. Once or twice he smiled across at John, who liked to share their mutual appreciation in that way. He was much relieved when the trio finished and he could rise to take his leave. John gave him the keys of the car.

"What are we to do about Haddington?" he said.

"We've done all we can about Haddington," Barbara decided. She had had her fill of upsets.

"We really ought to 'phone the police or something," John said.

"Perhaps he walked," Casey offered.

58

"Or climbed a tree," Ellis suggested. His effort was not appreciated.

The blind man had to be assisted. When they reached the car they decided to prop him up between them on the front seat. It was difficult in the darkness, but at last they got him fixed. Casey found the switch for the headlights and the half circle of gravel glared back at him suddenly. John waved good-bye. Barbara warned:

"Tomorrow morning early. For God's sake don't over-sleep."

"Don't worry," Casey shouted, "you'll have it back."

The bordering trees spun in a gleaming half-circle and they were off. Casey drove. Ellis held the blind man upright. It was a tight squeeze with the three of them in front.

"Not a very successful evening," Casey said, when they had been driving for some time.

"I got my ten pounds. I wouldn't complain."

Ellis lit a contented cigarette and looked out of the window to his left, where at regular intervals the beam of a lighthouse traced a golden passage across the calm waters of the bay. The night was heavy and still.

"Light me one of those," Casey asked. Ellis lit another cigarette and when he had handed it to him he said:

"I met Sara in the garden tonight and she was crying. Something his nibs here said to her."

"What was it about?"

"She wouldn't say."

Some minutes later Ellis took up the theme again. He sounded sleepy. But it was obvious that he had been turning it over in his mind.

"I don't think a woman has cried in front of me like that ever before. She's quite an alluring piece of stuff, the fair Sara."

"Remember your bachelor vows."

"Ellis will remain single. But not necessarily celibate."

"Hardchaw," Casey said.

He knew something of Sara's background, things Barbara had mentioned to him from time to time. It was a topic he did not wish to pursue. They made the circuit in silence and swung away from the coast road, encountering a long, hedge-lined suburban avenue and then, quite suddenly it seemed, a wide street, closed and shuttered shops, the first traffic lights.

"You're very subdued," Casey remarked.

"I'm trying to keep Father Rabelais here from falling off the bloody seat. He has me half strangled."

"How is he?"

"Still breathing – I think."

"We didn't ask him where he lived."

"No."

"I suppose you wouldn't have room ..."

"No."

"That's what I bought. No harm asking."

"Divil the bit. You're welcome."

That was that. Casey took responsibility for furnishing accommodation for the blind man. They had a job wakening him when Ellis was being dropped, but after a good deal of rough treatment he opened his eyes.

"Where am I?" he asked.

"Back in the city," Ellis said. "You'd better lean on your own shoulder from now on. I'm getting out."

X

There was a hint of greyness in the air when Casey got home. He brought the blind man up the steps and into his bedroom. He led him over to the bed.

"Where are you going to sleep yourself?" the blind man asked.

"In the car."

"That'll be cold enough."

"I'll take a blanket."

60

The blind man removed his boots and began to undress.

"Where do you keep the yoke?" he asked.

Casey was puzzled. The blind man got annoyed.

"Don't tell me you don't use a yoke. Everyone has a yoke in the bedroom."

Light dawned on Casey. "I use the toilet in the bathroom," he said.

"You can't expect me to be able to find that."

It was, Casey supposed, a reasonable point of view. He looked around. In an ornamental bowl by the window Mrs. O'Keeffe kept a depressing geranium. Casey removed the plant and handed the bowl to the blind man. It was a fancy bowl with teethed edges which were meant to represent the opening bud of a flower. The blind man ran his hands around it and began to criticise it.

"This is a highly dangerous contraption . . ." he began.

Casey cut him short.

"It's the only yoke available," he said. "You'll have to do your best with it."

He closed the hall door softly and realised that morning had come. He could see the houses opposite and below him the car, its shape misty with dew, black-skinned and moist like a large slug. He walked down past it and up the road, past the railings of the church, past the notice-board with its aggressive message and its unkept plot of graves and dandelions. They smelled sweetly and damply now in the early morning air. Then he turned back and as he did so he arrived at a decision. He was not going to Galway with Barbara. She would feel badly about it, he knew, but in the long run it would be better. It had been more than exciting, the whole prospect. She was beautiful, she was rich, so much so that her interest in him had always been something of a mystery to Casey. He was humble enough most of the time to wonder what she could see in him. She would suffer, of course. How much Casey could not venture to guess. Not very much he thought. In her world there were plenty of distractions. Besides, it would do her no harm. Out of some nightmare background of suffering, at some awakened memory of a family scattered and murdered, Sara had wept in front of Ellis. He had been touched to the extent that he desired to seduce her. And that was all. As for himself, he would retire once again to Mrs. O'Keeffe's room and the companionship of her favourite geranium, thinking now and then of the indignity to which circumstances had subjected its fancy container; thinking now and then also of a sunlit road, animal cries and the huddled, white gleaming of fleece.

Casey opened the door of the car and froze. Someone was sitting on the back seat.

"You," he exclaimed.

"You took a devilish long time," Haddington complained. "What on earth kept you?"

"How did you get here?" Casey asked.

"Come, come," Haddington said. "I was told to sit in the back seat."

Quite suddenly Casey saw that there was a simple explanation.

"My God!" he said. "You got into the wrong car."

"I waited quite a long time, then fell asleep. I appear to have slipped off the seat at some stage. When I woke up a while ago I was lying on the floor."

"We searched for you for hours."

"You mustn't blame me. After all, you knew there were two cars. I didn't."

"It never occurred to us."

"I have noticed myself," Haddington observed, "that the simple and obvious never really does. However, what are we going to do?"

"I don't know what you intend to do," Casey said, "but I'm going to sleep."

"Here in the car?"

"Yes, I have a blanket."

Haddington considered the matter while Casey settled down. Then he said,

"Could you spare me a corner of the blanket?"

"Certainly," Casey said. He rearranged it so that it covered both of them. He felt Haddington's head on his shoulder, a bony casket, which housed a rich store of erudition, a mind capable of fine distinctions which, in its time too, had probably differentiated between happiness and pleasure.

"I had a drink or two last night," Haddington confessed. Casey smiled quietly. Along the garden of the house outside a line of sunshine had appeared, the first thin manifestation.

"The sun has risen," Casey said.

Haddington gave careful thought to this latest intelligence.

"Alleluia," he murmured at last. Then they both slept — more or less.

The Scoop

A discreet glance to right and left assured Murphy that no undesirable interest was being taken in his movements. He tilted his umbrella, turned expertly into the alleyway and entered the Poolebeg by the side door. He shook the January snow from his clothes before mounting the narrow stairs, and once inside the lounge called for the hot whiskey he had been promising himself all morning. He then looked around to see who was present.

There was the usual lunch break crowd; some actors from the nearby theatre, a producer, a sprinkling of civil servants who, like himself, worked in the nearby Ministry for Exports. His friend Casey was in deep conversation with a group which included three of the actors. There was a stranger among them, who seemed to be the focus of their attention.

Murphy's head was not in the best of health. He found the friendly buzz and the artificial brightness a relief after the drabness of the streets. He curled his fingers about his glass and sighed deeply. It was comfortably warm to the touch. As he lowered it from his lips his eye met Casey's and he nodded. Casey in return winked broadly. At first Murphy interpreted the wink as a wry reference to their mutual drinking bout of the previous evening, an acknowledgement of suffering shared. But Casey followed the wink by indicating the stranger with his thumb.

So that was it. The stranger had fallen into the clutches of the actors and there was some joke going on at his expense. Strangers who entered the Poolebeg had to run that risk. The actors were adept practical jokers who had given the other regulars many a memorable laugh at some casual's expense. They were good fellows, whose companionship Casey and Murphy relished. Murphy, eyeing the group with added interest, smiled with fellow feeling. In matters of this kind, he was one of the initiates.

He had called for his second whiskey and was wondering who the stranger could be, when Casey stood up and came across to him.

"What goes on?" Murphy asked.

"It's priceless," Casey said in an undertone. "Come on over and join us."

"Who's his nibs?"

"An English journalist. Name of Smith."

Murphy, preparing to relish the fun, asked, "What's extraordinary about a journalist?"

"Do you know what he wants?" Casey said. "A photograph of the I.R.A. drilling and an interview with one of the leaders."

"He doesn't want much," Murphy said, his eyes widening.

"Someone told him the Poolebeg was an I.R.A. hangout. The actors are playing up to him. Come on over for God's sake. It's gas."

"Wait a minute," Murphy said. "I'll call another drink first."

He did so. This was one of the things that distinguished the Poolebeg from other houses. There was colour and life in it, the regulars were a cut above the ordinary. One could discuss philosophy and religion with them. They knew what they were talking about. Or poetry. Or, if the mood prevailed, horse racing and dogs. And there was always the chance of some well-manoeuvred joke, the telling of which would enliven the dull hours in the office of the Ministry for Exports.

Murphy got his drink and followed Casey. He was introduced as Sean O'Murchu. The use of the Irish form of his name puzzled him but after a while he concluded that it must be part of the joke. The journalist took an immediate interest in him. He spoke of several recent raids on Northern Ireland by the illegal army and of the interest which his paper took in them. The editor wanted photographs and an interview. Since his arrival in Dublin he had been trying to make contact. Murphy hid his amusement behind an unsmiling mask. Then the journalist said:

"When I got the tip-off about this place I wasn't inclined to believe it, Mr. O'Murchew. I don't easily despair, but I'd got several false leads already. But the moment I heard the Erse I knew you boys were straight."

One of the actors affected a guilty start.

"We were speaking Irish and he overheard us," he explained.

He said it directly to Murphy, in a tone of embarrassed apology, as though to forestall a possible reprimand.

"That's right," another added, "Mr. Smith here took us completely by surprise."

The first, fawning on Murphy, said:

"Oh – completely, sir."

The word "Sir" alarmed Murphy. He began to see what they were up to.

"What the hell do you mean by 'Sir'," he demanded.

"Sorry – it slipped out," the actor said. To Murphy's horrified eyes the actor appeared to blush.

He decided to take control of the situation at once. It was one thing to enjoy their leg-pull of an English journalist who was fool enough to think he could collect photographs of an illegal organisation such as the Irish Republican Army by walking into a public house and making a simple request. It was another thing if Murphy himself was to be pushed forward as an officer of that organisation and find God knows what dangerous reference to himself appearing in the English papers. Apart from the law, he was a civil servant and supposed to keep a mile clear of such things. It wouldn't do at all.

"Look here," Murphy said, with a show of tolerance, "I don't know what yarns these fellows have been spinning for you, Mr. Smith, but I know nothing whatever about the I.R.A."

"I appreciate your reticence, Mr. O'Murchew," the journalist assured him. "Don't think I'd betray anything. Or that our paper is going to be unsympathetic. We know the wrongs of the Irish. We've carried articles on the Irish question that have rattled the Tories. That's why we want these pictures."

"After all, think of the publicity," one of the actors suggested.

"That's right. The organisation needs it," said the other.

"A sympathetic review of *Aims*," the first urged.

It took Murphy some time to collect his thoughts. The combined attack petrified him. The journalist, interpreting his silence for indecision, looked on hopefully.

"Look here," Murphy said loudly, "I know nothing about the bloody I.R.A. I'm a peaceable man with twenty years' service in the Ministry for Exports. I came here to have a quiet, contemplative drink. . . ."

Casey suddenly gripped his sleeve.

"Keep your voice down, for God's sake."

This Judas touch from his closest friend made Murphy almost shoot out of his chair.

"Are you going to side with them too. Holy God . . ."

"No, no, no," Casey interrupted. "Look who's just come in."

Murphy looked up and immediately subsided.

A newcomer had taken his place at the counter and was ordering a drink with a grim inclination. He was tall, spare and hatchet-faced. He acknowledged those nearest him with a curt nod of the head and immediately excluded them again by studying his newspaper. Hempenstall was Murphy's immediate superior in the office. He seldom appeared in the Poolebeg. If he drank it was for a strict medicinal purpose. A sneeze in the course of the morning had caused him a moment of apprehension. Or a spasm of stomach cramp. Or a touch of 'flu. His world was essentially humourless and, since his wife's tragic death, a deliberately joyless one. His only release was the study of Regulations — all kinds of Regulations, which he applied rigorously. They were his only scruples. He spoke little, and that little only in the way of business.

"Do you think he heard?" Murphy asked in an undertone.

"If he didn't it wasn't *your* fault," Casey answered sourly.

Hempenstall was Casey's superior too. The journalist leaned forward avidly. "Who is he?"

"My superior," Murphy whispered, using only the side of his mouth.

One of the actors said, "The Wig."

"I beg your pardon?"

"No one must know his real name," the actor explained, "so we call him The Wig."

"Ah!" the journalist said, with complete understanding.

This was too much for Murphy. He tried to speak quietly, but emotion amplified what he had to say.

"Lookit here. This has got to stop. When I said it was my superior I meant my superior. I'm not going to sit here
. . ."

Hempenstall was seen to lower his paper.

"Keep your goddam voice quiet," Casey appealed. "He's looking straight over."

The journalist, who had formed his own conclusions, said:

"I suppose there's no use me making a direct approach to the . . . eh . . . Wig?"

The sudden change in Murphy's face gave him his answer. He added almost immediately: "Sorry, Mr. O'Murchew. I know how these things are. Forget it."

He lowered his voice further and asked for what he termed a tip-off. A photograph of a contingent drilling would complete his assignment. It would be used in a manner which would reflect nothing but credit on a brave and resourceful organisation.

"You might as well tell him," said one of the actors. "He's a sympathiser. I've read his articles before."

But the journalist was meticulous. It was the effect of

four hot whiskies.

"Not a sympathiser – quite," he corrected. "My rule is – Understand one another first. Then judge. Present the case. I mean – fair hunt. What my colleagues and I are proud to call British Impartiality."

"British Impartiality," the actor approved, with the hearty air of being man enough to give the enemy his due.

Impulsively his colleague said, "Shake."

The journalist looked at the outstretched hand in surprise, then gripped it with genuine emotion.

"Now tell him," the first actor said to Murphy.

Two matters troubled Murphy simultaneously. The first was the continuing presence of Hempenstall, who was uncomfortably within earshot. The second concerned the journalist and the actors. He found it impossible to decide which of them he would annihilate first – given the ability and the opportunity. He thought the journalist. He glanced around at the windows on his left and saw the snow dissolving in endless blobs against them. It tempted him with an idea for revenge. There was a mountain valley about seventeen miles distant, a lost, isolated spot which boasted a crossroads, a good fishing river and a public house. In summer Casey and he sometimes journeyed there by bus, for a little air and plenty of drink. In winter it was a godforsaken wilderness, frequently cut off from the outside world by deep drifts.

"Keep it very quiet," Murphy whispered. They all leaned forward.

"There's a valley about seventeen miles out to the south, Slievefada," he continued. "Go there tomorrow and visit John Joe Flynn's public house."

"How do I get there?" the journalist asked.

"Any of the car-hire firms will fix you up. Just tell them you want to go to Slievefada."

"And what do I say to Flynn?"

One of the actors took over.

"When you walk in just say Dia Dhuit."

"I get it – a password."

This was better than the actor intended.

"Exactly. If Flynn answers Dia's Muire Dhuit, everything's O.K."

"Do I mention Mr. Murchew sent me?"

"No. If he asks you that, just say — The Mask."

"The Mask."

"Now you've got it."

They spent some time teaching the journalist how to pronounce the simple Irish greeting which he had concluded to be a password and they wrote down the customary response phonetically so that he could study and recognise it. While they were talking Hempenstall left. Then the journalist found it was time to go too. His leave-taking was the occasion of a series of warm handshakes. As his bulk disappeared through the door, Casey felt the need of emotional release.

"Well . . . I declare to God," he began. But having got that far, words failed him. He looked at the rest and they began to laugh, the actors helplessly, Murphy uneasily. He was already apprehensive and inclined to regret his surrender to temptation.

His regret grew as the afternoon wore on. The office of the Ministry for Exports was an oppressive warren of corridors and offices, lit by hanging bulbs under ancient cowls. The whiskey had left an unpleasant aftertaste. He felt depressed. Life, from no tangible cause, bristled with vague but threatening uncertainties. On afternoons such as this the thought often suggested itself to Murphy that he was growing too old for the joking and the drinking, a thought he now and then discussed with Casey. They referred to the feeling mutually as a touch of Anno Domini. Sometimes they wondered if it would have been better to marry, even on the salary their modest abilities commanded. There was troublesome correspondence on his desk too. A Lady Blunton-Gough had started a campaign against the export of live horses to France for use as food. She had founded a "Save-the-Horses"

Committee. The trades unions had also made representation to the Minister because the horses were being exported. Lady Blunton-Gough had publicly praised the humanity of the working class. As it happened, prematurely. The trades unions had soon made it clear that they had no objection to the French getting their horse meat. They simply wanted to export the meat in cans, in order to provide employment for the butchering trade and the factory hands. As a result Lady Blunton-Gough and the trades unions were now at daggers drawn. It was part of Murphy's job to make a first draft of a letter to Lady Blunton-Gough advising her that her representations were being closely considered, and one to the Trade Union Congress to the effect that in view of the heavy unemployment figures their suggestion was receiving the sympathetic attention of the Minister. Both organisations would publicise the respective replies. He was struggling for the fifth successive afternoon with this unwelcome problem when the buzzer indicated that he was wanted in Hempenstall's office.

He found his superior sitting in an aroma of disinfectant, sucking throat lozenges from a box on his desk.

"What I have to say is not official," Hempenstall opened, waving him to a chair.

Murphy made signs which conveyed that anything Mr. Hempenstall cared to address to him would be avidly received.

"I speak in your own interest and that of the Department."

"I understand, sir."

"At lunch break today I visited the Poolebeg. I had a premonition of 'flu and felt the need of a preventative. You may have seen me?"

"Now that you mention it, I believe I did."

"I happened to overhear a remark of yours, a reference to an illegal organisation. I have no doubt that it arose in the course of conversation . . ."

"I assure you it did."

"Still, I think it my duty to remind you that even during his free time a civil servant remains a civil servant. Prudence requires him to avoid discussions of a political nature. Especially conversations involving the activities of an illegal army which operates in defiance of the Government he serves. I don't think I need labour the point. In mentioning it I have your career in mind. You are a long time with us."

"Twenty years."

"I thought even longer."

"I'd like to explain that the subject of the I.R.A. ...."

"Quite. I trust it won't be necessary to refer to it again."

"It arose, Mr. Hempenstall ..."

"Excellent. I won't keep you any longer from your desk."

Frustrated and upset, Murphy returned to his desk. He found it more difficult than ever to concentrate on the question of horse meat. The evening dragged on; against the darkened windows he could sense the silent melting of snowflakes. After some nervous reflection he 'phoned Casey, who seemed to be in remarkably good form, and said to him:

"That was desperate carry on."

"What was?"

"What-you-know."

"Lord, yes. Priceless."

"He seemed a bit of an ass."

"Who?"

"Who-you-know."

"It was good fun."

"Do you think he'll really go?"

"Where?"

"Where-you-know."

"It wouldn't surprise me."

"Look. Meet me after the office."

"The usual?"

"No. I think the other place."

"Dammit. I can't. I've got an appointment."

"That's a pity. Oh well. See you tomorrow. Lunchtime."

"In the other place?"

"No. Better make it the usual."

"Righto. By the way, I thought it very funny."

"What?"

"Calling you The Mask."

Murphy shuddered and replaced the phone.

Two days later nothing had happened and Murphy was beginning to see the bright side of the incident. The story of his sending the journalist on a wild goose chase to Slievefada had gone the rounds of the bars. In three different haunts he found himself invited to give the story to the *habitués*. It was received with tremendous hilarity. Here, their inner phantasies had been translated into reality. A man with a camera, armed with a harmless Irish greeting as a password, had gone off into the snow-bound wilderness for a glimpse of the I.R.A. It was as though Murphy had sent him hunting a Unicorn. Someone said it was typical of the English and showed that they lacked imagination. Another said it didn't. On the contrary, it showed they had too much imagination. Somebody else said imagination had nothing to do with it. It showed that the English had what the Irish always lacked, faith in themselves. Another said not at all; if it demonstrated anything it was that the English had faith in the Irish. Murphy, when asked for his opinion, modestly owned himself at a loss. It was dangerous to generalise. It was a matter of judging the individual character he said, weighing him up carefully and deciding how best to exploit his weak points. Of course, it was all easier said than done.

"And you were the man to do it," someone enthused. "I take off my hat to you."

Then they all took off their hats to him, even those who were not wearing them. Murphy found the experience pleasant. To be well thought of in such company was the only taint of ambition in his make-up.

Life had taught Murphy to believe in Fate. It had also taught him not to trust it, a fact of which he was reminded the following day when Hempenstall again called him to his office.

"You will remember our recent interview?" Hempenstall began.

"Of course, sir."

"Have you seen the *Daily Echo?*"

"No, sir, I don't get the English dailies."

"I have this morning's issue here. There is a photograph in it."

Hempenstall unfolded a paper and laid it before Murphy who bent down to examine it. His heart missed a beat. The photograph showed about twelve men, spread out in wide formation, advancing up a snowy clearing which was flanked by pine trees. The men were armed with rifles. The top caption read, *I.R.A. Manoeuvres,* and underneath, *Our Special Reporter scooped this candid shot of warlike preparations in the Irish mountains* (see below).

The accompanying article began:

Within twelve hours of his arrival in Dublin, enquiries sent our special reporter battling through snow and ice to a little known village less than seventeen miles from the heart of the Capital. The village — Slievefada, the mission . . .

"Slievefada," Murphy echoed involuntarily.

"You know the place?" Hempenstall said.

"Vaguely," Murphy confessed.

"You are hardly being frank, Mr. Murphy," Hempenstall accused. "You spent your vacation there two years in succession. We have it on your file. You will remember that during the recent war the regulations required everyone of this staff to furnish information as to his whereabouts when going on leave."

"Now I remember," Murphy said. "I was there for the fishing. Funny I should forget."

Hempenstall looked at him closely. He had the lowest

74

possible opinion of Murphy's intelligence, yet this new sample of its level surprised him.

"I show you the photograph because you may feel I was over-severe the other day. I realise, of course, that your choice of Slievefada as a holiday resort and the present picture have no connection. But I trust it will help to drive home my point about careless talk in public places."

"Very forcibly, sir."

"These English reporters are everywhere. Think of your situation as a civil servant if one of them were to overhear you and approach you."

"You make it very clear, sir."

"Good. I want no action of any officer under my control to reflect discredit on my Section. You may go back to your desk."

"Thank you, Mr. Hempenstall."

Murphy's appointment with Casey that evening was in none of their usual haunts. He was thankful for the darkness of the snowbound streets, thankful for the swarming tea-time crowds. He felt he might already be a hunted man. Now and again the picture flashed into his mind of a middle-aged body spreadeagled and lifeless among the shadows of some courtyard, the word "Informer" pinned to its shabby coat. The body was his. Casey was already waiting for him in the restaurant. It was a cheap and noisy basement with a multi-coloured juke box around which a group of teenagers wagged assorted bottoms. They drank two bowls of indescribable soup while Murphy urged the wisdom of going at once to Slievefada to question John Joe Flynn. Casey was disinclined.

"I don't see any sense in it," he objected.

"Maybe you don't. But I do. It's the talk of every bar that I sent the reporter out there. If the I.R.A. get to hear it God knows what will happen. They might even shoot me."

"That's what I mean," Casey said, making his point

75

clearly. "If we go to Slievefada they might shoot both of us."

"John Joe's a friend of ours," Murphy pleaded, "he'll advise us for the best and let us know how we stand."

"The roads are too bad," Casey resisted, changing ground.

"There's no harm trying."

"And look at the expense. Even if we persuade some driver to chance it, he's bound to charge us through the nose."

"Not if we hire a self-drive."

"And who'll drive it?"

"I will."

"You," Casey protested. "Not bloody likely. I'd rather give myself up to the I.R.A. and be done with it."

"All right," Murphy said at last, with a look of pitiable resignation. "I'll go by myself."

Two hours later Casey bitterly regretted the sense of loyalty which had made him yield to the unspoken challenge. He looked sideways at Murphy and wondered what strange love it was that induced him to stand by this thin, miserable, unprepossessing piece of humanity. He had a half bottle of whiskey in his lap which they had brought with them in case of emergency, but the potential comfort it contained failed to cheer him. The hired car slithered from ditch to ditch when they went downhill and slipped alarmingly when they climbed. Murphy crouched inexpertly over the wheel, his chin out, the rest of his face pinched and small with concentration and the cold.

"If I ever get back home alive," Casey said finally, "I'm going straight in to have myself certified."

The car swung wildly but righted itself. Murphy's nerves were in a bad way. He snapped at him:

"There you go — distracting my attention."

He crouched over the wheel once more. For some miles the headlights lit up a snowy wilderness. Soon it narrowed to a few yards. Slanting streamers of white surrounded and enclosed them. It was snowing again. The pine trees which marched up steep slopes on either side of the road disappeared. Once the near wheel slithered into the ditch and Casey got his shoes full of snow as he pushed and strained to lift it out. After less than a mile his feet were wet and cold. He stretched out his hand for the whiskey bottle. He began to grope about, calmly at first, then wildly.

"Holy God – it's gone," he said at last.

"What's gone?"

"The whiskey."

Murphy reacted automatically by pressing his foot on the brake. They careered from side to side, straightened, swung in a slow circle and, straightening once more, came to rest.

"How could it be gone?"

"It must have fallen when I got out to push you out of the ditch."

"What'll we do?"

"What the hell *can* we do?"

"Nothing, I suppose. We'd never find it now."

"You'd better drive on," Casey said.

As they drove his feet got colder and colder. He no longer gave a damn about the I.R.A. because he felt convinced he was going to die of pneumonia anyway. Once or twice he sneezed. After another half hour, during which they both thought more or less continuously of the whiskey bottle gradually disappearing under the falling snow, a view of the matter occurred to Murphy which he voiced for Casey's consolation.

"Ah well," he said, "thanks be to God it wasn't a full bottle."

At last they crossed the hump-backed bridge on the floor of the valley and swung left to the parking area in front of John Joe Flynn's. The two petrol pumps stood like snowmen, the blinds were down behind the windows, the door shut fast. John Joe could hardly believe his eyes. He dragged them in to the bar and over to the blazing log fire which reflected on the bronze and glass of the bar. Three or four times he repeated:

"Glory be to the Man Above Us, Mr. Casey and Mr. Murphy, well I declare to me daddy."

But he wouldn't let them talk to him until he had poured out a welcome, which he brought over in two well-filled tumblers.

"Get that inside the pair of you now," he said, "and take off the shoes and stockings. Youse must be soaked to the bone." He had a glass in his own hand too, which he raised.

"Sláinte," he said.

"Sláinte Mhór," they replied.

"You still keep a good drop," Casey approved.

"Hold on there now," John Joe said, "till I get you something to go with it."

He went down into the kitchen and they were alone for a while. Their shoes had left a trail of footprints on the flagged floor, their coats dripped wetly on the hanger. There was a smell of groceries, of drink, of woodsmoke. The oil lamp slung from the centre of the ceiling cast a yellow circle which was edged with black. It made a faint buzzing noise which they found comforting. John Joe returned with a pot of tea and a plate of meat which they dispatched ravenously. They talked of the weather, of mutual friends, of this and that. Then Murphy pushed aside his empty plate and said, deliberately:

"We had a purpose in coming, John Joe."

John Joe smiled and said:

"It occurred to me that it wasn't just to admire the scenery."

They acknowledged the joke. Murphy took the *Daily Echo* from his pocket and spread it on the table.

"As a matter of fact, John Joe, it was this."

"The photograph," he added, when John Joe looked puzzled.

John Joe put on his spectacles and studied the photograph gravely. "Well, I declare to me daddy," he said at last, "that fella was in earnest, after all."

"What fellow?" Murphy asked.

John Joe put his spectacles back in his pocket. They hindered conversation.

"This fellow the other day. He blows in here from nowhere with a bloody big camera and an English accent. He knew me too. 'Are you Mr. John Joe Flynn?' says he. 'That's what the priest called me when he poured on the water anyway,' says I, 'what's your pleasure?' He looked around once or twice as though he felt someone might be listening. '*Dia Dhuit,*' says he. '*Dia's Muire Dhuit,*' says I, surprised to hear an Englishman using the Irish. The next thing was he leaned over and whispered in me ear, 'The Mowsk sent me.' "

"The Mowsk?" Murphy echoed.

"I think that's what it was," John Joe corrected, "but I couldn't be sure. You know the funny bloody way the English has of talking. Anyway I left it at that and your man stayed the night. The next morning after breakfast he told me he was here to get a picture of the I.R.A. drilling."

"What did you say?"

"What would you say to that class of lunatic. I humoured him. I told him it was a bloody serious thing to direct anyone to I.R.A. manœuvres and asked for time to think it over."

"What did he say to that?"

"What he said before. The Mowsk sent him. He had this Mowsk stuff on the brain. Anyway, half an hour later, just to get shut of him, I told him there might be something stirring if he went down to Fisher's Point at twelve o'clock or thereabouts. And for the love of God, says I to him, don't on any account let yourself be seen. Dammit, but I clean forgot about the boys."

"The boys?" Casey repeated.

"An arrangement the boys had made here a few nights

79

before."

John Joe cocked his ear at the sound of a heavy engine which sent the windows rattling before it churned to a stop. "This'll be Lar Holohan and his helper. Hold on for a minute."

He went over to unlock the door and Murphy exchanged glances with Casey. Both had the feeling of being in the centre of a hotbed of illegal activity.

"He means 'The Mask'," Casey whispered. It was quite unnecessary.

"I know," Murphy answered. If anything, the whiskey had made his nerves worse.

The lorry driver and his helper sat down near them while John Joe got tea and bread and meat. It was a fierce night, the lorry driver told them, with a blizzard almost certain. When were they going back?

"Tonight," Murphy said.

The lorry driver addressed his helper.

"They won't get back tonight, will they, Harmless?"

"Not unless they has an airyplane," Harmless confirmed.

"We got ditched twice coming through the pass," the lorry driver said, "it's closed by now."

"Will it be right in the morning?"

"With the class of a night that's in it now, I wouldn't think so. Not for two days at least."

"Three," Harmless corrected.

The food was brought and they attacked it with gusto. When they had finished, John Joe asked Murphy for the *Echo* and spread it in front of the lorry driver.

"Have a look at that, Lar," he invited.

His eyes shone with expectation. Lar examined it thoroughly.

'Can you guess what it is?" John Joe asked after a while.

The lorry driver stroked his chin.

"It's not the I.R.A.anyway," he said at last. "I recognise Tim Moore and John Feeney."

"So do I," Harmless added. "I wouldn't accuse either of them of ambitions to shed their heart's blood for Ireland. Or anything else."

"I'll tell you," John Joe announced triumphantly, "it's the dog hunt."

The lorry driver guffawed.

"I declare to God," he said, "that's what it is."

"Dog hunt?" Murphy said with a look of enquiry.

"You may remember Matt Kerrigan that lived by himself up the mountain," John Joe began.

Murphy and Casey both remembered him, an old man who was something of a hermit.

"He died a few months ago," John Joe said, "but nothing would induce the bloody oul' mongrel he kept to quit the house."

"A ferocious-looking blackguard of a brute it was too," Harmless assured them. "Not a Christian class of a dog at all."

"That's not a word of a lie," said the lorry driver.

"It stayed on at the house," John Joe continued, "and of course after a while it went wild."

"It was never what you'd call tame," Harmless said. He had a grievance against the dog which had once bitten him.

"It did terrible damage to poultry, and latterly it began to attack the sheep. So when the bad weather came and the boys got together to help bring the flocks down to the lower slopes they thought they'd kill two birds with the one stone and shoot the oul dog if they could round him up as well. That's why they brought the guns."

"They got it too," Harmless said with relish, "shot it above at Eagle Rock. They said it was mad as well as wild."

"And that's the photograph the journalist got?" Casey asked.

"That's the photograph you see in front of you," John Joe said. "The boys' setting off to get the bowler."

"And he thought it was the I.R.A.," the lorry driver

commented, looking at the photograph with renewed relish.

John Joe proceeded to tell the lorry driver why. He described the visit of the journalist and about sending him down to Fisher's Point to get shut of him. Three or four times the lorry driver nearly fell off his stool.

Murphy looked over at Casey. They found it impossible to join in the general laughter. Outside it was snowing hard. A wind had risen which made a deep, rumbling noise in the wide chimney. They thought of the pass filling moment by moment with its barrier of snow.

"We may as well have a drink anyway," Murphy said; "we'll have whiskey all round, John Joe."

The lorry driver stopped laughing in order to hold up his hand and ask him to make his beer, explaining that he and his helper had had a skinful of whiskey already.

"It was when we were struggling with the lorry the second time we got ditched," Harmless explained. "Suddenly my foot kicked something. It was a half bottle of whiskey."

"Someone must have let it fall," said the driver.

"So we polished it off," Harmless concluded and then cocked an ear to the night. He considered carefully.

"At least three days," he added at last, meaning the Pass.

. . . . .

Harmless turned out to be right. Murphy and Casey stayed in John Joe Flynn's. There was nothing else they could do. They telephoned the post office and had a telegram sent on to Hempenstall, explaining that they were weather bound. On the same call John Joe sent a request to the post office to order a dozen copies of the *Daily Echo* and hold them. Every one involved in the dog hunt would want one for himself, he said.

On the third day, while Murphy was gazing out of the window the thought occurred to him that the telegram they had sent to Hempenstall would bear the name of

Slievefada Post Office as its point of origination. This was a fresh complication. It would be difficult to explain to Hempenstall. As he thought about it he grew pale. Even Casey noticed.

"What are you thinking about?" he asked.

Murphy's eyes dwelt in silence for a while on the snow-covered desolation outside. His pallor remained.

"Siberia," he said eventually.

Weep for Our Pride

THE door of the classroom was opened by Mr. O'Rourke just as Brother Quinlan was about to open it to leave. They were both surprised and said "Good morning" to one another as they met in the doorway. Mr. O'Rourke, although he met Brother Quinlan every morning of his life, gave an expansive but oddly unreal smile and shouted his good morning with blood-curdling cordiality. They then withdrew to the passage outside to hold a conversation.

In the interval English Poetry books were opened and the class began to repeat lines. They had been given the whole of a poem called *Lament for the Death of Eoghan Roe* to learn. It was very patriotic and dealt with the poisoning of Eoghan Roe by the accursed English, and the lines were very long, which made it difficult. The class hated the English for poisoning Eoghan Roe because the lines about it were so long. What made it worse was that it was the sort of poem Mr. O'Rourke loved. If it was *Hail to thee blithe spirit* he wouldn't be so fond of it. But he could declaim this one for them in a rich fruity, provincial baritone and would knock hell out of anybody who had not learned it.

Peter had not learned it. Realising how few were the minutes left to him he ran his eyes over stanza after stanza and began to murmur fragments from each in hopeless desperation. Swaine, who sat beside him, said, "Do you know this?"

"No," Peter said, "I haven't even looked at it."

"My God!" Swaine breathed in horror. "You'll be mangled!"

"You could give us a prompt."

"And be torn limb from limb," said Swaine with

84

conviction; "not likely."

Peter closed his eyes. It was all his mother's fault. He had meant to come to school early to learn it but the row delayed him. It had been about his father's boots. After breakfast she had found that there were holes in both his shoes. She held them up to the light which was on because the November morning was wet and dark.

"Merciful God, child," she exclaimed, "there's not a sole in your shoes. You can't go out in those."

He was anxious to put them on and get out quickly, but everybody was in bad humour. He didn't dare to say anything. His sister was clearing part of the table and his brother Joseph, who worked, was rooting in drawers and corners and growling to everybody:

"Where the hell is the bicycle pump? You can't leave a thing out of your hand in this house."

"I can wear my sandals," Peter suggested.

"And it spilling out of the heavens — don't be daft, child." Then she said, "What am I to do at all?"

For a moment he hoped he might be kept at home. But his mother told his sister to root among the old boots in the press. Millie went out into the passage. On her way she trod on the cat, which meowed in intense agony.

"Blazes," said his sister, "that bloody cat."

She came in with an old pair of his father's boots, and he was made try them on. They were too big.

"I'm not going out in those," he said, "I couldn't walk in them."

But his mother and sister said they looked lovely. They went into unconvincing ecstasies. They looked perfect they said, each backing up the other. No one would notice.

"They look foolish," he insisted, "I won't wear them."

"You'll do what you're told," his sister said. They were all older than he and each in turn bullied him. But the idea of being made look ridiculous nerved him.

"I won't wear them," he persisted. At that moment his brother Tom came in and Millie said quickly:

"Tom, speak to Peter – he's giving cheek to Mammy."

Tom was very fond of animals. "I heard the cat," he began, looking threateningly at Peter who sometimes teased it. "What where you doing to it?"

"Nothing," Peter answered, "Millie walked on it." He tried to say something about the boots but the three of them told him to shut up and get to school. He could stand up to the others but he was afraid of Tom. So he had flopped along in the rain feeling miserable and hating it because people would be sure to know they were not his own boots.

The door opened and Mr. O'Rourke came in. He was a huge man in tweeds. He was a fluent speaker of Irish and wore the gold fáinne in the lapel of his jacket. Both his wrists were covered with matted black hair.

"Filíocht," he roared and drew a leather from his hip pocket.

Then he shouted, "Dún do leabhar" and hit the front desk a ferocious crack with the leather. Mr. O'Rourke was an ardent Gael who gave his orders in Irish – even during English class. Someone had passed him up a poetry book and the rest closed theirs or turned them face downwards on their desks.

Mr. O'Rourke, his eyes glaring terribly at the ceiling, from which plaster would fall in fine dust when the third year students overhead tramped in or out, began to declaim:

"Did they dare, did they dare, to slay Eoghan Roe O'Neill?
Yes they slew with poison him they feared to meet with steel."

He clenched his powerful fists and held them up rigidly before his chest.

"May God wither up their hearts, may their blood cease to flow!

May they walk in living death who poisoned Eoghan
  Roe!"

Then quite suddenly, in a business-like tone, he said,
"You — Daly."

"Me, sir?" said Daly, playing for time.

"Yes, you fool," thundered Mr. O'Rourke. "You."

Daly rose and repeated the first four lines. When he
was half-way through the second stanza Mr. O'Rourke
bawled, "Clancy." Clancy rose and began to recite.
They stood up and sat down as Mr. O'Rourke
commanded while he paced up and down the aisles
between the seats. Twice he passed close to Peter. He
stood for some time by Peter's desk bawling out names.
The end of his tweed jacket lay hypnotically along the
edge of Peter's desk. Cummins stumbled over the fourth
verse and dried up completely.

"Line," Mr. O'Rourke bawled. Cummins, calmly
pale, left his desk and stepped out to the side of the class.
Two more were sent out. Mr. O'Rourke walked up and
down once more and stood with his back to Peter.
Looking at the desk at the very back he suddenly
bawled, "Farrell."

Peter's heart jerked. He rose to his feet. The back was
still towards him. He looked at it, a great mountain of
tweed, with a frayed collar over which the thick neck
bulged in folds. He could see the antennae of hair which
sprouted from Mr. O'Rourke's ears and could smell the
chalk-and-ink schoolmaster's smell of him. It was a trick
of Mr. O'Rourke's to stand with his back to you and
then call your name. It made the shock more unnerving.
Peter gulped and was silent.

"Wail . . ." prompted Mr. O'Rourke.

Peter said, "Wail. . . ."

Mr. O'Rourke paced up to the head of the class once
more.

"Wail — wail him through the island," he said as he
walked. Then he turned around suddenly and said.

"Well, go on."

"Wail, wail him through the island," Peter said once more and stopped.

"Weep," hinted Mr. O'Rourke.

He regarded Peter closely, his eyes narrowing.

"Weep," said Peter, ransacking the darkness of his mind but finding only emptiness.

"Weep, weep, weep," Mr. O'Rourke said, his voice rising.

Peter chanced his arm. He said, "Wail, wail him through the island weep, weep, weep."

Mr. O'Rourke stood up straight. His face conveyed at once shock, surprise, pain.

"Get out to the line," he roared, "you thick lazy good-for-nothing bloody imbecile. Tell him what it is, Clancy." Clancy dithered for a moment, closed his eyes and said:

"Sir – Wail, wail him through the island, weep, weep for our pride
Would that on the battle field our gallant chief had died."

Mr. O'Rourke nodded with dangerous benevolence. As Peter shuffled to the line the boots caught the iron upright of the desk and made a great clamour. Mr. O'Rourke gave him a cut with the leather across the behind. "Did you look at this, Farrell?" he asked.

Peter hesitated and said uncertainly, "No, sir."

"It wasn't worth your while, I suppose?"

"No, sir. I hadn't time, sir."

Just then the clock struck the hour. The class rose. Mr. O'Rourke put the leather under his left armpit and crossed himself. *"In ainm an Athar,"* he began. While they recited the *Hail Mary* Peter, unable to pray, stared at the leafless rain-soaked trees in the square and the serried rows of pale, prayerful faces. They sat down.

Mr. O'Rourke turned to the class.

"Farrell hadn't time," he announced pleasantly. Then he looked thunderously again at Peter. "If it was an English penny dreadful about Public Schools or London crime you'd find time to read it quick enough, but when it's about the poor hunted martyrs and felons of your own unfortunate country by a patriot like Davis you've no time for it. You've the makings of a fine little Britisher." With genuine pathos Mr. O'Rourke then recited:

"The weapon of the Sassenach met him on his way
And he died at Cloch Uachter upon St. Leonard's day."

"That was the dear dying in any case, but if he died for the likes of you, Farrell, it was the dear bitter dying, no mistake about it."

Peter said, "I meant to learn it."

"Hold out your hand. If I can't preach respect for the patriot dead into you, than honest to my stockings I'll beat respect into you. Hand."

Peter held it out. He pulled his coat sleeve down over his wrist. The leather came down six times with a resounding impact. He tried to keep his thumb out of the way because if it hit you on the thumb it stung unbearably. But after four heavy slaps the hand began to curl of its own accord, curl and cripple like a little piece of tinfoil in a fire, until the thumb lay powerless across the palm, and the pain burned in his chest and constricted every muscle. But worse than the pain was the fear that he would cry. He was turning away when Mr. O'Rourke said:

"Just a moment, Farrell. I haven't finished."

Mr. O'Rourke gently took the fingers of Peter's hand, smoothing them out as he drew them once more into position. "To teach you I'll take no defiance," he said, in a friendly tone and raised the leather. Peter tried to hold his crippled hand steady.

He could not see properly going back to his desk and

again the boots deceived him and he tripped and fell. As he picked himself up Mr. O'Rourke, about to help him with another, though gentler, tap of the leather, stopped and exclaimed:

"Merciful God, child, where did you pick up the boots?"

The rest looked with curiosity. Clancy, who had twice excelled himself, tittered. Mr. O'Rourke said, "And what's the funny joke, Clancy?"

"Nothing, sir."

"Soft as a woman's was your voice, O'Neill, bright was your eye," recited Mr. O'Rourke, in a voice as soft as a woman's, brightness in his eyes. "Continue, Clancy." But Clancy, the wind taken out of his sails, missed and went out to join the other three. Peter put his head on the desk, his raw hands tightly under his armpits, and nursed his wounds while the leather thudded patriotism and literature into the other, unmurmuring, four.

Swaine said nothing for a time. Now and then he glanced at Peter's face. He was staring straight at the book. His hands were tender, but the pain had ebbed away. Each still hid its rawness under a comfortably warm armpit.

"You got a heck of a hiding," Swaine whispered at last. Peter said nothing.

"Ten is too much. He's not allowed to give you ten. If he gave me ten I'd bring my father up to him."

Swaine was small, but his face was large and bony and when he took off his glasses sometimes to wipe them there was a small red weal on the bridge of his nose. Peter grunted and Swaine changed the subject.

"Tell us who owns the boots. They're not your own."

"Yes they are," Peter lied.

"Go on," Swaine said, "who owns them? Are they your brother's?"

"Shut up," Peter menaced.

"Tell us," Swaine persisted. "I won't tell a soul. Honest." He regarded Peter with sly curiosity. He whispered: "I know they're not your own, but I wouldn't tell it. We sit beside one another. We're pals. You can tell me."

"Curiosity killed the cat . . ." Peter said.

Swaine had the answer to that. With a sly grin he rejoined, "Information made him fat."

"If you must know," Peter said, growing tired, "they're my father's. And if you tell anyone I'll break you up in little pieces. You just try breathing a word."

Swaine sat back, satisfied.

Mr. O'Rourke was saying that the English used treachery when they poisoned Eoghan Roe. But what could be expected of the English except treachery?

"Hoof of the horse," he quoted, "Horn of a bull, smile of a Saxon." Three perils. Oliver Cromwell read his Bible while he quartered infants at their mothers' breasts. People said let's forget all that. But we couldn't begin to forget it until we had our full freedom. Our own tongue, the sweet Gaelic *teanga*, must be restored once more as the spoken language of our race. It was the duty of all to study and work towards that end.

"And those of us who haven't time must be shown how to find the time. Isn's that a fact, Farrell?" he said. The class laughed. But the clock struck and Mr. O'Rourke put the lament regretfully aside.

"Mathematics," he announced, "*Céimseachta.*"

He had hoped it would continue to rain during lunchtime so that they could stay in the classroom. But when the automatic bell clanged loudly and Mr. O'Rourke opened the frosted window to look out, it had stopped. They trooped down the stairs. They pushed and jostled one another. Peter kept his hand for safety on the banisters. Going down the stairs made the boots seem larger. He made straight for the urinal and stayed there until the old brother whose duty it was for obscure moral reasons to patrol the place had passed through twice. The second time he said to him: "My goodness, boy, go out into the fresh air with your playmates. Shoo – boy –

shoo," and stared at Perer's retreating back with perplexity and suspicion.

Dillon came over as he was unwrapping his lunch and said, "Did they dare, did they dare to slay Eoghan Roe O'Neill."

"Oh, shut up," Peter said.

Dillon linked his arm and said, "You got an awful packet." Then with genuine admiration he added: "You took it super. He aimed for your wrist, too. Not a peek. You were wizard. Cripes. When I saw him getting ready for the last four I was praying you wouldn't cry."

"I never cried yet," Peter asserted.

"I know, but he lammed his hardest. You shouldn't have said you hadn't time."

"He wouldn't make me cry," Peter said grimly, "not if he got up at four o'clock in the morning to try it."

O'Rourke had lammed him all right, but there was no use trying to do anything about it. If he told his father and mother they would say he richly deserved it. It was his mother should have been lammed and not he.

"You were super, anyway," Dillon said warmly. They walked arm in arm. "The Irish," he added sagaciously, "are an unfortunate bloody race. The father often says so."

"Don't tell me," Peter said with feeling.

"I mean, look at us. First Cromwell knocks hell out of us for being too Irish and then Rorky slaughters us for not being Irish enough."

It was true. It was a pity they couldn't make up their minds.

Peter felt the comfort of Dillon's friendly arm. "The boots are my father's," he confided suddenly, "My own had holes." That made him feel better.

"What are you worrying about?" Dillon said, reassuringly. "They look all right to me."

When they were passing the row of water taps with the chained drinking vessels a voice cried, "There's Farrell now." A piece of crust hit Peter on the nose.

"Caesar sends his legate," Dillon murmured. They

92

gathered round. Clancy said, "Hey, boys, Farrell is wearing someone else's boots."

"Who lifted you into them?"

"Wait now," said Clancy, "let's see him walk. Go on – walk, Farrell."

Peter backed slowly towards the wall. He backed slowly until he felt the ridge of a downpipe hard against his back. Dillon came with him. "Lay off, Clancy," Dillon said. Swaine was there too. He was smiling, a small cat fat with information.

"Where did you get them, Farrell?"

"Pinched them."

"Found them in an ashbin."

"Make him walk," Clancy insisted; "let's see you walk, Farrell."

"They're my own," Peter said; "they're a bit big – that's all."

"Come on, Farrell – tell us whose they are."

The grins grew wider.

Clancy said, "They're his father's."

"No, they're not," Peter denied quickly.

"Yes, they are. He told Swaine. Didn't he, Swaine? He told you they were his father's."

Swaine's grin froze. Peter fixed him with terrible eyes.

"Well, didn't he, Swaine? Go on, tell the chaps what he told you. Didn't he say they were his father's?"

Swaine edged backwards. "That's right," he said, "he did."

"Hey, you chaps," Clancy said, impatiently, "let's make him walk. I vote . . ."

At that moment Peter, with a cry, sprang on Swaine. His fist smashed the glasses on Swaine's face. As they rolled over on the muddy ground, Swaine's nails tore his cheek. Peter saw the white terrified face under him. He beat at it in frenzy until it became covered with mud and blood.

"Cripes," Clancy said in terror, "look at Swaine's glasses. Haul him off, lads." They pulled him away and he

93

lashed out at them with feet and hands. He lashed out awkwardly with the big boots which had caused the trouble. Swaine's nose and lips were bleeding so they took him over to the water tap and washed him. Dillon, who stood alone with Peter, brushed his clothes as best he could and fixed his collar and tie.

"You broke his glasses," he said. "There'll be a proper rucky if old Quinny sees him after lunch."

"I don't care about Quinny."

"I do then," Dillon said fervently. "He'll quarter us all in our mother's arms."

. . . . .

They sat with their arms folded while Brother Quinlan, in the high chair at the head of the class, gave religious instruction. Swaine kept his bruised face lowered. Without the glasses it had a bald, maimed look, as though his eyebrows, or a nose, or an eye, were missing. They had exchanged no words since the fight. Peter was aware of the boots. They were a defeat, something to be ashamed of. His mother only thought they would keep out the rain. She didn't understand that it would be better to have wet feet. People did not laugh at you because your feet were wet.

Brother Quinlan was speaking of our relationship to one another, of the boy to his neighbour and of the boy to his God. We communicatd with one another, he said, by looks, gestures, speech. But these were surface contacts. They conveyed little of what went on in the mind, and nothing at all of the individual soul. Inside us, the greatest and the humblest of us, a whole world was locked. Even if we tried we could convey nothing of that interior world, that life which was nourished, as the poet had said, within the brain. In our interior life we stood without friend or ally – alone. In the darkness and silence of that interior and eternal world the immortal soul and its God were at all times face to face. No one else could peer into another's

94

soul, neither our teacher, nor our father or mother, nor even our best friend. But God saw all. Every stray little thought which moved in that inaccessible world was as plain to Him as if it were thrown across the bright screen of a cinema. That was why we must be as careful to discipline our thoughts as our actions. Custody of the eyes, custody of the ears, but above all else custody. . . .

Brother Quinlan let the sentence trail away and fixed his eyes on Swaine.

"You – boy," he said in a voice which struggled to be patient, "what are you doing with that handkerchief?"

Swaine's nose had started to bleed again. He said nothing. "Stand up, boy," Brother Quinlan commanded. He had glasses himself, which he wore during class on the tip of his nose. He was a big man too, and his head was bald in front, which made his large forehead appear even more massive. He stared over the glasses at Swaine.

"Come up here," he said, screwing up his eyes, the fact that something was amiss with Swaine's face dawning gradually on him. Swaine came up to him, looking woebegone, still dabbing his nose with the handkerchief. Brother Quinlan contemplated the battered face for some time. He turned to the class.

"Whose handiwork is this?" he asked quietly. "Stand up, the boy responsible for this."

For a while nobody stirred. There was an uneasy stillness. Poker faces looked at the desks in front of them and waited. Peter looked around and saw Dillon gazing at him hopefully. After an unbearable moment feet shuffled and Peter stood up.

"I am, sir," he said.

Brother Quinlan told Clancy to take Swaine out to the yard to bathe his nose. Then he spoke to the class about violence and what was worse, violence to a boy weaker than oneself. That was the resort of the bully and the scoundrel – physical violence – The Fist. At this Brother Quinlan held up his large bunched fist so that all might see it. Then with the other hand he indicated the picture of the Sacred Heart. Charity and Forbearance, he said, not vengeance and intolerance, those were qualities most dear to Our Blessed Lord.

"Are you not ashamed of yourself, Farrell? Do you think what you have done is a heroic or a creditable thing?"

"No, sir."

"Then why did you do it, boy?"

Peter made no answer. It was no use making an answer. It was no use saying Swaine had squealed about the boots being his father's. Swaine's face was badly battered. But deep inside him Peter felt battered too. Brother Quinlan couldn't see your soul. He could see Swaine's face, though, when he fixed his glasses on him properly. Brother Quinlan took his silence for defiance.

"A blackguardly affair," he pronounced. "A low, cowardly assault. Hold out your hand."

Peter hesitated. There was a limit. He hadn't meant not to learn the poetry and it wasn't his fault about the boots.

"He's been licked already, sir," Dillon said. "Mr. O'Rourke gave him ten."

"Mr. O'Rourke is a discerning man," said Brother Quinlan, "but he doesn't seem to have given him half enough. Think of the state of that poor boy who has just gone out."

Peter could think of nothing to say. He tried hard but there were no words there. Reluctantly he presented his hand. It was mudstained. Brother Quinlan looked at it with distaste. Then he proceeded to beat hell out of him, and charity and forbearance into him, in the same way as Mr. O'Rourke earlier had hammered in patriotism and respect for Irish History.

It was raining again when he was going home. Usually there were three of four to go home with him, but this afternoon he went alone. He did not want them with him. He passed some shops and walked by the first small suburban gardens, with their sodden gravel paths and dripping gates. On the canal bridge a boy passed him pushing fuel in a pram. His feet were bare. The mud had splashed upwards in thick streaks to his knees. Peter kept his left hand under his coat. There was a blister on the ball of the thumb which ached now like a burn. Brother Quinlan did that. He probably didn't aim to hit the thumb as Mr. O'Rourke always did, but his sight was so bad he had a rotten shot. The boots had got looser than they were earlier. He realised this when he saw Clancy with three or four others passing on the other side of the road. When Clancy waved and called to him, he backed automatically until he felt the parapet against his back.

"Hey, Farrell," they called. Then one of them, his head forward, his behind stuck out, began to waddle with grotesque movements up the road. The rest yelled to call Peter's attention. They indicated the mime. Come back if you like, they shouted. Peter waited until they had gone. Then he turned moodily down the bank of the canal. He walked with a stiff ungainly dignity, his mind not yet quite made up. Under the bridge the water was deep and narrow, and a raw wind which moaned in the high arch whipped coldly at his face. It might rain tomorrow and his shoes wouldn't be mended. If his mother thought the boots were all right God knows when his shoes would be mended. After a moment of indecision he took off the boots and dropped them, first one – and then the other – into the water.

There would be hell to pay when he came home without them. But there would be hell to pay anyway when Swaine's father sent around the note to say he had broken young Swaine's glasses. Like the time he broke the Cassidy's window. Half regretfully he stared at the silty water. He could see his father rising from the table to reach for the belt which hung behind the door. The outlook was frightening; but it was better to walk in your bare feet. It was better to walk without shoes and barefooted than to walk without dignity. He took off his stockings and stuffed them into his pocket. His heart sank as he felt the cold wet mud of the path on his bare feet.

97

The Wearin' of the Green

JOSEPH the Fool did not evolve his idea of planting the suitcase with a time-bomb in it at the Festival Dinner in Murphy's Hotel in the studied and careful manner of the professional conspirator. He was not a conspirator. But to his simple and uncomplicated mind it seemed that the sooner Ballyconlan was free of Murphy, the man of power and property, and Lacey, the Chairman of the Gaelic League, and Father Finnegan, the Parish Priest, together with the lesser lights of the Gaelic League and the Old I.R.A., the better for Ballyconlan, and the better for Ireland at large. There was no difficulty getting the bomb. The bomb was in his possession since the time of the Troubles, when his brother did the difficult jobs and Murphy kept in the background, giving the orders and accepting the credit. It was a heavy and ungainly affair which had been made in the Fitting Shops of the Railway Co. in Dublin and smuggled out with several others for use, first against the British and later against the Irish themselves. Joseph knew how to set the mechanism and had no doubt whatever but that it would work. The suitcase idea had been handed to him readymade in the columns of the *Irish Catholic Times,* where a similar outrage on the clergy of Spain was reported and very much deplored. An Archbishop of Irish descent had died as the result of the injuries he received, so that no known detail of the occurrence had been overlooked. The only thing Joseph lacked was a suitcase. This he obtained from Purcell, the schoolmaster. It was on Purcell's behalf as well as civilisation's that he decided to blow the whole bagful up.

Purcell had been kind to him. It was the sort of kindness he had not experienced since his brother had been driven

98

away from Ballyconlan after an innocent but ill-advised attempt to elope with Murphy's daughter. The pair, who throughout the civil war and because of the close contact which had to be maintained between Joseph's brother and Murphy for the successful plotting of various jobs, had been thrown together at odd hours of the day and night and had fallen in love. Despite Murphy's rise to power and wealth and the young fellow's complete unsuitability (he had neither land nor cattle) the attachment continued secretly into more peaceful times. She had been disconsolate and fractious for months after her lover's banishment, but eventually agreed to marry an ex-enemy of her father, a man who had been on the opposite side during the civil war, but who was now a Town Councillor and a member of the Government. Naturally, Murphy saw no reason against letting bygones be bygones. In public they were bitter enemies; in private, two heads were better than one. It gave him a stake in both camps when eventually his daughter settled down contentedly. The news that Purcell, too, was leaving Ballyconlan at the behest of Murphy did something to the Fool's mind. It gave point and purpose to a confusion of resentments. He suddenly realised why he had kept the bomb by him all the years.

Purcell had taken to the Fool almost immediately on his arrival in Ballyconlan. Tipped-off about the schoolmaster's arrival by Patrick Hennessy, the cabman, Joseph met the newcomer at the station. He was well tipped for the help he gave, which encouraged him to hover near at hand in the ensuing weeks whenever Purcell came into the town for groceries. Purcell, on his part, liked and pitied the Fool. To see him loafing about town – being jeered occasionally by the children because he had a hare-lip and treated with suspicion by the shopkeepers – touched his always compassionate nature. Joseph seldom shaved, so that although he was mature in years, the hair on his face preserved the downy and untidy quality of adolescence. Purcell thought he looked hungry and hurt. This was not altogether true, for the Fool accepted a multitude of small hospitalities with well-concealed contempt.

"I see you've taken the Fool to the school cottage as a servant," Father Finnegan remarked to Purcell at the beginning.

"I have, Father."

"I don't know that your choice is entirely suitable. In the first place, he's known to be simple-minded."

"I know. I can suffer the little children, Father."

"Can you, Purcell?" (A knitting of the eyebrows.) "He doesn't attend Mass. . . . But I suppose you can suffer that, too?"

"It's a great pity. But perhaps if people treated you and me as they treat Joseph we too might hesitate about going among them."

"Your compassion does you credit, Purcell. But the real reason is that my curate condemned that brother of his who tried to seduce the young Murphy one. He said my curate was well paid for it."

Purcell smiled sadly.

"I know," Father Finnegan said; "any of my respected parishioners may say the same thing in a moment of misguided anger. But they would attend Mass." Father Finnegan was large, grey-haired and red-faced. When disciplining his temper he had a habit of stroking his nose with his curled finger, and he did so now. "He may not be completely responsible and possibly does not realise the wrong he does. Nevertheless it gives scandal."

Nevertheless Purcell took the Fool. They lived in the cottage just outside Ballyconlan on a hill from which at night they could see such drab lights as the town boasted. Ballyconlan lay in the valley between two hills. In the course of centuries it had shifted gradually away from the river, which occasionally flooded. In doing so, Ballyconlan jettisoned its last source of occasional excitement. Purcell, wandering from the main street to the railway station on the fringe of the town during the first month of his stay, found that when Murphy's Flour Mills closed, and

100

Murphy's button factory ceased work, to the wailing of the same hooter, there was nothing at all for anyone to do except moon around the central square where most of the pubs were located, or play pitch-and-toss at the green patch where the road forked right and left outside the town. Sometimes he followed aimlessly the hypnotic railway line as it climbed the hill to the moorland beyond, a long deserted tract of bog which reflected a lonely and indescribably poignant sky. He dropped into the bar of Murphy's Hotel now and then, where usually there was a commercial traveller to be found, drinking whiskey and making up accounts to fill in the couple of hours to bedtime. It was during this period of adjustment that he decided to start a Choral Society. He played the piano and organ and had produced end-of-term operas as a junior master in Dublin. Through the children in school he succeeded in gathering a sprinkling of adults – sons and daughters of the outlying farmers; and these in turn canvassed their friends among Murphy's factory staff. The rehearsals, at first small impromptu affairs, held in the dilapidated schoolhouse, proved extremely popular. Once a week the young people came along, most of them on bicycles, and eventually, when the rehearsals began to conclude with an impromptu dance, not all who attended were members of the choir. The Choral Society grew almost without Purcell's noticing it, and became the focal point of interest. The young people felt that at last there was something to do in Ballyconlan.

The fact that he had started something of importance was brought home to Purcell when he received his first letter from Lacey, of the Gaelic League, who wrote on behalf of his Committee, protesting against a talk given by Purcell on English Choral Music, while Irish music was being shamefully neglected. The letter filled him with an old weariness. He had not been a schoolteacher for some years without several brushes with zealots for the revival of the national language. But he lacked sufficient courage to ignore a letter which could call on the whole weight of the political machine to back it, so he invited Lacey to a rehearsal. He expected a *gauche*, tweed-clad patriot from some Atlantic-stunned parish on the western seaboard. Instead, he was confronted by a precise, bowler-hatted man with a worried expression which a neatly waxed moustache failed to disguise. He wore a spotless butterfly collar and a dark suit. A gold fáinne decorated his lapel. His waistcoat was dignified by the two symmetrical and massive loops of his watch-chain. He addressed Purcell in Irish, but seemed relieved when he was answered in English. The choir sang some numbers for him, which he gave the impression of hearing with impatient approval.

"A wonderful job, Mr. Purcell," he said, as though appraising a home-made table.

"I'm glad you like it," Purcell said. He rose from the piano and noted, with dismay, that a young man immediately seated himself at it and began vamping a dance number. He tried to lead Lacey out into the grounds, but found a young girl barring his way. She had been in the choir some months before, but after a few sessions had disappeared. Despite his anxiety to get Lacey out of the way, there was something about her which made him forget for a moment the importance of his visitor. Her name hovered in his mind just out of his reach, then came forward pleasurably.

"Sally Maguire," he said, "I thought you had deserted me altogether."

"It wasn't my fault," she said, "it was my father." Her eyes, ignoring Lacey's presence, challenged him with an uncomfortably brazen honesty.

"Has he changed his mind?"

She tilted her head and began to laugh. "I wanted the words of 'Drink To Me Only'," she said, avoiding his question. "I wasn't here when you gave them out."

He told her to take a copy from the bundle. His eyes following her involuntarily as she bent over his desk, he noticed the small bruise over her right eye and another on

102

her bare arm. They puzzled him. Meanwhile Lacey was unaware of this distraction.

"It's such a pity the choir is not attached to our Gaelic League Branch," he was saying, in the same rehearsed tone; "Mr. Murphy would welcome it – heartily. In fact, he told me to tell you so."

"It is very nice of him," Purcell said, "but doesn't he own enough of Ballyconlan already?"

"He's a man of much influence, who could do a lot to help," Lacey observed – rather uneasily, Purcell thought. "He has a wonderful national record."

"Did he kill a lot of people?"

"I expect so. He was in the War of Independence from beginning to end. And self-made, too." Lacey peered around him at the hedges and then ventured a confidence, "As a matter of fact, I can remember him as a gossoon without a seat to his pants." He concluded this with a startling and unexpected titter. The strains of a slow waltz drifting to them from the schoolroom set Purcell wondering irrelevantly if Sally Maguire were dancing with somebody. Lacey's watch-chain, with its pendulent football medals, began to chatter brightly. "The young people of Ireland do not know what men like Mr. Murphy did for them," he continued sadly. "They forget the wrongs of seven hundred years. Listen to that – that foxtrot for instance."

"Yes — a pretty tune, don't you think?"

"But English, Mr. Purcell."

"German. Besides, it's not a foxtrot, it's a waltz."

"Waltz or foxtrot," Lacey said, "it's foreign. That's the danger. These things shouldn't be encouraged. Now, if the choir was attached to our Gaelic League, we could see that only Irish music would be played. It could do a great service in preserving our National Heritage."

"In that case," Purcell said, "you ought to organise your own choir."

"We have tried," Lacey answered, "not here in Ballyconlan, but in other parishes. I'm afraid the young people won't come." He stared sadly at the dusky, sweet-smelling fields which were a small part of the Ireland only he and the Gaelic League knew how to love. Something in the tone of the voice touched Purcell. His compassion was suddenly aroused for this sad little man in the butterfly collar. He promised to do some Moore's melodies in the coming weeks. Lacey seemed relieved not to have entirely failed in his mission. When Purcell politely refused his final attempt to annex the choir he shook hands and asked rather sadly why he was so adamant.

"Because," Purcell said, "I think we should cultivate a thing for itself, not to serve a dubious political aim."

Lacey said regretfully, "You take the narrow view, Mr. Purcell."

A week later the Fool handed him a letter from the Gaelic League. Before he opened it, a thought struck Purcell and he said:

"Do you know Sally Maguire, Joseph?"

"I know the Maguires, Master; there's a tinker's tribe of them living in the cottage above on Knocknagen Hill."

"This is a girl of about eighteen, a slim dark girl. I noticed at the rehearsal the other evening she had bruises on her face and her arm."

"More than like — the father knocks hell out of them when the humour takes him. She is likely the one who works in Murphy's button factory."

He had betrayed enough interest in Sally Maguire for the moment and shifted the conversation.

"Murphy seems to have made plenty of money," he said. "I wish I knew his secret."

"He didn't make it, Master, he robbed it."

He smiled at this and said, "Was he not put in gaol?"

"No, Master. He's a patriot. During the Trouble it was a fine patriotic thing to hold up a bank or His Majesty's Post Office when the boys were short of funds and lift as much money as you could lay hands on. It was needed to fight the war, but if you put a few hundred in your own pocket to sweeten the risk, it was by way of no harm."

"How do you know all this, Joseph?"

"My brother told me. He did most of the work while Lacey was feathering his nest."

"Joseph," Purcell said, as he opened the letter, "why do they call you the Fool?"

"Because I'm not right in the head, Master," the Fool answered simply.

The letter was from Lacey on behalf of his Committee. Irish music, it declared, suffered more at the hands of gombeen men, like Moore, than through the suppressive activities of the Sassenach himself. The national ideal was to be sought, not in the foreign-dominated drawingrooms of nineteenth-century Dublin, but in the traditional songs of the people, sung in the people's traditional tongue. It also underlined the responsibility which the official educational programme placed upon Purcell, and hinted at possible representations to Father Finnegan, the school manager. A circular was enclosed with it, inviting him to attend a meeting of the leading townspeople for the purpose of seeking an increase in Old I.R.A pensions and soliciting his support. The inconsistency did not surprise Purcell in the least.

II

Sally Maguire's attendance at rehearsals created a new interest for Purcell. He had the gallant notion that any man who raised a hand to a woman was a brute, and what he had heard of her distressed him. He resolved to question her about it and decided the best way to make contact was to put her in charge of the music. When she accepted her new office without any fuss or pretension, he found his thoughts more and more preoccupied about her. Despite her rather brazen matter-of-factness she had an elusive charm, a gentleness which intrigued him. Though he did not for a moment think of her as someone he might love

(love was not a notion likely to occur to him in any case) he could not regard her dark hair and pale well-featured face without a new feeling of tenderness. Occasionally he walked some of the road home with her. He found she took as a matter of course the hammerings her father sometimes gave her.

"It was the mother's fault," she confided one night, when he asked about the marks on her arms and her absence from rehearsals. "She was complaining about me going out at night, leaving her to do all the work, and he heard her. He has the divil's temper."

"And he struck you?"

"He knocked hell out of me," she said.

"But your mother should speak to him."

"If she did he'd knock hell out of her too," she returned simply.

"Does he often do that?"

"Not very often. And after a while it's all forgotten. That's how I'm coming to rehearsals again."

During one of their talks he told her of the Gaelic League's opposition, and his decision to put the inpromptu social gatherings on a more formal footing. He was going to have a committee appointed and adopt as a name the Ballyconlan Choral Society.

"I'm going to suggest Sweeney as chairman."

"The ex-guard?"

"He used to play in the police band."

"I never liked a polis man," she pronounced sturdily.

"He's all right," Purcell answered. "He has no more love for the Laceys or the Murphys than I have. But I'm wondering what Father Finnegan will have to say."

"He'll try to stop you."

"I feel he will, though I can't see why."

"They hate to see a body enjoying themselves," she answered generally. Purcell was not unused to these over-simplifications. He let it pass.

When he was leaving her she said to him: "People are awful. They love something to gossip about."

"Are they gossiping about the choir?"

"Of course — but I meant about you."

"What about me?"

"About you leaving me home so often."

"Oh . . ." He said no more.

At first Father Finnegan received the proposal with a show of cordiality.

"I'm glad you've come to me, Purcell," he said, offering a chair. "I've had reports of your impromptu — functions."

"Not bad ones I hope, Father."

A half smile. "Not good ones, I regret to say."

"I'm sorry."

Purcell explained the proposal and gave the names of the committee.

"I had hoped you were going to ask myself or Father Keenan to act as chairman."

"Unfortunately the members have already made their choice."

"I see. But members should be guided in these matters. I presume you know I expect to be consulted."

"No, Father." As he answered, Purcell realised that that was a lie.

"It seems to me you are not prepared to consult any of us about this society. Is it some sort of undeclared policy not to do so?"

"Not at all, Father. As a matter of fact it started in a very small and informal way. It's because it has developed to such an extent that we got the committee appointed." Father Finnegan had close-cropped grey hair. It showed spikily above saturnine features in which the hue had perceptibly deepened.

"In social activities of any kind it is generally recognised as important to have someone capable of giving spiritual guidance. I am disturbed to learn that the idea does not seem to have occurred to you."

"I'm afraid the importance of spiritual guidance in the simple activity of singing together escaped me, Father."

"Any function where young people of both sexes are thrown together indiscriminately requires supervision. It's not the singing. There will be dances and drinking. I'm thirty years a priest and no fool. Nor are you, Purcell. You know as well as I do what these things lead to. What time do these rehearsals end at?"

"Oh — about eleven o'clock. Seldom later."

"About eleven o'clock. And at that hour young people are to set off home in one another's company — wandering three or four miles of fields at night time without let or hindrance. You may propose to encourage it. I certainly do not."

"With respect, Father — I can't quite see how having one of the clergy as chairman can alter that. In fact I don't see how my choir meetings can have any bearing on the moral behaviour of the young people of the parish — except perhaps to improve it by giving them something to occupy their spare evenings."

"And to give them an excuse for coming together without exciting comment."

"Should they not come together?"

"Under reasonable supervision, yes. That is my province, Purcell."

Purcell realised it was time to make a gesture of capitulation. There were many forces working against him. He saw no reason why they should, but he had been feeling the silent whispering of their small conspiracies for some time."

"If you suggest the safeguards you think necessary, Father," he said, "we will be only too happy to adopt them."

Father Finnegan accepted the surrender without any show of acknowledgement. He would consider the matter and let Purcell know. He had the air of one sufficiently the master of his own power to exercise forbearance.

Shortly afterwards a project to erect a statue in the central square, commemorating the insurgents of 1798, brought Purcell once more into contact with the leading townsfolk. Ballyconlan's connection with the rebellion was not quite clear to him. Everybody at the meeting, however, seemed quite assured about it. Father Finnegan was in the chair. Murphy, in his address, recalled that Ballyconlan had given its sons and daughters in the gallant fight and the blood of these martyrs cried aloud from every green field and every cobbled passageway for remembrance. In every generation patriots had arisen and it would be a sad day and a misfortunate day the day Ireland forgot them. Murphy, an official patriot himself, spoke with warm conviction. The project itself would be under the auspices of the Gaelic League, but the honour of collecting funds would be everybody's. Purcell's share would be to organise a musical entertainment in the Parish Hall which would feature his choir. After the meeting Murphy unexpectedly offered him a lift.

"Thank you," Purcell said politely, "but I like to walk."

"I wanted a word with you about the choir," Murphy said. "You can count on my help — of course. I'm an influential man — even if I say so myself. A business man — but not a musical one. Too hard a life, I suppose. . . ."

Purcell smiled at the implication.

"It's very kind of you," he said, "but I feel we can manage on our own."

"Two heads, Purcell." the other said "—better than one. You do the music, but who will handle the business?"

"The committee — in their own fashion, which is best."

"Business is business. I can do a lot to help. In fact I've wanted to talk to you for a long time, Purcell. The Choral Society can help me — a fair arrangement. I like to play an active part in any of the town's social activities."

Purcell saw that only a direct refusal would be taken as an answer. He summoned his will to give it, knowing that he was going to make an influential enemy. He saw quite

109

clearly that this was a moment of crisis.

"You are a public man, Mr. Murphy," he said, "and I appreciate your interest. But I am a schoolmaster, and what little I have learned from my experience convinces me that there is only one way to help our people. They must be allowed to develop of themselves. They must learn, however dangerously, to run their own affairs . . ."

"You mean you won't tolerate interference."

"Not at all. I mean to make the unpopular experiment of helping them to grow something their own way."

III

Purcell, poised on the stepladder with his hand outstretched to open the schoolroom window, heard the rattle of teacups and looked down at the gathering. Tea after rehearsals was one of the first innovations of the ladies on the committee. It invested the proceedings with an air of respectability sufficiently slight to increase rather than diminish enthusiasm. Sally Maguire was collecting music and putting it on his desk; a group of youths had gathered about the piano while another tried his hand at a popular tune; cigarette smoke in tapering ascent clouded about the naked electric bulbs. There was a warm odour from the tea urn which bubbled its friendly conversation in the far corner. These meetings of the Choral Society, these hands passing around tea and biscuits, the self-conscious badinage, even the occasional horseplay, had become very dear to him, the more so since he had seen its spontaneity threatened. Father Finnegan had cocked a nose to the wind and scented licence; Murphy recognised in it a new social unit and wanted it because he saw all such units as potentially political. The Gaelic League, having failed to impose its concept of music as an affair comprising kilts and bagpipes, sought to kill it. The crozier and the hurling stick were raised in menace. He opened the window and the cool autumn-smelling air made him suddenly aware of hushed, harvest-shorn fields, and winding laneways where leaves in odd unexpected movement surprised the darkness. It recalled for him the fact that besides announcing the opera which the committee on his advice had decided to undertake, he was also to arrange to operate Father Finnegan's suggestion for putting the moral side of things right. These dark fields with their harvest-heavy breath were dangerous. The girls and men were to go home after rehearsals in groups and not to go in mixed couples. As he got down from the ladder he realised that the actual announcement was going to cause him embarrassment. He went to the middle of the floor and clapped his hands. He tried always to forget he was a schoolteacher but there were occasional little mannerisms which betrayed him. When there was silence he cleared his throat.

"Before we continue, there's something I have to say. As you know we have been asked to give our support to the '98 Fund collection and your committee have agreed to produce a show in the Town Hall late in November. The decision is to produce *The Pirates of Penzance*, an opera with delightful music which I know you will enjoy rehearsing. The details are to be worked out later, but I can assure you here and now that you will find it much more difficult than anything we have attempted heretofore. It will mean more frequent and longer rehearsals. And that brings me to   communication which I received from Father Finnegan and which I propose to read to you."
When he had finished the letter he went over to Sweeney the chairman, who assured him the suggested arrangement would be carried out. No girl would go home alone in the company of a member of the opposite sex. There was a good deal of giggling over it. Purcell felt it provoked a new intimacy between the younger people by being too frankly suspicious. He had a feeling it would not be carried out. In the meanwhile he had his own problem. It affected his own walks with Sally Maguire which, without bother-

ing to consider why, he had grown to enjoy so much. Now he asked Sweeney to come some of the way with them.

"Do you think I'm a bloody chaperon?" Sweeney asked.

"I can't give a bad example."

"For the love of God, man — show a bit of sense."

"I am. Plenty of people in Ballyconlan would welcome the opportunity of pointing out to Father Finnegan that the schoolmaster was not treating his wishes with respect."

"But you're a grown and responsible man."

"For the sake of the society I don't mind being treated like a little boy."

So Sweeney, to Sally Maguire's obvious resentment, began to come home with them.

One night a month later he was losing heart and said to Sweeney: "Everything is going very well on the singing side, but I'm worried about expenses. These costumes are going to cost a lot to hire; the royalties are heavy. Maybe I should get Murphy's backing after all."

"No." Sweeney said, "keep that crowd out."

"What are we to do?"

"We'll pay for our own and have a subscription to help those who can't."

"Another matter," Purcell said. "I have a letter from the Gaelic League."

"Lacey?"

"Lacey signs it — but I expect Murphy is behind it. They object to the *Pirates* as a Sassenach production, likely to corrupt our Irish heritage."

"The seven hundred years."

"Precisely. But calling it that doesn't answer the letter. What am I to say?"

"Tell him to go to hell."

"I'm tired telling people to go to hell. I'm tired standing on my own. Isn't it time I got some help?"

"Then put it to the committee and *we'll* tell him. After all, rehearsals have gone too far now to start chopping and

112

changing. I suppose they still want Irish airs."

"They say they would be more appropriate to a '98 Concert."

"I know what they want," Sweeney said with feeling, "bits and scraps of things with neither taste nor smell about them. I went through it all I can tell you."

The committee agreed. They were going to do the opera. Apart from a general restiveness, an impatience with the traditional restrictions, they were keenly interested in the music. Besides, anticipation of footlights, colourful costumes and the long days of occupation and interest which promised ahead strengthened them. So they informed the League that rehearsals were too far advanced for any change to be practicable.

Another night as they walked home together Purcell said to Sally Maguire: "Sweeney is going down into town on some business. You'll have to trust me alone."

"Am I supposed to weep?"

Her tone surprised him.

"I'm referring to Father Finnegan's stipulations ..."

"Father Finnegan doesn't have to worry."

He smiled. "You can look after yourself?"

"Good God, no."

He puzzled for some time. Then he said, "I don't follow."

Her laugh answered him from the darkness.

"You're a bloody slow one." He was mildly alarmed.

Meanwhile nothing further come from the '98 Fund Committee. Various functions were held, including a football match which, though attended to capacity, yielded surprisingly little in cash (Ballyconlan exhibiting the traditional reluctance to pass through an official entrance when it could slip in over the fence); a Sale of Work in the Town Hall which did better; a Gaelic League Dance; a Whist Drive, which failed miserably because no one in Ballyconlan played whist. At last, Purcell wrote asking for assistance and after four weeks received a reply.

113

The '98 Committee did not consider the proposed performance suitable. As an alternative, a drama group from Dublin had been engaged to give performances in the town on the dates in question. It was an amateur group of proved ability and excellent national character.

He was unprepared for the anger with which the Committee received the announcement. "They're not going to get away with it," one of them said. The remark became a sort of standard about which they rallied. Hope of doing something really important had been raised too high to be crushed out so suddenly. In the past few weeks something unheard of and undreamt of in Ballyconlan had been shown to be eminently possible. With unusual disregard for good money they decided to pay for the entire production themselves by saving over a period of months. It meant postponing the performance, but since it no longer had any connection with the '98 Fund that did not matter. They agreed, tentatively, to aim at performances during the first and second week in the following July. When, after Christmas, it was announced that the statue would be unveiled during the first week of July, they fixed the time definitely. There would be people in town and the air of carnival would assure good attendances.

Naturally, word of their intentions got around. Opinion among those outside the society, at first divided, gradually, if secretly, hardened in favour of the Choral Society. Nobody cared much for Murphy, if for no other reason than that he was powerful. Gossip soon reduced it to a fundamental issue; the Schoolmaster against Murphy. People thought him a foolish young man, but liked him for it. The fact that the Parish Priest and the Gaelic League favoured Murphy was only to be expected. Power coalesced. It was circulated that it was an immoral opera and that Father Finnegan was going to kick up holy murder about it from the pulpit. Yet Sunday followed Sunday and Father Finnegan was silent. Near the end of May, Purcell was told by Sally Maguire of the first positive move.

"Murphy is putting us on overtime at the factory," she said. "It's all over the place."

Purcell was unperturbed.

"He's left it a bit late. It will make things difficult, but not impossible."

"Whatever he does, I'm coming to rehearsals. I don't care what happens."

"I wish everybody had your spirit, Sally," he said warmly. She looked at him quickly. But he was still platonic, the good father, the big brother.

He went to Father Finnegan.

"There's some talk that you consider the opera immoral, Father. I've brought you a copy of the script."

"I've already examined the script, Purcell," Father Finnegan said.

"Do you consider it immoral?"

"Personally, no, but a moral judgment is a difficult one to make. My parishioners think it immoral. It could be argued, therefore, that it is."

"How in God's name does that follow?"

"If it offends their sense of morality . . ."

"Your parishioners know nothing at all about it. They've never read the script. Most of them never heard of Gilbert and Sullivan. They are being told it's immoral and that you consider it so."

"I am doubtful about the character of Ruth. A lone woman with a band of pirates – to some of my parishioners the implications will be obvious."

"What of the character of the schoolmaster who selected it? There are implications there, too."

Father Finnegan looked directly at Purcell and saw that he was sincere. He turned away.

"In point of fact," he said, "I do not consider the script immoral." Then, as an afterthought, he added:

"While you're here, there is another matter I should like to mention to you. I am informed thet you have been

115

keeping company with the young Maguire girl."

"What is the ugly implication this time?"

The tone of goaded antagonism made Father Finnegan raise his eyebrows.

"I do not believe there is any ugly implication. There is gossip."

"The gossip is malicious. I know where it emanates from."

Father Finnegan's voice altered. "I'm no fool, Purcell," he said; "I've told you so before; and I can assure you that I will deal uncompromisingly with slander – whatever source it may spring from. It is only that I feel you should be warned. You are not any Tom, Dick or Harry here. You are the schoolmaster. That makes all the difference. And you are becoming bitter, against the institutions of the community, and against me. You are hardening your heart. That is dangerous."

It was the first human thing that had passed between them in their interviews. The fact that the initiative should come from the priest affected Purcell.

His mood quietened. "You're wrong about the bitterness, Father. I have my own was of looking at things, which I do not think is in conflict either with the Church or society. I've done no wrong."

"That's what the Pharisee said."

"In righteousness. I plead it in defence – not positively, but negatively."

"I don't doubt your motives for a moment," Father Finnegan said. Then he smiled. "If I did, I'd declare myself openly."

Purcell smiled too.

"Please God that won't be necessary, Father."

"Please God it won't."

They had established contact with one another, a mutual respect, which heartened Purcell considerably. For the first time in many months he saw some hope of success.

IV

Purcell checked his list of characters as Sweeney opened the boxes and examined the costumes which had arrived. There was an air of suppressed excitement in the schoolroom. Some of the cast were present, and the inevitable amateur was already seated at the piano, vamping a discordant bass to a popular tune. But those who worked in the factory had been kept back after tea on special work. Three or four rehearsals recently had been spoiled by these sudden decisions of the factory management. Purcell had advised them to work when they were instructed to do so. He was terrified of dismissals and consequent trouble. Tonight, however, Sweeney reported that they intended to walk out at eight o'clock.

"Is there no way to stop them?" Purcell had asked.

"A lot of irresponsible young ones – you know what they are when they get an idea into their heads," Sweeney answered. "I hope to God I don't lose my pension on the head of them."

"Flag – Pirate Chief," Purcell said, absently ticking the item with his pencil. "I think that's practically everything, except the orchestra parts. What did you order?"

At a quarter past eight most of those from the factory arrived. They had walked out. Purcell thought it a mistake and said so to Sweeney. "There'll be bloody murder," Sweeney said. "I'll bet it's all over town already."

But there was no use saying anything about it to them. Besides, he caught something of their excitement and felt the spirit of their revolt affecting him personally, as they undid parcels and changed into costumes. There was some horseplay and it was difficult at first to marshal them for the opening chorus. The rehearsal was hard to control, but it went very well. It finished near midnight.

When it was over, he remarked happily to Sweeney that nothing could stop the show from going on the

117

following week.

"What about the costumes?" he asked, looking around at the disorderly schoolroom where boxes and baskets lay scattered with clothes straggling untidily from them.

"It's very late," Sweeney insisted; "leave it all to me. You get some rest."

He walked with Sally Maguire up the hill from the schoolhouse. The sultry darkness was quiet about them, the wind soothing after so much excitement.

"Thank God Sweeney isn't with us," she said.

"You don't like Sweeney. I can't see why."

"I don't mind Sweeney at all. I – I just don't want him with us tonight."

Something in her tone excited him. He was suddenly conscious of her proximity and their aloneness together under a brown blanket of sky, and the warm wind on their faces which smelled of fields and flowers. Tenderly he said:

"Sally – won't you get into a hell of a row about what happened tonight?"

"We'd do more than that," she said off-handedly. "Don't you realise what it means to us – the Choral Society and the bit of gaiety there is since you started it?" She took his arm. "There was no life at all before it, not a thing from one end of the week to another. You came along and stood up to Murphy and his set. You were not afraid of Father Finnegan and the quality. There's something to look forward to now which they can't get their hands on and spoil. We couldn't let them stop us now."

"I can't understand why they didn't start anything themselves. Was there nothing in the factory?"

"Nothing at all – except some of the boys annoying you going home."

He said gallantly, "That's the penalty you pay for being pretty."

"Do you think I'm pretty?" she asked him openly.

"Of course I do," he answered. He felt the subtle

118

change which the remark made in their relationship and attempted a noncommittal note by adding, "The Ballyconlan Society is going to be noted for its pretty chorus." He realised immediately that he had said the wrong thing, but they walked for about ten minutes in silence before her arm left his as they came to a standstill. She went over towards the stile which led to the path through the woods. a shortcut for her, but one they never used. She said good-bye to him, over her shoulder, with the minimum of ceremony.

"I'm taking the short-cut," she said. "It's very late."

"You'll be mud up to the eyes," he joked, calling it after her, but she didn't answer. He hesitated. Then her sudden exclamation and the sound of her stumbling made him call her name. Impulsively he made for the stile. The silence under the tall trees on the far side alarmed him and when there was no answer he began to grope in the darkness with his hands. "Sally," he called again and again. "Where are you – Sally?" until a voice, almost at his ear, said softly: "I'm here."

"My God," he questioned, "are you hurt?" He bent down over her, discerning first the white outline of her face and then her slim form stretched out beside him. He put his arm about her shoulders. She tilted her face.

"Would you like to kiss me?" she asked blandly. For a moment he was angry. Then a sickly sweat of desire surged through him. He found her lips and for a long time he was unaware of anything except their moist softness. When at last he released her it was she who rose first. Without a word she began to run down the path. "Sally," he called, but softly this time, the passion she had roused, though controlled once more, still unabated. Her good night came back softly to him between the leaf-whispering trees.

Two hours later he was in bed but still awake, listening to the rain which beat incessantly on the roof of the cottage, when the knocking on the door startled him. The kitchen was fire-lit and warm as he crossed it to unbolt the door. The rain blinded him for a moment, but then he recognised her and his heart almost stopped beating.

"Sally," he said, "what has happened?"

He moved his own clothes, which Joseph had lit the fire to dry, and sat her down. The lamplight revealed a bruise on her cheek. She told him there had been a row when she got home over the walk-out at the factory. Her father had been waiting up for her. He had seen the mud of the ditch on her coat and come to the conclusion which Purcell, despite his rage, could not condemn as unjustifiable.

"He knocked hell out of me, and when I hit back at him he threw me out," she said. Then, as though in answer to a question, she added, "Who else could I go to?"

He roused Joseph, who took in the situation without any show of surprise. Over supper it was arranged she should have his bed, and in the morning he would find ways and means of getting her away. She wanted to go to Dublin. The decision she had taken, her long journey back through the rain, seemed to have exhausted her, so that she listened to him meekly and submitted almost without interest to all he said. Long after she had retired he lay awake on the makeshift bed which he had set up in Joseph's room. It was the most dangerous situation he had ever been in in his life and yet it was not that which occupied him chiefly. He found his thoughts straying again and again to the fact that she who had tried blatantly some few hours previously to seduce him was now a few feet from him in the darkness of the next room. Now it was he who was full of uneasiness and she who was passive, and, for the moment anyway, at rest. He recalled the sound of her voice, her pale face, the mockery which could light so quickly and so attractively in her eyes. He left her sleeping. But he slept very little himself.

The next day the postman saw her. He came up the hill at an unusual hour with a heavy parcel which Purcell found lying on the table for him when he returned from the village. The parcel had English stamps on it and was registered. She and Joseph were upset at their mistake, but

120

Purcell, after the first shock of it, accepted the situation like a man who had known that this must inevitably happen sooner or later. Victory had been coming too easily. He knew exactly how events would develop when tongues started to wag, as they would, almost immediately, and her father went to Father Finnegan to have him accused. His main concern was to get her away quickly and safely, which he succeeded in doing when the car he had engaged arrived early the following morning. There was a light veil of mist still crowning the wooded slopes of the hill and, as he said good-bye to her, he was aware of the peace which surrounded him, the sunlight on the lower fields and the birds testing the sweet-smelling air of morning. He would have liked to kiss her in token of what little existed between them, but the presence of Joseph and the driver of the car restrained him. Instead, he pressed her hand and told her to write to him, a request which he knew to be stupid and pointless when, later that evening, after a day spent in fruitless examination of the situation in which he was involved, Father Finnegan's letter arrived. It was as he expected. The priest appeared to be under the impression that she was still in the cottage, because he commanded him under God's Law to pack her back to her parents at once, and to attend at the priest's house in the morning for an interview, at which Father Finnegan would do his painful duty in response to the demands of the leading people of the town and with the blessing of every decent father and mother in Ballyconlan.

Purcell left the letter down and picked up the parcel which had started the talk. It contained the four or five band parts for the opera.

"Joseph," he said, "I want you to bring this to the post office first thing tomorrow to be returned to the sender. And when you come back I want to start packing. I'm leaving tomorrow evening."

"Leaving, Master?"

"Leaving, Joseph. What else is there to do? Every decent father and mother in Ballyconlan wants me to. So

121

do the leading townsfolk."

"But you did no harm."

"I did, Joseph. I didn't mean to. It seemed the most natural thing in the world to me to start a society which would keep the boys and girls of the parish amused. But I forgot the important people; the patriots and the priests, who must test everything first to assure themselves that the plan is set out on Irish-made paper which has been watermarked with the Sixth Commandment. Murphy, for instance, has a corner in patriotism. He sincerely believes that our forefathers wore kilts and played Gaelic football when they weren't writing Aislings. He has taken some pains to know about such things. What is to happen to him and his henchmen if there is a swing in favour of light opera and cricket? That would constitute a betrayal of the national idea, because Murphy is himself the National Ideal. Father Finnegan thinks he can make the marriage rate compatible with the birth rate by beating courting couples out of the national ditch with the walking-stick of morality. To argue with him at all is to attack the Catholic Church, because Father Finnegan is the be-all and end-all of Catholicism. Every priest his own pope. And, fundamentally, the couples have no belief in either of them, as their conduct when they get to hell out of the country, as I intend to do, amply proves. If the Gaelic League really want to sell the national ideal to the young people in the ditches, I could give them a slogan: Kilts are more Convenient. But Father Finnegan would object."

He paused and smiled, because he had been talking for the sake of talking. In his heart he was deeply wounded at the unexpected turn of events.

"Light the lamps, Joseph," he said.

Joseph began the nightly operation for the last time. In the darkening kitchen he pumped the kerosene lamp until its buzzing took on the sleepy familiarity of every night and became an unnoted background to their thoughts. "I'll leave with you, Master," he answered. The plan was already in his mind. It had come to him quite easily and

122

naturally as he pumped at the lamp. It filled him with peace. He stood against the background of his own colossal shadow, which filled the wall behind him, his eyes fixed in contemplation of his plan, his huge harelip slung like a drinking trough from his face.

"But where would you go?"

"I would go to a person I know – for a while. If I had a suitcase that would take my few things."

"You can have one of mine."

"Which one, Master?"

"Whatever one you fancy. One is as bad as the other. It's good we both travel light, Joseph."

"Tomorrow I won't travel light, Master."

Purcell dismissed it as one of the unaccountable things the Fool often said. But when he had gone to bed Joseph made himself busy. He fetched the bomb from its hidingplace and took its parts asunder, staring at them until slowly the procedure of long years ago came back to him, the routine of those far-off nights when he sat up to help his brother, who fought to establish a new Ireland by blowing hell out of the British Empire. Then he fetched out the three cases and, deciding that the faded green one with the unaccountable initials C. D. stencilled on it was the most suitable for his purpose, made it ready. The next morning, while he was bringing the three cases to Patrick Hennessy, who waited at the foot of the hill with his scrawny horse and ramshackle cab, he set the mechanism carefully for ten o'clock. He reckoned they would all be in the hotel by then. "These two," he explained carefully to Hennessy, "is the master's. They're to be left in the waiting-room below at the station."

"Right," Hennessy said.

"And this one," he said, "if you'll do a little turn for me . . ."

"Of course," said Hennessy.

" . . . you might leave at the hotel on your way down."

"Is it one of the quality's?"

"It is . . . a Dublin gentleman that's going to the dinner

123

tonight. It's to be left in the corner of the dining-room, beside the piano, so that he can find it."

Hennessy, who was wise about entertainments, said:

"I expect he's one of them conjurers."

"That's right," Joseph said, "he's a conjurer. I carried it down for him early this morning."

"Dammit, but you were quick enough getting back into business again, Joseph."

"I was."

Hennessy leaned over confidentially.

"Tell me this – about your man above . . ."

"What man?"

"Now, now – what man? The Schoolmaster. Tell me this."

"Not now. I'll tell you it all tonight after the train comes. But you'll be careful to do what I've told you about the case there."

"I'll do that – don't fret. Did you see them unveiling the statue this morning? I'll declare to God but it brought plenty to the town."

"It should have kept them away from the town," Joseph said violently.

Patrick Hennessy frowned down at him.

"You're a contrary bloody man," he observed in a puzzled tone, before flicking his whip.

V

The statue, the man, stood newly carved in stone, his pike tilted in slim menace at the unbelligerent houses opposite, where some children played marbles in the gutter and a dog with vigorous enjoyment scratched its mongrel belly. Purcell paused to look at it for a moment. Hoary Michael Hannigan was sitting on the seat near the statue, the only other adult in the square, sucking comfort from his clay pipe in the warm waning of the July

124

evening. In all the streets converging on the square, rows and rows of bunting dissected the sky into ragged drills. Purcell walked alone under the small flags which flaunted their triangular colours, and banners which blazed with slogans. Remember '98. A Nation Once Again. God Bless Our Pope. Warm odours drifting from the open windows of Murphy's Hotel informed him of the preparations for the festive dinner. From the distant fairground an amplifier pumped out patriotic music. It merely emphasised the loneliness of the hour and the loneliness of his own journey to the station on this evening, which was to have seen the presentation of the opera, his final triumph. Nobody had come to see him off. Even Joseph had disappeared without a word of farewell. As he moved out of the square to waste the hour which was left before it was time to catch his train, he felt that most of all. He found the lanes about the station deserted too, and full of the indifferent tranquillity of the evening. Lying back against a green bank, conscious of the drowsy meadowland, the hum of insects, the faint odours of cattle which hung about the lane, he lit a cigarette and began to go over it all in his mind, feeling like a Lear deserted even by his Fool.

Patrick Hennessy climbed down from his cab with the caution of his age and came over without a word to join Hoary Michael Hannigan. They surveyed the statue in mutual silence.

"That's a commendable piece of stonework," Hannigan volunteered at last. He was leaning forward on his stick, his grey hair falling untidily about the back of his upturned head.

"What does it say on the pedestal there?" Hennessy asked. He had had a good day's business, with plenty of free whiskey to keep him away from melancholy.

"Damn the bit of me knows," Hannigan said. "It's all in Irish."

"Nor Murphy either, for all his *cáirde gaels* when he was

125

unveiling it."

"Wait now," said Hannigan, who had moved around the side and was peering forward to counteract the slow waning of the long day's light, "it's in English here."

He began to read.

> *Erected By the People of Ballyconlan, to the*
> *Memory of the Men of The Insurrection Who*
> *in 1798 Fought and Died for Irish Freedom.*
>
> *By red wave of Slaney and Barrow they fell*
> *The tyrannous Saxon to conquer and quell.*

"They were fine men. You won't see the likes of them today."

"I wouldn't mind," Hennessy said, "but the get-up of a bloody gombeen man who unveiled it."

"There he is now – getting out of his car with Lacey of the Gaelic League."

"I can't see that far," Hennessy complained. "I suppose he's wearing his 1916 medal."

"The pair of them," Hannigan reported; "they'd catch cold if they went out without them."

"I wouldn't mind – but it's highly debatable if Murphy or Lacey ever got within earshot of a gun."

"They have their fine fat pensions for it, anyway," said Hennessy, "and their seats on the County Council."

The two old men watched the cars of the new social hierarchy arrive. Father Finnegan came next. He was joined by the doctor. Murphy shook hands with both of them and, as they ascended the steps, the committee members of the Gaelic League, who were speaking in Irish to one another, gave passage. Joseph the Fool came through the square and Hannigan called him. He stared at them with wide expressionless eyes, his closely cropped head a little to one side, his undeveloped body ungainly. The sleeves of his coat were so short that half of each forearm protruded nakedly.

126

"Are you not joining the quality?" Hannigan twitted him. Joseph ignored him and questioned Hennessy.

"You left the case in as I said?"

"I did that," Hennessy said, "in the corner by the piano."

"Are you sure?"

"I ought to be – I'm in and out and up and down that bloody stairs all evening. And very little to show for it – mind you."

Hannigan chuckled and interrupted him. "I saw the schoolmaster passing a while back. You'd wonder he had the neck after the carry-on of him with Sally Maguire."

Joseph narrowed his eyes.

"He did no harm," he said.

"I have it different, then," Hannigan answered.

"He did her no harm," the Fool insisted, "only the harm he did himself. He gave her his bed when her own father threw her out, and when she was hungry he put the bit of food in her belly."

"He put more than food in it," chuckled Hennessy, "if rumour has it right." Then, as an afterthought, he added, "God forgive me."

After a while, the old men left. Hennessy had money in his pocket which he invited Hannigan to help him spend. But Joseph sat on. He kept vigil with his elbows resting on his knees, his fists clenched under his chin. A burst of applause which overflowed into the square greeted Father Finnegan as he rose to begin the speechmaking. Everybody's thanks were due to Mr. Murphy, the President of the '98 Fund Committee (he said), a man who was a credit, a very great credit indeed, to the town of Ballyconlan. Murphy's Hotel, he would say, without fear of contradiction, was one of the best in Ireland, and his factory one of the most modern, for although we protected with jealous pride the traditional culture of our people, we were prepared, and rightly prepared, to examine and take to ourselves what was the worthy result

127

of progress in other nations, whose history – happier than ours – had allowed them to develop their industrial processes to a higher pitch of efficiency. He must not forget to thank ex-guard Sweeney, either, who presided so gracefully at the piano. Here was a confluence of sweet sounds to charm the ears of all, and to fill the heart with the proud knowledge that our native music could compare more than favourably with the best in the world. What could be more lovely than our Irish songs and dances? Of course, there were Irishmen – God help them (laughter) – who were prepared to ape the English taste for comic operas – and what could that be, after all, but a heathen taste; and others, of course, who wanted nothing less than Bach and Beethoven – he would refer to these gentlemen as the long-haired militia (laughter) – and who decried our native music for being too unsophisticated for their discriminating palates. But so far as he, personally, was concerned, and he was sure all present would agree with him, give him the good old Irish tunes every time. Give him these and he wouldn't give that (snap of the fingers) for all the symphonies and high falutin concertos of the Big Wigs.

So Father Finnegan went on, proposing the toast of Ireland, while the evening tarried above the town, and the fields of Ireland, which the blood of patriots had fertilised over long and painful centuries, lay passively and awaited its coming. Joseph sat so still that the old mongrel, forgetting the distrust of long experience, came and laid its muzzle on his knee. Joseph felt the warmth for some time before he pushed it away. It ambled for diversion over to the statue, a new amenity, and pissed wearily against its base. Hiss-piss-hiss sang its slaney-green wave from under a piky foot. Then it left Joseph to watch alone.

Purcell, who had the carriage to himself, watched the slow fading of the evening, too. It brought Sally Maguire to his mind. He wondered whether he should try to find her tomorrow or whether to let the whole business die. He would write to Father Finnegan, of course, and tell him what had occurred. After that there would be time to make up his mind; he had the long summer vacation in which to do so. He might go to England or, perhaps, further afield. Looking at his watch he found it was five minutes to ten. That gave him something over an hour before he would reach Dublin. He pulled one of the travelling cases, which the porter had left on the seat beside him, and lay it on the floor, wondering for a moment at its weight. It was the faded green one, with the unaccountable initials, C. D., stencilled on it. Stretching out his legs to rest his heels on it, he lay back. The train was travelling bogland once again, a brown and lonely expanse, dotted with poignant pools, in which the last light of the evening lingered and was drowned.

The Damned

HIS mother's hand shook his shoulder. When he opened his eyes she had the still-tall Christmas candle lighting on the dressing-table. It was the Christmas candle lighting but Christmas was three months ago. Its yellow unsteady light made him screw up his eyes. A solitary bell was ringing somewhere outside, somewhere far off across a space of cold, early-morning darkness. The blankets were lovely and soft and warm and lovely but his nose was cold.

Six o'clock, his mother said.

Warm dreamless sleep he longed to sink deep down back into but his mother's hand kept dragging him up from its fluffy depths, and his eyes opened, closed, opened like the cat's when she dozed at the fire. When at last they stayed open she said again six o'clock son and he could see she was smiling at him. She had a long nightdress on her and a shawl about her shoulders. All her face looked very old and tired and she had her teeth out. It frightened him to see her face worn and tired bending over him in candlelight and her teeth out. She was like dead and he would pray for her at Mass.

As he washed he made sure not to swallow any water because he was going to receive Holy Communion. His good suit was laid out for him and his shoes were polished.

Joe and Aunt Mary were here last night, his mother told him, they brought you a new shirt.

He murmured sleepily.

Aunt Mary is as good as gold, she added. He knew from her voice she was near to tears. Whenever she mentioned a kindness now it moved her to tears. Aunt Mary, her sister, had a habit lately of bringing little gifts. Since his father's death she would call and say: How are you, Ellen, in a warm voice. His mother said: Keeping the best side out. What else is a body to do. And once when he was there, pretending not to mind, his mother said: I'm worried about who-you-know. He's fretting. Who-you-know was him. Aunt Mary said: He saw it happen, the poor child. Is he still . . . I mean at night? He pulled on the shirt, which smelled nice and new.

His feet rang emptily on the path. Sometimes from a faraway street he heard feet as early as his own give answer; and now three different bells were ringing. The street lamps were on, which made it look like night, but the darkness was cold and more lonely than night darkness. From around corners a small sharp wind made ambush now and then and in the unswept gutters pieces of paper flurried and scraped. He passed the graveyard of the Protestant Cathedral. Once it belonged to the Catholics but the Protestants took it. They desecrated the Altar and the holy vessels. They would burn for ever in hell for that. He glanced fearfully through the railings at the leaning headstones and thought of their blackened tormented faces howling through the flames and their screaming, struggling nakedness, and then he thought of himself, his soul pure and white, hurrying through the dark, windy, early-morning streets to serve Mass and receive the Immaculate Host which was God Incarnate, the Unsuffering Victim, and he shuddered. Last night in confession he had told Father Rogan he prayed for the damned and Father Rogan said no, he must not do so. As he looked at the headstones a piece of white paper whirled past him with startling suddenness. The wind pinned it against the railings. It flapped and struggled. Then it went whirling and spinning again into the darkness among the tombstones, lost and helpless, pursued by the wind. He hurried on, frightened.

He put on his soutane and surplice and went into the vestry. Father Rogan, who was robed and reading his prayers silently, looked around at him. To avoid meeting his eyes, he pretended to see if the cruets were filled. Then

131

he took a taper and went out to light the altar candles. There were six tall ones at the back and a small one on each side of the tabernacle. When he turned, Father Rogan was ready. "Are you receiving – John?" he asked. "Yes, Father," he said. It was only a formality because Father Rogan knew. In confession he had promised Father Rogan to offer his Communion for the repose of his father's soul. The thought of his father troubled him for a moment as he preceded the priest on to the altar, but the holy things around him made him feel less afraid.

During Mass it grew very warm on the altar and the Latin came in low somnolent murmurs, so that he had to strain forward to know where to make the responses. Father Rogan's face became absorbed and pale and his eyelids drooped heavily. Sometimes he gave a great sigh. When a member of the congregation came in late you heard first of all the soft tread of feet and then the clap of padded doors, and quite a while later the candle flames wavered and danced and sent up little plumes of smoke. Then they stood still again, each tipped by its golden flame which burned like a pure soul. But if one blew out it was smokey and black, like a damned soul. Father Rogan looked at him very intently when he turned and said *Oratre Fratres,* but he knew he was not thinking of him at all. Father Rogan had been very angry with him in confession last night when he said he had prayed for the damned again. But now he had promised not to do it any more. Father Rogan had said the Damned hated God because God said to them, "Depart from me ye cursed into everlasting flames which were prepared for the Devil and his angels." It was useless to pray for these wicked souls who mocked at God's beauty and spat blasphemies in His face. It was dark and cold in the confession box and outside he had heard the clerk's keys rattling while he locked up the church. Then he forgot the cold and the keys and he thought only of God and heaven and hell.

Are many souls damned, Father? he had asked.

Father Rogan had breathed heavily and shifted and said

a little wearily: You think a lot about hell?

Did he think a lot about it now? Yes, he thought a lot about it, but he tried not to. When he prayed for his father he thought about it.

I dream often about hell, Father.

What do you dream?

About flames and black faces and being lost. He hesitated. One of the black faces he always knew.

There is something else, Father Rogan suggested.

I think of God, Father, when I wake up.

In what way?

The sweat broke out coldly about his eyes, but hot and moist where his shirt clung to his stomach.

Father . . . he attempted. His tongue with shame and blasphemy filled his mouth like a sausage.

Don't be ashamed, child, Father Rogan helped gently, you are not telling me – you are telling God. It was even harder to tell God, though God knew already.

I see God without any clothes on.

Is it an obscene image?

I – I think so, Father.

Do you entertain it . . . dwell on it?

Oh, no, Father, he said. His fervour satisfied the priest.

That's right, Father Rogan assured him, you must put it out of your mind. But don't worry or feel ashamed. The devil conjures up these evil visions to tempt and frighten you. Even the saints, very great and holy men, have complained of this.

I see, Father, he said. Then, without meaning to, he found himself saying again:

But are many souls damned, Father?

Father Rogan had hesitated. Then in an almost brutal tone he said: The Little Flower tells us that in one of her visions she saw souls falling to hell like leaves from the trees.

There was silence.

And Our Blessed Lady made known to us that more souls are lost through the sin of impurity than through all

133

the other sins put together.

More silence. The priest had waited and after a time leaned towards the grill.

Now, my child, the priest said very gently, you must try to tell me what is really troubling you.

Yes, Father, he said. Then a tear trickled down his nose and fell on his hand. The priest waited. He began to sob. He could not help now but to cast away all evasion and lay naked his heart.

Father, he said, I think my Daddy is in hell.

Father Rogan, his vestments rustling softly like the whispering of holy voices, turned his head indicatively but unobtrusively and began to recite the *Sanctus*. Catching the priest's voice almost too late, he reached out his hand and rang the altar bell. The congregation knelt. The sound of their knees meeting the wooden kneeling boards echoed like a long-drawn-out roll of distant thunder. The golden flames which tipped the candles wavered and steadied. Then it was quiet. He was to pray for his father. Father Rogan had asked him to tell him about the accident, and that was easy, for he remembered it all; his father's brown suit, the packet of biscuits with the white paper wrapping and the red seal which he tried to stick on his coat for a badge, but it fell off. His father handed them to him outside the pub and he was drunk even then. There were two other men his father had met.

Is that the eldest? one asked.

The eldest and only, said his father.

He's very like you, Michael.

His father pretended to be affronted.

I hope not, he said truculently. They laughed. It was then his father handed him the biscuits.

He's a good lad, he said gravely as he did so.

It was a warm July day. The whitewashed wall of the public house gleamed hot and white in the sun, and while he waited he picked little flakes off it with his nail. When he grew tired he sat among the clover by the roadside and heard the insects humming. The fields were full of

134

buttercups and daisies. Beyond them rose the hill with the mountain railway winding up towards the summit. It rose steeply with red sandstone cliffs and many furze bushes in sprawling yellow clumps. Here and there the sun flashed blindingly on the windows of small whitewashed cottages. His father came out at last and the two men were with him. They were singing. He frowned at them. They had been a very long time.

I suppose you'd given us up, his father said.

He looked down at the grass and sulked.

Well – then, his father said, casting round for something which would please him, we'll have a trip on the mountain railway – how's that?

He said all right without pretending to be much interested and the four of them set off. His father put his arm about his shoulders as they walked. He was disgruntled and hurt at being kept waiting and when his father lurched unsteadily it was an excuse.

You're drunk, he said.

I had a few, his father agreed tolerantly. It's our day out.

You mean it's your day out.

His father looked hurt.

Now, now, he said, squeezing his shoulder, you and I don't quarrel, son – do we. Life's too short.

He shouted at the other two in front.

Isn't that a fact . . . Joe . . . Dick?

What's that? they asked, turning around to grin. He began to sing life's too short to quarrel, hearts are too precious to break. He was in high good humour again and kept singing in snatches as they boarded the electric car. He stayed on the platform and the rest of the people laughed at him. But when the car started and the ticket collector ordered him aside, his humour became truculent and he began to argue. He heard his father using bad language and blushed scarlet with shame. Joe said to Dick: Prevail on him to come in before he gets us all arrested. His father came in with Dick. While they travelled he was very belligerent and kept abusing the conductor. The ticket collector went upstairs.

Didn't I pay my fare? his father demanded.

You did – of course, said Dick.

Like anybody else?

Like anybody else, Dick said. Now shut up like a good-mannered man.

I'll shut up when I bloody well like, his father said, tilting the bowler arrogantly over his eyes and rising.

Please yourself, Dick said with patience, but sit down anyway.

I'll sit or stand when I please, said his father, angrily, not at any man's behest. He pulled his arm free and went out on the platform. Joe looked imploringly at Dick.

For the love of God, he said, go out and fetch him in.

His father was on the platform, singing. He saw him swaying and then Dick catching him by the arm. His father pulled away.

Go to hell, he said and leaned out. He heard the sharp concussive sound and his father was no longer on the platform. The brakes made a loud grinding noise which filled the whole car. When they stopped he jumped off and went racing back along the tracks. Dick overtook him. He pulled him back as he reached his father's body. There was the body but no head. The conductor said: The man was drunk; there's a warning about poles. He stuck out his head. He felt his face being pressed roughly against Dick's waistcoat button. At that moment, his eyes no longer on the body, he screamed. Someone said, Take the child away – you fool.

He heard Father Rogan's boots creak as he genuflected and rang the bell. The white Host was raised. He saw it poised for an instant against the bars of the tall white candles. Eight golden flames, the souls of the Elect, stood still in worship. He tried to pray. But the paper fluttered against the weathered bars, lost its grip, and whirled in terror across the stones in the wind-raked field of the damned. He lowered his eyes. No matter how softly he flicked his wrist the bell wakened and hushed the church with echoes. It resounded in the body and chattered brightly in corners. He let it down with relief. Judge not and you shall not be judged, Father Rogan had said to him. It sounded frightening in the cold confessional. It came back now in the silence, after the din of the bell, a voice from a remote place speaking to him alone, so clearly that he looked around to see if it had been heard.

Did you love your father? Wasn't he kind to you?

He told people you won this in school and that for sports. Often he got angry but it was never for long. His mother said God help him, a kind word to him and you could twist him around your little finger. In the street you walked linking him and if you met the fellows you said this is my dad and you felt proud.

Yes, Father, he had said, his tears still falling. So inadequate was it, it felt almost like telling a lie.

If you loved him because he was good, how much more would God love him? We must not judge others, my son. God's mercy is infinite, and works in mysterious ways. Pray for your father and say to the Sacred Heart, when this terrible doubt troubles you, Sacred Heart of Jesus I place my trust in Thee. That will bring you comfort. You will do that, won't you?

Yes, Father.

For the moment he had felt at ease. But now it occurred to him that his mother loved him but that did not mean God would not send him to hell if he died in mortal sin. The doubts crept quietly upwards in him once more and he became so hot he felt weak and sick. The Host, the Living God, crackled very distinctly as Father Rogan's white fingers broke it. Behind him he could hear the quiet tread of feet as people came to the altar rails to receive. He tried hard to say Sacred Heart of Jesus but the blackened face appeared, smiled with gapped teeth, and dissolved before him. He pushed it violently from his mind. He rang the bell again when Father Rogan, striking his breast, his heavy eyes now almost closed, breathed the *Domine non sum dignus.* He thought he could pray and pray, all his life

137

he might pray, but he would never know where his father was. Father Rogan did not know though he was pious and holy. God alone knew and God rarely told, except perhaps in visions of His saints, or very occasionally in a secret half-heard whisper to the heart when you received Him in Holy Communion. One moment the sun beat down on the warm tracks, the people laughed, and you could tell people you were well or you were angry or you were hungry or you were sick. And then there was nothing at all; only a leg which could not walk and a mouth which was dumb and an eye which could not see. And somewhere inaccessible except to the dead themselves the flames leaped and the air was full of screams and God, no longer merciful or patient but terrible in majesty and Justice, called out a name which echoed from star to star.

Father Rogan turned around for the *Agnus Dei*. His stout white fingers held the communion particle over the ciborium. Father Rogan was looking at him curiously, waiting for him to go up to receive. But he could not rise. His eyes, resting on the tall candles behind the waiting figure of the priest, remained fixed there. Father Rogan delayed imperceptibly, then went down to administer to the people at the rails. He felt sick, but with an effort he rose and followed.

As he returned from the altar rails his eyes were drawn once more to the candle. The red point at the tip had now burned out. A thin column of smoke streamed up from it still. But the blackened wick had curled, acrid and damned, an unspoken message amid the golden beauty of the seven. He looked down at the priest's biretta. It lay before him on the altar steps. Soon he would have to take it up, kiss it, and hand it to the priest. But as he reached out his hand towards it he thought again of the candle and the biretta began to spin in front of him. It was a black and hideous face. The tassel parted in the middle and grinned widely at him. It began to roll down the white road. Steel tracks caught the sunlight and dazzled as they flung it back. Down the road rolled the head. Rolling and bouncing it rolled while he chased endlessly. It was exhilarating and he laughed. He caught up on it. Wielding his stick he began to roll it before him like a hoop. The wind, whistling past his ears, was odorous and hot like a furnace stream. Father Rogan, at the bottom of the steps now, crossed himself and began to recite the prayer for the dead. *De profundis clamavi, ad te Domine, Domine. . . .*

No response came. Father Rogan looked around at the pale face, the tense figure. He was unaware of the priest's eyes. Before him loomed great gates, under which the head rolled. He shook them with his hands and screamed noiselessly. The road dipped steeply into the sulphur-smelling darkness, the smoke choked him. Vile hands reached out and laughter resounded. Down through the flames and past the exulting figures the head passed, bouncing, grinning, spitting, mocking God, gathering momentum. He watched, and all the time beat futilely at the gates. He let his stick fall beside him. Daddy, he repeated silently, lacerated now by his guilt, his unkindness. Daddy. They were the gates of Hell. Yet he wanted to follow.

Father Rogan saw the perspiration on his forehead. Later he would call him to his room.

Fiant aures tuae intendentes, said the priest, making the responses himself, *in vocem deprecationes meam.*

The Half-Crown

THE man in the bookshop was suspicious. He had his hands in the pockets of his grey overall and he looked at you in a sharp knowing way which made you feel guilty.

"*A Hall and Knight's Algebra,*" Michael, embarrassed, said.

The eyes, cold and commercial, looked from the book to Michael. "Hocking it. Slipping it out of the house to flog it for cigarettes and the pictures," said the eyes. The hand took the book.

"A shilling," the man said, and sucked his tooth.

"That's not enough," Michael said, "it's worth more than that. It's worth three bob at least." The man turned the book over, pretending to examine it. He saw that Michael's sports jacket was too small for him and the ends of his flannel trousers were turned down in an attempt to conceal their shortness.

"Name and address?" he asked, as though absent-mindedly. That was written inside the cover. But if they really enquired and they got to know at home?

"What's that necessary for?" Michael countered. "You don't think I stole it?"

"I'm entitled to ask that," the man said. "Lots of books is pinched this time of the year. Besides," he added, "maybe your mammy doesn't know you're selling it." He used the word "mammy" very deliberately as an insult to Michael's self-esteem. "Well," he said, "how about one-and-sixpence?"

"It's worth more than one-and-six," Michael persisted doggedly. The man handed it back. "There you are," he said without interest, "take it or leave it." That was that.

The previous evening he had been so certain of getting at least half a crown that he had told Anne Fox he would meet her at the station. He had been out swimming with Mark, her brother, at Sandycove and when they came back she stood on the steps to talk to them. He had leaned over the borrowed bicycle with the togs and towel wrapped about the handlebars, enticed by her dark eyes, her slim bare knees, and moved by the cool and salty odour of his own body. He would risk a lot to be with her. Getting half a crown had seemed a small enough task. He thought she was very beautiful. At one point the thought so absorbed him that she said to him smiling, "A penny for them, Michael." But he had no words as yet for graciousness.

It had been the first thought to come into his mind when he was wakened too early that morning by his mother's hand stirring his shoulder. She was taking the child to the dispensary and wanted to be down early to be well placed in the queue.

"Michael son," she said at a quarter to eight. "Michael!" But the sun even at that hour was so strong in the bedroom he found it difficult to open his eyes. Without any intention of moving he said he was coming. At half past eight she again called him. "Your father has gone ages ago. You promised me you'd get up early," she said. But he pulled his shoulder away to show her how he hated her to touch him. Gradually over the past year he had felt hatred of her growing in him.

"I'm coming," he said angrily, "go and leave me alone." And when she had closed the door he turned over deliberately on his side. She had to be shown that shaking him would get her nowhere. But after a while, his anxiety to ask her for money had overcome his anger and he got up. She had fried bread for breakfast because it would save the butter, and when he sat down at table she served him with her hat and coat on. She had the baby in the pram. The rest of the children were with her married sister in the country. He said to her:

"We're going on an outing today. I want to know if you can give me half a crown."

141

"Half a crown," she said unhappily. "You got your pocket money on Saturday."

"You don't call one-and-sixpence pocket money."

That rebuffed her for a moment. She made another effort.

"Can't you borrow a bicycle somewhere?"

"We're going to Bray," he said. "The rest are going on the three o'clock train."

"Couldn't you arrange to meet them out there?"

Meet them out there? Tell them he had finished with school and could find no work and he couldn't help it if it meant being short of cash? He flung fried bread across the table.

"Keep your lousy half-crown," he had said, rising to go into the bathroom.

"Michael," she called after him, "you know if I had it I'd give it to you." He refused to answer. Then in a hurt tone she called to him, "I gave you two shillings last week." But he banged the door loudly. Later he had heard her take the pram down the steps by herself.

He stuffed the book back in his pocket. The sun, high over the tall buildings and the summer crowds, beat down on his bare head. Even under the striped awnings outside the shops in Grafton Street it was intolerably hot. There was an aroma of coffee in the air to stir his appetite, and flowers blazed yellow and red in vendors' baskets. Near the Green two girls on bicycles looked at him with interest. One was a tidy piece but she wasn't as nice as Anne Fox. He wouldn't think of Anne Fox in that way. None of the girls was as nice as Anne Fox. She was different. She wouldn't do that – no – she wouldn't let you – no. But if he couldn't go to Bray maybe Dorgan would see her home. He got on easily with girls and when he knew Michael was soft on Anne he would make sure to cut in on him. Dorgan loved to do that. He would invent stories for the rest of the gang, which he could tell in a way that made it hard not to believe them. If he did he would break his bloody neck. Then of course the rest would think it was sour grapes, but it wasn't that at all. Anne wouldn't let you do that; she was a nice girl but she was soft on him too. He knew by the way she looked at him last night on the steps, and the way she leaned her head back a little so that he could see her soft warm shapely throat and the way she laughed at what he said to show she liked him to talk to her. So nice it had been last night on the high steps under the green-gold, cloud-crossed evening sky to ask her; and now it was all being bagged-up because of a lousy half-crown.

His father and mother were both at table. He walked through quietly to sneak the book back on the shelf. The baby was asleep in the pram. It had blobs of white ointment on its face. Bits of bun lay on its dress and coverlet. He took his place and his mother rose immediately to fetch his meal for him. The tassels of a faded green cover hung down beneath the table-cloth. There was a hole worn in the centre when the table-cloth was not on but you covered it with a fern pot and that was more or less all right. He looked at his father slyly with the idea of putting out a hint for some money but his father's face was not a good-humoured one – in fact – no – it wasn't. His father's face was moist and flabby. Though it was so warm he wore a dark suit and a butterfly collar which was respectable because of his calling. He was a clerk in the office of Joshua Bright & Son, Timber Merchants. In good humour he told stories which always ended in Mr. Bright saying, "Kavanagh: you're a man after my own heart. How on earth did you fix it? I'm certainly indebted," or words to that effect. It always made you want to kick both of them in the fanny. But Bright was not on the menu today. There was something else.

"If I've told you once," began his father, "I've told you a dozen times that a razor should be dried and cleaned when you've finished with it. No one with manners a cut above those of a pig would leave a razor in the condition mine was left in. I've never objected to you using it –

143

though what in God's name you have to shave is beyond me – all I ask is that you dry it after you."

He remembered he had not dried it. He had left it down to put water on his hair in the absence of hair dressing and of course he forgot – well, he didn't exactly forget but he was in a bad humour over his mother.

"Razor?" he lied, pointlessly and brazenly. "I never touched your razor."

His father turned to his mother. "There's your rearing for you now," he said; "the lie springs easy to his lips. If he's going to sit there . . ."

His mother immediately tried to conciliate them. Too quickly, in her desire to placate them, his mother said, "You might have left it yourself, you were in such a hurry this morning."

"That's right," his father shouted, and let the knife and fork fall with a clatter on the plate, "stick up for him. Encourage him to deceive and defy his own father. I'll be a bloody lunatic before long between the pair of you."

"You can think what you like," Michael persisted. "It wasn't me."

"Michael," put in his mother.

"Then I suppose it was the cat," his father said with childish sarcasm, "or maybe it walked out of the case by itself. But I'll tell you one thing, you'll use it no more. You can get a razor of you own."

"I suppose you'll tell me how."

"Buy one. Do a little study to fit yourself for earning your keep."

"You must have studied a bit yourself in your day," Michael sneered. "You earn such a hell of a lot now."

He left the table. As he entered the next room a cup flew past his ear and shattered against the wall. It was unexpected and he jumped.

"You impertinent brat!" his father yelled after him. He locked the door hastily.

He came out when he was certain his father had gone. His mother took his meal from the oven where she had

144

put it to keep it hot. She had been crying. That sort of thing had never happened before.

"Have your meal, child," she said. "I don't know what's to become of us."

"I don't want it."

"It isn't right to answer your father like that; you should respect him. He works hard for what he gets."

"He knows how to hold on to it too."

She was silent. Then she said: "You know you'd get the half-crown if we had it. What were you ever denied that we had to give?"

"You can buy that baby in there sweet cake."

"A little penny bun. I'm ashamed of you, Michael."

That, unaccountably, slipped under his guard and stung him.

"You mind your own bloody business," he lashed back.

In St. Stephen's Green, children, their nurses watching them, were feeding the ducks from paper bags. And at the pond with the artificial sprays which spurted threads of pearly bright water into the thirsty air, children were sailing a boat. Michael lounged with his hands in his pockets. They were catching the train now.

"Michael Kavanagh is awful to be late like this," the girls were saying with angry little jerks of their heads, and the fellows were saying, "Oh, he'll come, don't bother, let's get a carriage." They were going to Bray to swim and after to lie in the bracken. They were going to eat ice cream and drink lemonade which the boys would buy for the girls, and eat sandwiches and make tea which the girls would bring for the boys. Anne would lie in the bracken. For the length of his own afternoon he could watch the people sleeping with newspapers over their faces and look at the flowers which blazed with a barren and uncommunicative joyousness. The sculptured face of Mangan brought some lines to his mind. "I could scale the blue air. I could walk . . . climb . . . I could . . ." How the

145

hell did it go? That was school. You knew these things when you sat for Leaving Cert. and then after a while you wondered how the hell did it go. You left school and watched the advertisements:

Junior clerk reqd. rep. firm Hons. Leaving Cert. Knowledge book-keeping asset. 15s. weekly to start. Good prospects.

Queue with the rest; don't stammer – oh – don't stutter – think oh, think. Cool – be cool and smile respectfully. Self-possession is nine-tenths of the law.

Your mother had pressed your suit and sat up into the small hours ironing and darning. She had already begun a Novena to Saint Anthony. (O please, Saint Anthony, send him work: O please. O sweet and good Saint Anthony intercede for my boy.) Your father gave you advice. He told you, take off your hat and smile easily and pleasantly. Don't fidget or sit on the edge of the chair, which wasn't to say, of course, that you were to put your feet on the desk. He had had a word with Gussy Gallagher who was said to have tons of influence since he hit it lucky in the auctioneering business. He was reputed to be a brigadier-general of something in the Knights of Columbanus. Now and then your mother looked across. "Pay attention to what your father is telling you," she would say. When she ironed late at night like that her hair fell in straggles over her face, her breath caught her now and then, her forehead so white showed moistly in the steamy light.

As you sat waiting to be interviewed you kept saying like an idiot over and over again something silly – like: "When Richelieu attained to office he was faced with the task of building a French navy."

Like when you were a child you went to the shop repeating in case you might forget: A pint of milk – a tin of beans – a duck loaf – and a half-pound of margarine and say the margarine is for baking. (That was a lie, but it was only a little white lie if your mother told you to tell it.)

But in the end someone else, like Harte or Joe Andrews, always got the job. Joe Andrews didn't know much about Richelieu, but he knew someone on the selection board with a bit more pull than Gussy Gallagher or Saint Anthony.

Knowledge weakened with winter, sickened with spring, withered and died in the hot July sun, giving place to new growths, to the contemplation of women, to long vacant hours, to quick greeds and slow lusts and jealous incessant neediness.

He sat down on one of the benches which were placed at secluded intervals along the quiet path. His mother was a silly bitch and his father a skinflint. His mother went out with his father to the pictures once a week and this was the night. It was the only night they went out but they could stay at home tonight because the other children were away and he was damned if he was going to stay in to mind the baby. That would be one way of getting his own back. The whole set-up was a bloody cod.

There was a thin white line running down the right side of his face, from his nose to the corner of his lips. He tried to relieve the tautness from time to time by rubbing his face with his hands, but failed because it welled up from inside him. Over him hung a wealth of almond blossom and opposite to him was a laburnum tree. It showered with perfect grace of movement to the tips of its trailing branches. Near it sat an old man and a child. He was a white-haired, serene-faced old man, whose ample waistcoat was crossed by two golden chains. On one end of the chain hung a watch. The little child was playing with it. She put it to her ear, listened, laughed. "Tick, tock, tick, tock," the old man said, making an attempt to imitate the sound. Frequently he bent down to chuck her under the chin or smile at her. Growing tired of the watch, she put her hand in his pocket to pull out a pair of glasses, a white handkerchief and a silver coin. The glasses and handkerchief were discarded, but she kept the coin. When she threw it, it flashed in the sun; when it fell, it

147

rang musically on the path and rolled round and round. It staggered in circles before flopping down. The old man, whom you knew to be old more by the stringy looseness of the neck behind his white butterfly collar than by any sign of age in the bright face, smiled an invitation to Michael to enjoy the antics of the child. But Michael only hated the child. He hated the child because a foolish and indulgent old man allowed it to play carelessly with a precious piece of silver. The milled edges of a half-crown were strong and comforting. You could stand a girl's fare and buy her ice cream, or buy cigarettes to smoke after a swim, and fish and chips to eat from a paper bag on the way home with the lads at night. The coin went up and down and he followed it greedily with his eyes. Sometimes it fell, a bright though tiny star, out of the child's reach, and the child would toddle across innocently to retrieve it. Sometimes when it fell, it staggered clumsily towards Michael. When the game had gone on for some time the old man lost interest and began to nod. Michael looked up and down the path. A keeper was examining a flower-bed some distance away. There was nobody near. But to rise, take up the coin and walk away quickly – that would be too obvious. The child might cry, or the old man open his eyes at the wrong moment. With half-closed eyes he followed the course of the coin.

To steal a half-crown could be mortal or venial. Three conditions were required for mortal sin and these were: (1) grave matter; (2) perfect knowledge; (3) full consent. It would be mortal to steal it from a poor man, but venial to steal it from a rich man, because it was dependent on the gravity of the injustice done. Not that he cared whether it was mortal of venial because he had committed sins of impurity which were always mortal and killed the soul, and it was eight months since his last confession. Automatically he almost said, "and I accuse myself of my sins." When the slide went click in the darkness the priest didn't say a penny for them he said well my child and with tongue stuck to roof and sweat of shame you had to

148

tell. If you were caught you were a (not-nice-word) thief.

The coin fell and rolled towards him. He watched it. It curved, glittering, towards his left. Gingerly he reached out his foot and stopped it. Then he looked sharply at the old man, whose eyes were still closed. He bent and picked it up.

"Go on," he whispered to the child when she came near him, "hump off." The face upturned to him was tiny and questioning. He could have raised his boot and crushed it without caring. But her bewilderment frightened him. When she began to cry he jumped up and said to her, "Here – we'll look for it in the grass."

He was earnestly searching along the verge when the old man stood beside him.

"Poor little pet," he said, "what's the matter now?"

"She lost her half-crown. I think it rolled in here."

They hunted for a considerable time. Michael kept his face averted. His heart thumped. He was afraid the old man might see it there thumping against his ribs, pulsing in his neck, calling out thief, thief so loudly that it must surely be heard. But the child began to sob and the old man comforted her by promising to bring her off to buy ice cream. After some time he told Michael he would have to leave it for the sweeper. "Finders keepers," he said regretfully but pleasantly as he was going.

Waiting impatiently while the old man and the child went off, Michael sat down again. He had no notion of the time. He should have asked the old fool before he went. They had gone in the direction of the station, but he would not dare to go that way lest they should meet again. The old man would want to chat. Where did he live? Was he still at school? What were his intentions? Suitable openings were hard to find for a young man standing on the threshold of life. A grunt. A stammer. There were no other answers to these things, none that he had found. They were simple expressions of amiability which always made the machinery of his mind lumber and clank, defeated and chaotic. He could never find responses.

149

He was afraid if the old man spoke to him, he would blurt out: "I took the half-crown and I'm sticking to it. You can do what you like about it." So he sat for half an hour and then went off in the opposite direction, taking a roundabout way to the station. He passed the university where Mark would soon begin to study to be a doctor. He always had money. Mark would never need to put his foot on a half-crown dropped by a child in a public park.

The street was so quiet he could hear his own footsteps echoing, and the building itself seemed peacefully asleep. There was a smell of dust and a sunlit silence. He thought of cool waters, of Anne Fox in her red bathing costume raising her round arms to let cool water fall from them glitteringly. She would climb Bray Head in her light cotton frock, slim knees bending, a sea-fragrance about her. It would not be easy to find them. She might go anywhere about the Head to lie in the bracken. She might lie in the bracken with Dorgan. He would have to search and search.

He hastened up the steps to the station, as though by hastening he could persuade the train to leave any earlier, or be with her any sooner. But when he reached the top he stood still. Just turning away from the booking office, holding the child by the hand, was the old man. The child wanted to carry the tickets. On the steps, an impassable barrier, stood guilt and terror. Instinctively and immediately he moved away.

At the corner of the Green, leaning against one of the pillars which had held the ornamental chains that one time bordered the pavement, he remained for a long time. He knew it was after six o'clock because people were passing in clusters on bicycles, and the hunger pains in his belly were worse. He should have taken his dinner. He was staring at the sky, golden and tranquil behind barred clouds, when his mother stopped beside him. She had been shopping and was pushing the pram with the baby in it. He knew it was she but barely moved to acknowledge her. Let her see him miserable. Let her see that he had only a corner to stand at and a sky to stare into. It would hurt her and that was something to know. Once he had loved them. When he was young, before the other children came along, he and his mother had often waited for his father at that very corner with a flask of tea and sandwiches and hot currant buns. They used to go into the Green to sit on the grass and have a picnic. But now he hated them. He had nothing to say to them. He had hated them for a long time now but they refused to recognise it. His mother waited. Then she said, "A penny for them, Michael."

Anne Fox had said that too, and now she was lying in the bracken with Dorgan. He made a sullen mask of his face and refused to answer. After a while, this time more urgently, she said, "Michael."

He grunted and shrugged.

"The baby isn't well," she began, once again placating him, trying to soften him, to bring him back to her. "I think I'll stay in tonight. You can go to the pictures instead. Make it up with your father at tea and then the pair of you can go off together."

"What is there to make up?" he asked. "You make me sick."

Hesitantly she suggested, "You weren't very nice to him at dinner."

"He wasn't very nice to me – was he?"

He looked around as he asked and was shocked to see tears in her eyes. But she averted her head and began to walk. He lagged behind, refusing to walk beside her. He saw in hunger and misery the squat steeple of the Methodist church, and over it the sky crossed regularly with clouds – a painted sea. Girls in the sea were slim and lovely. Girls in the sea had straight slim shapely legs. He looked at his mother's legs. They were very thin. They were encased in cheap unfashionable stockings, woolly, yellow in colour, wrinkled above the calves, much darned and dragged at the ankles. Her skirt was uneven as it swung about them. He watched the effort of her short step-by-step movement. He could not remember ever having looked at his mother's legs before. Now it stabbed him like a sword. His throat contracted. He searched for something brutal to say, something to protect himself against this fresh and unexpected onslaught of pain. She walked with her thin back towards him, her hands guiding the pram.

"We'll have to hurry home," she said brightly; "your poor father will be ages waiting."

He hoped to God she had wiped her eyes. He did not want people to see her. She quickened her pace and panted with the initial push.

"I have an egg for your tea," she added.

The brutality in him subsided. An egg for his tea. It made him want to laugh. But it also made him want to stretch out his hand to her, to touch her, to tell her he was sorry. But there were no words. He cast around for words. But when he even tried to think of them the grinding and turmoil in his head only became worse. Then his fingers touched the stolen half-crown. A flush of shame and unworthiness crept sullenly into his cheeks. It was suddenly without value. It could not buy what he wanted. Because he hardly knew what he wanted. He struggled with his own tears. He watched her now with immense tenderness, sorry for her, aching with love for her. But still something, his pride or his great shyness, would not permit him to speak to her or even to walk beside her.

In that way they went home; she walking ahead and unwitting, and he, who had no words for anything except churlishness or anger, followed silently.

Mercy

IN his own good time, in His own unpredictable way.
Martin Quinn. His soul and the souls of all the faithful
departed, through the Mercy of God ... Martin you are
gone oul' butty and I'm not long for the road. All our sins
for long enough was sinned together.

Morning sun shining brightly and warmly outside; tall
houses leaning over the street; bricks with age dark and
burned looking, but here and there coloured strangely
from weather, pale red and orange and slaty blue. After
dimness of church, traffic loud and repelling, light too
strong, sun-warmth seeping through clothes. Wait now.

He touched the money in his pocket, hesitated, then
with decision turned towards the vestry. The clerk, who
was putting away vestments, closed the press and came
over. He explained to the clerk.

"I want to have a Mass said – for Martin Quinn."
Feeling there was something missing, he fumbled a
moment before he thought of the phrase he wanted.
"Recently deceased," he added, satisfied.

"Certainly," the clerk said and reached for a book.

"And I want a second one offered."

"Two Masses for the repose of the soul of Martin
Quinn."

"No. The second is for someone else. I ..."

"Yes?"

"I don't know his name."

"That happens to us all when we get on," the clerk said
gently. "We forget in spite of ourselves. You can have the
second Mass offered for your special intention."

"Would that be for his soul?"

"That would be your special intention. A Mass to be
offered for the soul of your – friend. It's the same thing."

While the clerk wrote in the book, he took a ten-shilling note from his pocket and left it on the desk. His offering. That would leave him short. But God, who fed the sparrows, would not see him hungry.

"Thank you," said the clerk. "They will be the eight o'clock Mass tomorrow and the ten o'clock on Wednesday."

He put the beads in his pocket, dipped his hand in the holy water font and walked slowly down the steps. It had been a great shock, the priest turning from the altar and saying, "Your charitable prayers are requested for the repose of the soul of Martin Quinn, for whom this Mass is offered." After getting through the winter too. And he wouldn't have known a word because he wouldn't have gone to the Mass only the letter from the Ministry of Pensions had arrived that morning and he wanted to bring it to Fenlon. He had attained the age of seventy it said. He had, begod – no thanks to them. For long he had looked forward to it, talking about it to Fenlon and the rest, thinking how he wouldn't let on about the watching job he did now and then, in case it would interfere with it, wishing and worrying his few years away. And then this last few days he did not want to get it at all. And last night in the light of his torch a large brown rat had sat and grinned at him. On the ledge of the clock where he punched his card it sat, eyeing him, cerebrating. It was a summons. Like a crow on a telegraph wire or a beetle tapping its message through a wall.

He took the bottle from his pocket and went around the side of the church to fill it from the barrel with the rough white cross chalked upon it. He wanted holy water for his room. For that matter he could take some with him to the cutting tonight. It was lonely to sit in the watch box remembering bits and scraps of things, recalling faces, an old man not knowing the day nor the hour. A week of nights he had guarded the piled-up rubble, the tarred wooden sets, seeing the red lamps of warning growing pale with each dawn and waiting for the first footsteps to ring with morning hollowness on the pavement. Lately he would fancy them as the receding footsteps of life, or the approaching feet of death. With each dawn judgment came nearer. In the surface of the water were reflected the uncombed grey locks, the filmed, sleep-denied eyes, the grey stubble on his cheeks. They disintegrated in broken ripples as he plunged the botttle below the surface. He pushed the cork in tightly and went down High Street. The cutting was deep. It exposed the tunnels which honeycombed that part of the city, vaults which radiated from the Cathedral, ancient sewers which ran down Winetavern Street to the river. Once they had been drinking cellars and rebel plotting dens. Now the rats had taken possession. He remembered the clock. It hung beside a partition which sealed off an exposed vault. It was part of his duty to go down to punch it every hour. That was to make sure he inspected it. A pneumatic drill spattered as he passed, and the man nodded to him. "Bad luck to you," he murmured. But he was referring to the rats.

They were seated on the carved seats. Fenlon, Reeves and Hanlon, secluded in the sunny courtyard from the constantly passing people and traffic. Hanlon had turned a little away from the other two and leaned on a stick. Cronies. He was in no humour to join them, but he had the letter.

"More power, Fred," Fenlon greeted. "Sit down and take the weight off your legs." The sun-warmed stone felt comfortable against his back. He put the spectacles on the end of his nose, unfolded the letter, read Frederick Toner, Top Back, 23 Fenian Lane off High Street, Dublin, and passed it without enthusiasm to Fenlon.

"From the Government," he explained. "I got it at last."

"An unlucky breed," Reeves stuck in.

"But I can't get the gist of it at all; and there's a week's hard work filling in answers to questions."

"Them fellows go on with a lot of nonsense," Reeves complained, "and if you venture to ask them a question

155

you get nothing but the height of abuse. Johnny-jump-ups with a plaster of fountain-pens and the dung still fresh on their hobnailed boots."

"I'll fill in what you want," Fenlon said, "and bring it back to you tomorrow."

Age had failed to undermine Fenlon's great air of confidence, and the alertness which the waxed military moustache gave to his face was not entirely false. He knew his onions. No flies nor fears on Fenlon. But tell them.

"Poor Martin Quinn is dead."

"For God's sake. Where did you hear that?"

"At ten o'clock Mass. It was read from the altar."

There was a pause during which they raised unanimous hats.

"I didn't hear he was complaining," Reeves said, troubled.

"Nor I."

"That was a great butty of yours, Fred."

"He was. We soldiered together. The Boer War and after that in France. He was the heart of the rowl."

"He never looked after himself," Reeves said. "If he had he'd have been good for many a year yet." Aye. And if wishes were horses, beggars would ride. He could never warm to Reeves. An unsuccessful cattle jobber, generous to a fault in his day if you were fool enough to believe all the oul' guff he talked about himself. For myself, I never saw much of it. And a great man with the women – aye.

"Mind you," said Fenlon, "he had a power of money at one time."

"He had – enough money to build a chapel."

"More money than sense."

"God's truth, some people have all the luck," Reeves burst out, "the world is badly divided."

Divil thank the begrudgers. There was no mean drop in you, Martin. Spend it like water when you broke out. That time when the eldest daughter got married. The pair of us on the batter for a fortnight. At it all night and then up to the market first thing in the morning. And your

156

wife scouring the town for us. Poor woman, it was her money we were spending. Sheila Cassidy the publican's daughter from Macken Street. It put her early in her grave, Martin, the carry-on of the pair of us. Lovely she was at the time with her golden head of hair. Wistfully he murmured:

"She'd charm the birds down out of the trees," not meaning to say it aloud. That was age, too. They looked at him curiously.

"I mean his wife that's gone," he added, in explanation.

"Sheila Cassidy," Reeves said. "That's where the money came from. You'll find he still had a bit in the stocking. He always got the height of attention from the family."

"There'll be a contest between the daughters over his few ha'pence now," Fenlon said, "if I'm any judge in the matter."

Holy Hughie Hanlon in his greasy dustcoat turned a grey-bearded face with its gentle contemplative eyes and addressed them for the first time. As he moved, the rosary beads in his pocket, which he was for ever silently and secretly telling, rattled betrayingly.

"You will never see so many prayers as at a poor man's wake," he said, "but where there is a little money there is nothing but fighting and cursing."

"Well then," Toner remarked with forced gaiety, "I'll ger the prayers anyway."

"Me too — for what they're worth," said Fenlon. "I came into this world without a stitch and I'll go out of it without one."

That was true. You left it all behind. Naked and alone you walked the road to hereafter. Holy Hughie Hanlon smiled contentedly.

"There will none of us be heavy burdened on the road to heaven," he said.

At least there was conversation here. Not like at the cutting in the silence of the night, or lying down to sleep in his room with only the old mongrel scratching and

157

showing its age too. Here the Cathedral rose behind him, full of beauty and strength, and the trees were freshly in leaf. The apple blossom too was fresh and good to look on. Winter the worst enemy had passed. There were flowers once more and sunlight and children to run past now and then with shrieks of young laughter. Fear would have seemed far off, were it not for the patter of pneumatic drills which came to them, persistent but subdued; jabing with tenacious teeth which ripped raw wounds in the now untrafficked street. They would not let him forget. He thought of the rat. Then he thought of Martin, burdened with their common sin, and God knows what light of heavy load besides (had he the priest?) walking alone now the road to his judgement. He watched Hanlon's face for some time, and saw the lips moving soundlessly. They said he was a bit soft in the head. There must be great peace of mind in it anyway to let a man pray tranquilly like that. And no loneliness. He was about to tell them about the rat.

He said, thinking again of the scraping he heard every time he went down into the cutting and the flopping sound they made when they jumped:

"I got a bad shaking up last night."

"What was that?" Reeves asked.

But a young man, wearing his flesh proudly, not fearing rats, came towards them.

"Your son," Reeves said.

It was difficult for a moment to tear his thoughts from the thing in his mind, to look up at the young man who paused to greet them.

"I thought you were watching this week," his son said, "I didn't expect to find you here."

"I am watching, but I went to Mass instead of going to bed."

"A holy and wholesome thought," his son said brightly. His son's brightness embittered him, so that it crept into his voice.

"It was. A good friend of mine is gone."

158

"Who's that?"

"Martin Quinn."

"Is that a fact?"

"Well," his son added, "there's little the matter with you anyway. You're looking younger every day – what do you say, Mr. Fenlon?"

Encourage him. If he stops the watching he'll be a burden – what I never was.

"We'll have to shoot him," Fenlon said agreeably, "that's the only solution."

My son. My tall broad rearing a labourer in the Corporation in a fair way of becoming a ganger too, so they say. Faith and I watched you for more than long enough, me fine bucko Barney from Ballydehob. When it was daddy-I-this and daddy-me-that. A cute brew ever he was. Snooping round now about the pension, trying to find out if I'm picking up the few shillings that I never let on about. But it's too much trouble to you to call up to the room to me, to sit an hour with your father that reared you. Still my son for all that; my hope, my disillusionment.

"Your sister was with me last week," he said, giving him the rub. "She brought me a drop of brandy to keep in the house against sickness." Then more warmly, hoping for sympathy, falling into the trap experience could never teach him to avoid, he added, "I've been taking little turns." His heart. But it found no chink in the bright metallic armour of boisterous encouragement.

"Begod then," his son said, "I hope you told her you'd drink it while you had your health and your strength." He let a great guffaw out of him. "I'll be getting along," he said. "I'll drop up to you one of these days."

You will, when it's too late.

"That's a fine boy," they said smiling after him.

Aye. Fine for himself. Look after No. 1. Still – my son. Something of me there; me prudent; me looking after the pence. A ganger he would be. Then he would know the distrust of the men and feel the cold shoulder. He could have sat a few minutes for decency's sake if not for mine. Wouldn't the ganger's job wait a few minutes. I sat long enough with you, child. Couldn't he have asked me to walk down the road a stretch with him, to talk things over, to tell him what had happened. But it would be no use telling him about the rat. He would only laugh it away. Youse don't need me now, none of you. I'm not wanted now. When the mother goes, all goes.

"If he's half the man his father was, he'll do," he said. Sadly, bitterly, wearily, he said it.

After a while Reeves remembered. "You had something to tell us," he said. But the mood was gone. They would not understand. They would not be interested to grasp the deeper meaning of what he had to say, to know he had received a summons.

"Nothing," he evaded. "A bit of a dream. I disremember."

"I had a peculiar dream myself last night," holy Hughie Hanlon said. "I was dead, if you please, and was on my way to heaven."

"Do you think you'll go to heaven when you die, Hughie?"

"I have that hope," Hughie said simply.

His calm belief nettled Fenlon, so that he said with sudden bitterness:

"I hope you're not all disappointed. I mean about your novenas and your retreats, your heavens and your hells."

Reeves had been smiling but now he stopped.

"A nice collection," Fenlon pursued, "the three of you. Afraid of God and afraid of the devil. If there was a God up above there he'd burn the whole bloody lot of you – out of malice begod."

"Do you believe in nothing at all?" Reeves asked him.

"I do," Fenlon said. "I believe I'm like the tree – where I fall I rot."

There was an embarrassed silence. A young man might be careless of God's judgment and condemnation, but an old man nearing his end should be cautious of pride.

160

Toner's hand touched the holy water bottle in his pocket. Shame uprose and with it fear.

"There's no call for that sort of talk," he said uneasily.

"I was asked a question," Fenlon returned blandly.

By way of apology Reeves said: "Pay no attention to him, Fred. He's trying to rise you. He doesn't mean a bit of it."

Toner made an angry movement. Reeves expected he would ask them to have a pint with him on account of his having got his wages for the week's watching that morning. Reeves could wait then. He had come to them with the weight of his three score and ten, seeking reassurance and companionship, but what was there in them in the heel of the hunt. Fenlon's mockery, Hanlon's half-cracked holiness. Reeves' glib tongue smoothing things over because he did not want him to be angered. There was no warmth now in the sun. The seat was hard and painful against his back. He could not sit longer with them. It was bad to be lonely when you were alone. It was more unbearable to be lonely in company. He rose brusquely and broke the unhappy silence by saying, "I may as well go home and wet myself a cup of tea."

A little boy bumped into him, stopped to disentangle himself, and ran off again crying, "All in – all in, the game is broke up," a ragged little wretch with most of his three score and ten outspread enviably before him, his innocence as yet unsullied. No need there for the rosary beads and the offering of Masses. Fenlon's way was an easy one if it were only true – a sleep with no waking. At the end of the road came the shroud and the cold clay. Eyes rolled from their sockets and flesh peeled and putrefied. No gracefulness there, no clean crumbling like the tree. Pollution and the dark mouths of maggots, the stealthy scraping of rats. Body not like strong straight unsuffering tree, no. Because I was paid today youse are looking after me, thinking I might have asked youse to have a pint itself, not knowing that me money is given for Masses that I, God help me, and Martin too has more need of than

161

youse have of drink. And that's the deep interest youse have in me.

O Christ your face is bent on me, and your forehead thunderous beneath Its thorns. Mother of God me strength is all gone out of me, me body is feeble, me flesh is filthy, me soul is scarred and stained with a rime of sins. Holy Mother pray for me a sinner now and at the hour of my death. Jesus, Mary and Joseph assist me, now and in my last agony. Jesus, Mary and Joseph may I breathe forth my soul in peace with you. In peace. The book of my deeds is read and then there is heaven or there is hell. Not like the tree the soul which burns for ever, not like the tree the sin rotted soul. As he passed under the apple blossom he heard Reeves complaining bitterly.

"There he goes now, with his week's money weighing down his pocket, and never asked us if we'd a mouth on us."

The night was mild. In front of his watch-box the brazier glowed warmly. No one came near him except a passerby who delayed a moment to light a cigarette, offered him one, and remarked casually the old mongrel which lay curled beside him. He had taken it with him for company. It was old and useless but it came where he bid it. He rooted in his pocket and showed the blackened clay pipe in explanation. "Never could touch them, sir," he said, leaning forward painfully a moment from the dark warmth of the box. "Thank you all the same." The other moved away. A well-set-up young blade in evening dress with a cargo of drink aboard. A student, he thought, on his way to some diversion. They were the divils too. Drowsily he gazed after the figure until it receded first from his vision and then slowly altogether from his mind. He gazed until the seat he was sitting on was no longer warm and comfortable but suddenly cold and hard.

The sun was shining without heat in a clear sky, the little children ran past him, the apple blossom showered before him in delicate beauty. Martin Quinn was sitting

162

beside him. Seeing Martin beside him made his heart pump erratically.

"Martin," he began, trying to bring himself to speak it. But the sentence finished itself in his mind only, "you're dead."

Martin's face was tired and white. He wore the uniform of the Irish Guards.

"What are you doing here, Martin?"

"I can't get to heaven with the weight of my sins," Martin said.

"Isn't there Mercy?"

Martin smiled. "Do you remember the retreat from Mons when we shot down the Scottish Borderers. Because of what we heard they done on Bloody Sunday at Bachelor's Walk."

"Because they opened fire and murdered our flesh and blood. I do."

"Do you remember you and I came on one of them in a wood?"

"I've remembered little else all day. He taped what we were up to. He tried to hide."

"What did he say when we cornered him?"

"He said we're on the same side in this, Paddy, He said, Mercy Paddy, for sweet Jesus's sake Mercy."

"And what did we do, Fred?"

"We shot him in the head," Toner answered, his voice dying to nothing.

"You see," Martin Quinn said, "Mercy." He gripped his sleeve. His half-eaten fingers, which the gnawing rats had befouled, were cold.

"That was murder, Fred. We rifled the Temple of the Holy Ghost. Watch now and see it fall."

"What are you blathering about?" Toner asked in terror.

"Watch now."

Over the mountains, a small black cloud formed. It began to grow. As it grew and moved forward towards them it blotted out the sun, smearing the sky with alternate streaks of soot and blood. The traffic had stopped and the people, tumbling from cars and buses, were running away. But they made no sound. Silence lay on the street. His son rushed by without turning his head and in front of him Reeves gesticulated and pointed to the sky, while Fenlon shook his head in angry denial. Holy Hughie Hanlon knelt on the cobbles, his beads about his wrists, his face smiling and upturned. Then the railings bordering the close buckled as though with heat and pitched forward.

"Martin," he tried to say, "Martin – tell them I had a Mass said for his soul, tell them, Martin." But his lips moved futilely and made no sound at all.

"The temple of the Holy Ghost," Martin pointing upwards at the Cathedral said. "Look what we done."

He looked up. The spire tottered crazily. All the rest had gone. He looked at Martin's face. A wide grin distorted it and the left eye socket was bloody and empty where the rats had ravaged it. As the stonework split and toppled he held his hands above his head. "Jesus protect me," he cried. In the darkness his body sweated its fear, his heart pounded and sickened him. The smell of sulphur grew bodingly. He said struggling, it's a dream, I know it's a dream. Christ deliver me from the terror of this thing.

He beat about him with his arms, fighting with all his strength towards wakefulness. His opening eyes, anticipating the still, warm silence of his bedroom, sought hungrily for comfort and anchorage the statue of the Sacred Heart, one hand upraised, the other pointing mutely to the sword-pierced Heart. But there was no statue, no spot of light which the small red oil lamp always projected on the crumbling ceiling. Only darkness and the hard seat. Wait . . .

The dog whined and brushed against his leg. His fingers sought its rough, hairy coat. But it was to comfort himself, not the dog. Then he was aware once more of the red glow of the coke fire, the yellow smoke drifting thinly towards him, and beyond it the red lamps of warning

164

strung out on either side of the cutting. A dream. There was a wealth of meaning behind that if you only delve deep enough. All things, auguries, omens, signs; a crow on a telegraph wire, a snapped picture cord, a brown rat on a clock. "Good boy," he said to the dog. "Good chap." Its upturned, rheumy eyes fixed him with unremitting loyalty. Painfully, because of his heart, he said to it, stroking it roughly:

"Whistle and I'll come – yes – whistle and I'll come." It was by way of a vague joke. It was his long habit, in pain and danger, to make a joke. His watch told him it was past the hour. But he hesitated. Let them wait for him now, the cute brew who employed him, their clock which spied on him, the rats who coveted him.

"Where's the bottle," he asked the dog, "where did we leave it?" He rummaged in the box, took out a bottle and peered at it. There was a white liquid in it. The milk for when he was wetting his cup of tea. He sighed.

"I've no memory," he complained, "no memory these times at all." He rooted again and found the bottle of holy water under the sack covering in the corner of the seat. He sprinkled it about him. A drop sizzled on the fire.

"In the name of the Father and of the Son," he breathed, "and of the Holy Ghost." Then he grunted and rose.

"We'll pay our respects to the clock," he said. The dog ambled after him.

It was dark outside the radius of the coke brazier. The bells of the Cathedral chimed to mark the half hour, echoed in the empty street, and dispersed into nothingness under the thin stars. He picked his way among scattered, tarry sets, over mounded earth and crusted pipes which exhaled an odour of stale gas, stumbling sometimes and stopping when his heart made the effort too difficult. Under his feet passages honeycombed the earth. They radiated from the Cathedral with their coffined bodies in family vaults, historic fragments scattered about the stone web, decayed wings left and forgotten by the spider. At the entrance to the tunnel the dog stopped and growled. The electric torch played from wall to wall. They were dry. A scraping sound. The rat. "Come on," he commanded, "in we go."

His torch cleaved a path of brightness before him and made the darkness outside its beam more sinister and oppressive. With the earthy smell in his nostrils, he thought of a new dug grave.

I had a Mass said for you, Martin, and one for him, whoever he was. And when I'm finished the watching I'll go to the altar for him. I'll tell the priest in confession that I shattered the temple of the Holy Ghost. You see after all the years I know how to confess it now. And he'll say what do you mean my child, calling me his child and I old enough to be his grandfather, and I'll say I shot a man in cold blood, Father, and for these and all my grevous sins I am sorry. As they walked the dog sniffed and whined. The dog did not want to go on. He played his torch on the partition and found it still intact and untouched. His heart pumped fiercely as he did so. Who would go near it in the darkness? "All's well," he said to the dog, "we can go." But as he put his card in the clock the sudden scurry of tiny claws caused him to jerk violently. Pain shot across his chest, pain overpowering and blinding, so that he sank first on one knee, and then pitched forward. The torch shattered, he lay in the darkness, gasping for breath and fighting desperately the seizure, praying it would pass. The barking of the dog reverberated from wall to wall, filling the tunnel with noise. The sharp stabs of sound beat in his head. He lay in the noise-filled darkness, sweating his pain, praying assist me now and in my last agony. Not like the tree the body felled and suffering, the soul straining to its judgment. Claws they had to dig the holy ground, eyes to pry out flesh and entrails, teeth to ravage the toppled temple of the Holy Ghost. Is it me own blood I'm lying in or the holy water bottle I broke when I fell? Jesus Mercy, is it my poor heart has burst like a blood-filled balloon inside of me? Mass I had said for

166

Martin Quinn and for him. And for mercy him. Mary help.

In his own good time. In His own unpredictable way.

The dog stood trembling beside him, whining its fear, watching helplessly while he died. At the scrape of tiny feet or any stealthy movement it barked furiously. Throughout the hours it stood by his side. It stood whining, terror-stricken, guarding him, keeping them at bay, until morning came and with it the echoing of the first, lonely-sounding footsteps on the pavement above.

Dublin Fusilier

MARTY came swinging across town. Beneath the tall lamps and the broad white-faced clocks, by picture houses and odorous restaurant gratings, under the pillar where what was left of Nelson posed proudly against the sky, came what was left of Marty. The General Post Office pushed out its ponderous chest, and Marty did likewise. In the darkness white faces passed him, warm scents assailed him, shoulders brushed his shoulder. A newsboy bawled in his ear, '*Herald* or *Mail*, sir?' But Marty walked his own path in his own city, the present like a soft mist trailing past him. For Marty and Nelson were aloof. Nelson on his pillar stuck his head a little higher up into the dark arch of the night, and his stony fingers were curled irrevocably on his sword. And beneath him marched Marty with his satchel of grenades. Both bore arms always.

Marty with his pale foxy face, the nose of a snipe, the chest of a pigeon, the gait of a halty mongrel, walked his own lonely inaccessible way. There was a drop on the end of his nose, which he removed from time to time by wiping with the back of his hand.

Tramp, tramp, tramp, came Marty the Dublin Fusilier. Pride in me heart, said Marty, and porter in me belly. Tramp, tramp, tramp, thunderously across the city came Marty.

"Tell me, me dear Lord Roberts," says Queen Victoria, "whose them?"

"Them, ma'am," says Lord Roberts, "is the Black Watch."

"Hmm," says the Queen.

Tramp, tramp, tramp.

"And who," says the Queen, "is them?"

"Them, ma'am," says Lord Roberts, "is the Coldstream

Guards."

"Hmm," says the Queen.

Tramp, tramp, tramp.

"Quick," says the Queen, plucking at his arm, "whose them?"

"Them, ma'am," says Lord Roberts, "is the Dublin Fusiliers."

"Jasus," says the Queen, "them's Troops!"

Marty began to sing "Tipperary".

"It's a long way, to Tipperary, it's a long way to go."

"Are you going far?" asked the voice. It was dark on the bridge and hard to see. Marty squinted from his height of five foot seven at a silver button and a big helmet. He halted. "Attenshun," he bawled. So the policeman grinned broadly at the thin sick face under the peaky cap, and the sharp nose with its pendulent drop.

"So that's the way it is," he said.

That was on the wide bridge over the river. People passed and twisted to look closer, but did not stand because the breeze blew coldly from the river. Trams with lighted windows clanged past, with here half a man reading a paper or smoking, and there a girl staring straight ahead of her or perhaps patting her hair with deft fingers.

So the policeman grinned again and putting his fingers in his belt, turned and walked away.

Marty swung his grenades. Was he not Marty, an Irishman and a Dublin Fusilier? Son of no carey nor scab, but now and then the son of a seacook, and sometimes a son of a bitch, and always an oul' son of a gun. No sugarin' policeman would lay a hand on Marty. No dirty Jerry, nor snooping Boer, nor bloody Black and Tan. He'd banjax the whole issue, Marty would, all on his Barney Malone. But in the meanwhile, would you manage a pint, Marty? Would a duck swim, wha'? Willy is a bad fella. Right you are, oul' son, off we go for a loaf of Bolands.

Marty, letting out a shout, began to take his pint. A

young man sat at the bar with his back to a partition, his
raincoat unbuttoned, his hat on the back of his head. He
had been talking to two men about music.

"I've been rehearsing for three solid hours," he said.
"Bloody *Faust*. I've a thirst that a parish priest would sell
his soul for."

"All the same," said the pavior, "*Faust* is a lovely
opera."

"It's lovely," said the young man, "because it gives you
a lovely thirst after rehearsing it for three solid hours."

"Mick and me," said the pavior, "used to play in the
Trade Union band. We were thrown out for hocking the
instruments when we were short for a few pints. We used
to play selections from *Faust*."

"Rehearsing *Faust*," said Mick, "used to give us a lovely
thirst too."

"What band was that?"

"Tell him what they called us, Tommy."

"They used to call us The Sufferin' Ducks," said the
pavior reminiscently.

"It was very insultin' . . .' added Mick sadly.

Marty gave another yell out of him.

"That's Marty," the pavior said, "a harmless poor
divil." He put a finger to his temple and twisted it
significantly. His left eye winked..

"That was a terrible man once," said Mick, "that was a
holy terror."

"Poor Marty," said the pavior.

"I remember the band during the big strike. We were
marching down to a meeting at the docks. But when we
got to Butt Bridge every bloody policeman in the country
was there waiting for us."

"Drawn in a cordon across the street," put in Mick,
"standing about ten deep with their batons in their hands
and murder in their hearts."

"Your man Marty was the Bandmaster," the pavior
continued, "and he gave us the order to halt. 'Where do
you think you're going?' the Inspector came up and asked

170

him. 'Down to a meeting,' said Marty. 'My men are drawn across there in front of you,' said the Inspector, 'and if you try to pass them they'll leave the lot of you for dead.' 'Will they?' said Marty, and the Inspector walked away. So Marty turned round to us. 'Strike it up, boys,' he shouted, 'and forward on the double tap.' He waves his stick. 'Close your eyes, boys,' he says, 'and you won't feel the pain.' "

"It was slaughter, right enough," Mick commented.

"The police didn't like music," said the young man.

"They didn't like *our* music," Mick said sadly. "Marty had us playing 'The Peeler and the Goat'."

"That was Marty for you," concluded the pavior, turning to consult his pint.

Marty crouched staring in his corner, his head at an angle. The curate, who knew Marty of an old date, nodded his head towards him and then winked at the pavior.

"We're off," said the pavior, "pension on Wednesday and pop goes the thinking cabinet."

"We're over the top all right," said Mick. "Next stop Blighty."

"What's wrong with him?" asked the young man, upset because Marty was staring at him with violence and hatred in his eyes.

"Shellshock," the pavior said. "I soldiered with Marty in France." Then he said loudly, "How's tricks, Marty oul' son?"

Marty continued to stare.

"He doesn't know you," Mick said. "Maybe he'll come round later."

Marty lived in the same house as the pavior, and a married sister who lived there looked after him. The pavior said Marty was a fine Soccer player once. He played for St Patricks when they won the Leinster Senior Cup. That was against Sligo. They had a dinner after it in a hotel and then drove out to the Strawberry Beds on hacks and played melodeons and drank a lot of porter. But

171

that was in Oul' God's time. In those days you could get a pint for twopence and any amount of cheese and biscuits for nothing. They were on the counter. You wouldn't see the like of that today.

"Them days is done," Mick declared. "You'd see white blackbirds before you'd see that again."

The pavior spat into the sawdust, and then scrubbed his heavy boot over it so that it made a trundling noise on the floor. The young man regarded Marty with curiosity. Marty, however, was watching the fellow with the machine-gun. In France Marty had been going forward with his eye on that machine-gun when the explosion blew him off his feet. He woke up blind, with a buzzing in his head. The blindness went away after a while but the buzzing remained intermittently. When it became bad Marty crouched and watched. Sometimes he would throw himself flat with a sudden wild movement, a loud obscenity. If he did this where there was concrete, Mrs. White, his married sister, had to get the enamel basin and bathe away the blood. Quite often he did it where there was concrete.

Marty took a grenade from the satchel, bit out the pin and swung his arm in a slow loop. When the flame and smoke subsided he saw in front of him the three shiny handles, like rifle nozzles protruding above three shoulders, which were used for pulling pints, and beyond them the glass mirror with its gilt advetisement for DWD potstill whiskey, the yellow pear of the electric bulb with its white shade, hanging plumb and without movement from the ceiling, and the pavior's broad back. He heard also the hum of conversation and cars blowing horns now and then in the street. He found his pint almost finished. Would you have another, Marty? He would because a bird never flew on one wing. He fetched out a bright silver shilling from his pocket.

O Brian you've been drinking Brian O
I know it by your winking Brian O . . .

172

I took the Saxon shillin' for to do their dirty killin'
The oul' sergeant found me willin'

Molly o.

So Marty gave his bright silver shilling to the curate and in return he received his pint and a few pence in change.

"All the same," the pavior said, "*Faust* is a fine opera."

"I remember it well," Mick said. "The Devil has a bit to do with it."

"Too much," agreed the young man.

"He sells his soul to the Devil," continued the pavior thoughtfully, "for the sake of a slip of a girl."

"Shockin'," Mick said, "a bloody poor bargain."

"Many a man sold his soul for less, for a pint of porter or a piece of silver."

"That's the truth," Mick said.

"Yiz sold yer sowls for penny rolls and a cut of streaky bacon," quoted the pavior.

"No doubt about it," said Mick.

"Marty sold his soul for a shillin'," said the pavior with a finality which caused Mick, who did not quite follow, to shake his head in solemn agreement.

Marty gave his shilling. In the good days when he was young he would think himself well off with a shilling in his pocket of a Sunday morning.

One bright Sunday morning he left his mother's house in Patrick Street, his cap set gallantly, his shirt clean, his boots shining. Marty, young and vigorous, cocked an eye at the light cloud and the sun high up over the spire of the cathedral. The clamouring bells shook the street, St Audeon's, St Patrick's, John's Lane and Christ Church, shouting and singing above the rattling cabs and the slaty cobbles. "Come and worship all ye true followers of Christ." He was going to Mass but he was thinking of other things. The bells he had grown up with made his head spin.

"Come and worship, Marty oul' son," said John's Lane.

"Don't be dallying there with the sun warming your back and your eye giving the beck to the young girls with the feathers and the flowers in their hats."

"And them on their way to holy Mass too," said St. Audeon's. "Don't be hanging about there looking at the artificial sprays in the artificial ponds, and the dirty little urchins sailing paper boats in the close of St Patrick's, the little desecrators of the Blessed Sabbath."

"He's dreaming about the medal he'll wear in his chain when they knock the stuffin' out of Sligo," said St. Patrick's. "He's thinking he might give it to Annie."

"Taking her out to the hollow in the park or maybe down the Shellybanks, God forgive him, that's what's occupying him."

As he walked, the hand which was in his pocket holding the shilling sweated so that he felt a moist circle in his palm.

"Come in, Marty," said John's Lane, "and pray a while for your soul. It could do with it. And pray for the souls of them that's gone – a summer's day is a long day."

Everybody harped at him.

"Marty Callaghan," his mother had said to him previously, "are you going to Mass at all?" He said he was ready, he had lashings of time. "It's on your knees in the church you should be now, not polishing your boots. If it was a football match you'd be in time, never fear." Marty whistled and winked at his young sister.

He stepped out of the sunlight into the porch of John's Lane, and taking off his cap and dipping his warm brown fingers in the holy water font, he crossed himself and sprinkled some at the door for the poor souls in purgatory. A large dim church cluttered with poor people. A warm place, the air shimmering with the tapering flame of candles and sour with the smell of devout bodies. He was in time for the first gospel and came out after the last, leaving the women to light their lamps to Saint Anne, patron of childing mothers, and the old men with rosary beads and yellow faces to keep watch against the thief

174

who came by night. In the afternoon he walked with Annie through the Pigeon House fort where the soldiers practised firing, to the Shellybanks with their rough grasses which were sweet to lie in. They paddled in the shallow water and ate oranges, and Annie wore her blue dress. He asked her to marry him. Not immediately, he said, but soon. She said she didn't know really, she always thought she's have liked a soldier. Dinny Andrews was a soldier and she thought it was a brave thing that, to be a soldier. He said he always thought she cared for him more than Dinny Andrews, and she said she did too, honest. Her eyes were blue and she laughed when she saw that he was moodily plucking at the grass. The grass cut his finger. She became very concerned, and made him bathe it in the salt water. After that she thought she might marry him. He went down to the men's place to swim, his heart singing, his lithe body pulsing with a new excitement. When he came back they bought oranges and sweets from the peddling women and ate them lying in the sandy grasses, watching the boats and the people who passed, laughing at the antics of little children and making love to one another.

In the evening he left her home, and that night he sat for a long time dreaming at the kitchen window, until it was midnight, and the bells of St. Patrick's, having struck the hour, began as they always did at that hour to play a little tune, which stole quietly to him over streets and roof-tops.

Some nights later he told his father. He didn't know what to say to his mother. His father told her.

"Ellen," he said, "Marty's took the shillin'." He was sitting in a high armchair with his feet on the hob.

"I'm going to France, Mother," Marty said, twiddling his cap in his hands. "I'm a soldier."

That was in the kitchen where the picture of Parnell hung between two bronze horses with warriors tilting at one another across the mantelpiece, and the speech of Robert Emmet stood framed on age-spotted parchment. "Let no man write my epitaph; for as no man who knows

175

my motives dares now vindicate them, let not prejudice nor ignorance asperse them." Lovely round phrases which rolled in splendour from the mouth of his grandfather when he had a few jars in him.

One for the road and a bit of a song, Marty. Why not? It was a long time waiting for the war to be over. What would it be? Make it something Irish, was what they used to say to him.

Marty closed his eyes and turned his white face upwards. The sunken mouth opened and yellow molars stood up like cartridges. He sang "Danny Boy". His voice was cracked and wobbly, like his broken body. His voice was a thing sewn and stitched together, wrapped like a ragged bandage about his song.

"*There's* a bit of a tune now for you," said Mick. Marty had his eyes fixed on the ceiling, displaying a scrawny neck where his Adam's apple ran to and fro between two deep ridges when he paused for breath after each line. The three of them turned to stare.

"He's putting his heart into it," said the pavior. They laughed.

O Danny Boy, the pipes the pipes is callin'
From glen to glen and down the mountain side,
The summer's gone and all the flowers is dying
'Tis you must go, and so 'tis I must bide . . .

Two big tears rolled from Marty's eyes and lay on his cheeks on either side of his nose, matching the drop which now hung unmolested. The lower lids of both eyes, which sagged slightly outwards, were blood rimmed.

It was a sad song. Often his father had sung it at parties in their house in Patrick Street, because of course it was his father's song. It used to make his mother cry. It was always sad to think of the brave soldier marching off to the wars, leaving his father and his poor mother and the good kind people he loved. And his sweetheart too, who would wait

176

for him until he came back.

> In sunshine or in shadow,
> And I will stand, still waiting there for you.

But, as like as not, he never came back.

A very sad, beautiful song, just like all the old songs. "When the fields are white with daisies I'll return" had been his mother's song. Marty had a face which made the barman exchange another nod and a wink with the three, who looked on happily, and a heart which was broken for love of poor dead days and their poor dead people, a spirit which groped back, always back with tearing and torture to his mother, God bless her, and his good father who drank come-day-go-day God-send-pay-day may the sod rest light on him, to Mick his brother who'd give the shirt off his back and Little One his sister who said give us a penny Marty there's a darlin' Marty for to buy seedy cake and he always gave it to her, and to other poor souls dead and gone this many a long day, may perpetual light shine upon them, may they rest in peace. Amen.

Marty stared at the ceiling. His mouth remained open. He found he was walking down by Dublin Castle and the clock striking midnight. A moon stared down at him from the cloud-racked sky. His grandfather stepped out from the shadows.

"Remember your oul' grandfather," said the voice, "I cobbled boots for fifty years in Nash's Court. You used to laugh at me when my mouth was full of nails. You were only a dawny chisler then, Marty." He laughed again heartily at his grandfather, remembering the green baize apron and the cock of his hawky face over the boot. "An oul' cod," said Marty. He swung down the steep cobbles of Lord Edward Street.

"What about me," said a Callaghan with a greasy cloak, "that carried the keg of dynamite to the castle gate the time they pulled Kilwarden from his coach. They stuck twenty pitchforks in him to make sure he wouldn't

177

remember who done it. Emmet was bloody annoyed, I can tell you."

"That was a wrong thing to do," Marty said, "even though he was only a Protestant." His boots rang on the cobbles. Under a guttering lamp another joined him. He was long and broad-shouldered, but he had the hawky face.

"Did I ever tell you about 1534, Marty? I was keeping an eye on things after piling a bit of hay and me and Silken Thomas was having a drink together. 'Well, Fitzgerald,' says I, 'how's tricks?' 'Bad, Callaghan,' says he. 'They're after murdering the poor father. Do you see me sword of office?' 'I do,' I says. 'Well,' says he, 'as soon as I finish this mouthful I'm going straight over to the Abbey, and do you know what I'll do then?'

" 'I don't.'

" 'I'm going to take it off and throw it at the bloody Archbishop.'

" 'You'd be a foolish young man to do that,' I says.

" 'Foolish or not,' says he, 'that's the programme; and what's more, I hope it takes the bloody head off him, mitre an' all.' "

Marty yelled out loud at the idea of it. But a vague figure was following, whining and pulling at his sleeve. It had a death's head of a face, and a scrawny neck. "Fine talk," it said, "and fine men. But my potatoes withered in the ground and my youngest died with the green ooze of grass on his lips."

Said the Inspector to him, "My men are drawn across in front of you, Marty, and if you try to pass them they'll leave the lot of you for dead."

But that was poor Erin for you, the tear and the smile in her eye.

He would meet Annie on some cool summer's evening out at the Strawberry Beds. In the distance someone would play a melodeon. Or once again perhaps in Phoenix Park on a day when the fields were white with daisies and golden with buttercups he'd return and the sky would be wide and blue above them, and the river a silver girdle far below. But it was a long time waiting for the war to be over.

The glass he was holding was flung violently to the ground. Mick and the barman jumped. "My Christ, Marty," said the barman, rushing out, "what the hell do you think you're doing?"

Marty swung both arms out wide.

"Atten-shun," he bawled.

"Attenshun nothing," said the barman, "that bloody glass cost eightpence." Marty screwed up his face and glared.

"Forward," he commanded. "At the double," he bawled.

"Leave him alone," said the pavior, "you might as well talk to the wall."

"He's over the top," averred Mick sadly.

"Breaking glasses is a new one. What the hell am I to do if everyone that has a pint can smash hell out of me glasses without an after you or by your leave? It's all bloody fine."

"He couldn't help it, Joe," said the pavior soothingly.

"*Non compass mensit*," explained Mick.

Marty, brushing aside the commotion, drew himself up and with dignity demanded a pint.

"There you are," the barman complained bitterly. "Now he has the bloody neck to ask me for a pint."

"Give it to him," they said, "he's all right now." Marty got his pint. He was talking to himself. They heard him arguing and swearing. Then he swung his grenades into position and marched out.

Tramp, tramp, tramp, went Marty the Dublin Fusilier. Pride in his heart and porter in his belly. The night hung mildly over the city, the streets were quiet, the dark houses stood up like tall sentries. Some taxi men, who were waiting for the theatres to close, stood smoking at the great gate of Stephen's Green. A faint scent of flowers

179

hung in the air. Marty stood still at the corner. He stared ahead of him. Then he motioned with his arm. Then he stood still again. Then he howled an obscenity and began to lope forward. Now and then his arm swung in a wide loop. The noise of battle was about him. Once more in front of him was the fellow with the machine-gun. His cheeks were grey and streaky with sweat and dust but his bared teeth were blinding white. Marty shouted out Tipperary, flung grenades, ran and stopped. But the machine-gun continued to swing to and fro. When its black unwinking eye cocked itself wickedly in the centre of his regimental belt, Marty shouted and flung himself violently to the ground. His head struck on stone steps.

They said it was disgraceful that a man should get into such a condition. It was hard to know who was more to blame, the man himself or the publican who served him. A small knot had gathered when the pavior came along with Mick and the young man. The pavior knelt down and lifted him up. The pavior was the slightest bit tipsy.

"Marty oul' son," he said. Marty stirred.

"Come on, Marty, never say die. Old soldiers like you and me never die, Marty, we only fade away."

Marty murmured, "Attenshun."

"That's the spirit, Marty oul' son, that's the stuff to give the troops." He said to Mick, "For the love of God, will you take one side of him and don't stand there like a bloody statue."

Some money fell from his pocket as they lifted him, which Mick and the young man searched for while the pavior wiped blood from his face with his cap. There were traces of foam on Marty's mouth which he removed gently. "Have you his few ha'pence?" asked the pavior.

Mick, after peering around helplessly two or three times, said he didn't see any more. They helped him home. The spot where Marty had fallen was marked a little with blood, and in a corner by the iron railings where a little mound of dust had gathered winked a silver shilling. It lay waiting to be found by some passer-by with sharper

180

eyesight than Mick. They took Marty up the broad carpetless stairs, their boots kicking each step and echoing as they sturggled with their burden. Mrs. White, his sister, was in tears. "His poor face," she said when she saw him, "me poor Marty, what did they do to you?" And she got her green enamel basin and washed his face, and with her husband they put him to bed. Then she said there was tea waiting on the hob and they might as well have a cup.

"You're a good neighbour, God bless you," she said to the pavior. So they sat around drinking tea and saying Marty would be right as rain again tomorrow morning. But she kept saying, "What am I to do with him at all, at all? I can't be managing him for ever." And again she said, looking at her husband, "Wouldn't it be an unnatural thing to have him put away?" They talked until midnight in that way.

Marty lay in the little room. The window was open and let in the night noises, and the curtain stirred now and then faintly. The muscles of his hawky face twitched nervously, his mouth moved unceasingly. Sometimes his hands groped out for his satchel of grenades. St Patrick's sounded midnight and the room reverberated. The bells died away. It was quiet and peaceful once more, with only the murmur of voices from the next room to break the silence. Marty slept. Then the bells of St. Patrick's, with their time-mellowed tongues, began to play a little tune.

The Web

WHEN the Black and Tan lorry left the strand road to swing instead towards the centre of the town, the Dummy was lounging at the corner house. All evening he had stood there in the mild warmth of the October sunlight, and though he was startled he did not move. But when the lorry passed close to him, his eyes narrowed and his head inclined slightly towards the wide strand on the left. He counted the turns. The engine slowed, revved, dropped again. It was going towards Freddie's house. By the time it stopped completely he was hammering loudly at one of the small cottages which faced the strand. There was no answer. He sucked his thumb and looked over his shoulder. About half a mile out in the centre of the pool-pocked sands two men were digging for bait. Their bent figures were diminutive with distance. Beyond them he could see the first foamy ridge of water and then the barracks at the extreme end of the breakwater towards which the lorry should normally have gone. He began to force the part-open window. Niall was standing at the foot of a disordered bed. He held a revolver which pointed at the window. The skin over his cheek-bones and about his mouth was tight, and he held his gun steadily.

"I heard them," he said. "Tell Waxer."

The Dummy nodded and went swiftly through the hallway. In the kitchen he passed Mrs. Ryan. She had a loaf and a knife in her hands and her face was white. She followed him with wide eyes and moaned when his boots scraped on the wall of the small yard at the back.

When he returned she was with Niall in her husband's bedroom. It was disordered because Ryan had been cranky that evening and would let no one disturb him. His tea was cold and untouched beside his bed, and the buttered bread fouled with cigarette ash. Only his head was visible, a narrowed egg of a head and a face sunken and yellow.

"I'm a dyin' man, Waxer," he whined, "a dyin' man."

"We're all dyin' men," Waxer said. "You're not dyin' when it comes to finding your way to Tobin's of a Saturday."

He beckoned Niall and strode to the window.

"The stuff," he snapped without turning around. Niall bent over his father.

"Dad," he pleaded, "will you get up? Did you not hear them?"

"Am I ever hearin' anythin' else? They're goin' to the barracks."

"They're not," Niall said urgently. "They're goin' to Freddie's house."

His father shrank into an obstinate ball in the bed. His thin hands gripped the clothes tightly about his neck.

"What curse is over me?" he asked. "What possessed yiz to come in? There's no more guns goin' in here. I'm black and blue with the lumps under me mattress."

Niall gripped him by the shoulders and swung him to the floor. While the mattress was rolled back he stood bent and shivering by his bed. His left hand clutched the neck of his nightshirt, and when a fit of coughing seized him, his right pulled the bottom downwards for decency.

"Waxer," he pleaded, "am I to spend me latter days lyin' on a bloody magazine?"

"Come on, come on," Waxer snorted. "Get the stuff out of that."

He leaned forward to peer through the window. There were lorries about the block and the room quivered sometimes with the trundling of them. Suddenly he stiffened.

"Dummy," he breathed, "get the manhole open."

Niall's mother crossed herself. The Dummy went out quickly to the back. The boots of soldiers grew loud on the pavement outside, while another lorry thundered in from the strand road. They were surrounding the house.

Waxer motioned and Niall's mother followed them to the back yard.

"You'll have to put back the cover," Waxer said to her. "Lift it slowly and don't fuss. Then put your stool and the bathtub over it. Splash the water about as though you'd been washing."

Niall and she exchanged looks. She bit her lip.

"I will, Mr. Brannigan," she said," "I will."

The sun lay warmly on the little yard and the bin in the corner cast a long shadow. Waxer let Niall and the Dummy down first. Then he followed nimbly. Niall's shoulder brushed against the green ooze of the wall and the Dummy's nose wrinkled in disgust. Then the trap above was eased into position and the square of light narrowed and went out. They began to shuffle forward warily in the smelling darkness.

When the lorry pulled up outside Freddie's house the street was deserted except for a child with a white milk jug who stood to watch. The old men who used to sit on the low window sills were gone, and their dogs and their gossip. From an arc of wetness around a half-scrubbed doorstep, steam still rose lightly, and here and there a furtive curtain moved. The child went demurely up the street. She found Freddie with Phil Tobin in the back bar.

"Well?" he said.

"The soldiers are at the house," she panted. "I ran."

"Did they see you?"

"No," she said, "they didn't mind me. I was fetchin' milk."

Phil Tobin was twisting his white apron with his hands. He had fat stubby fingers. The apron was like a handkerchief against the width of his stomach. Freddie put his hand on her head.

"Good child," he said gently, "get the milk and bring it back and say nothing."

He became anxious.

"Remember," he insisted quietly, "nothing."

She nodded and slipped out.

184

Phil tugged at his sleeve.

"For God's sake make a move," he said. "They'll be in on top of us."

"That's right," Freddie answered. "They waste no time."

They picked their way through a tortuous passage and down stone steps.

When they were in the cellar Phil said: "I knew it. Someone informed."

"What makes you think that?"

"I'm no man's fool," said Phil Tobin.

"Unless we were seen, only yourself and the Ryans could know."

"People can talk," said Phil.

Freddie glanced round at the barrels which littered the cellar, and at the grating which opened into the lane above. There was a mattress in the corner and a roll of blankets. He stooped and took out a revolver. Phil crumpled his apron in his hands. The apple-red of his lusty face was wrinkled and perturbed.

"I don't know in the name of God what prompted youse to come in." he declared.

"Orders," Freddie said, straightening. "Don't ask me why." He settled himself facing the door.

"You'd best get back to the shop," he said. "If they find me, tell them I came in through the grating."

Phil closed the door and went off with a nervous jangling of keys, and Freddie sat down to wait.

The soldiers searched his house. They swore at his mother because she would not answer them. They took his father, struggling, with them. Other houses were ransacked also. But when the night came and they were spread watchfully throughout the town, nothing had been found.

When they reached the mouth of the tunnel the sun was down and the smell of the sea stronger because it was night. From the fern-grown opening of the disused drain they could see the whole wide expanse of the strand; the

185

lighthouse which stood beside the barracks at the extreme end of the breakwater, two miles of inkiness between, then the stringing of lamps along the coast road on their right, smears of blurred light through the misting rain. On the right, too, lay the Terrace and the house they had come from, Niall's house. The light was in his father's bedroom. He could single it out from all the lights along the strand road. When he was a child and night had overtaken his playing he had often walked to it in a straight line across the ebbed strand.

Niall stared for a long time at the light while they crouched in misery and felt the air damp about them.

"Somebody told," he said with sudden bitterness, "some rat."

"I know," Waxer said smoothly, "but who?"

"I don't know," Niall said; "someone."

He stared back into the darkness.

"They went to Freddie's house; I counted the turns."

"For all his smart talk," Waxer said, "Freddie is only a child; he wanted to be with his mother."

"He's got his bellyful now," Niall said. "You might as well talk to the wall." Waxer's mouth was closed tightly and his eyes looked to the right at nothing. He was thinking of several things at once.

But Niall's eyes moved restlessly, surveying the dripping walls, scanning the darkness.

"If they came to search here we're cornered. We can't get out."

Waxer smiled coldly. "We can get out the way we got in. You can always do that."

"No damn fear," Niall said, "not back through the house. I'm damned if we go that way."

"Who's giving orders?"

"To hell with orders," Niall said with heat. "That's one order you won't give." Waxer's mouth thinned.

"Who said so?" he asked evenly.

"I did. The mother is there and the da is a sick man, he's dyin'. If there was any trouble it would kill him."

186

Waxer smiled coldly. He sucked in his cheeks until the skin across the massive cheek-bones was white. He let the matter rest.

"Until we know what's outside," he said, "we'll stay put."

The tunnel was dismally cold about them and the rain spun thinly across the dark sands. Sound travelled easily across the open space, but tonight the familiar noises were hushed. The darkness of narrow streets echoed now and then as a lorry moved off or changed its position, and that was all. Niall crouched and looked back along the tunnel which ran right under his home. He wondered if the soldiers had stayed in his house, and what his father and mother were doing. He had a long sallow face which at the moment was strained and apprehensive, and eyes that were at all times wide and lustrous. Opposite to him crouched the stocky figure of Waxer. It was Waxer who had brought both Niall and the Dummy into the movement. At the language-revival classes Niall had more aptitude than Waxer, but when it came to military action Waxer was officer. It was Waxer who had thought of exploring the almost forgotten tunnel and had arranged with H.Q. for using it as a dump. He was checking the barrel of the revolver which was his sole certificate for scholarship.

Niall watched the house-lights on the shore go out one by one. He started at any unusual sound.

"All the same," he said later, "we shouldn't have come in. We were safe in the hills."

Waxer did not answer.

"Safer than here. It was bloody foolish to order four men . . ."

"Cut that out," Waxer said coldly. "Cut it out."

"I don't see . . ."

"Drop it," Waxer snarled.

The Dummy looked up mildly. He had taken possession of the bomb and was playing idly with it. Though he was young enough to wear knickerbockers, the legs beneath

187

his black stockings were muscular. His lips were turned up and slightly parted, as though smiling at his thoughts.

"When you've knocked off four officers," Waxer said grimly, "you're safe nowhere." He spat into the darkness. He looked at the Dummy and then lay back against the tunnel-wall once more.

"Yer a good soldier," he said drily, "you don't answer back."

The Dummy grinned and continued to play idly with the bomb. A long time later, when they were chilled and cramped and everyone had forgotten the context, Waxer said: "... Nowhere."

When Ryan walked up the plots the following morning there were fewer men than usual. They looked at him sympathetically and let him pass when he showed little inclination to linger. Nothing more had happened during the night. He had been wakened early by his wife. It was a clear morning of sunshine and light white clouds. The sun was on the front of the house and had filled the bedroom as he raised himself on his elbow to lean over the breakfast tray.

"Nuthin' happened?" he had asked, screwing up his eyes.

She glanced covertly at the soldier who sat in the window.

"What could happen," she had said indifferently, "and them miles away."

"That's right," he said, "of course."

He grunted uneasily.

"It's bright out, d'yeh think?"

"Like a summer's morning – thank God. You could take your walk."

"I will," he decided, "I'll take a turn down to the Bakery." It was his habit when Saturday was fine. He would walk down to the Bakery for his pension and then up the strand road for a pipe and a chat.

He showed improvement, the men sometimes said to

188

him. It pleased him and made him feel better. "It's the dry weather," he would say; "the doctor says I should go to a sanatorium. It'd cure me, he says."

But that morning he went by without a word. He shuffled moodily past them and stopped some distance away at the strand wall. They saw him huddle with his hands deep in his pockets, staring and staring at the bright pools which flashed in the wake of the tide.

One of the men said: "The soldiers were in the house all night. Isn't it a queer thing they should let him out?" and another: "He's waitin' for the band to play. They can't be hidin' for ever."

Phil was with Freddie on and off during the day. There was little doing in the shop. The soldiers were still in the streets and people did not go out without necessity. When he was taking away the remains of Freddie's dinner he said: "I sent that note you gave out. The youngster took it."

"Good," Freddie said. "If an answer comes, bring it immediately. Was there anything else?"

"Ryan was out and about."

"He goes down for the pension," Freddie said.

Phil said meaningly, "The soldiers are in his house."

"What about it?" Freddie asked irritably.

"Nothing," Phil answered mildly, "except that it's funny they should let him out."

Freddie ran his hands quickly through his hair.

He said, "No man would split on his own son." There were dark circles under his eyes and his face was pinched. His eyes were quick and nervous.

"Men do queer things, especially sick men."

Freddie shook his head. He looked around at the dust-encrusted walls, at the barrels tilted about the floor and the cobwebs which stretched like threadbare rags across every corner of the low ceiling. He began to pace restlessly.

"I wish to God I could get away from here," he said at last. Then: "Will Ryan be here tonight?"

189

"Always on a Saturday."

"Watch him," Freddie said, "and if an answer comes, let me know." The keys jangled and the beat of feet on the stone stairway dwindled once more into silence. There was still light in the cellar, and on the grating above loud feet clanged on occasion and passed. But there were long silences, during which he crouched in a corner from which he could command the door, smoking cigarettes, watching a spider spreading its dexterous web between two barrels. It stopped occasionally as though to stare at him. Now and then he blew smoke from his cigarette in a gentle stream towards the web. This would send it scurrying out of sight. His eyes narrowed as he considered the spider. Once he laughed suddenly. Then his mood changed. He broke the web in sudden disgust. It retired altogether for a time, but later came back and began to spin once more. It was inexorable. The streets grew hushed as the light failed and the cellar echoed not at all. The dust, smelling more strongly, foretold rain.

It began that night when the men in Tobin's were beginning to glance at the yellow-faced clock. At first, but for the diminutive drops which flecked the windows, it was hardly noticeable. But later it grew fierce. They sat and heard the wind rise and the rain sweeping over streets and little houses, over limp ropes and hanging nets and the dreary stretches of sand. There was little conversation. A stranger stood for a time at the bar, had some words with Phil and, when the rain was beginning, left. Ryan was there also. He sat nearer the right-hand end of the counter and lingered over his drinks. His overcoat was too big for him and pieces of fluff clung to it because of his habit of throwing it on the foot of the bed. He spoke to no one except Phil. He stared miserably into space and tapped absently at his chin with a bony finger.

Whenever Phil stood before him he took out a purse and fumbled awkwardly as he paid.

"It's a poor night," he said and looked down at his drink.

"It is," Phil answered, "for a man on his keeping."

When the men were leaving, Phil went down and stood before him with his hands resting on the counter. He looked down steadily at him.

"The sergeant is in the snug," Phil said levelly. "They were round at the house looking for you."

"Lookin'?" Ryan repeated.

"They want to question you."

"Question Phil. They'd have your soul damned into hell with their questions. They'd have you tormented." He looked right and left quickly. He reached out with bony fingers to caress Phil's arm.

"Phil," he asked, "have you word of Niall, do you know where they are?"

"Where?"

"I'm askin' you, Phil, you that knew them." He leaned forward. "Are they in the tunnel – I know there's a tunnel. Are they there?"

"You seem to know more than I do," Phil said.

Ryan looked down at his drink. His face was old and yellow-lined like a rotten apple. His eyes, like Niall's, swam with odd lustre, but they were sunken and peeped from a distance.

"I don't, Phil," he breathed, "I know nuthin'. I didn't even know they were coming back. But if they're in the tunnel it's not safe. I have word, I – I heard them talking last night in the bedroom . . ."

"You're keepin' the sergeant," said Phil coldly.

"Maybe I am, Phil, but I swear before God Niall is a good boy and I played fair by him. He'd tell you that. I reared him and I put the clothes on his back. I worked when I should have been at home in me bed. The doctor said a sanatorium would cure me, but it meant money and I couldn't see him hungry. There was nuthin' he had that didn't come from me." Phil's eyes mocked him.

"I wouldn't harm a hair on his head," he said almost to himself, "nor let others do it." A hand was laid on his shoulder. He turned around.

"There's a couple of questions I'd like to ask," said the sergeant, "so finish your business . . .'

Phil came in with the note and held the candle so that Freddie could read. The flame quivered and the grease dripped over and stung his fingers. The shadows retreated from the flame. They huddled in a ring about the two of them. Outside the rain ran in rivulets down channels, and the soldiers, scattered at their stations throughout the town, crouched miserably and swore. They looked up at the skies and wished for something to happen. Freddie stuck the note into the flame. They watched in silence while it burned.

"I've got to go," Freddie said. "I've got to find the rest."

"You'll find no one tonight, are you mad?"

"I'll find them all right. Put out the candle and help me to raise the grating."

"I won't," Phil said backing away. "Why can't you bide your time?"

"Quickly," Freddie said, "there isn't any time."

He listened acutely. There was no sound but the monotonous beat of the rain. He snuffed the candle and caught Phil by the arm. They began to build a pyramid of crates directly under the grating. When they had finished Phil's face ran with sweat. They eased up the gate cautiously. There was no creaking on account of the rain. Freddie let himself through. He crouched for a moment to listen. Phil stood by while the gate was lowered. Freddie signed to him, straightened quickly, and strode away.

He went casually through the darkened town, his shoulders hunched and his head down against the rain. Nobody passed; the streets were deserted; lorries stood here and there by the side of the road, vacant and dead beneath the swollen skies, like derelict ships.

But when he reached the strand there were soldiers at intervals along the wall. One was so near that he could hear the crunch of his boots and the irritable clank of equipment. He stopped dead. He was intensely aware of

the web that had been built around him, a web which for
months has been growing about him, a web he must break
from or perish in. The spider was spinning. His eyes
narrowed as each sense became suddenly sharpened. After
a while he dropped to his knees and made with painful
slowness towards the wall.

They crouched in the darkness, each withdrawn into
himself, so that they were three beings, three isolated
points of life in a vast solitude. The great ferns which
cluttered the mouth of the tunnel were swaying and
dripping, but when the wind dropped they could hear
sounds on the beach, lost sounds that were lonely like
eternity. Niall shuddered and when a fit of coughing
seized him he would bury his mouth in his cap in order to
stifle it. When shots rang out he licked his lips and glanced
through the darkness at Waxer and the Dummy.

His face was grey. The smell of the tunnel and the strain
of waiting had made him sick. His limbs were cramped
and stiff with waiting. He was fascinated when either of
the others moved or betrayed signs of life.

"Who the hell are they firing at?" he asked, his voice
rising.

"Maybe they're jittery," said Waxer, "shootin' their
shadows."

"We should have shifted last night, Waxer. We could
have made it."

"We waited for word."

"How could they send it?"

"If I know anythin' about it," said Waxer, "they'll find
a way. They won't let the dump go."

"If Freddie was caught . . ."

"Hush," Waxer said, "we've got to listen."

Niall hunched miserably. He squirmed and became
uneasy, chafing at his helplessness. He drew his knees up to
his chin, then stretched them full length; he turned on one
side. Then he shifted again, rubbed a cramped leg,
crouched once more over his knees. Sometimes he sighed.

193

But Waxer and the Dummy sat unmoved.

They were silent until the Dummy half rose and grunted.

"What?" Waxer snapped, and Niall jerked forward with his hand going automatically to his pocket. The Dummy jabbed his thumb towards the strand. They listened. Somebody slid down the embankment some distance away. A tin can clinked and then rolled noisily, and shots rang out.

"Christ," Niall said, panicking. He scrambled forward on his hands and knees towards the tunnel entrance.

"Back," Waxer growled, "you bloody fool, back towards the house."

The Dummy sat rigid, his mouth and eyes narrow lines. Niall still went forward.

"Them's orders," Waxer hissed, "and put that revolver away."

"Go to hell," Niall said. Waxer swore and pounced. Feet slithered on the embankment below and someone fell forward into the tunnel. Waxer flung sideways and came to grips.

"Who is it?" he snarled, and his fingers slipped swiftly upwards.

"Me," Freddie said simply.

Waxer loosened his grip. He felt his hands sticky.

"You're hit."

"Left shoulder," Freddie said. "They caught me when I'd crossed the wall."

"We'd better shift. Is it bad?"

"I can't say," Freddie answered. "I had a message from Cassidy. I burned it and came straight."

"Good work," Waxer said. He looked quickly behind him and then back at Freddie.

"Do you know how things are?"

But Freddie had slumped back against the wall. He was quite young, almost as young as the Dummy. His face beneath the shock of dark curls was pale. It was scratched and streaked with sand where he had fallen when the bullets struck him. His nose still bled slightly. Waxer and the Dummy looked on while Niall wiped away the sand with his handkerchief.

"See to his shoulder," said Waxer, "and bring him round. We don't want him on our hands."

"I don't want to strip his shoulder," Niall answered. "I think it might be dangerous in this atmosphere."

"That's right," grumbled Waxer, "do nuthin' you're told." But he made no move himself. He lay back and watched while Niall bent in silence over Freddie. The Dummy shaded a small torch with his body.

"He's bleeding like hell," Niall whispered in sudden terror. "Why don't you do something?"

"Wake him up," demanded Waxer, "I want to know all I can."

Niall shook Freddie.

"Freddie," he pleaded, "Freddie, don't sleep now. Do you hear me? We've got to get away from here."

Freddie murmured and twisted his head from side to side.

"What's he say?"

"He's wandering," Niall answered, frightened. "Something about spiders. . . ."

Waxer grunted.

After a while Freddie sighed with his whole body and opened his eyes. Waxer leaned forward.

"There's a first-aid kit in the bend by the dump," he said to Niall. "You'll get bandages there." He nodded to the Dummy. "Show him," he added.

When they had gone he spoke to Freddie. "Now," he said.

"Cassidy sent word by Phil. I was in the cellar . . . watching the . . . They're coming for the dump tonight."

"Are you sure of that?"

"Intelligence says so. You've to lay a fuse if you can and then get out. They'll have a car outside the Ivy Church . . ."

"The Ivy Church," Waxer said ironically, "that's a bloody good one."

"Someone informed . . ." Freddie added.

"Who?" demanded Waxer.

Freddie moved weakly and looked straight at Waxer. He hesitated.

"Niall's father," he said.

Waxer slid forward to the mouth of the tunnel. Here and there on the strand lights moved. They jerked in nervous bars in the blackness. He thought they were coming nearer, but very slowly. When he got back Niall was leaning once more over Freddie.

"They're coming," he said.

Niall looked quickly over his shoulder. Then he went on with his bandaging.

"Do you know who split?" he asked between clenched teeth. Freddie looked queerly at him.

"No, Niall," he said, "I don't know."

There was a short silence during which the Dummy's eyes turned with half understanding from Waxer to Freddie. Freddie looked away and Waxer's eyes focussed on the ground between his feet.

"We've got to make it quickly," Waxer said after a pause. "Can you make it, Freddie?"

Freddie nodded.

"Very well. We'll go back by the house."

Niall bit his lip. He seemed on the point of tears.

"Waxer," he said, "it'll kill me da, it'll be the death of him."

Waxer swore.

"Waxer," Niall appealed. "Supposin' they're still in the yard . . ."

"It's dark. If we go out shooting there's a chance. You and I will go first. Then while we cover them the Dummy will help Freddie through. Is that clear?"

Niall bowed his head. They nodded. There were noises from the strand as the ring drew nearer. They could feel the ring tightening on them. Waxer gestured with the revolver.

"All right," he said, "move."

He betrayd no emotion.

They followed, crouched, through the darkness. Once Freddie fell, and the Dummy helped him to his feet. They passed the opening of a tunnel on their right. It was at right angles to the main tunnel but had been blocked up about twenty yards from the opening. It contained the dump. There were bandages scattered here and there from Niall's searching. The Dummy paused but Waxer said, "There isn't time."

When they were crouching under the manhole which opened into Niall's back yard there were loud reports and shots ricochetted through the tunnel.

"Quick," Waxer said.

Niall went to his side and pressed his hands against the manhole. He took the strain with his wrists. Then he rose slowly and bent his arms. Waxer grunted and they pushed violently. The cover lifted with the sudden pressure. It went skidding across the yard. Then the rain was wet on their faces.

Waxer fired into the darkness, covering the scullery door and the opposite wall. Freddie gained the yard but the bin tripped him and he fell. He rose painfully, firing while Niall and Waxer broke for the back wall. "Freddie," Niall screamed, beckoning, "Freddie." But Freddie did not attempt the wall. He turned instead towards the house. After a while he was alone in the yard. He was dimly aware of lights and a kitchen table, and further away, like a long dark tunnel, the hallway and an open door. Beyond the door were soldiers. They opened fire. He shouted and lunged savagely forward. They closed around the hall door. They shot solidly until he reeled against the bedroom door. It swung inwards and he pitched headlong into the room. He moaned and breathed painfully. . . .

The Dummy lay back along the tunnel. They had followed him, forcing him slowly yard by yard back to

197

the dump. He was now quite dead. But though the bomb had rolled away from him, the pin which he had withdrawn was still clutched in his hand. It was intensely dark. In front of him and behind him, at about twenty yards' distance, were bars of light and cautiously approaching feet. . . .

When Freddie opened his eyes there was no one besides Ryan in the room. At first Freddie did not see him. He was watching the spider. It fascinated him. It crept across the floor, now stopping, now moving forward. It grew giant-like and after diminished; it became three spiders, and then ten, all marching or floating in a serried line. Sometimes they wavered and dissolved, sometimes all were spinning furiously. It became one again. Then slowly he was aware of a voice from the bed, an incoherent mumbling. He saw a head above the bedclothes and a thin hand which clutched rosary beads. He stretched his arm along the floor towards the revolver.

He said, "Why did you do it?"

The hand tightened.

Ryan sat up. He looked in terror at Freddie. He had been crying. He shuddered and said, "I didn't know youse were comin' back – I swear – youse told me nuthin' – what are you doin' with the gun?"

"It's not for you," Freddie answered, "it's for the spider." Ryan saw no spider. His eyes searched. His jaw fell open.

"Why?"

The spider, Freddie knew, had caused the trouble. The spider had made a web. It must be found. He raised himself painfully on his elbow.

Ryan yelled in alarm.

"Freddie – for the love of God – I didn't know youse were coming back. I only knew about the dump. There wasn't badness in that, not just about the dump."

"Why . . . ?" Freddie breathed.

He hardly knew he asked the question. He had found the spider. It was crawling slowly over the bedclothes towards the beads and the hand. As Ryan sank back against the pillow Freddie raised the revolver. He levelled at the spider, lost sight of it, then levelled again.

Ryan moaned and said, "How could I know youse were coming back?"

Then he closed his eyes. His voice, tired and almost inaudible, murmured: "I wanted the money. I wanted it for a sanatorium."

Freddie fired twice at the spider. It disappeared. He stared and saw the stain of blood growing on the sheets. Then suddenly his elbow gave under him and he pitched forward. His eyes were still open. When the explosion shook the room a moment later he neither moved nor heard.

But Waxer and Niall heard. They lay flat in the rain and the darkness. The little garden shuddered with the noise of lorries and about them they could feel the inexorable closing-in of the search. They looked sideways at one another.

Two blocks away, aeons away, looming over low roofs and intersecting walls, rose the Ivy Church.

Janey Mary

WHEN Janey Mary turned the corner into Nicholas Street that morning, she leaned wearily against a shop-front to rest. Her small head was bowed and the hair which was so nondescript and unclean covered her face. Her small hands gripped one another for warmth across the faded bodice of her frock. Around the corner lay Canning Cottages with their tiny, frost-gleaming gardens, and gates that were noisy and freezing to touch. She had tried each of them in turn. Her timid knock was well known to the people who lived in Canning Cottages. That morning some of them said: "It's that little 'Carthy one, never mind opening. Twice in the last week she's been around — it's too much of a good thing." Those who did answer her had been dour. They poked cross and harassed faces around half-open doors. Tell her mammie, they said, it's at school she should have her, and not out worrying poor people the likes of them. They had the mouths of their own to feed and the bellies of their own to fill, and God knows that took doing.

The school was in Nicholas Street and children with satchels were already passing. Occasionally Janey Mary could see a few paper books peeping from an open flap, and beside them a child's lunch and a bottle of milk. In the schoolroom was a scrawled and incomprehensible blackboard, and rows of staring faces which sniggered when Janey Mary was stupid in her answers.

Sometimes Father Benedict would visit the school. He asked questions in Catechism and gave the children sweets. He was a huge man who had more intuition than intellect, more genuine affection for children than for learning. One day he found Janey Mary sitting by herself in the back desk. She felt him, giant-like above her, bending over her. Some wrapped sweets were put on her desk.

"And what's your name, little girl?"

"Janey Mary 'Carthy, Father."

"I'm Father Benedict of the Augustinians. Where do you live?" Father Benedict had pushed his way and shoved his way until he was sitting in the desk beside her. Quite suddenly Janey Mary had felt safe and warm. She said easily, "I lives in Canning Cottages."

He talked to her while the teacher continued self-consciously with her lesson.

"So your daddy works in the meat factory?"

"No, Father, my daddy's dead."

Father Benedict nodded and patted her shoulder. "You and I must be better friends, Janey," he said. "We must tell your mammie to send you to school more often."

"Yes, Father."

"Because we must see more of one another, mustn't we?"

"Yes, Father."

"Would you always come?"

"I'd like to come, Father."

Father Benedict had talked with her for some time like that, the pair of them crushed clumsily in the desk and their heads close together. When he was leaving he gave her more sweets. Later the teacher took them from her as a punishment and gave them out again as little prizes for neatness.

She thought of Father Benedict until an old beggar who was passing said to her: "Are you whingin', child? Is there anything up with you?"

She lifted her head and looked stupidly at him, her mouth open and her eyes quite dry. He was a hump-backed man with broken boots and a bulbous nose. The street about him was a moving forest of feet; the stolid tread of workmen and the pious shuffle of middle-aged women on their way from Mass.

"You look a bit shook, kid," he said. "Are you after

taking a turn?"

"No, mister," she said, wondering. "I'm only going for to look for bread at St. Nicholas's. My mammie told me."

"Your mammie left it a bit late. They'll be going in for to pray." As though awakened by his words, the bell of the Augustinian Friary rang three times. It rang out with long, resounding strokes across the quivering street, and people paused to uncover their heads and to bless themselves.

Janey Mary looked up quickly. The steeple of the church rose clear and gleaming above the tall houses, and the golden slimness of its cross raced swiftly against the blue and gold of the sky.

Her mother had said: "Look till you find, my lady, and you won't lose your labour. This is the day of the Blessed Bread and if you get it nowhere else they'll be giving it out at St Nicholas's."

She turned suddenly and ran quickly up the length of the street. But when she reached the priory the doors were closed and the waiting queue had broken into small knots. She stopped uncertainly and stared for some time.

The priests, the people said, had gone in to pray. They would be back in an hour.

She was glad to turn homewards. She was tired and her bare feet moved reluctantly on the ice-cold pavement. Johnny might have been given some bread on his round with the sticks, or her mother might have had some hidden away. Her mother sometimes did that so that Janey Mary would try very hard to get some.

Picking her way amongst the debris-littered wasteland upon which houses had once stood, she watched her shadow bobbing and growing with the uneven rippling of the ground. The light of the wintry sun rested wanly on everything and the sky was dizzily blue and fluffed a little with white cloud. There were rust-eaten tin-cans lying neglected on the waste, and fragments of coloured delf which she could have gathered to play chaneys had she had the time. The children often went there to play shop;

202

they marked out their pitches with a file of pebbles in the form of an open square. When Janey Mary stood in one of the squares for a moment she was no longer Janey Mary. The wasteland became a busy street and the tracery of pebbles glittering stores. Her face would grow grave. It was that serene gravity of a child at play. But when she stepped out of the magic square she was again Janey Mary, a Janey Mary who was cold and hungry and whose mother was waiting impatiently for bread that had not been found.

"There was none," she said, looking up at her mother's face. "Nobody would give it and the man said the priests wouldn't be back for an hour." She looked around hopefully as she spoke, but there were only a few crumbs on the table. They littered its grease-fouled and flower-patterned covering. An enamel jug stood in the centre and about it the slopped ugliness of used cups. Now that she was home she realised how endless the morning's trudging had been. She realised how every door had been closed against her. Her mother's voice rose.

"Then you can do without. Are you after looking at all, you little trollop? Two hours to go the length of the street and around to the holy priests, and us all in a wakeness with the hunger. And Johnny going out with the sticks and him famished but for the little bit I had left away. Are you after looking at all?"

The enamel of the jug was broken in three places. The breaks were spidery, like the blobs of ink which used to fall so dishearteningly on her copy books. Down the side of each cup clung the yellow residue of dribbled tea. The whole table shifted suddenly and went back again, and her mother's voice seemed far away. Janey Mary wanted to sit down.

"Gallivanting," her mother said, "off gallivanting with your pals. I'll gallivant you. But you can go back again. There's nothing in the house. Back with you to the priests' house and wait like any Christian for what's going. And take the bag with you. You don't do a hand's turn till you do that."

Janey Mary stood with her hands clasped in front of her
and looked up at her mother. The thought of going back
again filled her with misery.

"I asked," she said. "I asked everywhere."

"Then you can ask again," said her mother. "You can
ask till you find," and swung away. Janey Mary went
wearily to the corner to fetch the bag. The kitchen
trembled and became dark when she bent to pick it up. As
she went out of the door her mother said:

"Put a bit of hurry on yourself and don't be slinging.
It's certain you'll never die with the beating of your heart.
The world and its wife would get something and mine'd
be left."

Once more she was out in the ancient crookedness of
streets, picking her way amidst the trundling of wheels
and the countless feet. Tiny and lost beneath the steepness
of houses, she went slowly, her bare feet dragging and
dirty. At this hour the shops in Nicholas Street were
crowded with women who haggled over halfpennies.
White-coated assistants leaned quickly over marble-topped
counters with heads cocked to one side and pencils raised
in readiness, or dashed from counters to shelves and back
again, banging things on the scales and then licking pencil
stubs while they frowned over figures. Sometimes Janey
Mary used to stand and watch them, but now she went by
without interest. When a tram went grinding past her, her
lips trembled, and though the rails after it and before it
gleamed in the sunlight, it was a pale cold gleaming.
There was no friendly heat in the sunlight. There was
nothing friendly. There were only trundling trams and the
tramp of feet, and once again the slim cross on the spire of
St Nicholas's.

On the Feast of the Blessed Bread it was the custom of
the priests to erect a wooden counter on the high steps
before the door of the priory. Here two of the brothers
stood to watch the forming of the queue. Janey Mary
looked hard through the veil which blurred occasionally

in front of her eyes, but could catch no sign of Father Benedict. No bread had yet appeared though the queue was growing. She took her place and kept close to the wall. In near the wall she found it easier to hold her position. It was very cold at first, but after a while more people came and the air grew warmer. They came, as she had known they would, with baskets and shawls, with torn shopping bags and ragged coats, and gathered thickly about her. There were men there too, old pensioners and men who had not worked for years.

"There won't be much going," they said. "There was a shocking crowd here this morning."

"Take your bloody hour," they said. "Who'd you think you're pushing?"

"Aisy, aisy, mind the chisler."

They talked like that for a long time. At first they argued furiously with one another. But later they became dour with impatience. They shuffled uncomfortably. They spat frequently and heaved long sighs.

After a while it became frightening to be in there so close to the wall, to be so small that everyone towered over you. Janey Mary felt weak and wanted to get out. When she glanced sideways or ahead of her she could see nothing but tightly packed bodies, and when she looked down there were feet, but no ground. She tried to look upwards, but could not. An hour passed before Father Benedict appeared on the steps.

"Father Benedict, God bless him," they said. "It'll be coming soon when he's here."

Janey Mary was lifted clear off the ground by the movement of the crowd and lost her place. Now she was behind a stoop-backed man with a threadbare coat and heavily nailed boots. His collar was flaked and greasy with dandruff and his coat was foul smelling, but it was the boots which held Janey Mary's attention. They clattered unsteadily on the pavement very close to her bare feet. There were diamond-shaped nails in double rings about the heels of them. She bent to keep her eyes fixed on the

205

boots and wriggled to avoid them. Her attention became fixed on them. To a man near her she said, "I want to get out, mister, let me get out," but even if he had heard her he could not have helped her now. She tried to attract attention, but they had forgotten her. They kept telling one another over and over again what each of them already knew.

"It's coming," they said, pressing forward, "it's coming." And after a while the murmuring changed and the queue surged.

"Look," they shouted, "it's here."

Janey Mary was lifted once more. Once more her feet were clear of the ground and her breathing stifled by the pressure of those around her. She was in danger now and clawed whimpering at the dandruff flaked collar. Through a whirl of arms and shoulders she had a view of Father Benedict, his broad shoulders tall and firm above the press of bodies. She tried to call out to him.

"The chisler," someone said, noticing. "For God's sake quit pushing. Look at the chisler." A man threw out his hand to grip her, but a movement of the crowd twisted him suddenly aside. She saw his hand grabbing futilely to her left. As the crowd parted she began to slip.

"Father Benedict," she called faintly, "Father Benedict." Then the man in front stumbled and the nailed boots crushed down heavily on her feet.

When her eyes opened again she was on the sofa in the visitors' parlour. Father Benedict and one of the lay brothers were bending over her. Someone had put a rug about her. An electric fire glowed warmly against the opposite wall and over it hung a gold-framed picture of the Sacred Heart. Her feet felt numb and heavy and the picture swam before her eyes. But it was warm in the parlour and the morning's searching was over. Then she remembered the bread and her mother's words. She moved suddenly, but when she tried to speak her ears were filled with noise. The lay brother had turned to Father Benedict.

"You were very quick," he was saying. "Is she badly hurt?"

Father Benedict, answering him, said in a strange voice:

"Only her feet.... You can see the print of the nails...."

The Eagles and the Trumpets

WHEN the girl crossed from the library, the square was bathed in August sunshine. The folk from the outlying areas who had left their horses and carts tethered about the patriotic monument in the centre were still in the shops, and the old trees which lined either side emphasised the stillness of the morning. She went down a corridor in the Commercial Hotel and turned left into the bar. She hardly noticed its quaintness, the odd layout of the tables, its leather chairs in angles and corners, the long low window which looked out on the dairy yard at the back. After six years in the town she was only aware of its limitations. But the commercial traveller startled her. She had not expected to find anyone there so early. He raised his eyes and when he had stared at her gloomily for a moment, he asked, "Looking for Cissy?"

One of the things she had never got used to was this easy familiarity of the country town. But she accepted it. One either accepted or became a crank.

"No," she answered, "Miss O'Halloran."

"You won't see her," he said. "It's the first Friday. She goes to the altar and has her breakfast late." He had a glass of whiskey in front of him and a bottle of Bass. He gulped half the whiskey and then added, "I'll ring the bell for you."

"Thank you."

His greyish face with its protruding upper lip was vaguely familiar. Probably she had passed him many times in her six years without paying much attention. Now she merely wondered about his black tie. She heard the bell ringing remotely and after a moment Cissy appeared. The girl said:

"I really wanted Miss O'Halloran. It's a room for a

gentleman tonight." She hesitated. Then reluctantly she added, "Mr. Sweeney." As she had expected, Cissy betrayed immediate curiosity.

"Not Mr. Sweeney that stayed here last autumn?"

"Yes. He hopes to get in on the afternoon bus."

Cissy said she would ask Miss O'Halloran. When she had gone to enquire, the girl turned her back on the traveller and pretended interest in an advertisement for whiskey which featured two dogs, one with a pheasant in its mouth. The voice from behind her asked:

"Boy friend?"

She had expected something like that. Without turning she said, "You're very curious."

"Sorry. I didn't mean that. I don't give a damn. Do you drink?"

"No, thank you."

"I was going to offer you something better than a drink. Good advice." The girl stiffened. She was the town librarian, not a chambermaid. Then she relaxed and almost smiled.

"If you ever do," the voice added sadly, "don't mix the grain with the grape. That's what happened to me last night."

Cissy returned and said Mr. Sweeney could have room seven. Miss O'Halloran was delighted. Mr. Sweeney had been such a nice young man. Her eyes caught the traveller and she frowned.

"Mr. Cassidy," she said pertly, "Miss O'Halloran says your breakfast's ready."

The traveller looked at her with distaste. He finished his whiskey and indicated with a nod of his head the glass of Bass which he had taken in his hand.

"Tell Miss O'Halloran I'm having my breakfast," he said. But Cissy was admiring the new dress.

"You certainly look pretty," she said enviously.

"Prettiest girl in town," the traveller added for emphasis.

The girl flushed. Cissy winked and said, "Last night he told me I was."

209

"Did I," the traveller said, finishing his Bass with a grimace of disgust. "I must have been drunk."

On the first Friday of every month, precisely at eleven forty-five, the chief clerk put on his bowler hat, hung his umbrella on his arm and left to spend the rest of the day inspecting the firm's branch office. It was one of the few habits of the chief clerk which the office staff approved. It meant that for the rest of the day they could do more of less as they pleased. Sweeney, who had been watching the monthly ceremony from the public counter with unusual interest, turned around to find Higgins at his elbow.

"You're wanted," he was told.

"Who?"

"Our mutual musketeer – Ellis. He's in his office."

That was a joke. It meant Ellis was in the storeroom at the top of the building. Part of the duties assigned to Ellis was the filing away of forms and documents. The firm kept them for twenty-five years, after which they were burned. Ellis spent interminable periods in the storeroom, away from supervision and interference. It was a much-coveted position. Sweeney, disturbed in his day-dreaming, frowned at Higgins and said:

"Why the hell can't he come down and see me?" It was his habit to grumble. He hated the stairs up to the storeroom and he hated the storeroom. He disliked most of the staff, expecially the few who were attending night school classes for accountancy and secretarial management in order to get on in the job. Put into the firm at nineteen years of age because it was a good, safe, comfortable job, with a pension scheme and adequate indemnity against absences due to ill-health, he realised now at twenty-six that there was no indemnity against the boredom, no contributory scheme which would save his manhood from rotting silently inside him among the ledgers and the comptometer machines. From nine to five he decayed among the serried desks with their paper baskets and their telephones, and from five onwards there was the picture house, occasional women, and drink when there was money for it.

The storeroom was a sort of paper tomb, with tiers of forms and documents in dusty bundles, which exhaled a musty odour. He found Ellis making tea. A paper-covered book had been flung to one side. On the cover he could make out the words *Selected Poems,* but not whose they were. He was handed a cup with a chocolate biscuit in the saucer.

"Sit down," Ellis commanded.

Sweeney, surprised at the luxury of the chocolate biscuit, held it up and inspected it with raised eyebrows.

Ellis offered milk and sugar.

"I pinched them out of Miss Bouncing's drawers," he said deliberately.

Sweeney, secure in the knowledge that the chief clerk was already on his way across town, munched the biscuit contentedly and looked down into the street. It was filled with sunshine. Almost level with his eyes, the coloured flags on the roof of a cinema lay limp and unmoving, while down below three charwomen were scrubbing the entrance steps. He took another biscuit and heard Ellis saying conversationally, "I suppose you're looking forward to your weekend in the country."

The question dovetailed unnoticed in Sweeney's thought.

"I've been wanting to get back there since last autumn. I told you there was a girl . . ."

"With curly eyes and bright blue hair."

"Never mind her eyes and her hair. I've tried to get down to see her twice but it didn's come off. The first time you and I drank the money – the time Dacey got married. The second, I didn't get it saved in time. But I'm going today. I've just drawn the six quid out of Miss Bouncing's holiday club."

"What bus are you getting?"

"The half past two. His nibs has gone off so I can slip out."

"I see," Ellis said pensively.

"I want you to sign me out at five."

They had done things like that for one another before. Turning to face him, Ellis said, "Is there a later bus?"

"Yes. At half past eight. But why?"

"It's . . . well, it's a favour," Ellis said uncertainly. With sinking heart Sweeney guessed at what was coming.

"Go on," he invited reluctantly.

"I'm in trouble," Ellis said. "The old man was away this past two weeks and I hocked his typewriter. Now the sister's 'phoned me to tip me off he's coming home at half past two. They only got word after breakfast. If I don't slip out and redeem it there'll be stinking murder. You know the set-up at home."

Sweeney did. He was aware that the Ellis household had its complications.

"I can give it back to you at six o'clock," Ellis prompted.

"Did you try Higgins?" Sweeney suggested hopefully.

"He hasn't got it. He told me not to ask you but I'm desperate. There's none of the others I can ask."

"How much do you need?"

"Four quid would do me – I have two."

Sweeney took the four pound notes from his wallet and handed them over. They were fresh and stiff. Miss Bouncing had been to the bank. Ellis took them and said:

"You'll get this back. Honest. Byrne of the Prudential is to meet me in Slattery's at six. He owes me a fiver."

Still looking at the limp flags on the opposite roof Sweeney suggested, "Supposing he doesn't turn up."

"Don't worry," Ellis answered him. "He will. He promised me on his bended knees."

After a pause he diffidently added, "I'm eternally grateful. . . ."

Sweeney saw the weekend he had been aching for receding like most of his other dreams into a realm of tantalising uncertainty.

"Forget it," he said.

II

Sweeney, who was standing at the public counter, looked up at the clock and found it was half past two. Behind him many of the desks were empty. Some were at lunch, others were taking advantage of the chief clerk's absence. It only meant that telephones were left to ring longer than usual. To his right, defying the grime and the odd angles of the windows, a streak of sunlight slanted across the office and lit up about two square feet of the counter. Sweeney stretched his hand towards it and saw the sandy hairs on the back leap suddenly into gleaming points. He withdrew it shyly, hoping nobody had seen him. Then he forgot the office and thought instead of the country town, the square with its patriotic statue, the trees which lined it, the girl he had met on that autumn day while he was walking alone through the woods. Sweeney had very little time for romantic notions about love and women. Seven years knocking about with Ellis and Higgins had convinced him that Romance, like good luck, was on the side of the rich. It preferred to ride around in motor-cars and flourished most where the drinks were short and expensive. But meeting this strange girl among the trees had disturbed him. Groping automatically for the plausible excuse, he had walked towards her with a pleasurable feeling of alertness and wariness.

"This path," he said to her, "does it lead me back to the town?" and waited with anxiety for the effect. He saw her assessing him quickly. Then she smiled.

"It does," she said, "provided you walk in the right direction."

He pretended surprise. Then after a moment's hesitation he asked if he might walk back with her. He was staying in the town, he explained, and was still finding his way about. As they walked together he found out she was the town librarian, and later, when they had met two or three times and accepted one another, that she was bored to death with the town. He told her about being dissatisfied

213

too, about the office and its futility, about having too little money. One evening when they were leaning across a bridge some distance from the town, it seemed appropriate to talk rather solemnly about life. The wind ripped the brown water which reflected the fading colours of the sky. He said:

"I think I could be happy here. It's slow and quiet. You don't break your neck getting somewhere and then sit down to read the paper when you've got there. You don't have twenty or thirty people ahead of you every morning and evening – all queuing to sign a clock."

"You can be happy anywhere or bored anywhere. It depends on knowing what you want."

"That's it," he said, "but how do you find out? I never have. I only know what I don't want."

"Money – perhaps?"

"Not money really. Although it has its points. It doesn't make life any bigger though, does it? I mean look at most of the people who have it."

"Dignity?" she suggested quietly.

The word startled him. He looked at her and found she was quite serious. He wondered if one searched hard enough, could something be found to be dignified about. He smiled.

"Do you mean an umbrella and a bowler hat?"

He knew that was not what she meant at all, but he wanted her to say more.

"No," she said, "I mean to have a conviction about something. About the work you do or the life you lead."

"Have you?" he asked.

She was gazing very solemnly at the water, the breeze now and then lifting back the hair from her face.

"No," she murmured. She said it almost to herself. He slipped his arm about her. When she made no resistance he kissed her.

"I'm wondering why I didn't do that before," he said when they were finished.

"Do you . . . usually?" she asked.

214

He said earnestly, "For a moment I was afraid."

"Of me?"

"No. Afraid of spoiling everything. Have I?"

She smiled at him and shook her head.

At five they closed their ledgers and pushed in the buttons which locked the filing cabinets. One after the other they signed the clock which automatically stamped the time when they pulled the handle. The street outside was hardly less airless than the office, the pavements threw back the dust-smelling August heat. Sweeney, waiting for Higgins and Ellis at the first corner, felt the sun drawing a circle of sweat about his shirt collar and thought wistfully of green fields and roadside pubs. By now the half past two bus would have finished its journey. The other two joined him and they walked together by the river wall, picking their way through the evening crowds. The tea-hour rush was beginning. Sweeney found the heat and the noise of the buses intolerable. A girl in a light cotton frock with long hair and prominent breasts brushed close to them. Higgins whistled and said earnestly: "Honest to God, chaps. It's not fair. Not on a hot evening."

"They're rubber," Ellis offered with contempt.

"Rubber bedamned."

"It's a fact," Ellis insisted. "I know her. She hangs them up on the bedpost at night."

They talked knowledgeably and argumentatively about falsies until they reached Slattery's lounge. Then, while Ellis began to tell them in detail how he had smuggled the typewriter back into his father's study, Sweeney sat back with relief and tasted his whiskey. A drink was always welcome after a day in the office, even to hold the glass in his hand and lie back against his chair gave him a feeling of escape. Hope was never quite dead if he had money enough for that. But this evening it wasn't quite the same. He had hoped to have his first drink in some city pub on his way to the bus, a quick drink while he changed one of his new pound notes and savoured the adventure of the

215

journey before him, a long ride with money in his pocket along green hedged roads, broken by pleasant half hours in occasional country pubs. When Higgins and Ellis had bought their rounds he called again. Whenever the door of the lounge opened he looked up hopefully. At last he indicated the clock and said, "Your friend should be here."

"Don't worry," Ellis assured him, "he's all right. He'll turn up." Then he lifted his drink and added, "Well – here's to the country."

"The country," Higgins sighed. "Tomorrow to fresh fiends and pastors new."

"I hope so," Sweeney said. He contrived to say it as though it didn't really matter, but watching Ellis and Higgins he saw they were both getting uneasy. In an effort to keep things moving Higgins asked, "What sort of a place is it?"

"A square with a statue in it and trees," Sweeney said. "A hotel that's fairly reasonable. Free fishing if you get on the right side of the Guards. You wouldn't think much of it."

"No sea – no nice girls in bathing dresses. No big hotel with its own band?"

"Samuel Higgins," Ellis commented. "The man who broke the bank at Monte Carlo."

"I like a holiday to be a real holiday," Higgins said stoutly. "Stay up all night and sleep all day. I like sophistication, nice girls and smart hotels. Soft lights and glamour and sin. Lovely sin. It's worth saving for."

"We must write it across the doorway of the office," Sweeney said.

"What?"

"Sin Is Worth Saving For."

It had occurred to him that it was what half of them did. They cut down on cigarettes and scrounged a few pounds for their Post Office Savings account or Miss Bouncing's Holiday Club so that they could spend a fortnight of the year in search of what they enthusiastically looked upon as sin. For him sin abounded in the dusty places of the office, in his sweat of fear when the morning clock told him he was late again, in the obsequious answer to the official question, in the impulse which reduced him to pawing the hot and willing typist who passed him on the deserted stairs.

"I don't have to save for sin," he commented finally.

"Oh – I know," Higgins said, misunderstanding him. "The tennis club is all right. So are the golf links on Bank Holiday. But it's nicer where you're not known."

"View Three," Ellis interjected. "Higgins the hen butcher."

"Last year there was a terrific woman who got soft on me because I told her I was a commercial pilot. The rest of the chaps backed me up by calling me Captain Higgins. I could have had anything I wanted."

"Didn't you?"

"Well," Higgins said, in a tone which suggested it was a bit early in the night for intimate details. "More or less." Then they consulted the clock again.

"It doesn't look as though our friend is coming," Sweeney said.

"We'll give him 'til seven," Ellis said. "Then we'll try for him in Mulligan's or round in the Stag's Head."

III

The girl watched the arrival of the bus from the entrance to the hotel. As the first passenger stepped off she smiled and moved forward. She hovered uncertainly. Some men went past her into the bar of the Commercial, the conductor took luggage from the top, the driver stepped down from his cabin and lit a cigarette. Townspeople came forward too, some with parcels to be delivered to the next town, some to take parcels sent to them from the city. He was not among the passengers who remained. The girl, aware of her new summer frock, her long white gloves, the unnecessary handbag, stepped back against the wall and bumped into the traveller.

"No boy friend," he said.

She noticed he had shaved. His eyes were no longer bloodshot. But the sun emphasised the grey colour of his face with its sad wrinkles and its protruding upper lip. As the crowd dispersed he leaned up against the wall beside her.

"I had a sleep," he said. "Nothing like sleep. It knits up the ravelled sleeve of care. Who said that, I wonder?"

"Shakespeare," she said.

"Of course," he said, "I might have guessed it was Shakespeare."

"He said a lot of things."

"More than his prayers," the traveller conceded. Then he looked up at the sun and winced.

"God's sunlight," he said unhappily. "It hurts me."

"Why don't you go in out of it?" she suggested coldly.

"I've orders to collect. I'm two days behind. Do you like the sun?"

"It depends."

"Depends with me too. Depends on the night before. Mostly I like the shade. It's cool and it's easy on the eyes. Sleep and the shade. Did Shakespeare say anything about that, I wonder?"

"Not anything that occurs to me." She wished to God he would go away.

"He should then," the traveller insisted. "What's Shakespeare for, if he didn't say anything about sleep and the shade?"

At another time she might have been sorry for him, for his protruding lip, his ashen face, the remote landscape of sorrow which lay behind his slow eyes. But she had her own disappointment. She wanted to go into some quiet place and weep. The sun was too strong and the noise of the awakened square too unsettling. "Let's talk about Shakespeare some other time," she suggested. He smiled

218

sadly at the note of dismissal.

"It's a date," he said. She saw him shuffling away under the cool trees.

When they left Slattery's they tried Mulligan's and in the Stag's Head Higgins said he could eat a farmer's arse, so they had sandwiches. The others had ham and beef but Sweeney took egg because it was Friday. There was a dogged streak of religion in him which was scrupulous about things like that. Even in his worst bouts of despair he still could observe the prescribed forms. They were precarious footholds which he hesitated to destroy and by which he might eventually drag himself out of the pit. After the Stag's Head Ellis thought of the Oval.

"It's one of his houses," he said. "We should have tried it before. What's the next bus?"

"Half eight."

"Is it the last?"

"The last and ultimate bus. Aston's Quay at half past eight. Let's forget about it."

"It's only eight o'clock. We might make it."

"You're spoiling my drink."

"You're spoiling mine too," Higgins said, "all this fluting around."

"You see. You're spoiling Higgins' drink too."

"But I feel a louser about this."

"Good," Higgins said pleasantly. "Ellis discovers the truth about himself."

"Shut up," Ellis said.

He dragged them across the city again.

The evening was cooler. Over the western reaches of the Liffey barred clouds made the sky alternate with streaks of blue and gold. Steeples and tall houses staggered upward and caught the glowing colours. There was no sign of Byrne in the Oval. They had a drink while the clock moved round until it was twenty minutes to nine.

"I shouldn't have asked you," Ellis said with genuine remorse.

219

"That's what I told you," Higgins said. "I told you not to ask him."

"Byrne is an arch louser," Ellis said bitterly. "I never thought he'd let me down."

"You should know Byrne by now," Higgins said. "He has medals for it."

"But I was in trouble. And you both know the set-up at home. Christ if the old man found out about the typewriter . . ."

"Look," Sweeney said, "the bus is gone. If I don't mind, why should you? Go and buy me a drink." But they found they hadn't enough money left between them, so they went around to the Scotch House where Higgins knew the manager and could borrow a pound.

IV

Near the end of his holiday he had taken her to a big hotel at a seaside resort. It was twenty miles by road from the little town, but a world away in its sophistication. They both cycled. Dinner was late and the management liked to encourage dress. A long drive led up to the imposing entrance. They came to it cool and fresh from the sea, their wet swimming togs knotted about the handlebars. It was growing twilight and he could still remember the rustle of piled leaves under the wheels of their bicycles. A long stone balustrade rose from the gravelled terrace. There was an imposing ponderousness of stone and high turrets.

"Glenawling Castle," he said admiringly. She let her eyes travel from the large and shiny cars to the flag-mast some hundreds of feet up in the dusky air.

"Comrade Sweeney," she breathed, "cast your sweaty nightcap in the air."

They walked on thick carpet across a foyer which smelled of rich cigar smoke. Dinner was a long, solemn

220

ritual. They had two half bottles of wine, white for her, red for himself. When he had poured she looked at both glasses and said happily:

"Isn't it beautiful? I mean the colours." He found her more astoundingly beautiful than either the gleaming red or the white.

"You are," he said. "Good God, you are." She laughed happily at his intensity. At tables about them young people were in the minority. Glenawling Castle catered to a notable extent for the more elevated members of the heirarchy, Monsignors and Bishops who took a little time off from the affairs of the Church to play sober games of golf and drink discreet glasses of brandy. There were elderly business men with their wives, occasional and devastatingly bored daughters.

After dinner they walked in the grounds. The light had faded from the sky above them but far out to sea an afterglow remained. From the terrace they heard the sound of breakers on the beach below and could smell the strong, autumn smell of the sea. They listened for some time. He took her hand and said, "Happy?"

She nodded and squeezed his fingers lightly.

"Are you?"

"No," he said, "I'm sad."

"Why sad?"

"For the old Bishops and the Monsignors and the business men with their bridge-playing wives."

They both laughed. Then she shivered suddenly in the cool breeze and they went inside again to explore further. They investigated a room in which elderly men played billiards in their shirt sleeves, and another in which the elderly women sat at cards. In a large lounge old ladies knitted, while in deep chairs an occasional Bishop read somnolently from a priestly book. Feeling young and a little bit out of place, they went into the bar which adjoined the ballroom. There were younger people here. He called for drinks and asked her why she frowned.

"This is expensive for you," she said. She took a pound

note from her bag and left it on the table.

"Let's spend this on drinks," she suggested.

"All of it?"

She nodded gravely. He grinned suddenly and gave it to the attendant.

"Pin that on your chest," he said, "and clock up the damage until it's gone."

The attendant looked hard at the note. His disapproval was silent but unmistakable.

"It's a good one," Sweeney assured him. "I made it myself."

They alternated between the ballroom and the bar. In the bar she laughed a lot at the things he said, but in the ballroom they danced more or less silently. They were dancing when he first acknowledged the thought which had been hovering between them.

"I've only two days left."

"One, darling."

"Tomorrow and Saturday."

"It's tomorrow already," she said, looking at her watch. Now that it was said it was unavoidably necessary to talk about it.

"It's only about two hours by bus," he said. "I can get down to see you sometimes. There'll be weekends."

"You won't though," she said sadly.

"Who's going to stop me?"

"You think you will now but you won't. A holiday is a holiday. It comes to an end and you go home and then you forget."

They walked through the foyer which was deserted now. The elderly ladies had retired to bed, and so had the somnolent churchmen with their priestly books.

"I won't forget," he said when they were once again on the terrace. "I want you too much."

The leaves rustled again under their wheels, the autumn air raced past their faces coldly.

"That's what I mean," she said simply. "It's bad wanting anything too much." Her voice came anonymously from the darkness behind him.

"Why?" he asked.

Their cycle lamps were two bars of light in a vast tunnel of darkness. Sometimes a hedge gleamed green in the light or a tree arched over them with mighty and gesticulating limbs.

"Because you never get it." she answered solemnly.

V

Sweeney, looking through the smoke from Higgins and Ellis to the heavily built man whom he did not like, frowned and tried to remember what public house he was in. They had been in so many and had drunk so much. He was at that stage of drunkenness where his thoughts required an immense tug of his will to keep them concentrated. Whenever he succumbed to the temptation to close his eyes he saw them wandering and grazing at a remote distance from him, small white sheep in a landscape of black hills and valleys. The evening had been a pursuit of something which he felt now he would never catch up with, a succession of calls on some mysterious person who had always left a minute before. It had been of some importance, whatever he had been chasing, but for the moment he had forgotten why. Taking the heavily built man whom he didn't like as a focal point, he gradually pieced together the surroundings until they assumed first a vague familiarity and then a positive identity. It was the Crystal. He relaxed, but not too much, for fear of the woolly annihilation that might follow, and found Higgins and the heavily built man swopping stories. He remembered that they had been swopping stories for a long time. The heavily built man was a friend of Higgins'. He had an advertising agency and talked about the golf club and poker and his new car. He had two daughters — clever as hell. He knew the Variety Girls and had a fund of smutty stories. He told them several times they must come and meet the boys. "Let's leave this hole," he said several times, "and I'll run you out to the golf club. No bother." But someone began a new story. And besides, Sweeney didn't want to go. Every time he looked at the man with his neat suit and his moustache, his expensively fancy waistcoat and the pin in his tie, he was tempted to get up and walk away. But for Higgins' sake he remained and listened. Higgins was telling a story about a commercial traveller who married a hotel keeper's daughter in a small country town. The traveller had a protruding upper lip while the daughter, Higgins said, had a protruding lower lip. Like this, Higgins said. Then he said look here he couldn't tell the story if they wouldn't pay attention to him.

"This'll be good, boys," the man said, "this will be rich. I think I know this one. Go on."

But Higgins said hell no they must look at his face. It was a story and they had to watch his face or they'd miss the point.

"Christ no," Ellis said, "not your face."

Sweeney silently echoed the remark not because he really objected to Higgins' face but because it was difficult to focus it in one piece.

Well, Higgins said, they could all sugar off, he was going to tell the story and shag the lot of them.

"Now, now," the man said, "we're all friends here. No unpleasantness and no bickering, what?"

"Well," Higgins continued, "the father of the bride had a mouth which twisted to the left and the mother's mouth, funny enough, twisted to the right. So on the bridal night the pair went to bed in the hotel which, of course, was a very small place, and when the time came to get down to certain important carry-on, the nature of which would readily suggest itself to the assembled company, no need to elaborate, the commercial traveller tried to blow out the candle. He held it level with his mouth but, of course, on account of the protruding upper lip his breath went down the direction of his chin and the candle remained lit." Higgins stuck out his lip and demonstrated for their

224

benefit the traveller's peculiar difficulty. " 'Alice,' said the traveller to his bride, 'I'll have to ask you to do this.' So her nibs had a go and, of course, with the protruding lower lip, her breath went up towards her nose, and lo and behold the candle was still lighting." Again Higgins demonstrated. " 'There's nothing for it, John, but call my father,' says she. So the oul' fella is summoned and he has a go. But with his lips twisted to the left the breath goes back over his shoulder and the candle is still lighting away. 'Dammit, this has me bet,' says the father, 'I'll have to call your mother,' and after a passable delay the oul' wan appears on the scene but, of course, same thing happens, her breath goes over her right this time, and there the four of them stand in their nightshirts looking at the candle and wondering what the hell will they do next. So they send out for the schoolmaster, and the schoolmaster comes in and they explain their difficulty and ask him for his assistance and 'certainly,' he says, 'it's a great pleasure.' And with that he wets his fingers and thumb and pinches the wick and, of course, the candle goes out.' " Higgins wet his finger and thumb and demonstrated on an imaginary candle. "Then the father looks at the other three and shakes his head. 'Begod,' says he, 'did youse ever see the likes of that, isn't education a wonderful thing?' " The heavily built man guffawed and asserted immediately that he could cap that. It was a story about a commercial traveller too. But as he was about to start they began to call closing time and he said again that they must all come out to the golf club and meet the boys.

"Really," he said, "you'll enjoy the boys. I'll run you out in the car."

"Who's game?" Higgins asked.

Ellis looked at Sweeney and waited. Sweeney looked at the heavily built man and decided he didn't dislike him after all. He hated him.

"Not me," he said, "I don't want any shagging golf clubs."

"I don't care for your friend's tone," the man began, his

225

face reddening.

"And I don't like new cars," Sweeney interuppted, rising to his feet.

"Look here," the heavily built man said threateningly. Ellis and Higgins asked the stout man not to mind him.

"Especially new cars driven by fat bastards with fancy waistcoats," Sweeney insisted. He saw Ellis and Higgins moving in between him and the other man. They looked surprised and that annoyed him further. But to hit him he would have had to push his way through them and it would take so much effort that he decided it was hardly worth it after all. So he changed his mind. But he turned around as he went out.

"With fancy pins in their ties," he concluded. People moved out of his way.

They picked him up twenty minutes later at the corner. He was gazing into the window of a tobacconist shop. He was wondering now why he had behaved like that. He had a desire to lean his forehead against the glass. It looked so cool. There was a lonely ache inside him. He barely looked round at them.

"You got back quick," Sweeney said.

"Oh, cut it out," Ellis said, "you know we wouldn't go without you."

"I hate fat bastards with fancy pins," Sweeney explained. But he was beginning to feel it was a bit inadequate.

"After all," Higgins said, "he was a friend of mine. You might haver thought of that."

"Sugar you and your friends."

Higgins flushed and said, "Thanks, I'll remember that."

Pain gathered like a ball inside Sweeney and he said with intensity, "You can remember what you sugaring well like."

"Look," Ellis said, "cut it out – the pair of you."

"He insulted my friend."

"View four," Ellis said, "Higgins the Imperious."

226

"And I'll be obliged if you'll cut this View two View three View four stuff..."

"Come on," Ellis said wearily, "kiss and make up. What we all need is another drink."

It seemed a sensible suggestion. They addressed themselves to the delicate business of figuring out the most likely speak-easy.

VI

The last bus stayed for twenty minutes or so and then chugged out towards remoter hamlets and lonelier roads, leaving the square full of shadows in the August evening, dark under the trees, grey in the open spaces about the statue. The air felt thick and warm, the darkness of the sky was relieved here and there with yellow and green patches. To the girl there was a strange finality about the departure of the bus, as though all the inhabitants had boarded it on some impulse which would leave the square empty for ever. She decided to have coffee, not in the Commercial where Cissy was bound to ask questions, but in the more formal atmosphere of the Imperial. She had hoped to be alone, and frowned when she met the traveller in the hallway. He said:

"Well, well. Now we can have our chat about Shakespeare." She noticed something she had not observed earlier – a small piece of newspaper stuck on the side of his cheek where he had cut himself shaving. For some reason it made her want to laugh. She could see too that he was quite prepared to be rebuffed and guessed his philosophy about such things. Resignation and defeat were his familiars.

"I see you've changed your location," she said, in a voice which indicated how little it mattered.

"So have you."

"I was going to have coffee."

"We can't talk Shakespeare over coffee," he invited. "Have a drink with me instead."

"I wonder should I. I really don't know you," she answered coolly.

"If it comes to that," he said philosophically, "who does?"

They went into the lounge. The lounge in the Imperial paid attention to contemporary ideas. There were tubular tables and chairs, a half moon of a bar with tube lighting which provided plenty of colour but not enough light. The drink was a little dearer, the beer, on such evenings in August, a little too warm. He raised his glass to her.

"I'm sorry about the boy friend," he said. She put down her glass deliberately.

"I'd rather you didn't say things like that," she said. "It's not particularly entertaining. I'm not Cissy from the Commercial, you know."

"Sorry," he said repentantly, "I meant no harm. It was just for talk's sake."

"Then let's talk about you. Did you pick up your two days' orders?"

"No," he said sadly, "I'm afraid I didn't. I'm afraid I'm not much of a commercial traveller. I'm really a potter."

"Potter?"

"Yes. I potter around from this place to that."

She noticed the heavy upper lip quivering and gathered that he was laughing. Then he said:

"That's a little joke I've used hundreds of times. It amuses me because I made it up myself."

"Do you often do that?"

"I try, but I'm not much good at it. I thought of that one, God knows how many years ago, when things began to slip and I was in bed in the dark in some little room in some cheap hotel. Do you ever feel frightened in a strange room?"

"I'm not often in strange rooms."

"I am. All my life I've been. When I put out the light I can never remember where the door is. I suppose that's what makes me a pretty poor specimen of a traveller."

"So you thought of a joke."

"Yes."

"But why?"

"It helps. Sometimes when you feel like that a joke has more comfort than a prayer."

She saw what he meant and felt some surprise.

"Well," she prompted. "Why do you travel?"

"It was my father's profession too. He was one of the old stock. A bit stiff and ceremonious. And respected of course. In those days they didn't have to shoot a line. They had dignity. First they left their umbrella and hat in the hall stand. Then there was some polite conversation. A piece of information from the city. A glass of sherry and a biscuit. Now you've got to talk like hell and drive like hell. I suppose he trained me the wrong way."

He indicated her glass.

"You'll have another?" he asked.

She looked again at his face and made her decision. She was not quite sure what it would involve, but she knew it was necessary to her to see it out.

"I think I will," she said.

He asked her if she liked her work but she was not anxious to discuss herself at all. She admittted she was bored. After their third drink he asked her if she would care to drive out with him to Glenawling Castle. There were not likely to be people there who knew them and besides, there would be dancing. She hesitated.

"I know what you're thinking," he said, "but you needn't worry. I'm no he-man." She thought it funny that that was not what had occurred to her at all. Then he smiled and added:

"With this lip of mine I don't get much opportunity to practise."

They got into the car which took them up the hill from the square and over the stone bridge with its brown stream. The traveller looked around at her.

"You're a pretty girl," he said warmly, "prettiest I've

229

met."

She said coolly, "Prettier than your wife?"

"My wife is dead."

She glanced involuntarily at the black tie.

"Yes," he said, "a month ago." He waited. "Does that shock you?" he asked.

"I'm afraid it does."

"It needn't," he said. "We were married for eighteen years, and for fifteen of that she was in a lunatic asylum. I didn't visit her this past eight or nine years. They said it was better. I haven't danced for years either. Do you think I shouldn't?"

"No," she said after a pause. "I think it might do you good. You might get over being afraid of strange rooms."

"At forty-five?" he asked quietly.

His question kept the girl silent. She looked out at the light racing along the hedges, the gleaming leaves, the arching of trees.

VII

They eventually got into Annie's place. It was one of a row of tall and tottering Georgian houses. Ellis knew the right knock and was regarded with professional affection by the ex-boxer who kept the door. They went in the dark up a rickety stairs to a room which was full of cigarette smoke. They had to drink out of cups, since the girls and not the liquor were the nominal attraction. There was some vague tradition that Annie was entitled to serve meals too, but to ask for one was to run the risk of being thrown out by the ex-boxer. The smell of the whiskey in his cup made Sweeney shiver. He had had whiskey early in the evening and after it plenty of beer. Experience had taught hm that taking whiskey at this stage was a grave mistake. But no long drinks were available and one had to drink. Ellis noted his silence.

"How are you feeling?" he asked with friendly solicitude.

"Like the Chinese maiden?" Higgins suggested amiably and tickled the plump girl who was sitting on his knee.

"No," Sweeney said, "like the cockle man."

"I know," Higgins said. "Like the cockle man when the tide came in. We all appreciate the position of that most unfortunate gentleman." He tickled the plump girl again. "Don't we, Maisie?"

Maisie, who belonged to the establishment, giggled.

"You're a terrible hard root," she said admiringly.

There were about a dozen customers in the place. One group had unearthed an old-fashioned gramophone complete with sound horn and were trying out the records. They quarrelled about whose turn it was to wind it and laughed uproariously at the thin nasal voices and the age of the records. Sweeney was noted to be morose and again Ellis had an attack of conscience.

"I feel a louser," Ellis said.

"Look," Sweeney said, "I told you to forget it."

"Only for me you could be down the country by now."

"Only for me you could be out at the golf club," Sweeney said, "drinking with the best spivs in the country. You might even have got in the way of marrying one of their daughters." The gramophone was asking a trumpeter what he was sounding now.

"God," Maisie said, "my grandfather used to sing that. At a party or when he'd a few jars aboard. I can just see him."

"My God. Where?" Higgins asked in mock alarm.

"In my head – Smarty." Maisie said. "I can see him as if it was yesterday. Trumpet-eer what are yew sounding now – Is it the cawl I'm seeking?"

They looked in amazement at Maisie who had burst so suddenly into song. She stopped just as suddenly and gave a sigh of warm and genuine affection. "It has hairs on it right enough – that thing," she commented.

"What thing?" Higgins enquired salaciously and was rewarded with another giggle and a playful slap from Maisie.

"Maisie darling," Ellis appealed, "will you take Higgins away to some quiet place?"

"Yes," Sweeney said. "Bury his head in your bosom." Maisie laughed and said to Higgins: "Come on, sweetheart. I want to ask them to put that thing on the gramophone again." As they went away the thought struck Sweeney that Mary Magdalene might have looked and talked like that and he remembered something which Ellis had quoted to him earlier in the week. He waited for a lull among the gramophone playing group and leaned forward. He said, groping vaguely:

"Last week you quoted me something, a thing about the baptism of Christ . . . I mean a poem about a painting of the baptism of Christ . . . do you remember what I mean?"

"I think I do," Ellis said. Then quickly and without punctuation he began to rattle off a verse. "A painter of the Umbrian School Designed upon a gesso ground The nimbus of the baptised God The wilderness is cracked and browned."

"That's it," Sweeney said. "Go on."

Ellis looked surprised. But when he found Sweeney was not trying to make a fool of him he clasped the cup tightly with both hands and leaned across the table. He moved it rhythmically in a small wet circle and repeated the previous verse. Then he continued with half-closed eyes:

"But through the waters pale and thin
Still shine the unoffending feet . . ."

"The unoffending feet," Sweeney repeated, almost to himself. "That's what I wanted. Christ – that's beautiful."

But the gramophone rasped out again and the moment of quietness and awareness inside him was shattered to bits. Higgins came with three cups which he let down with a

232

bang on the table.

"Refreshment," he said, "Annie's own. At much personal inconvenience."

Sweeney looked up at him. He had been on the point of touching something and it had been knocked violently away from him. That always happened. The cups and the dirty tables, the people drunk about the gramophone, the girls and the cigarette smoke and the laughter seemed to twist and tangle themselves into a spinning globe which shot forward and shattered about him. A new record whirled raspingly on the gramophone for a moment before a tinny voice gave out the next song.

> "Have you got another girl at home
>   Like Susie
>   Just another little girl upon the family tree?
>   If you've got another girl at home
>   Like Susie . . ."

But the voice suddenly lost heartiness and pitch and dwindled into a lugubrious grovelling in the bass.

"Somebody wind the bloody thing," Ellis screamed. Somebody did so without bothering to lift off the pick-up arm. The voice was propelled into a nerve-jarring ascent from chaos to pitch and brightness. Once again the composite globe spun towards him. Sweeney held his head in his hands and groaned. When he closed his eyes he was locked in a smelling cellar with vermin and excrement on the floor, a cellar in which he groped and slithered. Nausea tautened his stomach and sent the saliva churning in his mouth. He rose unsteadily.

"What is it?" Ellis asked.

"Sick," he mumbled. "Filthy sick."

They left Higgins behind and went down into the street. Tenements with wide open doors yawned a decayed and malodorous breath, and around the corner the river between grimy walls was burdened with the incoming tide. Sweeney leaned over the wall.

"Go ahead," Ellis said.

"I can't."

"Stick your fingers down your throat."

Sweeney did so and puked. He trembled. Another spasm gripped him. Ellis, who was holding him, saw a gull swimming over to investigate this new offering.

"It's an ill wind . . ." he said aloud.

"What's that?" Sweeney asked miserably, his elbows still on the wall, his forehead cupped in his hand.

"Nothing," Ellis said. He smiled quietly and looked up at the moon.

VIII

"Do you mind if I ask you something?" the girl said. "It's about your wife."

"Fire ahead," the traveller said gently.

They stood on the terrace in front of the hotel. Below them the sea was calm and motionless, but from behind them where the large and illuminated windows broke the blackened brick of the castle the sounds of the band came thinly.

"You haven't seen her for eight or nine years."

"Fifteen," the traveller corrected. "You needn't count the few visits between."

The girl formulated her next question carefully.

"When you married her," the girl asked, "did you love her?" The traveller's face was still moist after the dancing. She saw the small drops of sweat on his forehead while he frowned at the effort to recall the emotion of eighteen years before.

"I don't know," he answered finally. "It's funny. I can't exactly remember."

The girl looked down at the pebbles. She poked them gently with her shoe.

"I see," she said softly.

He took her hand. Then they both stood silently and watched the moon.

It rode in brilliance through the August sky. It glinted on the pebbled terrace. It stole through curtain chinks into the bedrooms of the sleeping Monsignors and Bishops, it lay in brilliant barrenness on the pillows of stiff elderly ladies who had no longer anything to dream about. Sweeney, recovering, found Ellis still gazing up at it, and joined him. It was high and radiant in the clear windy spaces of the sky. It was round and pure and white.

"Corpus Domini Nostri," Sweeney murmured.

Ellis straightened and dropped his cigarette end into the water below.

"Like an aspirin," he said, "like a bloody big aspirin."

The Trout

THE trout lay in midstream at a point where the sunlight lit the water with golden transparency. A little ahead of him a stone lifted clear of the stream and in the water which ribbed out on either side the images of trees bobbed and struggled yet remained firmly anchored. The surrounding mountains were almost lost in the heat haze. He was a giant among the dwarfed trout of the mountain stream. His eyes were wary, his underjaw a voracious jowl. As Denis watched, his rod useless because of the press of trees, the trout turned with an assured movement which brought it downstream to its lie beneath the bank. Denis noted the spot carefully before retreating.

That night he took Helen down to the public house. He felt her arms tight about his waist as the motor bike skidded and bounced on the rough country lane. After some miles they joined the surfaced road and stopped where the light from the two small windows of Flaherty's public house spilled out into the surrounding darkness of mountain and moor.

The men greeted them familiarly as they entered. There was a turf fire piled high at one end, not for the sake of warmth on this summer night, but because it was lonely country and a fire meant conviviality and company. Wisps of smoke escaping every now and then into the room gave a pleasant tang to the air.

In Flaherty's they were regarded as brother and sister. Flaherty himself had started the idea on their first visit.

"You're staying beyond in Glenbeigh Cottage?" he had asked.

"For a few weeks only."

"Isn't a great place for company," Flaherty had said, screwing up his eyes as he measured out the drink.

"There's plenty of swimming and fishing."

Flaherty disposed of these with a wave of his hand.

"That may be enough to content a young man like yourself. But company and a bit of dancing, I'm thinking, would be more to the liking of your sister here."

Flaherty bent down beside the paraffin lamp which he kept beside the till. It was convenient when he had to count change. A second swung from the centre of the ceiling.

Denis, wondering if an enquiry was intended, said nothing one way or the other. Flaherty left it so.

The trout still in his mind, Denis brought their drinks to a table in the corner and said:

"I saw the wisest trout in the river today."

"How do you know?"

"He was the biggest."

"Is the biggest always the wisest?"

"With trout — yes."

"Why?" Helen asked. She had a way of arching her eyebrows which made all her questions seem serious.

"They've lived the longest."

"It might be cunning, mightn't it," Helen said. "He probably eats everyone else's share."

Denis laughed and said:

"This one could be up to twenty years old. But his days are numbered. I'm going to catch him."

"How?"

"I don't know yet. I've got to plan it."

"You shouldn't want to kill things. It isn't fair."

"The trout kills things," Denis said reasonably.

"Because he has to," Helen answered, "but you don't. And you're much too nice to want to."

When she leaned over her drink her hair was the same colour as the liquid in the glass. And her eyes, alive and lovely, showed that inside her she felt what she said. He watched a moth banging against the centre lamp, bent on burning itself to death.

What she had said made him wonder Why? He rotated

237

his glass while he searched for a reason. Why would he kill it? The moment of sighting it was planted firmly in his mind. He could see the ring of mountains, the tree-lined bank, the water ribbing on either side of the stone and, still in centre stream, the startlingly large body, the almost imperceptible finny movements.

"He's the king of the river," Denis said at last, "and any decent heathen hunter will tell you that when you kill the king of its kind all his power enters into you."

"Madman," Helen said. But he had made her smile. More than that, his tone had troubled her love into wakefulness and desire crossed suddenly from one to the other. He slipped his hand over hers without thinking but she said, her voice trembling a little:

"No, Denis."

He remembered then that while drinking in Flaherty's they were to act as brother and sister. With an effort he withdrew from contact. Since the beginning of the holiday they had slept together only once. Then for some days it had not been possible, so they had slept in their separate rooms.

"When?" he asked.

"Tomorrow night."

"Are you sure?"

"Of course," she said gently. At the moment it seemed a long way away. He sighed and gave his attention to the bar. His body was pleasantly heavy after the strenuous day, his cheeks and arms tingled from the long hours in the sun. A newcomer had arrived and was seated at the fire with a melodeon on his knee. They were asking him to play. Seeing the music about to begin Denis signalled for more drink and, as the first notes caused the company to fall into attentive silence, Helen lay back and said contentedly:

"Lovely."

They stayed late, held by the music and the spell of the warm fire.

That night he dreamed about the fish. He stood at the

river's edge, the trees pressing about him, the night arching softly above him, the river itself noiselessly moving, a blackness streaked here and there with unaccountable red light. Somewhere below, its tail making perpetual and unseen movements, lay the fish. It kept vigil with wide night eyes, a thing of knowledge. That was all that existed in his dream: the fish; he himself; the night.

He was digging for bait the next morning when he heard the car. He left the spade on the bank of the river and looked to his right, where the road curved over the slender arch of the bridge. At first he saw only the segment of the mountain road. It was unsurfaced and sandy, with tiny flecks of mica flashing in the sun. Then the car passed and stopped. Denis, going up by the track through the ferns, recognised Carew's back before he turned around.

"Denis," Carew greeted, holding out his hand.

Denis took it.

"Your motor bike is parked a few yards back," Carew explained, "I recognised the number."

"You must come up to our cottage," Denis said.

"Cottage?" Carew enquired, with a smile.

"Helen is with me," Denis said. He saw suspicion of the Unspeakable manifesting itself by degrees on Carew's face.

"Alone?"

"Only the two of us," Denis acknowledged. He led the way, talking as they went of the accommodation and the ideal weather and what they were paying for the month, but hoping to God, as he spoke, that this morning of all mornings Helen would be properly dressed when she opened the door to them.

As it happened she was lying in the front garden, attired, as Carew obviously felt, very casually indeed. Denis said to Helen, "This is Robert Carew."

"I've heard so much about you," Helen smiled.

And to Carew he said, "This is Helen."

"Ah . . ." Carew said.

For the moment it was the best he could do.

"You're just in time for lunch," Helen said. Denis excused himself and followed her into the kitchen.

"What a thing to happen."

"To blazes with him," Helen answered.

"He's engaged to my sister Maura for the past eight years. And greatly admired by the family for his rectitude."

"Imagine carrying an umbrella on a day like this. God."

"He'll feel it's his Christian duty to tell them. It's a pity you were . . . I mean his first sight of you . . ."

"It was the last thing I expected."

"You didn't look surprised."

"I hadn't time. You let him practically walk on me."

"Oh well," Denis said, resigning himself to it. The damage was done anyhow.

It was Helen who suggested that Denis and Carew should climb the mountain together. That was when they had coped with him all through their meal and had shown him over the cottage. He had poked his head into bedrooms, looked into presses, murmured words of surprise at the bellows which was built into the wide fireplace, the heavy kettle suspended on its primitive arrangement of bars and chains. He was polite and yet his unspoken disapproval seemed to linger in everything he touched. Carew was reluctant about going at first, then suddenly he seemed to think it a fine idea. She packed food for them and sent them off, after some indecision on Carew's part about bringing his umbrella. They assured him it was unlikely to rain and drew his attention to the colour of the sky and the absence of wind and cloud.

"Still, I think I'll bring it," he decided at last, having considered these various matters carefully.

"Whatever you like," Denis agreed.

As they struggled up through the forest of pines Carew removed first his coat and then his collar and tie. Denis let him set the pace. At first the umbrella, the braces, the

240

collarless shirt with the useless stud still sticking out at the back depressed him. Then he forgot about it as the forest grew deeper and the pines, tall and straight on the lower slopes, marched uphill with them and enclosed them in a green gloom.

Once again the trout took hold on his mind. During the morning he had worked out a plan. He would go down at dusk to the point of the river he had noted so carefully. Then he would wait until the light had gone and the sounds of his coming had been forgotten. For bait he had dug up a grub which he found deadly in other parts of the river, a mud coloured grub which curled on the hook but which opened out to display a white underbelly when dropped in the water. If he dropped it in gently, as though it had fallen from an overhanging branch, it might tempt the trout. One day when he was short of flies he had tried the grub without much expectation and discovered its value by accident. He thought it strange that of all nature's profligacy, so many lures should be next to useless and yet this one should prove so deadly. One could spend a lifetime classifying the life forms to be found in an acre of earth. He was about to remark on this to Carew, but stopped himself. Carew, no doubt, would see in it the Omnipotence of God.

After a couple of hours they were clear of the forest. It happened suddenly. One moment they were surrounded by gloom and silence, the next they were in a world of vivid colour and overpowering light. There were islands of loose, weathered stone in a sea of heather and gorse. All this brightness burst suddenly about them like a loud shout, so that Denis straightened for a moment, listening rather than looking, the trout, for the moment, forgotten. Higher up, by a small stream which tumbled through a miniature gorge, there was a cool patch of grass which looked inviting. They decided to rest.

Carew opened his umbrella and used it as a sunshade. "I knew it would be wise to bring it," he said.

Still the unspoken questions hovered between them. He

241

looked ridiculous under the black umbrella, like a great bat in the sunlight. Denis, raising himself on his elbow said, "You can see the cottage from here."

"Where?" Carew asked, also moving.

"Follow the line of the stream and look left near the floor of the valley." Carew saw it. It nestled against the mountain side, with bright red window frames and gleaming white walls, surrounded by its snug garden and small fruit trees.

"It looks very beautiful," Carew admitted, but grudgingly, his mind obviously troubled.

Denis, finding the constraint tedious, decided to kill it. He said, half smiling, "The tents of the robbers are prosperous, and they that provoke God are secure."

Carew scuttled back quickly under his umbrella, like a huffed snail drawing his shell about him.

"I am thinking of your parents," he said very deliberately.

"What they don't know won't worry them."

Carew took that under the umbrella with him too and chewed on it. He changed his approach.

"I hope you don't mind if I speak to you, Denis. I am, in a way, one of the family."

"Not at all," Denis said.

He could not see Carew now. The sun was too bright on his eyes and the great black umbrella had swallowed the other so that the voice seemed to speak to him from the depths of a cave.

"I am disappointed in you," Carew began. Denis refused to give him any help.

"I'm not suggesting that there is anything . . . sinful . . . between you and . . ."

Denis waited. He wouldn't say Helen. He didn't.

". . . this girl. But there's such a thing as the occasion of sin. What would your father and your mother say if they knew? Your brother John is now a priest of the Church. Think of the pain it would cause him if he heard you were living alone with a young girl in a remote place such as this."

Denis maintained silence. He was watching the stream, its swift movement, its urgent conformity, its helter skelter of obedience to forces with which it could never pause to argue.

"And Maura. She and I are to be married. We love each other. What do you think her answer would be if I were to suggest that we should holiday together as you and this girl are doing?"

Denis plucked a piece of grass. It was thin and fine here on the mountain and almost silver in colour. Down in the valley it was broad and dark green. Maura and Carew were eight years engaged. If that was love it could not be very exciting.

"Don't you ever want to?" Denis asked.

"I beg your pardon?"

"Want to go off and live together?"

"We shall do so," Carew said impressively, "when circumstances permit and we are ready to ask God to bless our union."

Once again the tone tempted Denis to smile. It was as though Carew were announcing his determination to form a Company. Robert and Maura Ltd. The appropriate steps would be taken.

"But not until then?"

Carew stuck his head forward from under the umbrella.

"May I remind you," he said, "that you are speaking of your own sister."

"I know," Denis said.

"Maura is a good Catholic. She knows better."

"Yes," Denis said. "You are both better at knowing than at loving."

Carew pulled his knees up to his chin and clasped the umbrella between them. He brooded for some time. He said, unhappily, "I am very clumsy at expressing myself and you are adept at saying things which sound well but don't seem to mean very much. At least they don't seem to *me* to mean very much. But surely you must acknowledge that you are living in sin or, at the least – in the occasion of sin."

"I don't deny that," Denis said quietly.

"Ah," Carew exclaimed.

The admission brought him out from beneath his umbrella to suggest that they should eat. The suggestion, Denis knew, was only by way of an adjournment.

They made tea. Carew got water and gathered sticks. Denis improvised a wooden support for the billycan. Carew got on his hands and knees and with his nose six inches from the ground began to blow the fire into life. Denis unwrapped the sandwiches and sorted them. Helen had made them. The thought was oddly pleasing.

He leaned back against the rock and surrendered himself to the moment. Before him stretched the slope of fern and rock and below that, where the pine trees began, a swift flood of green swept down to the valley floor. He had not known green could be so many colours. That was another thing one could devote a lifetime to classifying – the colour green. Beyond the mountains lay the world of parents and priests, where prejudice and necessity compounded to produce the communal will and make war on individual desire. It was inescapable. The community was even now at his elbow, fanning a fire under a billycan. It said, "How do you know when this thing is boiling?"

With an effort he gave it his attention.

"Hold the handle of a spoon against the side," Denis answered. "You'll feel the vibrations."

Carew did so. A smile lit his face, brief, but for the first time genuine.

"So you can. Extraordinary."

He took the billycan off the fire and removed the lid. Carew said that food tasted differently in the open. Perhaps it was that one had a sharper appetite. It was a good argument for the outdoor life. He said all this from under his umbrella, to which he had again retired. Meanwhile Denis had been thinking.

244

"Are you going to tell them?" he asked.

"Have I touched your conscience?"

"A little perhaps, but it's not that. Worrying them won't undo anything."

"It might stop you."

"It won't."

"I can't believe you'd inflict pain on them."

"That's up to you," Denis said, with finality.

"Denis," Carew said, putting his cup from him, "I think I'll tell you something now. You didn't ask me why I happened to pass this way. Or where I got the car."

"No."

"The answer is that I haven't got a job anymore. The old firm has closed down. That's something Maura and I had been afraid of all along."

"Is that why the two of you waited?"

"That's why I waited. Maura was willing to take a chance."

"You believe in God. But you don't trust Him very far."

"He gave us foresight and prudence. We must use His gifts."

Denis felt a twinge of compassion, for Carew and his sister Maura and their eight years of unrewarded patience.

"I'm sorry about the job. I thought you were having a few days break from the office."

"I had the chance of another and asked a friend for a loan of the car. In fact I was driving down for the interview today. Now it's too late. I've missed it."

Denis looked at him closely, wondering if he was mad.

"Did you delay simply to talk to me about Helen?"

"I stopped to say hello. But when I found out what you were doing I felt it my first duty to speak to you."

"You could have done so without spending the day about it."

"At first that's what I intended. But then I saw that a few words would be useless. I hoped, if I spent the day with you . . ." Carew sighed. He was obviously deeply troubled. "Does what I've told you make any difference?"

"It makes me feel a bit miserable," Denis said honestly, "but it doesn't alter my decision about Helen."

"And you're content to go on like this, offending God day after day? I can't understand that."

"I'm not like you," Denis said. "I don't really believe in God. I believe in what you see around you; in mountains and rocks and rivers. Man should live peacefully in places like this, taking what pleasure there is. There's nothing before or after it. It doesn't know anything about you and it doesn't expect anything from you. And you can treat it with the same indifference."

What he was saying surprised him. He had not really thought about it until now. Carew said nothing.

"I'm sorry," Denis said.

Carew still remained silent. He looked quite forlorn, disappointment etched on his face.

Denis thought once again of the trout. Not the trout alone but the whole scene: the rock and the ribbing water, the crowding trees and the watchful mountains. He wanted to have time to get down there when Carew had left. After a while, with a feeling of impatience which he did his best to hide, he said, "We ought to be getting back."

When they reached the road again Carew refused to go back to the cottage. As he reversed the car he said, "You may as well know that I won't tell them, particularly on Maura's account. She's upset as it is."

"What will you say about missing the interview?"

"I hadn't told her about the interview. She gets so anxious about things like that. I mightn't have been successful anyway."

"Something will turn up," Denis said. He found it hard to believe. Carew's age was beginning to count against him. And his qualities, although they were useful, were ordinary and not by any means self-evident. You had to

246

know him.

"With God's help," Carew said, and drove off.

Later, when Denis was changing into his waders, Helen said, "Are you going fishing?"

She sounded surprised.

"I'm going to have a try for that trout. I want to get down to the river before the light goes."

"Can't you leave it alone?"

She put her arms about his shoulders. The room was in half light now. They were a pleasant and persuasive argument. Her voice too, which could disturb him with an inflexion, had the note of desire in it. But he resisted gently. There would be tonight.

"I have a plan," he said, and went on with his preparations. His tone told her that his mind was made up. She moved away.

Dan O'Sullivan, their nearest neighbour, was at the door of his cottage as Denis passed on the way to the river. The cottage was small, with a corrugated iron roof which had been covered with tar. The walls, once white, had yellowed over with weather, as had the stiff stepping hens that wandered in the mud about the front door.

"Are you after the fish?" Dan shouted as he passed.

Denis held up the rod and wagged it.

"You'll be losing the light soon," Dan shouted again.

Denis tilted his head and scanned the sky. It was on fire behind the deepening black of the clouds. He could feel the wind freshening too. It blew coolly through the back of his sweater.

"So long as the rain holds off," he answered, by way of courtesy, and struck down through the woods.

It was darker than he had expected. At first the trees were well spaced, with clearings at intervals. They grew thicker as the slope increased, so that he had to stoop frequently to make a passage. But he went quickly, groping in the semi-darkness, his ears fixed on the growing murmur of the river. It was a relief to reach it and to find he was within a few yards of the spot he had in mind. He saw the water ribbing on either side of the stone, well upstream to his left. His coming had been unavoidably noisy. He had slipped several times in the soft mud and branches as he grabbed at them had snapped loudly. He fixed his lure, lit a cigarette and squatted in the silence and half light. His heart thumped uncomfortably but he knew he must master his impatience. He must wait, without movement, without noise. At first a curtain of midges screened his view of the river. The smoke drove them away.

The river clung to the last of the light. It hoarded light as a miser. When everything else had surrendered to darkness the river doled out from its store of light drop by drop, particle by particle. It was watchful. It was never wholly dark. If it was wholly dark it would die.

One night when Dan O'Sullivan was walking home with them from Flaherty's he was sad with drink and he stopped at the graveyard and showed them sadly where his father and mother lay buried. There was a moon and tall, sweet-smelling grass which stroked damply against their hands. He said that at one time long ago his father and mother and six brothers and sisters lived in the small cottage and they were happy. Then one by one the others went to America and he was left alone with his father and mother. Then his father died. Then his mother. He was alone. At first he lay awake and alone at nights and prayed to his father and mother to talk to him. Nothing happened. He thought it was God who would not allow it so he prayed to God to let one of them come to him, just for one, brief moment. He asked God to have pity on his great loneliness. But nothing happened. Night after night he prayed and night after night in the silence between his prayers he heard nothing only the ticking of the clock and the creak of ash in the dying fire. Until one night it became so unendurable he rose again and dressed. Something drew him to the graveyard. He stood at the grave and entreated his mother and father to speak to him.

248

But nothing happened; nothing stirred in the little graveyard; there was nothing at all. And as he listened to the nothingness that made no response no matter how hard he implored and begged and wept, the thought for the first time came to him that there was nothing to beg from. He was talking to nothing. If God were there He would have let them come; if his father and mother were there they would have come in spite of God because they would have heard how he was suffering and they loved him before everything. He did not blame God. He was not there. He did not blame his parents. They were not there either. In the graveyard that night he found out that beyond the little span of years granted to each man and woman there was only silence and emptiness. Instead of God and Heaven, there was Absence and a Void. That was what Dan O'Sullivan had told them.

Denis finished his cigarette and, in his abstraction, almost flicked it into the river in front of him. When he dropped it at his feet it glowed for a moment, then sizzled and surrendered slowly to the wet mud. Despite the darkness the river glimmered, almost soundless, its surface wrinkling when the trees in their upper branches shivered in the strengthening wind. A rat flopped clumsily into the water. He watched it as it crossed diagonally, its little snout uptilted towards the sky. He became conscious of his own isolation. Before him there was the river and behind half a mile of tangled briars, crowding leaves, dykes and fences; the sky's darkness pressing on everything and the wind tormenting the branches. It would be as well to get done with it.

He paid off some line and manoeuvred the tip of the rod outwards, allowing it to hover above the water, until the wind began again at the back of the woods. He marked its gradual swell and calculated its progress, until it roared in the leaves immediately above his head. When the water wrinkled under it again he dropped the line close to the bank. For a second or two nothing happened. Then a light tap passed through the rod, followed almost immediately by a powerful tug. The line shot swiftly through his fingers – then stopped. His heart pumped madly. The fish, if it was the fish, had made no run. It had dived for the bottom. He abandoned the rod and took the line in his hand, putting weight on it until it stretched dangerously. He relaxed some of the weight but kept a light strain on it. It held fast to the bottom and for minutes nothing happened. Then the pull eased. Imperceptibly Denis drew upwards. Just at the right moment, when the head had barely surfaced, he lugged powerfully and swung the short line back on to the bank. The fish hit the mud, lay still, then gave a panic stricken jerk into the air. He lashed powerfully at it with his fist, driving it down deep into the mud and sprawling full-length himself. There was nothing to kill it with so he dragged it after him while he searched. He found a broken branch. With this he hit it on the head over and over again. Eventually it lay still. He plunged his fingers through its gills, dismantled the rod as best he could and struggled upwards blindly until he reached a clearing.

Here he rested, trembling violently. All about him the trees tossed in the grip of the wind and just ahead of him a branch, dislodged by its force, tore its way heavily through tangled foliage and crashed to the ground. His wrists were torn by brambles, his cheeks too. On both his hands his own blood mixed with the slime and blood of the fish. The fish still bled through gills and gaping mouth. It had a murdered look.

Late that night Helen said, "It's a good thing Carew decided to keep quiet."

"Yes," Denis said. He had been silent a long time, lying beside her in the darkness. His hands, clasped on his breast, felt smooth and strange.

"I mean it would be so unpleasant."

What she was saying seemed irrelevant. He was listening to the wind. It was sweeping in desolate blasts over mountain and forest, graveyard and cottage. Over river and rock. On out into emptiness.

250

"You're thinking of something."

"The wind. I wish it would shut up."

"It'll be gone tomorrow," she said.

He lay very still. At last she said, "Well – goodnight, darling."

Her tone was inconclusive. He knew she had been waiting for him but he was unable to respond. He said, tenderly, "Goodnight."

When he closed his eyes it happened again. The branches crowded over him, the wind wrinkled the river in agonised spasms, the mouth of the fish gaped and bled. It was Carew and Dan. It was Helen. It was the World. It was a loud cry. But there was nothing to hear. Was there no one, even, to blame?

He stretched out his arm and touched Helen. She was asleep.

The Plain People

THE tread of Tonman Byrne's feet outside drew Mulligan's attention from the woman who sat opposite him. His eyes, turning imperceptibly ceilingwards, almost betrayed his relief. For an hour he had sat listening to her, trapped in his shabby office, behind the dilapidated table which held a telephone, a very dusty dictaphone and a number of minute-books relating to the affairs of No. 6 Branch of the Trade Union. She was a widow who was looking for a job for her son. She had been in several times already.

Normally, Mulligan was a patient man. Twenty years' service as an unimportant Branch Secretary had taught him that virtue. He was also a disillusioned one. He seldom expected the people it was his duty to deal with to accept a perfectly reasonable explanation, or to take someone else's No for an irreversible answer. But this morning he was suffering. A bad night had left him with a head that throbbed and palms which sweated. The sunlight, mitigated though it was by the thick dust on the windows, hurt his inflamed eyes. He was a shabbily dressed man with a well-lined, putty-coloured face. His dearest wish at that moment was to get out, even for ten short minutes, to the public-house next door.

There was a time when he would have thought nothing of stopping for one on the way in. Back in the old days, the Union was small and a Branch Secretary enjoyed certain freedoms. Now, things were different. Head Office had been set up in an imposing building in a fashionable part of the city where the executives had polished desks with telephones and intercommunication apparatus and floors covered by acres of soft carpet. They had left Mulligan behind them in the rickety little Hall near the quays, where he could be in close contact with his difficult members. But, knowing Mulligan, they had not left him solely to his own devices. They asked for reports. They telephoned frequently and expected him to be there to answer. If he was absent, they expected his delegate, Tonman, to be able to say where the hell he was.

On his entry, instead of interrupting, as Mulligan had hoped, Tonman stood back deferentially to wait for the widow to finish, an eventuality which Mulligan had long ceased to expect.

"All I want for my son is a fair hunt, Mr. Mulligan," the widow insisted.

"And a fair hunt is the thing he's going to get," Mulligan said, for the tenth time. "Isn't he on the list?"

"He's been on the list for the past eighteen months." It was beginning all over again.

Mulligan looked at Tonman with murderous politeness. "Did you want to see me?" he almost shouted.

Tonman, waking up and taking his cue, said: "Terrible urgent."

"You heard that, didn't you, Ma'am?" Mulligan said. "You'll have to excuse us."

The widow did so with bad grace. When she had left and was out of earshot, Mulligan turned on his delegate furiously.

"A right bloody hour you turn up at."

"Wait a minute," Tonman pleaded. "In the first place, I wasn't feeling too well——"

"And how the hell do you think I was feeling?" Mulligan demanded. "After what you walked me into last night!"

To the best of his recollection Tonman thought it had been the other was round, but he said nothing. He was used to being blamed. Besides, there was a more urgent matter on his mind.

"I see you haven't heard the news," he said. "The trimmers are on strike."

Mulligan's face, which had been long enough, grew

appreciably longer.

"Not again."

"Yes," Tonman said gloomily, "again."

"Where are they working?"

"They are not working," Tonman explained patiently.

"Don't pick me up on everything I say," Mulligan bawled at him. "I'm not able for it this morning."

"Sorry," Tonman said. He was a huge man, with an indefinable air of sadness about him, who always sounded short of breath.

"Where are they striking – if that pleases you better?"

"Down at the Basin."

"Holy God," Mulligan groaned and reached for his battered hat.

They went down together into the sunlit street. The Basin was at the farthest point of the wall. There was no public transport. It meant a two-mile walk through narrow, evil-smelling streets, past a hospital which catered for those victims of venereal disease who were too poor to keep their troubles private, and by line after line of groaning cranes, clanging buckets, trundling floats and smoking ships. Mulligan gathered the details over a curer in a public-house called "The Sailor's Rest" and ruminated on them in silence. It was the third strike in his Branch in three months. A sharply worded letter from the Executive on the subject of unofficial stoppages lay on his desk at that moment. The letter pointed out, among other things, that such stoppages could often be traced to the failure of the responsible official to take early and adequate steps to deal with minor grievances. Mulligan knew that the Executive were acting under public pressure. The press had launched a trenchant campaign against the frequent unauthorised strikes which always hit, as they put it, "at the man in the street". The Government had threatened legislative action if the Unions were not prepared to act on their own. The Union leaders had made pious speeches proclaiming their determination to discipline members who took the law into their own hands. The employers

254

threatened several times to Lock-Out. Yet no one cared to be the first to move. The employers feared a chain-reaction of sympathetic walk-outs. The individual unions were reluctant to take any action that might cause a breakaway among their members. The Government, with a shaky majority in the House, disliked the idea of introducing legislation which would be jumped on by opponents as an attempt to curb the worker.

"Why does it always happen to us?" Mulligan asked.

"It's the dock workers," Tonman said, "no respect for God or man."

"The Government can't handle them, the employers can't handle them, the Executive can't handle them. How the hell are you and me supposed to handle them?"

"There I leave you," Tonman said. He found some loose change in his pocket and counted it anxiously. He heaved a sigh of relief. "Have another of them," he added.

"No," Mulligan said. "I better get down to them. I want you to go back to the office and stall off Head Office as long as you can. If they call, explain that I'm out on a job but you don't know exactly what it is."

"I have you," Tonman acknowledged.

"Don't tell them about the stoppage," Mulligan elaborated. "Just say I'm on a job all right, but you haven't the details."

"Rely on me," Tonman answered him.

They parted company.

After the bustling life of the quays, the scene at the Basin was one of startling inactivity. A ship was lying idle under a grab, the bucket poised half-way between the hold and the crane arm. In his cabin the craneman was smoking a cigarette. From time to time he leaned out, measured carefully and spat. In the middle of the bridge the Singer-Out rested with his elbows on the rail, petrified in abstraction. The trimmers stood in a group. With everything at a standstill, the only people who looked as though they couldn't care less were the trimmers. Mulligan sighed inwardly at the fate which had tied him to such a bunch of tough, intractable and unpredictable bowsies. As he approached, the stevedore also joined them.

"Here's Mr. Mulligan now," he said with relief.

"Never mind Mr. Mulligan," Duffy, a burly trimmer, with a cap, said. "How did you get on?"

Mulligan remained cautiously silent. He wanted to find out what he could.

"I telephoned again," the stevedore began.

"Who this time?"

"The Assistant Chief Engineer."

"What did he say?"

"Just what the Marine Supervisor said."

"So he won't pay."

"That's what I keep telling them, Mr. Mulligan," the stevedore said. "They're wasting their time."

"You told him it was oxide?" Duffy persisted.

"What do *you* think?" said the stevedore. He hated Duffy. Mulligan understood the emotion. It often afflicted himself.

"And that it's dirty?"

"No," the stevedore corrected carefully, "I told him you *said* it was dirty."

Duffy rubbed his chin.

"You told him no dirty money – no work?"

"Listen. There's no dirty money. I told you. The Marine Supervisor told you. The Assistant Chief Engineer tells you."

No one said anything. The stevedore, thinking he detected a weakness, began to hustle.

"Now come on. Into the ship. Start unloading."

The rest waited for Duffy, who looked up at the craneman and waved.

"Gerry," he bawled.

The craneman locked his controls, dropped his cigarette over the side and climbed down.

The stevedore got red in the face.

"Mr. Mulligan," he appealed. "The agreement says no

256

stoppage without seven days' notice first. Is the Union going to stand for conduct like this?"

While Mulligan hummed and hawed, torn between the necessity for applying the brake and the immediate unpopularity of trying to do so, Duffy shouted to the Singer-Out. The figure on the bridge thawed out, unlooped itself and began to make its way towards the gangplank. In the face of such determination Mulligan did the only thing possible.

"We'd better talk about this," he told the stevedore.

He had a discussion with the trimmers and found they wanted sixpence a ton dirty money. He was persuaded to step into the hold to judge the justice of their case for himself, a gesture which, in his delicate state of health, nearly killed him. He then went into the stevedore's office and telephoned in turn the hierarchy of company officials. Finally, he got through to the General Manager – a Mr. Beggs. He was, Mulligan thought, a comparatively new man. He decided, however, to chance his luck.

"This is Mulligan."

"Who . . . ?"

"Mulligan. Secretary No. 6 Branch of the Union."

"Oh."

The General Manager's tone conveyed that, while the name was oddly familiar, he did not welcome telephone exchanges with people of Mulligan's lowly status.

"It's about the trimmers."

"One moment, please. You are the men's shop steward."

"No. Their Branch Secretary."

"An official of the Union?"

"A paid official."

"Quite. Then I trust you have done your duty by informing them that their action is highly improper, a breach of a clear-cut agreement between your Union and this company and therefore entirely unofficial."

This was an unexpectedly tough line. Mulligan dithered.

"Well – Yes . . . No——"

"You appear to be uncertain."

"Well, naturally it's unofficial——"

"One moment. You confirm that it is unofficial."

It was the voice of one who makes meticulous notes on his desk-pad. Mulligan began to sweat. He was dealing with a pedant. That was inconvenient.

"Hold on a minute," he began.

"I beg your pardon."

"I don't mean it's unofficial——"

"Are you implying that it is official?"

Mulligan had a fleeting vision of the General Executive, solemn men, severe men.

"My God – no——"

"But it must be one or the other. Will you kindly say which? We must know where we stand."

"All right. Let's say it's unofficial. That's not what I phoned about. I thought you might care to discuss the claim."

"You say the strike is unofficial. In that case it is your plain duty to instruct the men to return to work. If they refuse, then it is the business of your organisation to suspend them from membership and supply us with men who will abide by their Union's agreement. As an official you ought to know that."

"I see——"

"I beg your pardon?"

"I said – I see."

Mulligan rang off, regretting the impulse which had tempted him to negotiate at so high a level. He tried to reason with the trimmers.

"Look, boys," he said. "I know the cargo is dirty——"

"So do we."

"But there's no use taking the law into your own hands. Give us a chance to submit the claim in the normal way."

"When the work is already done and they can tell us to lump it," Duffy said. "Not bloody likely."

"Now, now, now. We have an agreement about giving

notice of a stoppage. There's the machinery of negotiation."

"Stuff that," Duffy told him.

"Then all I can do is get back and report to Head Office."

"Do that," Duffy said cheerfully. "You're caught up in the rules. We don't blame you."

All agreed it was not Mulligan's fault. After all, he had been twenty years with them. He was not brilliant, perhaps, but they knew him and he them. If they stuck to the old, tough methods they nevertheless recognised that the kind of trade unionism which sat around conference tables and attended Labour Courts was as remote from Mulligan as it was from them. Unfortunately, he was an official and had to follow the form book. But they were not going to undertake a dirty job without compensation just because business or Union executives liked to draw up neatly argued documents which were signed at the bottom by five or six brass hats. So they left their long-handled shovels back in the stores, adjusted their caps, hitched up their belts and went off to discuss their grievance over several drinks.

Tonman was sitting faithfully by the telephone. To Mulligan he looked like the dog on the gramophone records, waiting to hear his master's voice. There had been no call from Head Office, a fact which puzzled him until he telephoned to make his report. There was no one to receive it. The General Officers were away attending a convention.

They both adjourned to the public-house. Tonman, who had been thinking while he waited, expressed the fruits of his efforts.

"It's a bad situation," he said.

"You needn't tell me. The management won't budge. I phoned Beggs."

"Beggs?"

"He's the new General Manager. He wanted to know was it official or unofficial."

"That was an academic class of a question," Tonman observed. "Is it trouble he's looking for?"

"It looks like it."

"Holy God, he picked a nice time. The trimmers have been working the big American boats for the past month. They've money to burn."

"I had that in mind. A spell of good weather and plenty of money for beer. They'll be in no hurry to settle."

"Then there's the match."

"Match — what match?"

"The big match in Dalymount tomorrow — Ireland Selected versus Arsenal."

"Holy God. We'll have them all in it."

"I knew that hadn't struck you," Tonman observed.

Evening found most of the striking trimmers drunk. In the public-houses along the dockside the story of their grievances spread and was discussed. The quay workers and the deep-sea dockers had been working the American boats too. The fact that there was a football match of more than usual importance had not escaped them. The cargo of oxide became dirtier and dirtier. The men had been refused masks. The management had threatened to introduce non-Union labour. At the psychological moment the evening papers reached the area. One had a big headline:

LIGHTNING STOPPAGE AT BASIN UNOFFICIAL, SAYS T.U. OFFICIAL

It went on to describe "an assurance, given to the Company by a Mr. Mulligan, Branch Secretary, that the strike was unofficial. It trusted that, at long last, appropriate steps to deal with lawlessness and irresponsible members would be taken by the Union."

Mulligan opened the paper in the bed-sittingroom which he occupied in a seedy house not far from the Union Hall. The headline almost knocked him off his chair. He read it, with horror, several times, while his tea grew cold on its tray.

He kept away from the Union Hall. He guessed, accurately, as it happened, that there would be newspaper men waiting there to see him. He also guessed, and again quite accurately, that they would be accompanied by an infuriated deputation of coal trimmers. He forgot for the moment about Mrs. Lynch. She too was there, on the fringe of the crowd. She had thought of another firm Mulligan might write to in the morning on behalf of her son.

The morning papers brought further bad news. They reported that the Union declaration that the strike was unofficial had caused considerable bad feeling among the men, who felt the pronouncement had been made without a thorough investigation of their case. Steps taken by the Company late the previous night to release the boat and divert its cargo to another port had been answered by a walk-out on the part of the sailors, who struck in sympathy with the trimmers. Once again, the public were to be held up to ransom. A leader remarked that it was good to see that at last the Union was going to face up to the situation.

Mulligan read it all at breakfast and went back to bed. That was where Tonman found him around midday. Mulligan held the blankets tight against his chin and most of the time Tonman had to talk to a frightened pair of eyes.

"I had to come for you," he said, "everybody is looking for you."

"Tell them I'm sick," Mulligan said.

"You don't look sick."

"You can have pains in your chest and your legs, can't you," Mulligan mumbled, "without looking sick. And queer spots floating before your eyes."

"You were all right yesterday."

"I know. I must have picked up something in the hold of that ship. A germ or something."

"The sailors walked out last night."

"So I read. It's all this bloody football match."

261

"There was a murderous mob at the Hall last night — looking for you."

Mulligan groaned. The eyes above the sheet rolled a little.

"And three times this morning there were trunk calls from the Convention in Cork."

"The General Secretary?"

"Yes. He wanted a report."

"I'm, sick, Tonman."

"What in God's name, made you say it was unofficial? It wasn't your place to do that."

"It slipped out, Tonman. I didn't mean it."

"It's landed everyone in the soup," Tonman said. "If you'd kept your mouth shut things might have rested for a while."

Mullligan blamed Beggs. In the ordinary way the job would have been left idle while the management protested in well-measured notices in the press. The Union would have spent two or three days pretending to deliberate on whether the strikers should be expelled from the Union or whether the matters in complaint were so urgent that the sudden stoppage should be excused. Meanwhile, both sides would have made sure to find a solution before any real danger of having to face the issue arose.

That afternoon the quay workers struck in sympathy. A record attendance at the football match saw Ireland Selected beating Arsenal by three goals to one. The result gave Mulligan no satisfaction. The headlines were more distressing:

UNOFFICIAL STRIKE SPREADS
PORT OF DUBLIN THREATENED

And then on another page, some reporter had chanced his arm. A report that the Union was going to take disciplinary action had a headline:

MULLIGAN INFLEXIBLE
LAWLESS STRIKES MUST STOP

262

The inflexible Mulligan returned to bed and remained there throughout the next day. He was the subject of discussions in the office of the Minister for Industry and Commerce.

"Who *is* this Mulligan?" he asked his secretary.

"Some remote official," said the secretary, "probably mad."

"Any information from Union Headquarters?"

"No. There will be later. They're all at a Convention."

"Conventions – and the whole port closing."

"Keeping out of the way probably."

"Damned cowards. Expect us to carry the baby – as usual."

"By the way, the Minister for Justice has been on."

"For God's sake, stall him off. Things are bad enough without that chancer butting in."

"It seems the trimmers are picketing. The Superintendent of Police doesn't know what steps to take. Strictly speaking, he should issue orders for their arrest."

"That would make matters a good deal worse. The whole shooting gallery would walk out."

"Yes. But a picket is legal only when the strike is official. There's something in the Trades' Dispute Act."

"Tell him to forget the Act and hold off for a while. And make another effort to contact someone responsible at Union headquarters."

"It looks as though Beggs *wants* a close down. The man seems to have been a bit of a fool."

"Yes. I'm getting Bullman to deal with him. This could become a general strike."

"It's not a good time for facing issues. Look at our trade deficit."

"I've been looking at it for the past six months. Do what you can."

The secretary said he would. But he had a hopeless air which discouraged the Minister. These permanent officials, however friendly, were all fatalists. The Minister sighed and lifted his telephone.

Tonman was reaping a mixed harvest. After a day spent in the hourly fear of a summons to Head Office he moved out for a quiet drink. The quay workers, his life-long butties, froze him out of three of the familiar haunts by turning their backs when he entered. He left in deep gloom and walked through the streets of dockland. There were police at intervals along the quays, bulky men who were taking the place of the striking night-watchmen and being bad-tempered about the extra work. Ships lay idle, cranes rose up bonily above the poor lighting. The night sky had few stars and threatened rain. The windows of an occasional public-house splashed the footpaths with light. Animated conversations, falling on Tonman's ears and then dying away as he passed, filled him with a feeling of homelessness. Tonman had known other days. He had been handy with the fists. He had been the equal of any two policemen. He could lead a deputation and bargain with simple directness when tough words and reckless courage were all that were required of a negotiator.

Now all was changed. Writing and telephoning, points of order and terms of reference, Tonman had no head for such things. But he had a heart, soft and loyal. During his walk as an outcast, it pained him so much that he had to stop every so often to ease it. Whenever he did so the river and the cranes, the wind stirring the refuse which always littered the quayside, the stone houses and outlines of great containers looming at him out of the darkness, made him so disconsolate that he had to start walking again almost immediately.

Eventually, they drove him once again into a public-house. There were sailors in it but they were English and barely knew him. He was drinking on his own when a stranger interrupted him.

"You're a Union Official," the stranger said. Tonman shrugged away his thoughts and said yes.

"Thought I saw you around. Name of Mulligan?"

Tonman said no.

"Know him?"

264

Tonman asked the stranger who he was.

"Reporter. I want to get a story. This strike..."

Tonman interrupted to ask if by any chance he was Labaour Correspondent to the paper which had first carried the headlines about the strike being unofficial.

"That's me," the reporter said, with justifiable pride. "Now I want the follow-up."

There was a provident streak in Tonman's nature. He carefully finished his pint and moved the glass out of the way. The sound of the blow stopped the conversation of the sailors. They looked with curiosity at the outstretched form of the reporter and then in admiration at the huge man who managed such things so quietly and neatly. The barman signalled to two attendants, who dragged the limp reporter outside.

"Did he insult you?" he inquired. He was cleaning a glass.

But Tonman was in no mood for aimless conversation.

"He wanted the follow-up," he said. Then he left.

"That long chat I had with Bullman was worth while," the Minister said. It was the third day of the strike but he was remarkably cheerful.

"It bore fruit?" asked the permanent secretary.

"It will. It appears that Beggs is a new man from England. He came the heavy with this man Maloney."

"Mulligan," corrected the permanent secretary. He had a tidy mind.

"Whatever he's called. Anyway Bullman gave Beggs hell for pinning Maloney down and then releasing the fool's statement that the affair was unofficial. It gave no time for fencing."

"It takes a senior director," approved the secretary.

"Bullman agreed all the way. He's too long in the tooth to want a show-down in the dock area."

"What's to happen?"

"I am to write suggesting an Umpire. The company and the Union will write accepting."

265

"Under protest, I suppose."

"Inevitably. The board will kick up about interference from outside, in order to keep up appearances. But they'll concede the claim. It seems there are fair grounds for it."

"Pistol-to-the-head stuff. I know the line. But how is the Union to negotiate without declaring the stike official?"

"The Executive Officers were away. They will admit that there was gross mishandling. In the circumstances both parties overlook the . . . er . . . irregularity."

"Ah. Gross mishandling. So someone walks the plank. Poor Mulligan."

"But the man is a fool. He committed the Executive without a shred of authority to do so. Incidentally, I heard unofficially that he has taken to his bed. . . ."

"What about Beggs? In strict justice——"

"Come, come," the Minister reproved gently. "What is · strict justice?"

The secretary sighed.

"A philosophical abstraction. I am reminded that the Minister for Justice has been on again."

There was one subject on which the Minister found it impossible to contain himself.

"That bungler," he interjected.

"There's been a complaint of assault. A Union delegate punched a journalist in some public-house. I asked them to go easy."

"Good. We don't want the introduction of a martyr in the cause of Labour at this point. What was the row about?"

"God knows. The journalist involved was the one who splashed the story that Mulligan had declared the strike unofficial."

"Was it serious?"

"A broken nose, I believe."

The Minister's good humour returned. "Excellent," he said, rubbing his hands, and smiling at nothing in particular.

On the fifth day, the strike was fixed and the men returned. The Union had undertaken to investigate the circumstances surrounding the stoppage; the Minister had had some stiff words to say about the plain people of Ireland being held up to ransom; the board acknowledged that there were unusual factors in the case and conceded the demand. It cost approximately twenty-four pounds — there were only twelve trimmers directly involved in the claim. Thus a dangerous situation was averted, yet honour on all sides remained unsmirched. Only Mulligan failed to rejoice. In response to a summons from the Executive Committee and on the urgent advice of Tonman he rose from his bed and attended before that body the same night. They sat looking at him stonily as he entered with his delegate, the heavy-breathing, heavy-hearted Tonman.

The General Secretary read out the lengthy list of similar stoppages in Mulligan's branch in the past. He deplored Mulligan's off-the-cuff statement that the strike was unofficial. Had it not been for the most delicate handling, the company would have had to insist on a return to work before any negotiations had been entered into and the Union, in compliance with its agreement, would have had to take disciplinary action against the trimmers by expelling them from the Union. This might have set up a reaction of sympathetic strikes all around the Port. It would certainly have led to breakaways from the Union, a situation which would have been welcomed by the membership-hungry rival Unions operating in the same area. Mulligan, he concluded, had proved himself hopelessly incompetent and unable to handle a comparatively small number of members.

Mulligan, in his shabby suit, with his putty-coloured face looking even more downcast than usual, made confused answers throughout the interview. At one point he pleaded illness.

"You mean you took to your bed in an attempt to avoid responsibility."

"No. I was sick. Tonman here will tell you."

"It's not a very likely story. I doubt if you'll find one member of the Executive who believes it." Mulligan looked around. The stony faces registed unbelief.

"He looked very poorly when I called up to see him," Tonman supported loyally.

"Because he was in a blue funk. That's the worst feature of it. First he commits the Executive. Then he hasn't the moral courage to face the music. Mulligan's sudden illness is the most unbelievable ingredient of an incredible bungle."

After that, Mulligan kept his mouth shut. But when the interview was over and he was asked if he had anything to say before they requested him to withdraw, he swallowed a few times and looked around rather hopelessly at the unfamiliar dignity of the appointments: at the long, polished table, with the ashtrays and scribbling-pads, at the portrait of the last General President which graced the wall opposite him, at the carpeted floor which completed the taste and quiet luxury of the surroundings. Then he began to speak.

"I made a bit of a bags of it, I know. I'm not what you might call a handy man with the pen, or at making out reports. I'm not a very brilliant negotiator." Here somebody said Huh very loudly, and made a noise with his chair.

"I know all that as well as you do. Back in the old days I was more useful. There were police and scabs to be dealt with then. Tonman and me were able to deal with them. The membership was small and the Union was a room over a dockside pub. It was always broke. Tonman and me often went without our wages. We often paid out strike pay and walked the streets together, wondering how we were going to get a bit to eat and a shake-down. But we used to be good at getting the dockers together and I was a good man at telling the employer what we wanted, and what we'd stand out solid for until it was got. I don't think I have anything else to say. Times is different. There was no such things as Labour Courts and Conciliation

Boards twenty years ago. And then, the crowd I deal with are different. They're like me and Tonman. They use the old methods. They don't understand agreements. There were very few agreements in the old days. They live in an old world, I suppose. I guarantee you won't change them any more than I can. But even though they're out to lynch me at the moment I'll say they're a good bunch. You won't find better. They stick to their idea of fair and square. I think that's all I have to say."

When they were going home afterwards, Tonman told him it was a most eloquent plea.

"For all the good it does," Mulligan said.

"Don't belittle yourself," Tonman comforted, "it was a powerful speech. I'm sure it'll have an effect on them."

"Never," Mulligan said. "It's like trying to draw tears from a glass eye."

The Union's decision to suspend Mulligan from duty for three months might have closed the matter, had it not been for its effect on Tonman. The news upset him deeply. He brooded over it all through Sunday. On Monday night it drove him back to one of the familiar pubs which he had been avoiding up to then because of the attitude of the trimmers. He remained on his own, drinking whiskey, with the vague intention of cleaning up the joint at some point by way of revenge. At first the coolness of the others fed his desire. But, for once, the drink worked in the opposite direction. Sadness overcame him. He stood alone at the counter, silent, reflective, drinking vast quantities of whiskey until, to the surprise of everybody, two tears trickled down his massive cheeks.

"A gallant bunch of boyos," he said aloud.

Everybody turned to listen. Duffy, the trimmer, heaved himself up from a chair and went over.

"What's wrong, Tonman, oul' son?" he asked.

"Don't 'oul' son' me," Tonman said, "I forbid you to talk to me."

Duffy saw two more tears gather and fall. He was appalled at the sight of this gnarled mountain of a man weeping.

"Godalmity, Tonman, what's upsetting you?"

"Fair-weather friends," Tonman said.

"There's none of that kind here."

"Fine talk. Mulligan and me know to the differ."

"What do you want us to do; make him a presentation of a watch and chain? He tried to sell us out."

"He didn't. It was Beggs who twisted what he said."

"Then why didn't he deny it?"

"He couldn't. He'd no right to, without the Executive. He's over twenty years with you and when he was in trouble you let him down."

"Why didn't he tell us Beggs pulled a fast one on him?"

"How could he?" Tonman said. "Wasn't he sick?"

Duffy invited him to have a drink. At first he refused. When Duffy insisted he accepted.

"Let bygones be bygones," Duffy said, raising his glass for the toast.

"That's easy said. But what about Mulligan? The Executive suspended him."

"They what?"

"For three months."

Duffy was astounded.

"Doing the stevedore act," he said, "that takes the bloody biscuit."

"Trade Unionism," Tonman observed, "is all a bureaucracy, nowadays."

It was an expression Mulligan sometimes used.

"How do you mean?" asked Duffy.

"Like the Employers. They have the mode and outlook of the capitalist class."

That was another of Mulligan's expressions. Tonman admired it.

Duffy took a very serious view.

"We'll see about changing that tune," he declared.

270

That was how Mulligan found himself in the headlines once more. The trimmers and the quay workers, after a long argument over tea-break, walked out, to demand his reinstatement. They were led by the Joseph's Brass and Reed Band, which happened to cross their route on a practice march and which was prevailed on to join in the affair. They carried banners. Some read simply "No Victimisation". Others, more specific, proclaimed their thirst for justice with the words "We Want Mulligan". Bullman, the senior director, phoned for the Minister for Industry and Commerce, but was told by his permanent secretary that the Minister was already involved in a long telephone conversation with the Union.

"Shall I tell him you're willing to negotiate?"

"What is there to negotiate about? Can I reinstate some blasted Trade Union secretary? Don't be a fool, man."

The permanent secretary, who did not like to be referred to as a fool, even by a senior director, thought carefully.

"I meant," he said, "will you let them resume if we find a solution, or will you decide to lock-out or something like that?"

"I want them back at the earliest moment. Do you think we can carry on with the Port opening and closing like a goddam melodeon?"

"In that case," said the permanent secretary, who had been poised for this from the moment the senior director had requested him not to be a fool, "I strongly advise you to keep Mr. Beggs away from the gentlemen of the Press."

He went in to the Minister to report.

"Never mind Bullman," the Minister said, "I've been on to the Union. I told them if these eternal stoppages are not curbed I'll have legislation outlawing them. They tell me they believe they can fix it."

"By reinstating Mulligan?"

"Yes. It's the obvious thing to do."

"Do you really think you can outlaw these things?"

"I could do it tomorrow. And I could count on a fair

271

share of popular support."

"But it wouldn't be democratic?"

"Exactly. Next to his right to work, a man has the equally important right to refuse to work. Somewhere deep down in me, I sympathise with Mullarkey. I shouldn't say so, but there it is."

"Oddly enough, so do I. Do you think, perhaps, despite the philosophers, man is not a rational animal?"

"I wouldn't know. My only interest in man is as a political animal."

"Speaking of politics," said the secretary, "it will be interesting to see how the Union contrive to reinstate Mulligan and save face as well."

The Union proved equal to the occasion. A short statement appeared in the Press:

"A mischievous rumour, to the effect that a Branch official of the above Union has been suspended from duty, has already led to serious misunderstanding among sections of our members. The facts are, that the official concerned, who assisted the Executive in their investigations into the recent friction around the Port of Dublin, had been taken ill during the week and was granted three months' sick leave with pay. The official has since indicated to the Executive that he is sufficiently recovered to wish to return to work and, in accordance with his own express desire, will take up his normal duties as from tomorrow morning."

Tonman and Mulligan were joined that night in their celebrations by many of the trimmers. Next morning the cranes lumbered again into life, the horse-drawn floats clattered on the cobbles, the long-handled shovels flashed busily in the dust-laden holds. A copper-coloured sun took some time to squeeze its way through the warm haze which hung in the sky. The flags of the ships hanging limp and the oily colour of the river were a measure of the morning's calmness as Mulligan made his way to his office.

272

Mrs. Lynch was waiting for him at the door. He gave her a chair and composed himself to listen to her. He was feeling terrible. From time to time he wondered where Tonman was. All the time she spoke he waited, with growing impatience, for the welcome tread of heavy feet on the stairs.

Finegan's Ark

IT was while he was pushing his way through the Christmas crowds in Moore Street, Finegan told us, he remembered the Noah's Ark the Granny and the Aunt had bought him in that self-same street well over 40 Christmas Eves before.

It was a sudden and vivid memory, he said – the kind that hits you in some vital part of the machinery and makes everything grind to a stop. Did we ever experience anything of that kind?

Joe left down his glass to say he had. I did the same and said I knew what he meant. Casey avoided comment by picking flakes of cigarette ash out of his whiskey with the help of a pencil. A stout man and a nondescript kind of a man with a muffler whom none of us knew leaned over from their table in the corner and listened carefully.

Apart from the two strangers at the table there were only the four of us in the Snug. Normally we would have been in the bar, but what the Boss called "The Grand Xmas Draw" was to take place that night and this year the four of us had been selected to draw out the tickets and to ensure that all was conducted in accordance with the requirements of justice and fair play.

It was the custom on Christmas Eve to segregate those so honoured from the riff-raff in the public bar. Why, I don't know – perhaps as a precaution against corruption and malpractice and to lend dignity and a sense of occasion. Anyway, there we all were, waiting for the Boss himself to give us the word that everything was in readiness.

"When I looked around," Finnegan said, continuing

274

with his Epiphany, "dammit if everything wasn't exactly the same as on that evening 40 years ago."

Then he went on to describe the scene: the fog under the lamps, the thronging people, the carol singers shaking their collection boxes and the traders with barrows jamming both sides of the street, all bawling out their novelties under a forest of balloons. It was a very affecting description.

"I like carol singers," the stout man told us. "When I hear the carol singers I do get a lump in my throat."

"What class of an Ark was it?" Joe asked.

"A wooden one," Finegan said, "with a figure of Noah and a collection of animals to go with it."

"That's a nice gift for a child," the sout man approved. "I believe in gifts that encourage a fitting respect for our holy religion in the child."

Casey, I noticed, looked across at him sourly, but then Casey was looking sourly at practically everything bar his whiskey that night, so nobody minded.

"I remember asking the shopkeeper would it float," Finegan continued, "and he told me it would and he patted me on the head."

"That was for the benefit of the Granny and the Aunt," Casey put in.

"I think that was very nice," Joe said getting soft, "an Ark that floated."

But Finegan shook his head and said that that was the ugly part of it – that was what he was coming to. After five minutes in a bathtub the joints had opened and Ark and animals had gone to the bottom.

Noah had floated a bit longer than the rest, he told us. And then he described Noah lying on his back staring up at him with saucer-blue eyes, unable to believe that God had let him down.

Joe was astounded.

"That'd shake your faith in anything," he said.

"There's terrible rogues and liars loose in the world," the stout man said. And for the first and last time that night the man in the muffler took his nose out of his hot rum.

"A poor little child," he said, unable to believe it.

Then the Boss brought more drink to us and said everything would be ready very soon. The pair in the corner had more hot rum and the stout man, remarking the notice of "The Grand Xmas Draw" on the wall, said he'd like a ticket for that and the Boss sold him one. Casey gave him another sour look and turned to Finegan.

"I didn't know the Granny was a Protestant," he remarked.

Finegan was astounded.

"The granny was no bloody Protestant," he said, putting his glass down to bang the table, "and I'd like to know who's spreading a rumour like that about me and mine."

"In the name of God," Joe said to Casey, scenting a row, "what made you say a thing like that?"

"It struck me that a Noah's Ark is a very Protestant class of a toy – that's all," Casey said, very coolly, I thought.

At that moment, by good fortune, the Boss arrived in with more drink, which had a soothing effect on everybody, especially the stout man, who now butted in to mollify all concerned.

"Let's all remember it's the Eve of Christmas," he said, "and listen to that lovely singing there outside."

There were tears in his eyes. The sound of a carol drifted in and when I looked around I saw silhouettes against the frosted glass. The smaller figures, the children, held candles that flickered behind cardboard shields. Looked at through the glass, each flame wore a nimbus.

It made Joe remember in his turn going down Moore Street as a child. It was the Granny and the Mammy *he* used to go with he told us – God be good to them, for they were both long since in their clay.

"I remember often enough," he said, "standing outside the public-house waiting for them. I knew well enough they were in there coaxing themselves to a couple of hot

276

clarets on the sly, but of course – so as not to give scandal or bad example – they used to pretend to me that they were short taken."

Casey looked up at heaven. The stout man lowered a man-sized mouthful of the rum and said that it only went to show what a shining thing Irish Catholic motherhood could be, and that Christmas, when all was said and done, was really a time for the children.

He used to sing in the Church choir himself at Midnight Mass, he said, which was the happiest days of his life. Where would a man be without his Irish mother and the comforts of God's Holy Religion. We all agreed with him.

"Listen to that, for instance," he said, pointing a finger at the ceiling.

We listened. It was shaking under the weight of scores of merrymakers in the upstairs lounge.

"The majority up there," he said, "is young blades getting parlatic on the smell of a cork, the holly and ivy drinkers out of our so-called Catholic university. Not to mention the young bits of girls with them, that should be at home helping the mammy to stuff the turkey and wash the kids for early Mass in the morning."

"Ah, now," Joe said reasonably, "suffer the young. Sure we're only young once."

"I agree with our friend," Finegan said severely. "If they were daughters of mine it's sore bottoms they'd all have. That's what they'd suffer from."

Then the Boss himself came in with another drink and said that all was in readiness for the draw. So Joe raised his glass to everybody and said: "Well, here's a happy Christmas."

"A happy Christmas," we all said.

"With knobs on," Casey said, and glared again at the stout man.

We trooped up the stairs. A large box full of raffle tickets stood in the centre of the Boss's sitting-room and about it were set out the prizes – turkeys, hams, bottles of whiskey, port and sherry, packets of cigarettes, rich Christmas cakes, boxes of chocolates.

We began the draw, and of course the inevitable happened. The first ticket out was number 445 and we all remembered it belonged to the stout man.

"There's the luck of the draw for you now," Joe said. "We're drinking here all the year round and a stranger comes along and has the coolness to win first prize."

"He has," Casey said, "and do you know who that stranger is?"

"A Protestant, no doubt," Finegan said, his resentment flaring up again.

"Whoever he is," Joe said peaceably, "he's a decent poor divil anyway, with a nice, natural upbringing. Did you see the way he cried when he heard the children singing the carols?"

"Let me tell you who he is," Casey said, glaring at him. "He's a notorious bloody receiver of stolen articles – a fence. And that skinny little gurrier with him is just out of the gaol after a sentence for burglary."

Casey works in the Courts, delivering summonses and all that class of thing, so none of us dared to doubt him. The Boss got pale.

"Merciful God," he said, "ruined."

We all understood what he meant. If it got noised abroad that fences and burglars were taking to frequenting his premises in such numbers that they won prizes in his Grand Xmas Draw it would do his business no good in the world. It was a time for swift decisions. Casey looked at the Boss, then at us. Without a word he took ticket number 445 and tore it up.

"Is that agreed, boys?" he asked.

We all nodded. There was no need to ask what he meant.

"Right," Casey said, "now, in the name of God, let's start the draw."

When it was over we went back to the bar and certified that everything had been done in strict accord with honesty and fair play and we announced the results. We returned to the Snug again for more drink, this time on the house. The Boss had one with us and so had Muffler and the stout man.

The carol singers outside began again. The stout man wept copiously, so that the tears splashed into his hot rum. Casey, raising his glass, gave us a toast.

"Here's to Noah," he said, staring hard at Finegan. I looked into my glass and saw two unbelieving, saucer-blue eyes.

A Touch of Genius

I MET Danny O'Donnell in the main street of Ballyross at about eight o'clock on that winter evening. At the best of times Danny was a miserable, half-starved looking oddity who owned the skinniest, most woebegone example of an Irish terrier you ever clapped eyes on, and that evening, with a hint of snow in the air and the wind making a chimney of the narrow street, I found myself feeling sorry for him – a dangerous luxury so far as Danny is concerned, because he's the greatest toucher in Ireland, with an infallible instinct for any hint of softness in the heart of a likely client. I should explain, in case you might think me hardhearted, that everyone in Ballyross gave Danny food and clothes to try to improve him – but it never seemed to have any effect, good, bad of indifferent. Danny could eat five meals a day and still manage to look half famished.

"Where are you off to, Danny?" I asked him.

"Up to meet the bus," he said, "to see if I can raise the price of a pint."

In the matter of drink Danny had made a fine art of providing for himself. He was an old soldier, with an old soldier's perpetual thirst, who drank his way through his pension two days after he drew it and it was his habit, when he was broke, to try raising a few bob by meeting the bus at the top of the main street, and singing for the passengers during the half-hour wait. He always took the dog with him, knowing of course that the woebegone spectacle of the pair of them was enough to draw tears from a glass eye. It was alright in summer, but in winter I didn't fancy his chances and I said so.

"You'll be lucky if there's anybody at all to sing to," I said to him."

"I'll have to take that chance," Danny said. Then he

looked at me out of the corner of his eye. "Unless, of course, you were feeling like saving me the trouble."

"I'll ramble up to the bus with you, Danny," I said to him. I'd stood him three free pints that week already and that was the limit I'd laid down for myself.

When we got as far as the bus Danny let an oath out of him and when I had a look for myself I saw why. The only people in it were an elderly gentleman and a youngster of about eight – his nephew, by the looks of things. Naturally, there was no sense at all in singing to a house as poor as that.

"You're bunched, Danny," I said.

"Don't be too sure," said Danny and off with him into the bus.

There was a cocky note in his voice that made me hang around to see what would happen, because I'll say this for Danny, he was a resourceful man, not easily put off the trail of free drink. I saw him talking to the elderly man and after a while the nephew and the gentleman got up and left. They went off in the direction of the village, while Danny followed at a distance. It appears he'd told the old man there was half an hour to kill and that the whiskey in Tim O'Leary's was as good a cure for frozen feet as anything devised by a benevolent providence.

"And where were you thinking of going yourself, Danny?" said I.

"Down to Tim's for a pint," said Danny, "what else."

He was as cocky as you please and I knew now that getting a pint had become a question of honour with him.

"And how much have you got?" said I.

"I've tuppence," Danny admitted.

"You won't get a pint for that," I reminded him.

"If I don't," said Danny, "I'll have a damn good try."

The upshot was I followed him into Tim's myself. I expected he'd have a go at what I called the dog trick and I was right. The dog was as cute as a christian and whenever a stranger came into Tim's it used to go over, plant its skinny chin on the stranger's lap and look up at him with that adoring and trustful look that all dogs can conjure up when occasion demands it. Danny had it trained to this, of course, and he used to come over after a while and apologise at length for the dog's unmannerly behaviour. Nine times out of ten it led to a conversation and ended in the stranger asking Danny to have a drink. I fell for it myself on my first visit to Tim O'Leary's the previous summer, so I know what I'm talking about.

However, the elderly gentleman was in no mood for skinny animals. He was at the counter coaxing himself to a ball of malt and when the dog planted its chin on his knee he gave it a push with his hand that nearly dislocated its jaw. Danny called the dog to him with a great show of anger, gave it another wallop for good measure – to teach it manners, moryah, and then went over to the nephew, who was sitting at a table with the blank look on his face that all kids seem to wear when they're working their way through a packet of biscuits. I watched closely. Danny patted the nephew on the head and said in a loud voice that he was a fine little man. Then he started a rigmarole, asking what age he was, was he going to school, what book was he in – all that class of blarney, for about ten or twelve minutes. You could see the old uncle at the counter beginning to lap it up. Then Danny said the boy must have another packet of biscuits.

"How much is the biscuits?" he shouted over to Tim.

"What they always were – twopence," Tim shouted back. You could see Danny's antics had him feeling a bit impatient.

"Throw us over a packet," said Danny. Danny caught the biscuits and gave them to the nephew.

"A bird never flew on one wing, son," he said, "isn't that a fact now." The voice would put you in mind of Daddy Christmas.

The kid lit into the biscuits right away and Danny went up to pay for them.

"You shouldn't have done that," the old man said to him.

"Yerra — what's a packet of biscuits," said Danny, as though not taking much interest, with such a grand wave of his hand that you'd think he was the factory that made them.

"Were you going to have a drink?" asked the old man.

"I was thinking of it," said Danny.

"Just a moment, then," said the old man He rooted in his pocket, slapped a half crown on the counter and said, "You'll have this one on me."

Danny looked surprised.

"Indeed then and I won't," he said, firmly.

"I insist," the old gentleman said, and I don't think I ever saw a man so anxious for the honour of standing another man a drink. It was the packet of biscuits that had done the trick, of course, I could see that.

"What will it be?" the old man insisted.

Danny hesitated beautifully. Then, with the look of a man who is only doing it to be agreeable, he gave in.

"I'll have a pint, so," he said.

When he was raising it to his lips he had a look over his shoulder at me, to see how I was taking it, I suppose, and I raised my glass with his.

"You're the greatest chancer in Ireland," I told him, when the old gentleman and the nephew had left.

"I'd want to be," said Danny, with such a hard look at me that I found myself breaking my rule and buying him another.

The Boy on the Capstan

I SAW Dobbs for the first time that summer evening when I turned the corner of the street that led to the Work's Gate. We were both due on shift work at ten o'clock and already we were late. He was about thirty yards ahead of me, an undersized man with his supper in a parcel under one arm, and he was standing quite still. That surprised me, I remember, because Dobbs was one of the most meticulous timekeepers on the job. I stopped too, not wanting to pass him. It was a wide, dusty street, quite deserted at that late hour, with a summer peace over it that comes even to the dockside when the wagons and the floats have drawn their last loads and called it a day. There were discarded cigarette cartons lying here and there in the channel. They had curled up throughout the heat of the long day. I can remember the sky above the works glowing with red and gold and, outlined against it, the great chimneys sending up their steady black smoke.

Dobbs had his head a little to one side, listening for something. After a while it came – a rumbling sound, distant at first, which grew and grew until the street was full of it, and then slowly receded. It was the Wexford Mail, thundering southwards. I thought of my father in the little cottage by the railway line and knew he was going over to the kitchen dresser to check the alarm clock by it. He was a shift worker too, and he had been doing that as long as I could remember. That evening the thought made me sad, because any day now I'd be leaving him to try my luck somewhere else. Three weeks as a trainee with Dobbs had convinced me that there were better things in life than playing nursemaid to a conveyor belt from ten at night to six in the morning. I loved my father, I suppose, but I was twenty-three at the time, an age when summer skies make promises they don't always keep.

Dobbs was already at the time office, talking to the gateman, when I took my card from the rack and put it in the clock.

"Fifty years I'm in it," he was saying in a voice that was not quite his own.

I remembered then that he was being retired the following day. It was his last night on shift work. The clock made a tiny ping of sound when I pressed the lever but neither of them noticed — they had heard it too often. I lit a cigarette and began to listen, my hands in my pockets, my eyes looking down the works yard, where the telfer, suspended from its rail, was making a slow and graceful parabola high above us.

"It isn't long going over," I heard the gateman say. He sighed. He was an old man too.

"Not in the heel of the hunt," Dobbs answered.

"Still," said the gateman, "it'll be good to be finished with the shift work. You'll be able to get into bed at night and up in the morning for a change. That's a hell of a lot better than vice versa."

"More Christian anyway," Dobbs said.

"More natural altogether," the gateman insisted, and I could hear they were both trying hard to be cheerful about it, to be cheerful about the fact that time passed and years ran out all too quickly.

"I left that message out at the Chief Engineer's house," Dobbs said.

It explained why he had been late. I'd been out there once myself, because we often had to leave out lists of pressures and details about what we called "The Makes". It was a large house down the coast with an orchard and a tennis court. The beautiful daughters entertained their boy friends there. I'd seen them.

"Did he have anything to say to you?" asked the gateman.

Dobbs began to talk fifteen to the dozen. It was unlike

him, but I suppose the idea of starting the last shift of his life was upsetting him. Anyway, he said the Chief Engineer knew he was retiring and brought him into the house and made him drink a glass of whiskey and had one with him. He called the wife, too, and explained about Dobbs being fifty years in the job and she had a glass of sherry or something. Then he gave Dobbs a pound note and shook hands with him.

When Dobbs had told all that and said a lot more about what the room was like and so on, he produced the pound note from his pocket and showed it to the gatekeeper. The gatekeeper couldn't resist the temptation to point it out to me. I pretended to take notice of them for the first time and laughed at them.

"You're made up," I said. I couldn't help it. As I say I was twenty-three and that was the way we talked.

"The Chief Engineer himself gave it to him," the gatekeeper said. And you'd think he was talking about St. Francis or the Pope or something.

I laughed again.

"Oul Starve-the-worker," I said. I put out my cigarette and moved away. Before I was quite out of earshot the gateman told Dobbs I was nothing but a pup.

That annoyed me. I went into the great furnace house where Dobbs and I worked in a gallery set high about the furnaces. Our job was to service the conveyor belt from a catwalk which stretched like a steel thread away up above the smoke and the glare. But instead of climbing the narrow ladders I went straight through the house and out on to the quayside which bordered it, where the trimmers were working one of our ships under arc lamps that looked pale and weak because the sky and the river were still clinging on to the last of the light. I'd meant to talk to Byrne, their No. 1 man, about London or New York (he was a well-travelled character), but found him grumbling because there was no money to buy beer for the gang. The company allowed them to have porter on the job when a cargo was dirty, but Callaghan, the foreman, wouldn't lend them the necessary because he'd had some kind of difference with them and, of course, the furnace hands were all broke – as per usual.

"Oul Dobbs has a pound," I said without thinking much about it, but Byrne's eyes lit up immediately.

"Thanks be to God," he said, "get it off him for us. We'll pay it back tomorrow."

The trimmers were a good crowd to pay back, I knew, but somehow I hadn't Byrne's faith in Dobb's generosity. However, I went back into the house and left my coat and things beside Dobbs' in the locker on the ground floor before climbing the ladders that led to the top gallery.

Dobbs had a greasing gun in his hand and already his face was black.

"I suppose you expect the bloody hoppers to fill themselves," he growled.

"No hurry," I said, not very concerned. The catwalk led to a large window at the end of the house, beneath which there was a platform where we usually took our meals. I stood for some time looking out at the long vista of the river, the sprawl of warehouses and shipping, that vividly coloured, heartbreaking sunset in he sky. I thought of the large house way down along the coast, far away from dirt and poverty, and then I thought of money and then I saw the trimmers working on the quayside directly below me and remembered. I went down to Dobbs.

"The trimmers have no beer money," I said to him. "They want to know if you'll lend them your pound."

"Not bloody likely," he said immediately.

"Come on," I coaxed, "don't act the miser."

"I'm going to keep what's my own."

"And let your mates go dry," I said, with all the bitterness of my twenty-three years.

"I never saw them any other was," he said. "Come-day go-day-God-send-payday."

That was that. I pretended to do a bit of greasing for the next hour or so and then I slipped down again and gave Byrne the bad news. He had the trimmers natural gift of languages and let himself go. I didn't blame him.

"The pound is in his coat pocket, in the locker," I said.

"Inside?" Byrne asked, jabbing his thumb in the direction of the furnace house.

"Beside mine," I said.

"He might miss it if he comes down for his grub parcel at supper break," Byrne said.

"Don't worry," I said, "I'll keep him occupied."

The result was that at the supper break I brought up Dobbs' grub and the can of tea for both of us. He started when I appeared beside him. He was standing on the catwalk, the greasing gun limp by his side, his other hand curled tightly about the thin rail, looking down from his eyrie at the sweating furnacemen far below. I knew he was listening to the hum of the belt and the rattle of buckets and that for him all the beauty of the world lay in the glare and glow of that vast house and its dust-laden galleries. I showed him the food and he followed me to the rest platform under the great window. He thanked me for bringing up the food and said I wasn't a bad lad after all. I could see he was genuinely pleased, thinking, I suppose, that I was showing him respect because it was his last night. I began to feel uneasy and mean, but I had promised Byrne to keep him talking and I began to do so. After all, the trimmers would give him back his pound the next day, so what did it matter anyway.

"Tell me about the old days," I said to him. "What it was like when you were a youngster."

He fell for that. He began to tell me that when he was a child of twelve or thirteen he used to bring down the lunch basket to his own father, who was a trimmer with the company. He was a bright lad, able to read and write, which was unusual then, so when lunch was finished the men used to give young Dobbs the paper and gathered round while he read it out to them. Dobbs stood up when he got to that part of it and led me over to the window.

"Do you see that capstan?" he asked me, pointing down. I said I did. I noticed while I looked at it, that the trimmers had stopped work. They were getting their cans ready.

"They used to stand me up on that," Dobbs said, "and they'd gather round me and I'd read them all the news."

"I'll bet you were proud," I said. I was beginning to feel like Judas. He was such a small man and so worn and with so little life left to him.

We stood watching. Just then Byrne returned with a bucket and began dishing out the beer. There were shebeens all over the docks at that time and they dished out the stuff to the trimmers at any hour of the day or night. Dobbs noticed and said:

"They got their beer money somewhere." Then he said, "I'm sorry about refusing the pound."

"Forget it," I said.

"No," he said, "I'd like to explain. If it was a pound that I had of my own it'd be different. But the Chief Engineer gave it to me himself."

"I know exactly what you mean," I said. But he kept on.

"I'm fifty years here," he said, "and a pound I got like that is something the missus at home would like to see and handle for herself."

I said nothing. The trimmers below had seen us. They were a tough crowd with a tough sense of humour and they were holding up the cans to us, making a great mockery of drinking our health. For them it was all a great joke.

"What are they doing that for?" Dobbs asked.

I felt he was going to tumble to it at any moment and began to gather the cups without answering him. I went out casually on to the catwalk, moving away all the time. When he finally tumbled to it and let a shout out of him, I was halfway down the ladders. The fierce glow of open furnaces, the sweat glistening on half-naked bodies, the burst of blue smoke, almost directly under me, told me the furnace men were making the new draw. I got down to the floor of the house just in time. The smoke and fumes grew thicker each moment. Under the apertures of the roof orange and green and violet and blue began to twist and billow in fantastic tracery. I could see the dust particles swimming and eddying and knew that Dobbs would have to go back to the platform under the window until the draw was finished.

When he got down at last he made straight for his coat, searched it for his pound and then rushed out on to the quayside. He was shouting at the top of his voice.

"A pack of bowsies," he kept saying, "a bunch of hill-and-dale robbers."

He was face to face with Byrne when I caught up with him.

"My pound," he was yelling at him, "where's my pound?"

Byrne, a great hulk of a man, only grinned down at him.

"It was a joke," he said, "you'll have it back tomorrow."

I thought Dobbs would go berserk at that.

"I want no truck with robbers," he shouted, but stopped suddenly when Byrne gripped him by the shoulder. He wasn't grinning any more. He tightened his grip.

"Easy on the name-calling," Byrne said.

I got between them and manoeuvred Byrne away.

"Come on," I said, "he's an old man. Leave him alone."

That only made Dobbs turn on me instead.

"You're an elegant bowsie yourself," he shouted at me. "I have you well taped. You kept me talking so that they could lift my pound."

"Come on," I said to Byrne, "enough is enough."

We walked away a bit and turned round. One of the trimmers had left an empty can on the stone capstan. Dobbs crossed to the capstan, grabbed the can, and flung it into the river so violently that for a moment I expected to hear it striking a sound of thunder from the water. It

290

landed quite noiselessly and began to drift steadily towards the open sea as the turning tide caught it and directed it. Dobbs watched it and as he did so all his anger seemed to leak away from him. I saw his body drooping and his head cocking a little to one side, as though he was listening. I thought again of the Wexford Mail. He leaned his hands on the warm stone of the capstan. I looked up at the sky. The light had left it. After a while Dobbs began to stroke the capstan, gently and thoughtfully, and we watched him. He was thinking, I suppose, of his father – as now years afterwards I sometimes think of mine – and thinking, too, I suppose, as I often do now, of how surely things pass. Hurt, passion, anger, jealousy, pain, the moments of triumph, the lovely days of our innocence, all go bobbing out into the darkness like an old tin can in the grip of the turning tide.

I drew my time next day and Dobbs was beside me, drawing his last pay packet. He didn't speak to me and I couldn't find anything to say that would help matters. When I came back many years later and saw the overhead telfer describing its slow and graceful parabola above the works yard, both he and my father were dead.

Ferris Moore and the Earwig

THE long, thin, unmuscular body which lay supine in the sunny field was, Mr. Ferris Moore eventually conceded, the property of Mr. Ferris Moore. For the moment at any rate. Mr. Ferris Moore had been inhabiting the body for close on sixty-two years. Or rather, Mr. Ferris Moore qualified (his eyes closed contentedly and his ears gratefully aware of the sound of the nearby river) a succession of bodies not by any means similar in shape and health had been inhabited for that period by a succession of mysteriously related individuals who might be referred to collectively, though unsatisfactorily, as Ferris Moore. For instance, Ferris Moore pointed out to himself, the brown-limbed boy whose sad little ghost had been haunting his thoughts for some moments past, could only in the most loose and general way be considered Ferris Moore. The boy had once played cowboys and Indians in this very meadow. He had climbed trees. He had, for a period of now forgotten duration, owned a pet rabbit to which he fed lettuce from the kitchen garden, something which Aunt Emily, long since departed from the last body of all, had expressly forbidden. If that remotely remembered little being was also Ferris Moore, then it became necessary to distinguish. He had been Ferris Moore Eight. The long, thin body, presently conscious of the sun, the smell of grass and the sultry hum of insects, was Ferris Moore Sixty-Two.

Ferris Moore should have been relieved at achieving this little measure of clarification, but he was not. Something – an indisposition of the body juices perhaps, kept him melancholy. He raised himself into a sitting position and leaned over the river bank to see if the earwig was still there. It was. He had felt it would be. It clung to the steep, damp bank, its near pincers stiff and erect against the threat of its enemy. It clung to a small dry patch of the bank, encircled by the water which oozed in a thin stream on every side of it, so tiny a stream that it would hardly wet the top of the finger of Ferris Moore Sixty-Two. But it would sweep the earwig away if it tried to crawl through. Plainly, the earwig was trapped.

Or rather, the earwig believed itself to be trapped. It could not know the thought in God's mind. It could not know that Ferris Moore (sixty-two) had determined, at some later moment still to be more precisely determined, to rescue the earwig. Not out of love or pity, but because Ferris Moore had decided to demonstrate that the will, in spite of the doctrine of Epicurus and the arguments of the Determinists, is free to choose. In other words, that he had the faculty of inward self-determination to action.

The last phrase required considerable formulation and for the moment it exhausted Ferris Moore's desire to concentrate. Relaxing, he began to speculate lazily about the earwig and its plight. How had it got there in the first place? Had a bird dropped it from its beak? Had it been questing along the bank for food or for ambulatory pleasure while, all unnoticed, the natural drainage increased and the banks began their deadly ooze? Ferris Moore decided that he could not say. He felt critical, however, of its general behaviour. There was no sense in offering a threat to, or trying to evoke terror in, a watery ooze. To raise the rear pincers in such circumstances was an unnecessary betrayal of the emotions. The sustained muscular tension it called for must have the effect, on such a day, of making the earwig uncomfortably warm. If earwigs suffered from that sort of thing. Ferris Moore was not sure.

It was undoubtedly a very beautiful day. Too beautiful. Beauty, Ferris Moore had long observed, was conducive to sadness. Perhaps it was not the indisposition of the juices after all. He felt a gentle pleasure in the warmth of the sun which seeped through his clothes, but underneath that

293

pleasure there was pain. In some dark cave of his consciousness Death, he felt, was making preparations to take over where Ferris Moore would be obliged to let go. When he closed his eyes this deeper part of him seemed to feel the silent spinning of the world on its tilted axis and its simultaneous forward motion through the great void of space. Searching for some expression of this mood, Ferris Moore remembered poor Dick, of whom Housman had written:

> Fall, winter, fall; for he
> Prompt hand and headpiece clever
> Has woven a winter robe
> And made of earth and sea
> His overcoat for ever
> And wears the turning globe.

Searching for a homelier expression of the mood, Ferris Moore remembered the words of an old gardener who returned at the age of eighty from the funeral of a friend and, being asked how he had got on in the cemetery, replied: "The gravedigger shook his shovel at me."

But these were unpleasant thoughts for so perfect an afternoon. Tonight, at dinner, he would open another bottle of wine, whatever his sister might have to say about it. He had had some words with her at lunch. She was older than he and although they had lived for years together in the lonely house their parents had left to them, they frequently had words. Not noisy words, but polite, frigidly controlled expressions of ill-feeling.

He had been reading a book throughout the meal, in order to avoid speaking to her.

"I wish you'd speak to me," she had complained at last.

"I am reading, my dear."

"You are always reading. Poetry, Pamphlets, Making-And-Mending, Philosophy, War diaries, Detective novels, Dictionaries."

He had said nothing.

294

"Anyway," she resumed, "I don't believe you are reading at all."

"You express yourself strongly, my dear."

"Your book is upside down."

Ferris Moore had not missed the note of triumph.

"Of course. Why not?"

"It seems unusual."

Thinking quickly, Ferris Moore replied. "It is recommended as a cure for astigmatism."

"What is astigmatism?"

"An uneven tension in the muscles of the eye."

"Is it very painful?"

"Only when one talks about it."

At one time he had felt it might have been better to marry a wife, but now he realised that it would have amounted to the same thing. Unless, of course, there had been children and that would have been disastrous. Children trampled on flower beds and stole fruit. It was best to be as alone as one could. Life in itself was sufficiently unintelligible without additional complications. We came, we went. The sun rose. Things grew. Cold and emptiness enveloped this little blob on which there was action but no apparent purpose. Was there a God? Possibly. Did He care? Hardly.

It was that thought which first drove Ferris Moore to drink. Not to drink too much, but to drink at all. It happened at the age of fifty. He had never drunk up to then, but over the years the round of his life lost its flavour. It seemed senseless just to potter about the garden or walk to the village and back again; to read the papers at breakfast and sleep a little after lunch; to play string quartets on the gramophone (his was an old-fashioned house) or write articles of local historical interest which he never felt quite interesting enough to show to anyone.

His sister had objected to the drink and pointed out that he was bound by his promise to his dead father to abstain from powerful waters for life. He had felt himself a little bit guilty at first but eventually he worked it out in the form of a dialogue which ran so satisfactorily that now and then he still took it from his desk and read it.

A. Do you deny that you promised your dead father to abstain from powerful waters?

B. Most emphatically.

A. Your own diary asserts the contrary.

B. The diary is imprecise.

A. In what particular?

B. The diary is that of Ferris Moore Twenty-eight. I am Ferris Moore Fifty. I can hardly remember Ferris Moore Twenty-eight.

A. But he exists.

B. He does not exist. Any more than Ferris Moore Eight does.

A. Who was Ferris Moore Eight?

B. Simply someone I once knew. He used to chase butterflies and kept a pet rabbit. He also climbed trees. I am Ferris Moore Fifty and quite incapable, as you see, of climbing a tree or chasing a butterfly. This flesh is not the same flesh, this form is not the same form. This voice and the mind which directs it, they are not the same at all.

A. Then where are they? Where are Ferris Moore Twenty-eight and Ferris Moore Eight?

B. Why ask me? They have both gone away. They have left leaving no address.

A. Ah – but there is something else.

B. What else can there be?

A. Uniqueness. A uniqueness which is common to Ferris Moore Eight, Ferris Moore Twenty-eight, Ferris Moore Fifty. This uniqueness is constantly present in the arithmetical progression of bodies which is the physical manifestation of the journey of Ferris Moore through Time. From this we must imply a continuation of responsibility.

B. The philosophers, I know, speak of this uniqueness but I am not altogether convinced of it.

A. You will never shake us on Uniqueness. Without it there would be no responsibility, no culprit for any crime, no basis for law.

B. Does this uniqueness continue outside of Time?

A. Well-brought up people believe so. It is only fair, however, to rule that the question is beyond the competence of the present enquiry.

B. In that case I am free of my promise. If, for the sake of argument I concede Uniqueness, I can maintain that the Uniqueness which was my father has moved out of Time. If I believed in a benevolent and personal God I might still hesitate. But I do not so believe. For me God died some years ago, quite suddenly. I was gardening at the time. I thought of my father. He had planted and his work surrounded me. I looked up into the blue sky. It was deep. It was worse than deep. It was empty. The heavens were blue and beautiful and empty. At that moment my father's uniqueness became a remote possibility. And even if it still Is, I argue that there can be no basis in law for a compact between a uniqueness which abides in a body and moves in Time and one which is pure spirit, remote, moving beyond Time. Death is unbridgeable. I am now going to have my first drink.

He did so. He had found it helped, too, despite his sister's disapproval. If softened the outlines of Reality. It blurred the menacing shapes of things without a Maker.

The doomed earwig on the steep side of the bank caught the attention of Ferris Moore more closely. As with it, so with him. He was surrounded on all sides by a flood from which there was no escape. He placed it in the order Orthoptera. Somewhere under its horny case there were wings. Why did it not use them? Probably, Ferris Moore conjectured, they were used only for the nuptial flight. If so it was a great waste of wings. Under the horny case too lurked a soul and an intelligence. The earwig Was. It knew that it Was. It was obviously uncertain, however, that it was going to continue to Be. Ferris Moore would attend to that presently. But only temporarily. That was the sad thing.

The realisation that he was sad about the earwig

297

brought Fereis Moore into a sitting position once more. He had not been sad about another creature for a long time. During the middle twenties a vague sympathy for the lower classes had suggested itself to him because, despite their boorishness and their undeniably outrageous behaviour about which his sister had remarked adversely, it seemed unfortunate that so many should be hungry and hopeless. On another occasion, when a little boy smiled at him he had felt a strange pang of sympathy too – illogically this time since the child was happy and healthy. After that there was nothing to be moved about, except in a way when, listening to the Schubert Quintet, he felt it a pity the composer should have died before the work had been performed. Or again, when the King died and a pang of genuine regret pierced him. And now the plight of the earwig which he was about to rescue suggested once again the idea of inter-relationship or responsibility or, in so far as he could formulate the emotion, a sense of familyhood under an All-Fatherhood. Perhaps Love best expressed it, although it seemed extravagant to consider a trapped earwig and describe the resultant emotion as one of Love.

Ferris Moore stirred himself and searched around stiffly and painfully for a stick. Eventually he found one and returned to the edge of the bank. He sat for a while in a mood of recollection. It was really a very beautiful afternoon. At a distance from where he was sitting a belt of pine trees formed a semi-circle around the flower-scattered meadow. The blue sky above displayed here and there a small, fat, white cloud. It was a world which even God might condescend to walk in, always assuming of course that the idea of an intelligent and sympathetic God was compatible with the awe-inspiring irrationality of certain aspects of His Creation. Ferris Moore, his rejection of such an idea weakening under the benign assault of sunlight and scenery, found that he was no longer acting under his original impulse. The rescue would not be designed to demonstrate his possession of the faculty of inward self-determination to action. It would be

298

an acknowledgment of kinship and brotherhood, an acceptance of universal inter-responsibility dictated by an All-Fatherhood, interested or disinterested, caring or uncaring, capable, if so desired, of being investigated more closely at a later date, if he so determined.

Ferris Moore leaned over the bank and found with relief that the earwig was still there. Very carefully Ferris Moore let down the stick. At first the earwig backed away from it. It was suspicious. It did not trust this strange arrival. But Ferris Moore had patience and intelligence. He let the stick hang perfectly still just about an inch from the earwig's head. In a few minutes, as Ferris Moore had cunningly anticipated, it crawled over slowly, made its necessary investigation, then crawled on to the end of the stick. Ferris Moore smiled with quiet triumph. The brown water below reflected the smile back at him. Ferris Moore saw his own face and for a moment allowed the smile to distract his attention. It startled him. He had not smiled at himself for quite a long time. Now it was his undoing. The stick jerked awkwardly. The earwig lost its grip. Ferris Moore realised what had happened when the small point of a splash dissipated his smiling image. He was thunderstruck. The earwig, a bright brown speck on a dark brown tide, drifted slowly downstream, until the failing eyes of Ferris Moore Sixty-two could no longer distinguish it. When it had gone and the shock had spent itself he shrugged sadly and dropped the stick into the river too. Then he lay back once more and stared into the blue sky. He was thinking ...

Beyond the blue lay the darkness of outer space, and beyond the limits of outer space, at the remote point of Infinity, without length or breadth or thickness, abided the mind of God, towards which all things travelled at an unreckonable speed; including Ferris Moore Sixty-two, his unloved sister, the King, the little boy with smiling eyes and the small, drowned earwig on the brown bosom of the waters.